LAKE OF FIRE

PRAISE FOR THE ALLISON COIL MYSTERIES:

Lake of Fire:

"*Lake of Fire* swirls into an environmental inferno that reads all too true—Mark Stevens writes like wildfire."

—Craig Johnson, author of the Walt Longmire novels,
basis for the hit series *Longmire*

"Don't miss it. Mark Stevens is at the top of his game."

—Margaret Coil, *New York Times* bestselling author
of the Wind River Mystery series

"Mark Stevens is one heckuva storyteller, and *Lake of Fire* is a riveting page-turner of the highest order."

—Scott Graham, National Outdoor Book Award-winning
author of *Mountain Rampage*

"Mark Stevens just gets better and better … An absolutely must-read thriller!"

—Chris Goff, author of *Dark Waters* and the
bestselling Birdwatcher's Mystery series

"You'll revel in Mark Stevens's painted descriptions and sharp dialogue. And most of all, you'll root for the smartest, coolest heroine this side of the Mississippi: Allison Coil. Try not to tear the pages as you turn them furiously."

—James W. Ziskin, author of *Stone Cold Dead*
and the Ellie Stone Mystery series

Trapline:

"A chilling tale."

—*The Denver Post*

"Allison's third adventure … combines a loving portrait of a beautiful area with an ugly, all-too-believable conspiracy that could have been ripped from today's headlines."

—*Kirkus Reviews*

"Readers will enjoy the fast-paced action."

—*Mystery Scene*

"A well-executed and suspenseful narrative … The book is a thrilling read."

—*The Aspen Times*

"Stevens has a clean style and keeps the plot moving."

"Thrilling, complex, and well-crafted with more twists and turns than a high road through the Rocky Mountains … No doubt about it, Mark Stevens is an author to watch!"

"*Trapline* rings as true as the beautiful mountains and valleys that frame this exciting, tense drama of today's Colorado."

Buried by the Roan:

"*Buried by the Roan* is flat-out terrific. Everything you expect from a first-rate mystery is here: Savvy sleuth Allison Coil, hunting guide on-top-of-her-game, gorgeous Colorado mountain setting, gripping story where the pages practically turn themselves, and eloquent writing to boot. If you haven't yet discovered Mark Stevens, this is your opportunity!"

"Mystery fans can delight in Mark Stevens."

Antler Dust:

"I stand ready to devour the next one."

"The Colorado crime scene has gained a strong new voice, as well as a new character to watch in Allison Coil."

"With its unique setting and diverse cast, Antler Dust makes a fast-paced, intriguing addition to the list of new thrillers."

"This book was a thrill to read."

"A page-turner with all the makings of a great mystery: two deaths and a variety of characters who aren't really what they appear to be."

LAKE OF FIRE

AN ALLISON COIL MYSTERY

MARK STEVENS

MIDNIGHT INK
WOODBURY, MINNESOTA

FIRST EDITION
First Printing, 2015

Book format by Teresa Pojar
Cover design by Lisa Novak
Cover photo by iStockphoto.com/19699798/©jonbeard
Editing by Patti Frazee

The song verse from *Lake of Fire* used with permission from Meat Puppets Music, LLC (Curt Kirkwood)

Midnight Ink, an imprint of Llewellyn Worldwide Ltd.

Library of Congress Cataloging-in-Publication Data

Stevens, Mark, 1954–
  Lake of fire / Mark Stevens. — First edition.
      pages ; cm. — (An Allison Coil mystery ; #4)
    ISBN 978-0-7387-4363-9
    I. Title.
    PS3619.T4914L35 2015
    813'.6—dc23
                                        2015014201

Midnight Ink
Llewellyn Worldwide Ltd.
2143 Wooddale Drive
Woodbury, MN 55125-2989
www.midnightinkbooks.com
Printed in the United States of America

This one is for Mark Graham, my longtime pal in words and stories

ACKNOWLEDGMENTS

Thanks to Dan Schultz for writing about the tragic slaying of Cortez Police Officer Dale Claxton. *Dead Run: Murder of a Lawman and the Greatest Manhunt in the Modern American West* is a fascinating account of anti-government sentiment. Schultz's research of those 1998 events provided key themes here.

Overdue thanks to Al Marlowe. His guidebook, *The Hiking and Camping Guide to Colorado's Flat Tops Wilderness,* has served as an ever-handy research tool throughout this series. In the latest edition (so glad to see the update), he is joined by co-author Karen Christopherson. Editor Shana Kelly helped shape an early draft and offered keen insights into character. Shana's ability to see inside a story is remarkable.

Thanks to Patti Frazee and Leroy Smith (yes, Leroy X of Denver rock and roll fame) for spot-on line edits and clean-ups. Much appreciation to a short-lived writers' group—Christine Goff, Linda Joffe Hull, Jennifer Kincheloe, Christine Jorgensen, Suzanne Proulx, and Melisa Ford—for terrific comments on the opening chapters.

Private detective David Keil offered considerable detail to my questions about investigations. Thanks again to Colorado Parks and Wildlife District Wildlife Manager Frank McGee for a careful read and insights about the wilderness and how humans and hunters behave when they go there. Thanks also to Rio Blanco County Sheriff's office and Deputy Sheriff John Scott for the extended ride-along.

My good friend Stephen Singular generously shared a piece he wrote about a meeting with the late Randy Udall; I drew some key ideas from Stephen's words (and may have borrowed an image or two). Writer pal Amy Kolquist gave generously of her time for reading and brainstorming. Thanks to David Akerson and Katie Reinisch for the use of a retreat space for a final writing push.

The Short Story Book Club was there when I needed them most, at the semi-raw stage. The SSBC members are Ted Pinkowitz, Susan Fox, Dan Slattery, Parry Burnap, Laura Snapp, and my wife, Jody Chapel.

Thanks again to two fabulous daughters, Ally Chapel and Justine Chapel, for all their support. Thanks to Sami Jo Lien for all her help behind the scenes. Thanks to the cast of thousands at both Rocky Mountain Fiction Writers and the Rocky Mountain Chapter, of Mystery Writers of America.

Thanks to all the folks at Midnight Ink for their solid support and non-stop enthusiasm. And heartfelt thanks to Terri Bischoff for her friendship, leadership and, well, help with everything. In my world, Terri is a rock star. And final thanks to Renée Rumrill. I wouldn't be here without you.

"And the beast was taken, and with him the false prophet that wrought miracles before him, with which he deceived them that had received the mark of the beast, and them that worshipped his image. These both were cast alive into a lake of fire burning with brimstone."

—The Book of Revelations

"Where do bad folks go when they die?
They don't go to heaven where the angels fly
They go down to the lake of fire and fry
Won't see them again until the Fourth of July"

—The Meat Puppets

1

ONE:
WEDNESDAY
LATE AFTERNOON

NATURE KILLS AS MEAN as man.

A one-hundred-foot spruce exploded like a giant sparkler. Smoke flowed thick like London or San Francisco fog. Take your fucking fog pick. The cloud stung her eyes and for a moment the burning lollipop bubble of orange on the tree faded behind the wall of smoke and she slowed to a walk, unable to see much beyond Sunny Boy's snout.

Pincers of flame threatened to close off the mouth of the ravine that she needed to clear in order to not become a fleshy morsel of skin and bone amid the fire's otherwise steady diet of crispy-dry timber.

Her heart flared. Sweat coated her forehead. Smoke whipped around and another tree caught the lollipop disease with a snarling crackle. High-definition, 3D movies rolled in her head that showed various scenarios for how the next minutes might play out. None of the clips ended well.

The gap with the lobster claw pincers of flame might, in fact, be a trap. She might be getting seduced by the appearance of an exit— an opening—when in fact the best route out would be where the two fires on her flanks converged.

Allison Coil tugged the reins and turned Sunny Boy around, back uphill.

"Trust me," she said out loud. With authority. "And I'm not saying you don't."

Sunny Boy's ears flattened. He jerked his head up like he'd seen a snake.

"I know," she said.

She shoved away the rising dread. At least, she faked it. She needed Sunny Boy's complete dedication. He would sense her uncertainty. She pulled her kerchief up over her mouth, put her head down. She turned one stinging eye in the direction she had pointed Sunny Boy, shot the gap between two trees that cooked in relaxed fashion like a couple of logs at a campfire. From the ground up, fire wrapped each tree in wicked bursts of orange. Dragon's breath. Dragon in the form of climate change and beetle kill and aberrant, menacing storms. And her demise. A minor loss in the big scheme of things. Katrina to Sandy to the monster tornadoes from Missouri to Oklahoma.

In flashes, the heat surged with intensity. Trudy's bread-baking oven times three. More bite. More weight. Less room to back away.

Allison inhaled a lungful of heat. Sunny Boy jerked his head from side to side. No doubt his eyes stung too.

All smoke. White-gray smoke. Chewy smoke. Fresh, thick gobs of the stuff.

Allison found an open patch. A clearing. She stole a glance up— *blue sky*. Happy-normal grass under Sunny Boy's feet. Fire on all sides and still the smoke, but this scrap of oasis, like the way some tornados leave one house unscratched in a city of devastation, offered proof that fire and nature and man-made accidents were all capable of unexplained bits of random kindness.

No time to linger.

She kicked Sunny Boy toward the thickest, smokiest exit. Smoke charged her. Sunny Boy tensed. She may as well have coaxed a whale to the beach. His front legs stiffened. He had the urge to rear up, to shake off his parasite, determine his own fate.

Allison contemplated her own. Colin flashed—and Trudy, too, right there. Her parents and family. Was this it? What would she miss? Time before birth was as unknown as the time after death—shouldn't you also be afraid of what you didn't experience before your birth? Or as jealous of what you missed? Why was one's birth the starting point for zealous ownership of life?

Family obligations kept Colin out of this pickle. No doubt spotters would have reported the fire. Maybe a response was already being organized. Maybe Colin knew she was in this area, given the timing and her anticipated trip over. Maybe she should say goodbye to him, even though he wouldn't hear. To Trudy too. She coughed to relieve the ache in her lungs. To no avail. Should she climb down, press her nose to the ground and hope for a smoke-free snort of air?

If a human caused the fire, did that disqualify it as a natural event?

Sunny Boy relented.

He shot forward as if to say, "Get this over with."

Allison ducked. The smoke was so thick she could be heading for a low branch. Or smack into a tree. She hoped Sunny Boy's sonar was up and running.

"Go," she said, head down. "Go."

A hand on his withers came away soaked from worry and sweat.

TWO:
WEDNESDAY EVENING

FINDING THE EDGE OF the burn scar was a snap. On one side of the random line, trees thrived. Their tops shuddered in the breeze. They showed no sign of remorse for their doomed brethren.

On the other side of the random line, blackness reigned. Still-smoldering blackness. Smoke oozed from the pores of the dying trees. Stray wisps—last gasps.

Devo marveled at the thoroughness of the destruction.

And it pissed him off.

The fire was no act of nature. Or lightning.

He had been up on the flank of Rat Mountain when the orphan thundercloud rolled through the valley. It generated mist, not rain, and it produced occasional and lazy lightning. But none of the strikes were down here where he had seen the first puffs of smoke.

The cloud had stayed to his left, rolling in from the west. The fire had started in the sun-splashed timber a solid five miles of woods and scrubby undergrowth to the north. He had taken his bearings and headed off.

By the time he had reached the ignition point, the fire was a blowup. Full-sized trees snapped like cracking bones. He caught glimpses of flame as he followed the general direction of Marvine Trail. Devo had stayed off the trail. He wasn't fit for civilization. He avoided contact. He cut his own path, as he was prone to do. The fire had started on the west side of the Marvine Trail. Devo had started on the east. He crossed the trail when the line he'd chosen brought him to it. He could hold a straight line better than a crow. He could hide better than a well-fed wolverine.

The risk of being spotted up here, even around the well-traveled Marvine Trail, was remote. Traffic in the Flat Tops was minimal—hikers, campers, fishermen. Horse riders too. The drought made the wilderness no fun. And no campfires. Devo didn't need the newspaper to know that much—he hadn't seen a campfire in weeks.

But you couldn't be too careful.

At the spot where the fire started, the trees had not burned completely around the circumference. It wasn't untouched bark on the downwind side, but the burn wasn't as thorough. It was easy to see which way the fire had blown. What he saw here lined up with what he had seen from the ridge—yellow-orange sheets of flame that had kicked up twice the height of the treetops and then the frenzy churned to the northwest with an unlimited supply of its favorite food ahead.

A normal west-to-east weather pattern might have put his camp —*their* homestead—in the crosshairs. "Camp sounds so temporary," Cinnamon always insisted. "It's a homestead. Our place on the edge of the new frontier."

The wind direction was a fluke.

He looked for signs of where lightning might have struck the trees, even though he knew it hadn't. He knew lightning could travel a long way, but the thundercloud had been so confined and distinct, and its lightning shots so straight down, that he knew something else was responsible. He looked for a shattered or exploded trunk or any black, linear gouge in the bark. Nothing. It was possible a lightning scar could get concealed by the fire itself but not here. There had been no goddamn lightning.

Devo stood and took in a deep breath. He was alone. He'd slipped away, pre-dawn. He usually had a cameraman or camerawoman who followed every move. The television show captured every burp and scratch. But not today. He had made it look like a routine walk to take a pee and then he slipped off. It was his right. The show was his idea. Occasionally he needed the break. He needed breaks to think. And relax. Around-the-clock cameras were exhausting.

Devo stopped. His senses were so keen that his body seemed to know things ahead of his brain. His eyesight had sharpened, but his nose led the way. The shift had been subtle. It wasn't overnight or anything like that. He once sensed a herd of elk slipping through the forest a full half hour before he had come up behind them. He had known they were there. His nose told him the size of the herd. It sensed the weight of their collective smell. Elk were a fairly easy test, however. Their funk could linger in bedding areas for at least a day or two. He once stalked a pool of elk pee for hours. The elk? Long gone. He could smell bear and deer, both before and after the rut. He had long since merged his scent with the land. He hadn't used a man-made product to clean himself since he had left the city. At some fundamental level, he emitted a human scent. He hoped the elk thought, *oh that animal*. But his ability to move softly, coupled with a growing sixth sense about the patterns and movements among the animals, made him feel at times utterly at home.

It worked.

Devolution worked.

Shedding the city worked.

When the new recruits arrived, he could see the difference too —how far he'd come. They were up to nineteen now. Twelve women, seven men. The new recruits were hardly unfamiliar with outdoor life and outdoor survival, but committing yourself to the habitat, year-round, changed the dynamics. He could see them look around at the camp—*the homestead*—and study the more experienced tribesmen and start to process the fact that all their food would come from their work and prowess, that their survival would depend on their skills, smarts, toughness, teamwork. And that they were each other's only source of friendships. They would have to work together.

Devo could see them look.

For now, the fire bugged the living shit out of him. In these conditions, the idea of a firestarter on the loose was worrisome, to say the least. While lush and dotted with lakes, the Flat Tops looked now like they had been forgotten in a kiln. Lakes and ponds sported shores triple the normal width. The remaining water in the lakes and ponds looked inert and dying. For ideal working conditions, a firestarter could ask for nothing better than this summer in the Flat Tops.

If this had happened near his camp, their camp—their homestead—they wouldn't have had time to outrun it. He shuddered to think.

He found no signs of lightning. He drifted into the burn scar, zigged and zagged along the line between healthy and blackened trees. He was forty yards east of the Marvine Trail and that, too, suggested something other than lightning.

Convenience. Access.

He was in a dense stand of lodgepole pine, weaving along the random line of fate, when he almost walked right into the small fire ring. It was no bigger than a dinner plate—seven stones in all. The inside was flat and, of course, black. It still held heat. And so did the trees.

Ignition point.

Devo stood back, walked away. The burn scar ran in a wide V-shape, fanning out and away.

Carelessness? Somebody so desperate for a campfire that they had to sneak off and light one? There was no obvious sign of where any tents might have been pitched and no sign of a campsite at all except for this pint-size ring.

Something was not right.

Devo inhaled, turned his nose up and turned his head off to the side, trying to pick up something on the breeze.

Something cooked. Like goat. A roast on a spit. But not quite. Heavier. A metallic whiff in the mix too. He turned his nose up like a dog getting the news off a flow of morning air. The whiff reminded him of a city barbecue.

Frying fat.

He straddled the line at the edge of the fire—pristine wilderness to his left, utter blackened devastation underneath and for miles on his right—and dropped down in a crouch. He moved on all fours. His compact frame liked the change. He'd grown more flexible and lean, of course, and the position didn't bother him, even a stranger spotting him now might think the Flat Tops had long hidden the lone ape in North America. The move worked. His knuckles enjoyed getting in on the tactile action.

Nose inches off the ground, the odor of crispy goat or pork hung to the air. The trail dissipated and he backed up, course-corrected. Followed further.

Maybe the firestarter had gotten caught in his own blaze.

Devo stood.

He had smelled enough, seen enough.

This was the spot.

The investigators would have no trouble confirming what he now knew—as long as they made it up here in the next day or two. An arson investigator would nail this as the spot, the V where it all began. Maybe there was a way to test the shattered bits and blackened remnants of wood.

Wood and—

Skull?

Twenty feet from where he stood, the skull lay resting on its back. Staring up.

Devo waited a moment, studied the ground he was about to step over and then crossed the steps as if seconds mattered.

They didn't.

The skull was burned. No hair, no eyes. Mouth open, teeth exposed. The smell of meat mixed with burned guts and the copper-sulfur pungent stew from blood and hair.

In his first three years living in the woods, death was a daily issue. Rabbits, squirrels, deer, and elk. There wasn't a species of bird he hadn't tasted.

But a still-smoldering human carried a heavier definition of death.

Why? Really, why?

He already wanted to find a way to report that the fire wasn't caused by lightning. He already wanted to report he'd found the spot where it started. He already knew he'd have to find a way to communicate to the big civilized world out there. And he knew the implication for his brothers and sisters in camp.

In *the homestead.*

Cinnamon. He would have to secure her approval. They were a group now.

And groups meant one thing he hated more anything else.

Politics.

"What the hell?" he asked the charred skull. "What the hell? Tell me what happened, would you?"

THREE:
WEDNESDAY EVENING

"As far as I'm concerned, pre-evacuation alerts or pre-evacuation orders or whatever they want to call it are a bunch of government bullshit. What the hell does it even mean? Get ready, you might lose it all so start packing the animals? Load the ark? Like they know what the hell direction the fire is going to go and they want to get the whole valley scared out of their gourds?"

Earl McKee didn't comment. He held court. He relished an audience. In this moment, he had a big one. Three sons—Daniel, Garrett, and Colin.

Allison had fallen for the runt of the litter. Colin was the McKee most her size, below average in height and weight. She always found herself sitting up straight at the McKee's dinner table. Dan and Garrett were twin towers of the family, an inch or two taller than Earl. You might not notice Colin at first, but when you watched his sure movements and started to make a list of all the things he could do—and do well—size didn't matter.

Along with the male offspring were Daniel's wife, Gabriella, and Garrett's girlfriend, Jayne. Jayne was the newest face. Allison met her for the first time this afternoon. Garrett hadn't been super lucky in the girlfriend department and even now, Allison didn't like his odds based on how Jayne had paid him any scant attention over the past couple of hours. The fourth female was Earl's wife, the quiet force behind the McKee Empire, Charlotte. *Char.* Nobody's fool. A Beagle puppy, Rex, was passed around for ear scratches and cuddles. He was twelve weeks old and his brown ears were soft like velvet.

In these gatherings, Allison tended to sit back and sip margaritas. Or straight tequila. She kept her head down in the swirling stew of McKee testosterone. The topic of the day generally involved some government screwup. Earl's prodding quizzes about her operation carried the not-so-gentle implication that this phase of her life was exactly that.

They were gathered on the McKee's back deck, a sprawling cedar beauty that served as the McKee exterior living room for three months of the year. It came with a gas grill the size of a small car. Plunked next to the grill, a well-stocked wet bar with one flavor of beer—Coors. Daniel McKee had opened his laptop on the long table. He was switching back and forth between Grand Junction and Denver stations. The news was all fire all the time, from the foothills west of Golden to a "monster" blaze near Paonia. On the size-of-fire scale, no doubt "monster" spoke of both sheer acreage consumed and its willingness to be tamed. News anchors must take a special class in learning when to assign such meaningless shorthand monikers. The beleaguered incident commanders stuck to droll facts-are-facts briefings. The wildfire she encountered wasn't big enough to have joined the revolving news recaps.

But it wouldn't be long.

The "pre-evacuation" order had come via recorded message on a reverse-911 call a half hour earlier as the elk tenderloins were coming off the grill.

"They let the Big Fish Fire burn in '02 at first," said Earl. "That whole wilderness, let-nature-do-its-thing approach didn't quite work and when it threatened to come off federal land they stepped up and knocked it down." Earl took a swallow from his glass of golden beer. "It's mostly luck every time."

One positive about these visits was the welcome reminder that she had hooked the one offspring in the brood, Colin, who believed there were more questions than answers.

Earl overstated to make his points, but had raised his sons to believe that all you needed was a firm grip on the reins to get what you wanted out of all people, animals, and opportunities.

"Well, finally," said Daniel, punching up the volume on the laptop. Well-gnawed corncobs were strewn on the table. Char produced a fresh pitcher of margaritas, made with fresh lime juice and triple sec. The pitcher was jammed with ice, but none of it would last long. Jayne helped herself to a fresh topper.

Daniel flipped the laptop around for all to see and punched up the volume. The news anchor from Grand Junction held a grim stare: "…a new fire near Trapper's Lake in the Flat Tops Wilderness is the latest threat, although the area is lightly populated. Roadblocks are being set up to limit access to the scenic byway that runs across the north of the wilderness from Meeker to Yampa."

The McKee gathering grew church-like, except for Jayne. "Holy smokes, here we go. What's gonna happen? Holy smokes. I knew it. I've been afraid of this all summer long. Oh my *gawd*."

Jayne's flashy makeup was overdone for a simple backyard barbecue. She wore tight blue jeans and wedge shoes made of cork that jacked her up a couple inches. The blue jeans quit in time to reveal matching barbed wire tattoos circling each ankle. She hadn't looked Garrett's way in about an hour, but fiddled with a stone necklace draped where her purple top opened up. She was skinny in an unhealthy way and not one thing about her suggested what she might be good at, other than the obvious. Earl never missed a chance for an eyeful.

"They are calling this the Rat Mountain Fire and winds in the area are making this situation unpredictable." The news anchor was chatting, not reading from a script. He was weary. This was all so familiar. "There aren't a lot of houses in the area, as we saw with the six hundred homes destroyed on the Front Range last week, but another fire there could discourage hunters from booking trips and hikers and campers too. So to the folks who are trying to decide how best to prioritize all the battles around the state, you've got a tough job and limited resources."

Most summer nights in the mountains of Colorado required a light jacket. Something. But not this stretch and not this July. The deck came with a sun shade, but sweat came as natural as sitting. Allison estimated it was 90 with a gusty, dry breeze. Her smoky jean jacket was inside. She was down to her smoky riding shirt—blue checked, cotton long-sleeve—and her smoky Wrangler jeans. There was promise of a hot shower and she owed a check on Sunny Boy, who could use a scrub-down and de-smoking too. He was down with dozens of other horses in the thirsty, miserable grassland by the White River. Sunny Boy would no doubt have troubled dreams about their harrowing moments with the fire. So would she.

"They won't give a flying crap about Buford—you know it. I know it." Earl leaned back, plucked a stubby cigar from a shirt pocket. He fired up the smoke with a silver lighter that snapped shut with metallic authority. The ritual required mere seconds. Even Jayne understood he hadn't relinquished the floor. "They'll evaluate it, then the governor will check his list of contributors and see who deserves the big jets and the slurry drops. So, Ms. Allison, how far up was this when you tangled with the fire?"

Now Earl McKee was in decision-making mode and, at last, listening. "Five miles. Most likely less by now," said Allison. Wolf criers and worriers were Earl's least favorite types, although he had a long list of least favorite types.

"If it runs into where the Big Fish Fire took down the forest in oh-two, it'll run out of gas." This was Daniel, the oldest, not an Earl echo chamber. But all the sons seemed to defer, Garrett especially.

"If it started near Rat Mountain, it could come down three or four different ways," said Garrett. "Wouldn't mind if it stays put up high where it belongs."

"You had lightning last night?" said Earl.

"More lightning than rain," said Allison. Two flashes were so close she'd climbed out of her sleeping bag to check on Sunny Boy, who was plenty agitated. The smoke in the morning wasn't a shock, given the conditions.

"But you thought you could get around it?" said Garrett. "I would have just headed the other way."

Garrett tried a protective arm around Jayne, but the arm did nothing to close the awkward gap of space between them. Jayne had checked her watch five times in the last minute. She was cute in a small-town way, but she tried too hard. Allison slapped herself for judging. Jayne's fourth cocktail was already half-drained. With Daniel and Gabriella, who barely touched the beer she was poured, Allison smelled a touch of religions and morals—and the whiff reeked of steady judgment. With Garrett and Jayne, she wanted to know if they had met yesterday or last week and which online dating algorithm had a serious flaw.

"I thought I had an angle around," said Allison, making a point to minimize the number of words uttered aloud. "It was a calculated risk."

"Uh oh," said Daniel. He'd switched from watching the laptop to staring down a spot on the ridge. They all followed his view.

High to the south, a dull orange glow pulsed. Silent. Against the sweep of the dark night, the orange flicker wasn't much but the flames waved hello. *We are coming for you.* The pulsing waves of fire were careless, offhand, and powerful. The edges of the light throbbed. Allison had no problem adding her own soundtrack, that exploding lollipop effect she knew so well. Someone produced a pair of binoculars from the kitchen—Char was a back-deck birder—and they took turns trying to discern its intentions.

"She's coming hard," said Daniel, apparently missing the double meaning. "Mann Gulch in Montana? Killed all those smokejumpers back in the 1940s? They figure it was moving four to five miles per hour."

"She?" said Allison. "Why a she?"

"Mother Nature," said Earl. "All her kids—tornadoes, hurricanes, floods. They're all a bitch."

"Hurricanes get boy names now. Andrew, Igor," said Allison. "Sandy could have been either one."

"Government for you again," said Earl. "Always trying to even things up, when everything was fine the way it was." Earl took his turn with the binoculars. "Holy hell she looks angry."

Jayne stood up. "Let's get out of here, please." Allison appreciated Jayne's sense of urgency. Jayne steadied herself with an arm on Garrett's shoulder. Garrett took the opportunity to hold her but nothing about the gesture looked smooth. "That shit scares the daylights out of me."

Allison took pride in her resistance to panic, but the fire challenged those instincts. In this case, drunk Jayne was dead on. The ranch house stood in the middle of a field on the northern banks of the White River. It was an idyllic spot close to Buford, nothing more than a cluster of closer-together houses, a gas station, and where the road from New Castle ended. The McKee location afforded splendid views, but they were limited to this spot in the valley. The big problem with any fire was a stand of eight towering cottonwoods that protected the house, like bodyguards, to the south. The shade kept the house cool in the summer but could now play the role of deadly fuse. Candles to the cake, in this case old clapboard. At the rate the wildfire was cooking, it would spew red-hot embers that could skip ahead on the fire's own pumping, angry thermals and then land willy-nilly in dry timber downwind. Fires had their own selection process for destruction and it lived somewhere between random and nonsense. Once the fire had worked its way down to the southern banks of the White River, the McKee Ranch would be ripe fuel. The fire wouldn't pause to burp.

The match head on the high horizon had swelled. Through the binoculars, the fire filled Allison's view. Individual trees stood black against their tormentor. The sight churned up fresh memories, mere hours old.

"Could work its way down overnight," said Daniel. "And we know the state won't attack anything up this way until tomorrow."

"At the earliest," said Garrett.

Daniel stayed at the table, monitoring the laptop. Gabriella and Charlotte busied themselves with the cleanup. Allison knew they would wonder why she didn't join the chore.

How about this once? Channel your inner Trudy, Allison chided herself. Your best friend would never let a kitchen-related task happen without pitching in, so couldn't she get off her ass?

Allison gave Colin a high sign and a smile like "watch this." She stacked dirty plates and grabbed empty dishes in an ungainly pile.

Her arrival in the kitchen was greeted warmly, though Allison worried she smelled too much like a week of camping. Or a month. No doubt she was spraying a scent like adrenaline-tinged sweat shaken with eau de forest fire. Neither Char nor Gabriella were prone to fingernail polish or fussiness, but the big gatherings at least called for a clean shirt and a comb through the hair. A look. Gabriella wore crisp new blue jeans. Charlotte—*Char*—sported a bright turquoise top. Nearing sixty, Char was a feisty presence who put her head down and did one thing at a time and did it well. Char managed chores around the ranch—working the vegetable gardens, keeping the house shipshape, keeping the family well fed, and attending to a variety of church and school organizations in Meeker, a booming metropolis compared to Buford's blip.

Char stood at the sink, conducting the orchestrated cleanup attack. Gabriella hand-dried bowls and pots with a towel. Through the kitchen window, Allison could see Garrett with his arm around Jayne at the deck's railing, staring up the valley. Her attempts to keep her distance from Garrett were now a constant source of amusement and Allison almost felt sorry for the guy.

Inside, Char spoke first. "If he decides to go, we've got a lot of animals to haul out and a ton of stuff to pack. But he might stay and fight."

"You don't have a say?" Gabriella was a dark, beautiful woman whose Mexican-born parents were successful owners of a restaurant in Glenwood Springs, *El Conejo*. Gabriella was five months pregnant with the McKee's first grandchild. The attraction between Daniel and Gabriella was obvious—her beautiful golden-brown skin, dark eyes like black beads, and a trim figure that sported the baby bulge like an appealing element of femininity. A temporary one. Pregnancy wouldn't change Gabriella. Even Allison wondered what it would be like to kiss her sleek mouth—sharp corners and screaming white teeth. It was easy to think some beauty might rub off.

"A say? He lets me think so." Char smiled.

"This summer is terrible," said Gabriella. She and Daniel had made the trek up from Denver for a week's stay at the ranch. "You get the feeling the whole state is on fire. Or about to go up. Makes you appreciate the normal years."

"Just don't mention global warming," said Char. "Not tonight. Not ever."

Allison knew Earl McKee wasn't the last non-believer in Colorado. There were bunches of them out there who walked around with the old ostrich mentality down pat. It was all a government hoax or a longer-than-normal shift in temperatures. By now the non-believers had dived deep underground, but they were out there crawling around in their secret tunnels and meeting up to mock what was happening to the water supply and the coastline. Her client base of hunters included the occasional denier. The idea that anyone could dismiss global warming was the equivalent, Allison thought, of dismissing east as the direction where the sun would rise. In all ways she could think to measure and weigh, Colin was perfect long-term material. The lone complicating element was how much she might be expected to interact and tangle with the McKee family as time went on. Tongues could be bitten for only so long before they started to bleed. Maybe she needed to homestead with Colin in backwater Alaska. Or the Himalayas.

Dishes clacked into the washer. Gabriella wiped down the half acre of counter. Everything about the house was double or triple in size and scale. Daniel showed up carrying two stray beer mugs with his laptop tucked under one arm. Jayne sat alone by her margarita. Her glass had magically refilled itself. Garrett remained by the railing.

"I guess that huge fire down south has got Paonia in the cross-hairs so the Denver station is going to full-time coverage," said Daniel. Garrett drifted into the kitchen, Jayne on his fingertips, not even palm to palm. Jayne looked woozy. Daniel was the better groomed of the two older brothers—a fresh shave and bit of polish. He cared about his shirts and hair. The look said he cared. Garrett kept scruff and country grunge alive. He was prone to plaid flannel shirts and his jeans looked tired and ill-fitting. He had long, scraggly hair. Now that Daniel and Colin had moved off, Garrett helped around the ranch, home to the fine horse collection and a large herd of beef cattle kept on separate sides of the property. Garrett could strap on a distant gaze like he had taken full advantage of Colorado's legalization of weed. She hadn't had much reason to nail down the details of Colin's two brothers—in part because Colin deflected probes on the general topic. "They already lost some ranches and barns outside Paonia and it's a skip and a jump into town."

Allison snuck a glance at the big picture window over the sink. The wedge of orange jabbing its way down the ridge had tripled in size in the last ten minutes.

"Thanks for all the help," said Char. "Many hands, you know."

"No problem," said Daniel. An old, tired joke. "I needed another drink after all that work."

"I'm afraid sons one and two learned the old-school separation of roles from their father," said Char by way of explanation to Allison. "You got the one who doesn't draw distinctions."

Earl McKee entered the kitchen like he was conquering new territory, Colin right behind him. Earl had left his cigar outside but a discernable waft of the sticky smoke trailed him like dust following a pickup down a dry dirt road.

"We're not running," said Earl.

"No?" said Char. "We're not? You see what I see?"

"We're going to stay and fight. Water from the river. We've got a pump and a generator and since I still don't know what the hell a pre-evacuation order even means, we're going to pretend we never heard the goddamn message."

Something told Allison that the comfortable guest bedroom, and Colin's body wrapped around her in a happy, tequila-induced haze, was not in her near future. Earlier, she had visions of a quiet screw in the first-floor guest room, about the size of a normal master bedroom, as her thank you to the world for escaping the flash fire and her payback to Colin if she had ever, for one minute, taken him for granted. Garrett's awkwardness made her appreciate Colin even more.

But "alone time" vanished.

Time for battle.

And Allison's usual low-key optimism had squirreled itself into a dark hole.

No matter the size of the farm's pump or hose, Allison doubted it could generate the pressure to soak the tops of the sixty-foot trees. Colin slid around his brothers and stood next to her in the now-immaculate kitchen.

"If it gets us, it gets us," said Earl. "At the very end, we can let the horses go and we can make a run for it if it comes to that. But we can soak all this down real good and hold the line on our own. You see any sign of help? I've got four hundred feet of good hose in the barn and we can move the pump and generator down to the river in a pickup." Earl already had it all figured out. "We'll have to stand and watch it tonight but about an hour before she gets here we start hosing everything down and we keep it up for as long as we can. And we hope to get lucky with the winds. But I am not running. I've got too much sunk into this place. We all do."

"Fun way to end a party." Colin said it with a disapproving bite.

"And you want to run? Leave it at that? Take our chances?" Once set, nobody bumped Earl McKee off a plan.

Colin didn't mind squaring off and Allison silently cheered him on. "Your hose and a wet-down won't be enough if it comes to that. And the firefighters might take one look at the lack of defensible space on the south and just mark this all off as a goner. And if they want to drop slurry or do anything else in here and you had refused an order to evacuate—"

"It's a pre-evacuation order—" said Earl.

"Whatever," said Colin. Nobody else wanted to mix it up; nothing unusual there.

"Yeah, whatever that is—" said Earl.

"Well, the next call is coming in about an hour. Or two. And they are going to want you out of here." Colin spoke with the calm authority of an independent consultant.

"Who made you the expert?" said Garrett.

"It's the same thing every year, every fire," said Colin. "Whether it's Black Forest or Waldo Canyon. It's all about defensible space."

"We aren't running," said Earl. "We'll open up the gates and let the cattle and horses go if we need to and we'll get them later. But the house and the outbuildings, I'm not leaving them to the whims of the government. No way. No how."

FOUR:
WEDNESDAY EVENING

"You can't worry about it unless it affects us."

"It's not an *it*. *It* is a person. Or was. And the fire was set," said Devo. "On purpose."

Cinnamon Nation had taken to devolution like a trout to a mountain stream. She was already halfway there when she first appeared.

"Where do you draw the line?" she said. "We're either doing our thing up here, or we're not. Are we the eyes and ears of the National Forest Service? I don't think so."

"Someone was killed," said Devo.

"Or to put it another way, lost their life." This was T-Bone. A half-dozen had joined the verbal fray and T-Bone, a former computer programmer turned survivalist from Utah, sided up with Cinnamon. He towered over Devo and came ready for devolution, with a prominent Neanderthal brow. "How far do you take it? They'll find him—*somebody* will be looking—and they *will* find him."

"Every day matters," said Devo. "That was no accidental fire—the fire ring was goofy staged shit. If there's someone out there running around with a box of matches, it's a whole new deal."

"I'm with Devo. What's it going to hurt?" There were three women who gave Devo unwavering support—Jasmine, Lyric, and Nancy. Lyric wasn't known for expressing her opinions. "He gets the message out—the authorities deal with their thing, we go back to ours. There is a basic, you know, responsibility here."

Lyric was small, like Allison Coil, but darker with black hair, dark eyebrows, and brown eyes. She was tireless. She was one of the new recruits from this summer's batch of ten—more than doubling the size of the tribe. She held a certain softness, but through her application and screening process, Devo learned she had hiked the Pacific Crest Trail solo and had kayaked a remote gorge in China. Of the women in camp, she was easily the most attractive. To his way of thinking, they would make a good-looking couple. Did it matter? Out here? He didn't get much of a chance to study his own looks, but he knew that the years in the woods had added toughness and wiriness to his body. Even with the long hair and beard, he expected he was easy to look at. The cameras liked close-ups. Of course he was the star, the show's battery. They might reject modern-day distinctions about beauty and sex appeal, but even out here Devo sensed social sorting based on looks and types. Lyric matched his own body. She was small, tight, and trim. The nuts and berries diet hadn't altered his underlying features—strong, slightly bent nose and a high forehead. Twice at casting calls during his city days he was told he could be the younger brother of Daniel Day Lewis.

"He slips the message to the right person, and that's the end of it," said Lyric.

The tense conservation had drawn in most of the group. Devo knew it was good theater, but he would stick to his guns because that's what he wanted to do.

"They'll figure it out on their own," said Cinnamon. "They'll find him, same as if it happened in the next mountain range, the next state, anywhere. We got lucky. Let's get back to our work here and call it good."

A camerawoman circled. She was one of four. The cameramen and camerawomen rotated in and out. They usually shot for about a week, then took a break. Devo saw the faces come and go. They had all become more or less familiar. He wasn't supposed to develop relationships *with them*. They were there to record the progress— the regress—of Devo and the growing family of devolutionists as they shed city softness for backwoods toughness, working together to develop a new breed that grew and nurtured true grit and would re-infuse determination DNA into the American spirit. There were plenty of people and tribes living straight off the land in unforgiving conditions, but not in America. Even American Indians, once one of the toughest groups going anywhere on the planet, had been softened and babied and pampered into an unrecognizable shadow of their former selves. Who could build Mesa Verde today? Who could hunt buffalo with a spear today, if needed? Who had undaunted courage? Who lived instinctively with the land?

Devo and his erstwhile followers were determined to put the brakes on the deterioration that comes from television, fast food, cruise control, video games, fifty kinds of ice cream, Wal-Mart, celebrity worship, celebrity gossip, fried chicken, cotton candy, spa treatments, facials, Internet porn, Handi Wipes, pre-mixed margaritas, and the endless list of things that contribute to American complacency. The gene pool was *puffy* and needed to be slammed in reverse. Perhaps it would start with the flock Devo had assembled.

That was the subject of *Latitude/Longitude,* the biggest hit the History Channel had ever aired.

The show's name came from Devo's approach. The flock of devolutionists didn't live in Colorado or the United States. Government was irrelevant, state boundaries were meaningless. Devo had a major head start on the others. The camp where the men and women were reacquiring long-lost skills was, for all intents and purposes, nowhere. Their homestead was tucked into a hidden pocket in a steep ravine near an underground spring that Devo had discovered in his solo second year, before he sent out the YouTube invitation to any others who wanted to join. No outsider had ever seen the camp. It was doubtful any outsider ever would. The camera crew had been sworn to secrecy. It wasn't in their interest to have the camp destroyed or to have the devolutionists dispersed. TV ratings soared. They were all making money.

Cinnamon Nation was forty when she had arrived the previous spring. She moved like she was twenty. She was spry, nimble, and energetic. Her calves were broad and muscular. They were born to work, scrunching up like cartoon biceps when she squatted in the garden or climbed a tree to wait for a squirrel on its morning rounds. She wore a one-piece brown dress made from hemp she'd grown on her farm. She believed in occasional bathing to clean key parts of the body but also believed in building up natural oils and had done so, in fact, for years. Three weeks into her stay, she took off her one-piece wonder of hemp while they were out foraging and asked if they wanted to "get it over with." They might pair up, she had said, and besides, who didn't need the release? Sex was simply one of her routines. Like cleaning or milking the goat. It was over in five minutes and Devo never felt in charge. She massaged his balls, sat on him, and smiled. She leaned back and looked up at the trees. She sat up and hugged her breasts. She pumped him slowly. She said something about taking care of all needs and urges. They finished with him on his back, looking up at her swaying, slender, workmanlike boobs. They hadn't been corralled by a bra since who knew when? Full natural hippie. She rolled off him, dressed, and stretched. "Invigorating," she had said. "Thank you." Screwing became part of the routine.

"How are you going to send word, anyway?" said Cinnamon. They never used more than first names, and you got to decide whether to keep the one you came with, just as he had when he slipped away from civilization, alone, and started the YouTube channel that had blossomed into the full network contract. Devo, short for devolution, was the obvious choice as he wriggled free of his city skin. "March into town. Make a telephone call from Trapper's Lake? Smoke signals?"

"I'll figure something out," said Devo. "You just reminded me—I saw Allison Coil."

"Here we go again," said Cinnamon.

"She is real," said Devo.

"You have a fixation."

"So would you, if you met her." Devo had told pieces of the stories many times—how he had worked with Allison and how she had helped him.

"You saw her?"

"From a distance—but she was heading north. On her horse. It was before the fire started, in fact, and kind of in that direction."

"You're going to find her how?"

"She lives on the other side, so she's going to head back. She has to."

He would wait for three days or a week along Marvine Trail if it meant a chance to work together again—though he didn't want to wait that long to report the body.

"How do you know she hasn't already?"

"Already what?"

"Gone back."

"A feeling," said Devo. "Just a hunch."

"And that's your plan? Waiting for Allison?"

Somewhere along the line, he had ceded strategy to Cinnamon. And, in the same process, to the group. Discussions? Nobody could brood or stew or suck their thumbs better than this crew and Cinnamon held sway. Her knowledge translated to better crops, planning, and organization. Devo was treated with respect. His suggestions weren't ignored. But Cinnamon arrived with vision. She knew the homestead needed structure to thrive. She had already been living off the grid, in Paonia, for ten years. She knew more about soil management than Devo thought possible. She knew about harvesting and collecting mushrooms and berries. She knew how to flavor a pan with leeks and garlic before frying grubs. She made a mean cricket fried rice. She had a hundred tips for holistic health management. Devo knew similar stuff, too, of course. But Cinnamon demonstrated the techniques with enthusiasm and confidence. Her swirl of certainty had healing power. Devo had grown weary of the teaching role, but Cinnamon relished it.

"It's as good a plan as any," said Devo.

"And Allison Coil shows up, then the cop types and the authorities types and all the uniforms show up," said T-Bone. He was taking this argument more seriously than it deserved. Devo was sure the producers were digging the confrontation. "So then they start asking how the body was discovered, etcetera, etcetera, and we aren't that far from where all this took place. They'll want to talk to the person who found the body."

"Allison found the body," said Devo. "She'll cover for us. She won't give us up, if that's what you're thinking."

"Why would she do that?" said Cinnamon. "What makes you so sure she's a friend, anyway? You haven't had contact in how long?"

"I know she is a live-and-let-live type. I know her heart." Allison, in fact, had saved Devo's life one night in a snowstorm. There was no doubt in his mind that she would do it again. Although now, with their growing encampment, it was possible her attitudes had shifted.

Of course, the one problem was that once the story got out, some of this conversation on television would confirm that *Latitude/Longitude* was filmed in the Flat Tops and the discovery of the body might triangulate location details for those on the hunt for their camp, their homestead.

He had been warned, from a producer's note, that devolutionist wannabes had been spotted wandering the woods trying to find the *Latitude/Longitude* set. One had died, apparently, early last winter. The eighteen-year-old had left a note in his Nederland home, and his body had been found in the wilds near Red Feather Lakes, hundreds of miles away. The producers were good about concealing critical location information. The death and related details—articles and reviews—were slipped to Devo in a pre-loaded handheld device with one long message each week. He swapped out the devices each week.

"I think we take a vote," said Cinnamon. Most likely, she had counted her votes. She had a good sense of the political winds.

"We're not all here," said Devo. About half the population was off cleaning, gathering, hunting, foraging.

"If you're here, you get to vote," said T-Bone.

Devo could count on Jasmine, Lyric, and Nancy. They were Devo loyalists. Cinnamon had T-Bone and seemed to have the head-nodding support of Jimi, their lone black guy, and Feather, their most senior recruit and a woman who had arrived in the first batch the previous summer. Feather was a big-boned woman who loved to work and held quiet sway. Sky would likely be the tie-breaker. The recent college graduate and crop expert was their resident nerd and approached all decisions like it was the analytical challenge of the century.

"What we must weigh is Devo's comfort level with the rest of us if we don't give him the opportunity to follow through on what he sees as the right thing to do," said Sky. He was slender, wore as little as possible. "This whole thing is his idea. He wouldn't take an unnecessary risk, at least in my view."

They voted by standing by Cinnamon or Devo.

"Allison has to go back," said Devo when he had four others beside him. Cinnamon had three. "It's not a matter of if."

FIVE:
WEDNESDAY EVENING

THE EMBER HOVERED LIKE a flying saucer with bits of fiery shrapnel dancing around it. The whole night sparkled orange like an invasion of fireflies or new, fast-moving constellations.

The fire that birthed the ember engulfed the forest across the White River producing waves of heat across the water and the fields. One of those waves had lifted the ember straight up, like a spaceship being recalled on a light beam to its home planet in a distant galaxy.

They all watched the ember. Allison aimed the oversized hose at it and all its pesky brothers and sisters and cousins. She had the hose tucked under her left arm. With the water surging through it, the hose wriggled and kicked. She wrangled it off and on for an hour, taking turns with Daniel McKee, who was as tough and capable as his brothers and father. The water spurting from the hose, stretched to his full length, was enough to spray the side of the house. It couldn't reach any part of the trees above the roofline or the roof. The cottonwoods made a perfect, picturesque river valley windbreak—eight stoic soldiers guarding the house in tight formation. But now they stood like eight potential wicks for the fire, each capable of having their crispy-dry tops explode at the mere mention of fire, let alone having an ember land in a branch like a messenger from the sun.

"Get the hell out of here," shouted Daniel at the ember. His fists held the nozzle of the hose in a death grip.

"If it were spring, the river would be wider," said Allison. "If it were a normal summer, same thing. What about the livestock tanks?"

Those who knew the ranch in detail—that is, everyone else— were busy cramming vehicles with valuables from the house or loading prize horses onto trailers. For the rest of the animals, the plan was to leave the gates open and hope for the best if it came to a fast exodus. Earl's plan to stay included a get-ready-in-case effort at packing up. The only one who was already gone was Jayne. She had driven off alone in her pickup, but only after Char made her wait an hour to sober up.

Allison left Daniel with the feisty hose. The grounds were slick. She ran gingerly until she found solid footing beyond the immediate perimeter of the house. The fire roared. Flames doubled the height of the treetops as tentacles of heat danced and swayed. The river created a natural fire break and the McKee side of the river was open pasture, not tinder-dry forest, but the field wouldn't repel fire. Shards of fire—shrapnel from the exploding trees across the river— rained down from the sky. They were stray fireworks, random bits of space junk taking aim at fresh turf. Advance troops. It was a matter of time. Or luck.

The glow from the fire helped her spot the livestock tank, halfway between the barn and the river's edge. The surface of the water reflected a flash of the fiery mayhem in the distance. But how much water was there? Ropers weren't ideal for jogging, but she made them work. Her feet barked complaints from the pinching and strange commands. She had jogged in high school, where the head coach of her track team believed her small frame and lean body made her a good candidate for the cross-country team. "Low to the ground," he called her style. "Efficient." Allison was flattered. She tried for about a month to find "the zone." And the point. Why would she want to go anywhere fast? Or faster than anyone else? She had a severe case of athletic disinterest, though she briefly liked the idea of "team." Maybe. Track was kind of a team sport and sort of not. The ability to shine as an individual held appeal, but she failed to find motivation to win. At least, back then.

The livestock tank was three-quarters full. Not being a farmer, she wasn't sure of the tank's capacity, but in her mind's eye she pictured the water in front of her pumping through a hose and imagined it would take a good half hour to empty. It would be a shame if the water sat here, unused, and the house burned to the ground.

The pump hummed in the distance. Out by the road, a line of cars and trailers awaited Earl's final evacuation orders, which wouldn't come until the house was engulfed. Between all the McKees, there were enough trucks and SUVs to start an auto dealership. Where was Colin? She had headed off with Daniel on the pump team, and she hadn't seen him in a couple of hours. Colin might be helping with the animals. He knew how to get them to move. Now, she needed him to evaluate her plan. Was the closer water worth it? Was the closer tank enough to get the hose up higher? Would it be enough? How much time would it take to move the pump and put it back by the river if her scheme flopped?

The fire answered her questions with a fresh growl. A new squadron of embers swarmed into the night sky.

Allison jogged back to the house, veered along the hose line toward the river. Daniel dropped the hose when he saw her arm-waving excitement and the hose spat and spewed in the mud like a freshly beheaded snake.

At the river, Daniel silenced the pump with a flick of a switch. They lifted the apparatus into a trailer hitched to a mud-splattered ATV. The fire's heat couldn't be ignored. It shortened Allison's breath. Flames billowed out over the river. The idea of rolling into the river, fully dressed, held appeal. The light doubled down here with the flames reflected in the wide, slow-moving water. It would take years or perhaps a decade or more before this fire's giant burn scar would stop turning the river into a squalid gutter from all the topsoil runoff when it rained.

Assuming, of course, that it ever rained again.

Daniel's movements were swift. He was a city boy now, but he possessed the innate McKee inner strength. He worked as if this was all another inconvenience. His actions suggested they would retreat soon to the porch for another round of beverages and perhaps they could roast marshmallows using long sticks. He fumbled to find the start switch on the ATV. Then the machine jerked and stalled when he tried to put it in gear.

"It must not approve," he said. "Hateful thing." Matching eye teeth flashed in his wide grin. His tone was disaffected and cool, but his cheeks glowed with sweat. He looked unconcerned about the ember shower or the fact that he had failed to spark the ATV to life.

A tree exploded across the river like a bomb of light and death.

Allison straddled the quad, yanked on the clutch, jabbed the starter. It roared to life. "Don't tell Colin." Daniel hugged his head in mock shame. "Or Dad."

"Make sure the hose doesn't snag on a rock or a bush while I drag it across," said Allison.

She charted a course off the corner of the barn, put the ATV in low gear until she knew whether the thick hose was prone to snagging. It was a race in slow-motion across the open scrubby field to the tank—ten minutes.

Unload the pump—another minute.

Jam the hose into the livestock tank—five seconds.

Start pump. It balks. Try again. It balks again. Try once more.

"No, wait," said Allison. "We could never carry a running hose up the ladder—it would be too heavy, too unwieldy."

"Probably right," said Daniel. "And we'll need a ladder."

"One of us will have to come back."

They both stared at the machine. Who would have the mechanical touch?

They raced back across to the ranch house, trailer bouncing behind—three minutes.

Now they had slack in the hose but they had to hope the water pressure would be tree-top height. Sparks floated and swirled in the air, fanned by a cruel, erratic wind.

"We need a ladder—quick," said Allison.

"There's one on the west side of the house." The voice came from behind. Normally exuding the calm of a brain surgeon, Colin's voice carried an edge.

"It's an extension ladder," Colin added, already running.

"A timely ghost," said Daniel. "Informative, too."

Locate and carry extension ladder to east side of house, tip it up, and find a good angle—four minutes.

"I'm not a big fan of heights," said Allison. The ladder flew up, the rung locks clanking like gunshots. The top cleared the eave by one rung.

They dragged the hose to the base of the ladder through the sopping, muddy grounds. Allison slung the hose over one shoulder and clamped it tight with her right arm, the nozzle dripped on her jeans and Ropers. Mud splattered everywhere. It would be sort of fun if there wasn't so much at stake. At least the mud was cool.

Daniel started heading back to the ATV. "Just give me the signal. I should be able to see you when you're up there."

"Go," she said, hoping he didn't fumble restarting the pump.

Daniel zipped away.

Would there be enough pressure? Could the pump handle it? Would an ember land on the roof and catch the house on fire as she watched? She envisioned every single way this was such a dumb idea.

The first ten rungs weren't so hard, but the hose grew heavier as she climbed. They should have spooled the slack at the base of the ladder. She was dragging the weight of the hose, too, shouldering added weight. The hose angled straight back, and she feared that it could tilt the ladder perpendicularly, plucking her from a rung and tossing her across the sparkling, fiery night like the flick of a serpent's tail.

By the time she reached the top, she told herself this was all her mind playing tricks and she wasn't in an airplane. She draped the hose across the top and shimmied up and over, ignoring the shifting ladder as she pushed off and kept her slight weight close to the roof.

She rolled over, sat up, and tugged on the hose as she scooched her butt farther from the edge.

"Start her up!" she yelled into the night. A lung-full of smoke forced a cough and stung her eyes. The light flared and pulsed.

The fire's size and ferocity created an odd sensation—daylight in front of her face and nighttime above.

Daniel waved back to her. She and Daniel had no cheering section or witnesses, which may have been a good thing.

"Come on baby," she said to the pump and to the night. On general principle she would be indifferent about the loss of personal property to the forces of nature, but now that she had a personal stake in the outcome and had pursued and promoted this particular approach to saving the house, she wanted to succeed.

A throaty purr drifted across the night. She braced herself for the weight and life of the water. She jammed the nozzle of the hose between her knees. She sat, suddenly aware of the strange sexual sensation and gender reversal. The hose shuddered—it *throbbed*—and she shook her head. It was a gusher!

The water jetted in a steady, beautiful arc as she flashed the hose back and forth across the tops of the trees, scaring away the floating embers or at least transforming them from chunks of fire to wet bits of harmless flying flotsam, too heavy to stay aloft.

The trees started to droop and no doubt the branches wondered about this strange sensation on their bark. It had been so very long.

SIX:
THURSDAY MORNING

From the ridge high above the homestead, looking west as dawn broke, smoke shot up in near-volcanic proportions. Dense blankets of grays and blacks climbed into the well-smudged sky. Devo imagined he could hear the fire chewing through and spitting out the giant swaths of timber he knew so well. He imagined all the animals and birds on the run, wondered if the squirrels and the chipmunks could run fast enough—or long enough—to stay out of harm's way. The insects couldn't. Neither could the butterflies or the grubs and pine beetles. The voles and moles were already dead.

The fire would also consume the authorities. Good. Except the dead body would draw them back, which wasn't so good.

Without the body, Devo and the devolutionists might have caught a reprieve from the government's so-far lame efforts to find their homestead. They had all seen the wildlife officers scouting, trying to pick up a trail. They were forced to devise a foolproof route for exchanging producers and crew through a backdoor of sorts.

Devo and Cinnamon and the others all figured it was a stalemate. Surely the government types had a rough idea of the homestead's location. But did they have the public relations wherewithal? From late spring to early fall, the camp wasn't critical—theoretically they could all live on their own and scatter around, communicate by an underground railroad. But living apart made it difficult to share any sudden bounty, like a good-size deer killed in a fall trap. And they needed to work together. It was more efficient, more productive under Cinnamon's guidance. Come winter, they had to work together to keep warm and nourished. Nine of his devolutionists had gone through the last winter with Devo—but it had been mild as winters go. Winters were usually rough, not for the borderline types. It was a mind game. This year, there would be nineteen holding out together. The occasional snowstorm caused major disruptions to their ability to hunt, but only for a day or two. Or maybe three.

"What are you thinking?"

He'd forgotten the camerawoman was there. Devo stared off at the fire. Light poured into the valley and, soon, the sun would awaken the forest. The blaze roared through the timber far in the distance, the giant burn scar smoldered in the foreground. Devo zeroed in on the ignition point far below and the charred body right where he'd left it.

Her camera was always pointed at him, part of the deal that fattened his Denver bank account.

"I'm thinking I'm glad that the fire is burning away from camp, at least for tonight." They had coached him to speak in a near-whisper, as if he was worried about being overheard. "Looks like it's heading down the ridge. I can imagine all the scrambling going on in places like Buford and down that way."

41

The message to the public was that the money from his contract would go for legal expenses and a non-profit to support teaching survival skills to youth, a National Outdoor Leadership Academy that would start with pre-teens. It would be NOLA on steroids for all to spread the gospel, to feed the need.

The "story" about the contract was a good story. It wasn't the whole story.

"Have you thought about any emergency plans if you had a fire near camp?"

Ninety percent of the questions they asked were ridiculous. They were the mind set of modern society. Ruth Suggs was one of his favorite *Latitude/Longitude* crew members. Maybe she had to ask what the viewers might be thinking. He could picture their production meetings in Denver.

"We'll have to deal with it at some point, I'd imagine," said Devo.

He could smell Ruth's nearly overwhelming lavender shampoo. They had tried to get the crew to go natural for three weeks before filming, to mingle better scent-wise, but not all complied. Devo admired the smooth, white skin of her cheek. She was lean and tall with a wide mouth. She could be a model for a dental hygiene commercial. Her cheekbones gleamed, her ponytails grazed her shoulders and her biceps flexed. She wore long white socks, hiking boots, and shorts that left at least a mile of leg exposed.

"We caught a break with the way that fire headed," said Devo. "If it was a couple days ago, with the winds we had, it might have been a whole different story."

"And how do you think things are going with the new recruits?"

This was a question in regular rotation. New blood, new conflicts, new rhythms, new resentments. A three-month course back in civilization, on the "top side" as Devo called it, helped newbies transition their diet, learn the wilderness hygiene drills, and revisit survival basics and extreme situations, too. They learned to make atlatls and how to skin and cook squirrel. Still, actual camp was a shock. The three months was a decompression chamber of sorts, but camp involved another set of tremors to digestive systems and modern comforts.

"I'm always worried," said Devo. "It's a tough transition. It's hard on the body and even harder on the mind. You start making lists of all the things you miss—the things you could be doing. You have to push through, so you can reach the point where your mind accepts this. Believes that you are capable, and this is the new norm. That these things and that whole lifestyle out there no longer exist. And they have to make that transition before winter, because that's a whole other deal."

"But let's say you get bigger, and they think out there that your camp is becoming more of a nuisance, won't size be an issue? It's not like you can go into town and vote for someone who will protect you or your squatter's rights up here, is it?"

Ruth gave a look like it was an easy question, like "which way to the mall?" Camera rolling. Who knew what shots they actually used? The handheld device he was given each week included both ratings and bank numbers. The figures were stunning. Some of the money was going to the non-profit. He was starting to realize he had a substantial nest egg waiting for him at home.

"Not our problem yet," said Devo.

"But someday soon," said Ruth. "Complaints that you're hunting up here without licenses. That you're camping illegally in the Flat Tops—"

"—if that's where we are."

"Yes," Ruth conceded. "The allegation might not be true but it might become fact if enough people repeat it and pressure the authorities to come root you out like a bunch of Deadheads who think it's 1974 and the party is just hitting its stride."

Producers ferried questions and answers to his top side lawyer, the one who handled the contract with the History Channel. He'd never seen an actual episode, though presumably they could load episodes on the handheld devices to show him. He was told they didn't use the producers' or videographers' questions on the show. So they could say anything they wanted to prod and poke. They used only his voice as if he was an oracle prone to spontaneous monologues narrating the devolution. They talked to all members of the camp in the same way, pulling them aside for one-on-one running commentary. Devo knew the thing they wanted to hear from tribe members were complaints, spats, and disagreements about the direction of management. The side interviews were like the water cooler bitch session.

"I don't know," said Devo. He had to hide his feelings. His old training as an actor, informal as it was, helped. "With the conditions up here, the drought, the stress on the whole landscape for lack of water and lack of rain, I think the bigger problem is fire, and I think they know it down in the towns and cities too. When the fire wipes Buford off the map or roars down through New Castle, there will be a bunch of people wishing they knew a thing or two about survival, wishing they weren't so soft in the middle."

"So the fire is a good thing?"

The producers sent notes. *Don't hold back. Be blunt. Keep it simple. Say what needs to be said.* The main thing was to show how devolving changed a person's attitude about nature. The producers, on the other hand, sometimes seemed overly fascinated by the health aspect for newbies and any romance or romance-related tiffs. *Latitude/Longitude* was one-part reality show about rapid weight loss and one-part *Real Housewives of the Cave.*

"Fire isn't good or bad," said Devo. "It's another element you have to deal with. It's more of a problem if you've got stuff to protect. You worry about your possessions going up in smoke. We're more like animals. We just have to stay ahead of the flames. Some places haven't burned in so long that the old forest and all the dense undergrowth, well, the fire gives them a new start—they need to devolve too. Start the fuck over."

They liked the occasional f-bomb, though they bleeped them. *Not to worry.* But whenever he slipped one in, he felt he was giving in to the top side lingo and urban vernacular. Shouldn't they be developing their own language to go with their new culture? That would kill the ratings unless they wanted to start using subtitles. The language was a distant thought anyway. They had enough to worry about.

"So?"

"So it was weird, that's all. There was no lightning down that way. I don't mind fire when nature is taking her course, but if others are trying to meddle? That's fucked up."

"So what are you going to do?" said Suggs.

"You mean now?"

"Yeah, sure. Now."

"I'm going to go down and look for Allison Coil."

"You're going to report it—everything?"

"And I'm going alone," said Devo.

She flipped the camera off, or at least pointed it down and away. "I can't let you do that. A dead body? Can you imagine the ratings?"

"I'm going alone."

"I was told to follow you. I stocked up. I've got a backpack ready—food, batteries, plenty of digital chips, water."

"You're going to have to tell them that I lost you. Or else I will, and then you'll be fucked."

Devo could outrun anyone, especially a fully loaded camerawoman and her backpack. All he would have to do is walk fast.

"First, I could be down there waiting for a day or two. Second, let me go do my thing with this deal. All I'm going to do is get word to the top side, dust my hands, and come right back. It'll be as if it never happened. You know, a tree falling in the forest."

SEVEN:
THURSDAY MORNING

DAWN'S ARRIVAL MEANT THEY had worked all night. Allison felt it all in her weary head. Dawn also meant the sun, of course, and daytime would revive the fire, give it a fresh shot of juice.

The McKee Ranch stood. The trees dripped, but that would end the second the sun hit the valley. The pump had been moved from the now-empty livestock tank back to the river, just in case.

Across the river the undergrowth had been licked clean from the floor of the forest. It was incinerated, smoldering, smoky, black, blacker, and gone. The roaring lion had eaten and was beginning to circle around and look for a spot to recline. Blackened tree trunks vented sadly defeated puffs of gray. Technically, the forest across the river remained "on fire." It wasn't contained. But the fire had done all the damage it could—and it had moved on down the road to terrorize another family, another town. Smoke from the forest rose lazily into the flat morning sky. Allison couldn't help but think of all the wildlife, the small critters—insects, squirrels, mice, voles, and foxes, and others who might run hopefully to their holes and their homes. Dirt was an excellent insulator from the heat, but the smoke could find them, and then what was left for cover if they did survive? They'd be easy prey for the birds, the owls, and any snakes that survived.

It was a bad summer to begin with. Bookings were low. Why bother with overnight horseback rides deep into the wilderness if you couldn't sit around a campfire sipping whiskey while the Milky Way gnawed its way into your soul? The statewide campfire ban took care of that. Based on where the fire had started and the size it had now reached, it was laying waste to prime hunting ground, and she couldn't begin to imagine what the fire would mean for her business and all the outfitters. But one thing was sure—anywhere this fire roared, it would take a half century before this land could restore itself as prime hunting ground. Investigators around the state had their hands full with all the fires, but if some idiot had set this blaze in her precious ground, there would be no patience for due process. She'd never led a lynch mob, but an arsonist taking advantage of the current conditions might be plenty of reason to form one.

Sleep beckoned. A couch, a bed, a spot in the barn. It didn't matter. She had planned to ride back across the Flat Tops to Sweetwater this morning with Colin, but that could wait. The area between the McKee Ranch and the road up to Trapper's Lake would be choked with firefighters and all their equipment. She might be better off borrowing a pickup and a trailer to move Sunny Boy back over to Sweetwater, but she couldn't imagine the mayhem this fire was causing down river around the outskirts of Meeker.

She found Colin in the kitchen, waiting on a pot of coffee to finish dripping.

"A man who understands survival skills," said Allison. She fell into him for a smoky, tired embrace. Colin was the shortest McKee, but his relative height made her feel protected. The notion was ancient and primal and all about her amygdala, but there it was.

"Mom put the coffee on," said Colin. "I can't take credit."

Allison kissed Colin on his sweaty, sticky cheek. She tasted salt and, of course, smoke. "I hope she's prepared to make more," said Allison. "Like one pot each?"

Caffeinating would have minimal impact. Her body cried for a corner to curl up and crash. No chemical stood a chance in that tug of war.

Colin pulled two thick-handled mugs from a cupboard. The front door slammed. Char and Gabriella carried boxes so heavy they both walked with an awkward gait.

"It's not like there's a rush," said Char. "Seems like we were moving out just ten hours ago."

"That's because we were," said Gabriella.

"I say let the stuff sit in the trucks for now. Make sure," said Char. The boxes went on the kitchen counter, with Colin's help. They rattled when they landed. Earl McKee found himself suddenly sentimental about his dinnerware.

Gabriella wore boots, jeans, and a turquoise cowboy shirt with a small bolo tie closed by a square, shiny black stone. The hair was high maintenance. Char had worked through the night in a sturdy white T-shirt that said MEEKER across the top and featured an image of a bugling elk, now faded by the years. Allison had to admire Char's plain-style spunk. Her work boots were muddy. Gabriella's were ready to head for the dance hall.

"He wants to unpack?" said Colin. "Already?"

Allison needed to find something to do. Maybe the pump or the river needed checking. She could climb the ladder and monitor the fire. Or climb the ladder and wait for the first passing helicopter to drop a line and hoist her out of there. She would almost rather fly than help carry boxes of McKee crap back inside the house. What was the rush?

"That's what he says," said Char. She poured a glass of water toward the sink. "I do believe the threat isn't what it was at midnight. What fire is left doesn't seem to have the power to leap the river."

"And not a peep from our so-called government." Earl McKee carried an ornate clock that belonged on the fireplace mantle tucked under one arm and a photograph of their first Beagle, Duke, under the other. "Screw it, you all are right. We'll leave everything packed in the car."

"Makes sense," said Char.

Gabriella closed her eyes long enough to look like she'd fallen asleep standing up. She took a breath and shook her head. "Okay," she said. With Earl's blessing, they now had permission to droop.

"What a pain in the ass," said Earl. "One big royal pain in my hairy ass."

The coffeepot and the conversation moved outside where the margaritas had flowed hours, or was it weeks ago? Char and Gabriella assembled melon slices and biscuits followed by scrambled eggs. A plate of sizzling link sausages came next. Somehow Char made the transition from refugee to model hostess without a hiccup.

"Better get those others back here unless they like cold eggs," said Char.

From her corner of the porch, Allison could see "those others" out across the field by the livestock tank. One of the black behemoth SUVs was parked with its nose sticking out of the barn. From time to time she caught a flash of movement from inside and once she glimpsed one of the brothers.

"What's the rush out there?" said Allison to nobody in particular.

"I think Daniel needs his SUV for something later on," said Gabriella. "And not full of stuff."

Perhaps they had loaded up the saddles and tack—Earl McKee was partial to the best of everything for the horses. With the price of a good saddle sky-high, the priority made sense.

The driver's side door closed and the SUV pulled out. It had to be a quarter-mile view across the fields. Details weren't sharp but Allison would have sworn that the departure was done with attitude, or at least haste. Perhaps they smelled breakfast.

"Done is done," said Allison.

"Suppose so," said Colin.

"Shit," said Earl. He was on his last bite of eggs. Was he complaining about the portion sizes? "Not one helicopter took a look, not one fire truck came up this way to check on diddley squat."

"Probably building lines in town," said Colin. Closer to Meeker, houses dotted the south banks of the White River. "Maybe they assumed we were okay."

"All I know is little Miss Allison Coil saved our bacon," said Earl. "That was some quick thinking."

"Daniel was right there," said Allison. "Total team deal."

"I think I can see why Colin thinks you're so special," said Earl.

"Anyone would have seen the problem," said Allison.

"But not the fix," said Earl.

"Take it," said Colin. "Besides, it's true. And anything you do well makes me look better, so—"

"Partial credit for having her here," said Earl. "That's it."

In the complicated dance around Earl's ego, Allison preferred the role as wallflower. Her adopted strategy to survive these visits started with being naïve and giving off a sense that she was still learning the ropes, which was half-true anyway.

"I'm going to take my truck to see what's what down the road," said Earl. "See where the fire is now, and see how long it takes to find anyone who gives a shit."

"Want some company?" said Colin.

Earl shrugged. "Stay here," he said.

Good. She wanted Colin's help to come up with a plan to get her and Sunny Boy back to Sweetwater. They were due to lead a group of riders on an overnight trip set up by a guest ranch near Eagle, though she had the feeling the cancellation call would come any minute. Either the fire would force the National Forest to ban all such trips into the Flat Tops or the riders would decide not to horseback up into jeopardy.

"Help keep an eye on the place, okay?" said Earl. "I don't know what I might say or do if I happen to run into one of them bureaucrats who are deciding if it's time to start fighting this fire."

"Maybe they are punishing you," said Gabriella, a well-conditioned Earl sympathizer. "Maybe they have their favorites. The city never forgets to pick up the mayor's trash, you know."

"Possible," said Earl. "Or maybe they were too weak-kneed to make it this far upriver. I'll have to go ask. I'm sure they'll tell me why my tax dollars didn't amount to squat on the night I could have used them the most."

It was impossible to imagine Earl McKee watching the river flow or the campfire crackle. Unlike Daniel and Garrett, Colin had grown up uninfluenced by the original Earl McKee agenda, to populate the county with strong, independent offspring who would be taught from the get-go about manifest destiny.

When Daniel was fifteen and Garrett was fourteen, Earl had tested his boys by dropping them off deep in the Flat Tops. They had to find their own way home. He gave them matches and a small axe—nothing else but the clothes on their back. They had one day's notice to think through what to wear, but they couldn't hide any secret items. They left at midnight and Earl drove around in circles, the boys blindfolded, before putting them on horseback. It was a bright night with the moon but the boys had no idea where they were. The blindfolds came off. They rode for three hours before the sun came up and then all day. The drop-off point was on a high ridge covered in a thicket of dense pines. It was late afternoon. Earl took the horses and headed back. The boys had a rough idea of direction but the lesson was survival and route-finding. It was a test. Allison had pieced together parts of the story from Colin over the years and Earl referred to bits here and there, but the bottom line was a tale that bordered on child abuse because they both got soaked in a day-long rain, and Garrett spent two weeks in the hospital fighting off pneumonia. It had taken them three days to find their way, and they hadn't found or consumed the calories they needed for the effort they were exerting. They didn't sleep. Their attempts at shelter failed. They stumbled home. They had followed the one rule Earl had laid down—not to rely on another human being. They weren't angry, but Daniel could barely stand.

Earl hadn't put Colin through any such gauntlet. Colin's interest in the woods came naturally. Perhaps by the time Colin came up through the ranks, Earl let him be. No agenda, no expectations. Allison didn't know all the details but gathered in a general way that the whole survival test had been conducted over Char's heavy protestations. It wasn't hard to imagine that son number three faced no such survival exam.

The older brothers held nothing against Earl. They were too stuck in the shadows of Earl's outsized presence, and likely also viewed the government as "them." Colin had taken to the woods like a lime takes to tequila, even without the wilderness challenge. He had forged his own reputation as a hunter and had surpassed his father's capabilities and experience in the outdoors.

For having gained Colin as a partner, Allison had to expose herself to Earl's opinions two or three times a year—and usually no longer than a barbecue and a couple of margaritas.

Earl exited. Char went to round up more eaters. Gabriella gazed out over the surreal remains across the river.

"Ride or drive?" said Colin. "If we ride, we'll have to put in somewhere other than Trapper's. We'll need to start further east to avoid the burn."

"And downstream is going to be mess," said Allison. "It's got to be a zoo through Meeker with the fire. I'd rather be on a horse." Plus, if they trucked around they'd end up with an extra trailer at Sweetwater and then need to figure out how to get it back. "You can get your honorable discharge?"

Colin smiled. "What do you mean?"

"From active duty to the homestead, you know. Are you free and clear to go?"

"You make it sound like I'm a conscript."

"Family obligations," she said. "Like gravity. Only more demanding."

"I was here, I helped. You helped. Everyone pitched in."

"Just an observation," said Allison. "Take it easy, cowboy."

Colin was never one to grow prickly or defensive, but also didn't appreciate this line of analysis. With Colin, you did what needed doing and you did it well. Head down. Forthright. Well-meaning. No excuses.

"Then let's quit the chatter about the stuff that doesn't matter," said Colin. She was short, and he was medium height, at least it was a generous definition of the word. The fit was perfect, including how she tucked against him for a hug. The night's hustle in the heat coated his neck and T-shirt in grit and salt. The sun punched through smoke and again reiterated its monotonous, relentless message. Two months to go in summer. Plenty of earth-baking time remained. The chance of saving the fall hunts were dwindling with each scorching day.

"Horses or trucks back to Sweetwater?" said Colin. "I suppose the other option is to avoid Meeker and head east to Yampa and then back south the long way around."

"A long ride in a truck on a dusty washboard road or a couple of days on horseback in the Flat Tops. You don't think I consider that a real choice," said Allison. "Do you?"

Allison and Colin focused on their horses and supplies for food and the trip back. Earl McKee decided at the last minute to give them a young mule named Hercules to replace Eli, who had died that spring. It was always great to have a mule in the mix for their hybrid vigor and sure-footedness. Allison liked the way mules thought, and she wanted to bond with Hercules the way she had with Eli, though it would take a year's worth of trips. The plan was they could leave a pickup and a trailer at a trailhead, maybe Marvine Lake. They would skirt the fresh burn and get out ahead of any invading army of firefighters. In a day or two, the brothers would come collect the pickup and trailer.

Getting ready involved side projects Earl dreamed up for Colin. A trip to the barn to retrieve something or other and some tinkering with a stubborn trailer hitch on one of the SUVs. By the time they were ready to load Sunny Boy, Merlin, and Hercules in the four-horse Cimarron trailer, it was later than they had hoped. They were putting the mule up the ramp when a mini-convoy of authorities turned off County Road 9 and headed down the straight-shot dirt road that ended at the McKee's. One pale green pickup, Colorado state logo on the door. One Rio Blanco County Sheriff's squad car, lights swirling. One U.S. Forest Service pickup bringing up the rear.

"They're gonna ask if we've seen a fire." Earl McKee was focused on rigging a halter for Hercules. He paused long enough for a glance. "Fuckers," he muttered. "What could they possibly want?"

The vehicles stopped in a tight row, nose to tail. Allison admired the attempt to appear efficient and organized out here next to nowhere on the outskirts of Buford, but even she had to wonder whether they didn't have better things to do or fires to track.

Each vehicle held two men. Five of the six sported too-clean matching yellow Nomex as if they were headed up to dig trenches on the front line. The sixth was a sheriff's deputy who stuck to his olive greens and obvious badge. All men who knew their roles. Perhaps they were working their way up river, doing preliminary damage assessment. She feared for them all if Earl McKee said what he was thinking.

One self-appointed leader offered a handshake that Earl took with zero enthusiasm.

"Everybody safe?" He introduced himself as Deputy Sheriff Joe Campion. His skin was pocked. His long face ended in a jutting jaw. The uniform gave him a look of authority and it was one size too big. He might have been trying to add some heft. She didn't recognize him or anyone. But why would she? Sheriff Christie was still in office but it had been two years since the death of Josh Keating and the whole ugly thing with Austin Rayburn. She never looked over at the Keating place when she drove upriver, and she hadn't been involved or tangled up with authorities in Rio Blanco County since.

"We made it," said Earl.

Allison hung back from the inner circle as the White River National Forest something or other introduced himself. She was under the impression that the older brothers had been off on another meaningless mission, but there they stood as if space and time were concepts for mortals to wrestle down.

"The house is okay?" asked Campion.

"Thanks to a stroke of ingenuity," said Earl. "And fighting for our lives all night. No sign of any help, unless you're it."

"The fire has jumped the river. We've got our hands full downstream."

"So if you're here to help me unpack, let me show you—"

She couldn't leave soon enough. These soldiers of bureaucracy had met their match. They had no clue. Earl McKee's bitter sarcasm could get volcanic. The fire wouldn't be their only problem if they looked the wrong way or said the wrong thing.

"You're in the evacuation zone."

The wrong thing—like that.

"Thank you for the notification," said Earl. "I already evacuated and came back. Sorry you weren't here to see it."

Deputy Sheriff Campion's tone was matter-of-fact. He expected compliance and reason. He explained that the forecast was for the winds to turn. It might look close to burned-out down by the river, but there was a whole chunk of untouched forest up on the ridge that could "blow up every bit as much as what we all witnessed the day before." They had an army of firefighters on the way.

"The woods are burning," said Campion. "It's far from over. We'll be working all through here. We need good access to the road that runs from Buford south to New Castle and this whole area. We can't guarantee anyone's safety."

The fact that Earl McKee didn't say anything did not imply, Allison knew, that he believed this new information had merit. Gabriella kept her distance up on the porch. Garrett came out of the house behind her, holding a midday beer. He lifted the glass as she caught his eye for a morning toast. Garrett looked wiped out or maybe he'd kept the beers going all night. Daniel came out behind Garrett, coffee mug slung casually.

"So you can't guarantee you can protect my house, either? I mean, if we leave?" Earl's tone was of the "making conversation" variety, but Allison heard the indignation an inch below the surface.

"All I hear the forest fire guys say is they want to find a spot to draw a line and hold it."

"If the fire comes back this way, it would be like picking through the garbage at an old dump," said Earl. "There's nothing left."

"This area is our access to the battlefield, and believe me when I say you don't want to be here—the noise and the activity around here will be insane for weeks."

"Then find another spot for your war," said Earl. "We're done being jerked around. Not a call or a morsel of assistance when shit was happening last night, and now you're telling me to go when the threat is over? You gotta know that's fucked up."

Earl turned around, spotted Garrett on the porch and gave him a quick finger flip. *Come here.* Garrett shuffled over with the pace of a pallbearer. Maybe to piss off his father. Maybe to be strange. When Garrett was halfway, Earl repeated the finger flip and stared, his expression cold and blank, at Allison.

"Earl let's just—" Char tried to interject, but stopped. She had been pacing on the perimeter of the cluster. The three words were enough to draw her husband's attention, but she hadn't considered the risk of showing the authorities a break in the family ranks.

"Let's just what?" The general mocked the idea that key tactical advice might come from a fresh troop in the rear guard.

"Go," said Char. Her suggestion lacked oomph. "Get out of their way, you know. The main thing is moving all the animals. Let them fight the fire, and we'll come back."

Allison hadn't budged an inch, giving Char space to make her case, and now Earl repeated the finger flip in her direction at the same moment as Garrett arrived.

Earl nodded as if he was contemplating Char's counsel. He greeted Garrett with a firm shoulder grab.

Allison stepped up. How slow could she move? Earl's hand came around her shoulder when she got within range, and his grip squeezed like a clamp.

"You know what these two did last night?"

"It was Daniel," said Garrett, to Earl. "It was Daniel and Allison."

"Right," said Earl. "My mistake."

"I don't care what—"

Campion stopped mid-sentence. They all heard it at the same time. It was a noise she knew well.

It haunted her dreams, both the day and night varieties. There were times she watched her personal plane crash from the perspective of someone standing on the end of the runway and the dreams—nightmares—always featured this same overpowering scream.

This jet flew so low that it might be on final approach to the nonexistent Buford International Airport. Or maybe it was planning to put down in Earl McKee's pasture. The jet's nose tipped up. It swooped over the house, the fuselage so close Allison could make out the paneling pattern of aluminum on its underbelly. Acid soaked her stomach. Salt water lapped at the back of her throat. She stood smack back in the cold murky waters off Long Island Sound. Jets cruising at altitude had lost their psychological punch. They chose random times to gnaw at her soul but this one threatened to fall like a rock straight out of the sky and bash them all like bugs. What were the odds? You survive a crash of a commercial jet at a big-city airport but your fate is waiting for you a decade down the road in a spot where a DC-10 nose-dived and splattered all over a remote pasture.

The roar crushed them. Char plugged her ears with her fingers and bent over at the waist, as if an extra foot or two of distance might lessen the impact. Gabriella, on the porch, ducked.

The giant jet scraped the high ridge to the south. Its belly hemorrhaged bright red-orange guts and blood. The engine whine rose an octave. Then it was gone after a drawn-out diminuendo. Finally, there was room to speak.

"The fire is right up the hill," said Campion. "You all need to evacuate."

On some invisible cue, the remaining Nomex-clad authorities stepped forward.

"Whoa," said Earl. "You got no legal right—and you know it. Get the fuck off my property now."

Deputy Sheriff Joe Campion reached behind him. It was a quick move. Allison imagined a set of handcuffs dangling from a rear loop. The Nomex gang had numbers.

Char let out an audible gasp. She saw it coming. Allison, having moved back while the jet roared overhead, also saw it coming. Deputy Sheriff Joe Campion never saw it coming.

Earl McKee was a lefty. The punch started fast, ended faster with follow-through, a sickening pop, hard to the jaw.

Deputy Joe Campion spun around. His arms didn't come up to protect himself from the fall.

EIGHT:
THURSDAY MORNING

"WHAT THE HELL WAS that all about?"

Allison stared straight ahead. Colin drove. The pickup strained, tugging two horses and a mule. Riding to the trailhead might have been faster.

Calling in medical care for the deputy, whose face was bloody and smashed, hadn't taken long, but figuring out where to go and what to do had taken hours.

"You think I was having fun?" He looked over, shook his head, and shuddered. "I couldn't wait to get out of there."

"I mean that thing right before the punch when your dad wanted me to come up with Garrett?"

"Maybe he was going to say that you saved the house once and you could save it again."

"What was happening during all of that anyway?" said Allison. The question gnawed at her all night.

"Huh?" said Colin.

"Huh—what?" said Allison. "What was everybody doing all night?" She refrained from replacing "everybody" with "you."

"What do you think?"

"I don't know," said Allison. "Seemed odd to make me and Daniel the bucket and hose brigade."

"And you did great," said Colin. "We were moving stuff—you know, packing as much as we could. Every damn vehicle was crammed to the gills. I could sleep for a week starting right now, all the shit I lifted and carried."

"So we had the easy job?"

"I didn't say that. All I know is he gets his mind made up. Once he fell into a rhythm loading up, nothing was going to change until the house started burning or until we were done."

In fact, when Earl McKee talked, you sometimes got the feeling his opinions were rooted down in his boots.

"I wasn't being critical," said Allison.

"Don't think I love hanging around that place," said Colin. "Especially when the whole crew is there, wives and girlfriends and all. I can't keep straight all the things I can't say so I tend to go numb."

The pickup rounded a corner and the road pitched up, slowing them further.

Allison could feel the pressure lift. With Earl headed to jail, Daniel and Gabriella headed back to Denver. Garrett had his own place in Meeker; it didn't sound like much. Allison's head turned to the Flat Tops, and she wondered what kinds of views they would have of the fire when they climbed up on the plateau.

They would need one night under the stars, given the late start. It wouldn't hurt to catch a trout or two, if they had time. Colin had swiped some frozen homemade chili from the McKee's refrigerator, and they rode over with the usual stash of snacks and crackers and Fig Newtons. They would arrive home tired and hungry, Allison imagined, and that was fine because at least they would be out from under the McKee mayhem.

The horses and the mule smelled like smoke when they came out of the trailer. They would all need a thorough scrub-down. With meager supplies and minimal camping gear, it didn't take long to pack and saddle up, including a check of the three animals. The high sun pounded the sandy pull-out where they worked. It was so hot Allison wondered if the forest would provide its usual relief. Whenever it was working, and whatever it was destroying today, the wildfire was no doubt feeling encouraged by the mother ship, the orange orb in the sky that squeezed any last bit of moisture from the fuel in its path.

A pickup pulled in behind the horse trailer. It stopped, spewing a cloud of dust. They'd seen no other vehicles all morning. This one came at them with purpose. It looked familiar. Colin tipped his head back, signaling resignation.

The sun's reflection off the windshield blinded her view of the driver, but Colin seemed unworried.

"What now?" he said to nobody in particular.

Garrett climbed down from the pickup, extra wide and black with running boards and a front grille that mimicked a semi. He left the engine running.

"Don't shoot the messenger." Garrett shook his head. "I followed Dad to jail and he wants you back to stay with Mom."

Solo would suck.

"Tell him you missed us," said Colin. "Tell him we were long gone up the trail."

That seemed reasonable.

"He wants you to help watch the place," said Garrett.

"Shit," said Colin, matter-of-fact.

Merlin snorted. Allison understood. *Let's go.*

"I was gone," said Colin. "We were gone. You found an empty trailer and an empty truck. Can't you work with that?"

"I'm a terrible liar. The worst."

"Then you'll have to do better."

"He won't believe me." Garrett furrowed his brow as in imitation of someone who was thinking. "He'll know there wasn't enough time for you to get saddled up."

"We're quick," said Colin. "And we're traveling light."

Allison knew when to stay on the sidelines, her Team Colin pom-poms tucked away. Not a peep. Not one dewy eye. Allison knew Colin would not budge.

And that Garrett wasn't done trying.

"If Colin comes back with me, you'll be fine by yourself, right?"

Allison took her time answering, for effect. "Not ideal with a two-horse string."

"We'll take Merlin back with us," said Garrett.

"He should get out of the smoke," said Allison. "And it's a long ride solo with a mule and a horse on the string."

Garrett sighed. "Guess I'll have to tell Dad the same thing I told you."

"What's that?" said Colin.

"Don't shoot the messenger," said Garrett.

"But you didn't even see us," said Colin. "Tell them you hiked up the trail, knew then you wouldn't be able to keep up."

Garrett headed back to the pickup. "Like I said, I'm a terrible liar. He'll see right through me."

NINE:
THURSDAY AFTERNOON

DUNCAN BLOOM SMELLED SMOKE. He'd been waiting for a whiff. His windows were open. His crusty Camry gobbled up County Road 8, heading west from Yampa. The sky through the trees looked innocent, clueless, and basic Colorado blue. He couldn't see the smoke, but his nose said *hello*.

Duncan Bloom had covered his fair share of Colorado wild-fires—the Red Canyon blaze near Carbondale a couple years back, the massive Hayman fire that burned for weeks and weeks along the Front Range in 2002, back when Bloom was a Front Range reporter working at *The Denver Post*.

This one sounded like it had the potential to be the biggest one yet, although it didn't have the dollar damage potential of the Black Forest Fire in 2013 that trashed 500 homes near Colorado Springs.

Bloom slowed to a crawl. A thick white column of smoke blotted the sky. Its stalk was bent to the wind. A thousand feet up, maybe higher, the column smashed into an invisible ceiling, and the smoke pancaked into a messy blotch that smudged the whole northern sky.

Bloom stopped the car and snapped off the motor. His air conditioner was feeble to begin with, but the blast of outdoor air suggested that he should be more forgiving of its efforts. He stood with his camera and recorded what he could with the longer of his two lenses. He wouldn't make it to any Wi-Fi before Meeker to download the pics to his laptop and ship the digital images back to his editor. The fire roared west of Buford. If a checkpoint had been put up there, he was screwed.

Bloom's cell phone squirted an electronic beep that cut through the stillness like a clarion. He'd left his car door open. The air conditioner would have to start all over again, climbing Mt. Everest starting from sea level at the Indian Ocean. It didn't matter. He couldn't have left the car running. Now that he was with Trudy Heath, whose every breath respected the Earth and its resources, his habits had changed.

The cell phone squealed again.

"It's Coogan. Where are you?"

"Making my way," said Bloom. "From where I'm standing, this fire will be cooking for a long time to come."

"Dante Soto is missing," said Coogan.

"How do you know when a recluse is missing?" said Bloom.

"Riddle of the day, I guess," said Coogan.

"He's a hiker," said Bloom. "Since when?"

"Not sure," said Coogan. "Just got a tip called in, that's all. All I'm saying is you've got more than the fire to cover. You've got sources. You should have an edge."

It had been one of those profiles he had reported and written over the span of four months, snagging interviews and telephone conversations as he could. At some point along the way, he had let it slip to Dante Soto's friends and cohorts that he was Trudy Heath's partner or boyfriend. The next thing he knew Soto was lured out of the shadows and had joined them in Sweetwater for an off-the-record evening of in-depth conversation. In addition, Bloom had made four separate trips to Meeker to talk about the Dante Soto phenomenon and once made the long drive up a winding road to Soto's remote yurt.

Soto, sort of the Hispanic J.D. Salinger of the environmental movement, didn't grant interviews. In a couple of op-ed pieces, he slapped the media for its role in exacerbating every issue. The media found no ratings or advertisers by engaging thoughtful, solution-oriented analysts, Soto asserted. The rise of the insatiable consumer culture was due to the toxic yeast sprinkled on society by Giant Media and the advertisers who convinced us, post-World War II, to overspend, overuse, and overeat.

The end result, Soto argued, was that as citizens we had lost touch with our relationship with the planet. We had no real concept of what fed us and fueled us. We had no idea what was behind a $79 round-trip discount airfare to go visit grandma at Thanksgiving. We had no idea what it took to fill our gas tanks or heat our homes.

Soto didn't laud the heroes of the anti-fracking crowd, nor did he demonize those who wanted to drill. He didn't believe that a new balance would be propositioned by lawmakers in either Denver or Washington, D.C.

For the most part, Soto shunned the limelight, but the fact that he was an intellectual Hispanic, one who had made the environment his top priority, gave the messages a nifty new twist.

Soto had attracted millions of loyal followers and had developed a large network of friends and influencers, including none other than Trudy Heath. But Soto's big plan had yet to get rolling. And Meeker was the place where he had wanted to start. As he gained traction, it wasn't hard for Duncan to imagine he had stepped on some toes and awakened a beast. Status quo.

TEN:
THURSDAY AFTERNOON

THE PUNGENCY OF A horse, Devo liked to say, at least to himself, was a whole different animal. The sweat produced a sharp odor that cut through the forest just like trout frying over a campfire or a meadow of July wildflowers basking in the sun. He smelled them before he heard them, heard them for a good ten minutes before he saw them.

Allison Coil and her guy both up on horses and a mule too.

Devo's nose had picked up a wrinkle in the horse sweat and now all was explained—the mule.

He hadn't had to wait more than six hours. And there she was, coming right up alongside the edge of the burn scar. It was a short quarter-mile more south to the body but he had found a spot to wait and hide off in the unburned side of the Marvine Trail.

He stepped out onto the tree-lined trail, good as having a stoplight in the goddamn forest.

Allison Coil rode in front, the mule stringed to her horse. And the guy, that same guy from the last time he'd seen her, brought up the rear.

The horses stopped. Allison shook her head. "Holy shit," she said.

ELEVEN:
THURSDAY AFTERNOON

"Point," said Allison. "Point to the spot. I want to go in alone."

One reason was to get away from Devo's harsh bouquet. She knew from previous experience that it took some getting used to, but it was possible. She also wanted to step in as if finding it herself. The third reason she couldn't quite specify, but she flashed on the fact that she had barely escaped this very fate, becoming a pile of charred bones in the woods.

"About forty yards in." Devo pointed the line to follow. "Right close by the base of a trunk. Can't miss him."

Sun blasted the scene. A sci-fi movie set. Dystopian. Bombed-out. The day after the end of time. With the forest canopy torched, more of the surrounding forest could be seen except it was no longer forest—and wouldn't be again for a long time. It would reincarnate as itself but perhaps one micro-evolution more, something—tougher? More fire-resistant? Lightning-resistant? With water more precious than gold, this time the forest might be forced to re-germinate on a thinner diet. The implications could alter the species of all the critters that would someday depend on it for shelter and food and a place to call home.

Fire was a natural force, part of the cycle, but she found herself concentrating on the critters who sensed the need to flee but who didn't stand a chance at self-preservation given the scale and ferocity of the blaze. The news reporters would quantify the square miles covered by the fire; Allison wanted them to report the toll on the animal populations and the devastation to the hunting grounds that provided cover for the prey that fed her business.

This guy stared at the open sky except there were no eyeballs, only sockets. No flesh survived the heat, only bone.

"You smell it?" said Devo. He had followed her in. He spoke in secrets. The air was still. Voices carried.

Allison preferred not to inhale. "Maybe," she lied. "Not sure."

"Almost overpowering to me," said Devo.

Colin stayed back on the trail. Nothing had been said, but she was glad someone decided to keep watch.

The owner of the skull looked like he had laid down to take a nap. The bones were charred black. His body was oriented so his toes pointed northwest, the direction the fire had blown. They also pointed downhill; the grade was steep. His head rested a good foot higher than his toe, close to the base of a tree as if he might have been napping and got surprised.

Allison crouched and spotted one area on the left side of both legs where the flesh hadn't burned away—consistent with the direction the fire had moved.

The flash of crispy skin and fat made the remains more human. Allison suppressed a strong surge of nausea and wondered about the definition of "corpse." Bones alone seemed somehow less like a previous human being. The remnant of flesh put death back closer to the land of the living. It made the loss of life more vivid.

"Goddamn it," she said.

"What?" said Devo.

"No sign of anything he was carrying, so maybe he's out for a day hike and he runs into this? And can't get out?"

Maybe he had carried a backpack, and it was underneath him. There wasn't a scrap of anything to suggest that was possible.

Devo showed her the stone fire ring. "We're right on the edge of the fire here—the whole thing," said Devo.

It took two hands to pick up the smallest stone, about the size of bowling ball, but heavier. Scorch marks blackened one side while the other was pristine. "But why bother with the stones?" said Allison.

"Careless campers?" said Colin. He had abandoned his post on the trail to take a closer look at the whole scene.

"On their first fire?" said Allison. "And why would you camp here? So random, just a place off the trail."

Allison put her face down into the ring, studied the blackened surface. She caught a whiff of something odd, out of place, and asked Devo to give it a closer sniff. He stuck his nose into the blackened ash and wriggled his nostrils like a bloodhound.

"What the hell?" said Devo. "Greasy potato chips—takes me right back to eighth grade lunchroom."

"You serious?" said Colin.

Allison counted fifteen paces from fire ring to body. She walked the whole scene in a circle, walked six more paces further out from the body and repeated the circle in the opposite direction. Her circles took her back to the Marvine Trail and, as she expanded the radius, on the east side of it too. Finally she stood on the trail at the closest point to the fire ring. Devo and Colin huddled over the ring, chatting. Colin kept his distance upwind. She put her back to them and plunged directly off the trail in the opposite direction from Devo and Colin, her head down and scanning. A firestarter wouldn't take to the trail—too obvious. Allison scanned right and left. She counted one hundred steps into the healthy-forest side of the trail, hoping for a piece of litter or an impression from a boot.

Nothing.

"I'm telling you," said Devo. She was back at the fire. "My nose has gone Airedale. So much more powerful. So much more interesting."

"How's your flock?" said Allison, making conversation. She kept moving, scanning the ashy ground. What had she missed?

"It's not my anything," said Devo. "We're a team."

"Bet you didn't mind that mild winter." Allison continued to circle, now without a pattern, more random, looking for anything out of place. "Least amount of snow in fifty years or something like that?"

"Winter's a bitch," said Devo. "It's all part of it. But we've got our huts now, actual roofs. And all we have to do is plan ahead since we've got a place. It's not like we're Lewis and Clark coming over the Bitterroots."

"How far from here?"

"The Bitterroots?" said Devo. "Seven or eight hundred miles."

Allison smiled.

Devo leaned against a tree like an overgrown cartoon chipmunk. He wore some sort of tight-fitting loincloth made out of buckskin. His dreadlocks fell past his shoulders, thick ropes of fuzz in various shades of brown. His beard was ragged, but his eyes were bright. He looked like he could climb straight up the tree as easily as walk back to the trail. Underneath it all was a decent-looking dude, but a barber and bath wouldn't be a bad start.

"I'm not telling you where the camp is—what we call the homestead now," said Devo.

"Did you see anything?" asked Allison. "Anything at all?"

"Enough to know it sure as hell wasn't lightning. Not down here. Not that day. Up on the ridge, yes. Higher, sure. Much higher."

"Where were you?"

"Southeast of here about five miles, up higher. Sweeping view. I know my good vantage points. No way was this started by a big spark from the sky."

"I think I know where this is going," said Colin.

"You mean, where we're going," said Allison.

"I don't want to, but we could split up," said Colin.

"You're going to do it." Devo looked giddy. "Police, forest rangers, authorities—the whole bit?"

"Why are you so keen on cops?" Colin had maintained a steadfast dozen feet of distance between himself and the woodland creature.

"It's not obvious?" said Devo. "We can't have some pyromaniac up here starting fires. We've got a legitimate community up here and, no, I ain't saying where, but if a fire came racing up the hill we would be in deep shit. Or dead."

"And then there's the body," said Allison.

"That you found," said Devo.

"We'll see," said Allison, loud enough for her ears only.

Colin's idea of splitting up held no appeal. Sending him back north to find someone from the sheriff's office put him back in the throes of the mess at the family ranch. Getting the cops' attention might be a challenge, given the scale of the fire around Meeker, but if they were going to split up it made more sense for her to retrace her steps and lead authorities back to the spot and then catch up with Colin in a day. Or two. Or...

"You take the mule back home," said Allison.

"Bad idea," said Colin.

"Why?"

He had been thinking this through too.

"We're better off together."

"What I was thinking from the get-go," said Allison. She was lying.

"Hey, great," said Devo. "Tell them you two found the body. Keep my name out of it."

"And how am I going to explain that I just happened to find the body?" said Allison.

Devo stared at his lightly sandaled feet, some sort of buckskin moccasin type of footgear. He shook his head. The whites of his eyes were snow. "I don't know," he said.

"So what if I need to come find you?" she said.

"You better not," said Devo.

"But what if?" said Allison.

"We'll watch for you," said Devo. "Camp, say, in this general vicinity. Anywhere a couple square miles east of here, light a small camp fire—"

"Campfire ban," said Colin. "Whole state. Apparently these fuckers didn't get the memo."

Devo shrugged. He tightened his lips and stroked his matted dreadlocks. "I think they'll have their hands full. Make it a small fire. We'll keep an eye out."

"Small campfire," said Allison. "How about a more specific place? You know, to speed up the process if we need you?"

Devo stared at her for a moment, then Colin. "I guess I can trust you. Slide Lake. You passed it about thirty minutes ago."

"I know it," said Colin.

"But don't mention anything," said Devo. "Say you stopped for a break, wandered into the woods to look at the fire and, bang, there he was. Simple."

Allison flipped open her years-old mobile phone. No cell. No surprise. Trapper's Lake Lodge might be their best bet, and she plotted the route in her mind—Marvine Trail to Oyster Lake Trail and hang a left. Twelve miles? They should be there by early evening. The route would take them around the southern end of Marvine Peak. Trapper's Lake Lodge should be far enough east of the fire that it wouldn't be too overrun with fire equipment and gear, but it wouldn't surprise her if it was being commandeered as a headquarters or base camp. It might be evacuated too. At least there were land lines, if they worked. If they could get in to use them. She and Colin could wait there for authorities and guide them back. Not the worst assignment. She was with Devo on one thing—if this monster burn had been arson, something had to be done. Soon—as in now.

TWELVE:
THURSDAY EVENING

Duncan Bloom sailed through Buford like a local. No checkpoints. His Camry was as good as putting an "outsider" sign on the roof. He needed a pickup, a cowboy hat, a shotgun rack, and a dog in the back—maybe two.

Bloom snaked down the long road from Buford that followed the White River to Meeker, then headed north toward Craig about fifteen miles before taking a sharp right that left the pavement behind and headed up. The car throbbed on the dirt washboard. The air conditioner was no match for the attack from the sun. Bloom cracked a window, but that made it worse.

Back to the south, down the valley past Meeker, smoke billowed high. It felt odd to be driving away from the main event. If something had happened to Dante Soto, he wouldn't be the last reporter up this road. He knew, however, he was the first.

Meeker was a special place. When he had needed to run up here to cover a story, he liked to travel with Trudy. The teaming up saved gas; she visited accounts in Meeker too. The Blue Spruce Inn was nobody else's idea of romantic getaway, but it was whistle clean and a friendly hotel a block off the small downtown. They had their first deep heart-to-hearts at the Blue Spruce, only six weeks after they had worked together on the story about the for-profit prisons and the cruelest kind of hunt Bloom could imagine. That was the trip that sealed their relationship. Thinking back on it took his mind off Soto and put him in a kind of peaceful reverie.

She had transformed him. In ten months, he had shed ten pounds. No meat. Piles of vegetables. One glass of wine per week. Long, relaxing rounds of sex as needed. Three times a week at least. "Purifying," said Trudy. "One thing that's impossible to multitask." Long runs or long walks, it didn't matter.

Bloom had never been with a woman who needed so little time to prep. Deodorant, lotion, brush, and out the door. Ready for this, ready for that, but never in a rush.

The biggest downside was his commute down Sweetwater Road and through Glenwood Canyon to get to work. He used to go eight blocks, now he went thirty miles. But now he saw Allison Coil regularly and his earlier mad crush faded into genuine friendship.

Bloom went back to chipmunking sunflower seeds he kept in a loose pile on the empty seat next to him. The shells formed a slag heap in a paper cup. He slugged water to wash the salt around and to stay hydrated. Good air conditioner or not, this air would suck anyone dry, an invisible and insidious alien.

The road rose up. Thick stands of forest parted by the dusty brown cut—humanity's intrusion into the backwoods. A pickup came at him. The driver's two fingers popped off the steering wheel in a rural routine. Cowboy hat. Sunglasses. Giant poof of dust that obliterated the road. Following out of the cloud, a sheriff's pickup.

Bloom spotted the colors and at the last minute, flashed his lights and pulled over, popped open the door and stood there.

The cop slowed and Bloom gave him a slight head bob like "what's up?" treating the flying sheriff's pickup like it was the tourist information center.

The car stopped and Bloom kept his hands down and low and struck an unassuming, unalarmed attitude. The officer, alone, stared back. Bloom felt the rush of icy air from the cop's cool interior as the power windows came to half-mast. The blast was the equivalent of a modern walk-in freezer by comparison to the Camry's A.C., which packed the punch of a picnic cooler.

"I'm a reporter from Glenwood Springs," said Bloom. "Any updates on Dante Soto?"

There had to be precisely one reason to be on this particular road on this particular day if you were not involved, somehow, in managing the chaos around the fire.

"All the information is routed through the sheriff himself." He seemed polite, at least. Part of the routine. The cop filled the driver space like a football player, but no gut. His left arm was propped over the steering wheel like a ramrod. "Do you need a telephone number?"

"No," said Bloom. "I got that."

"There's not a lot of point in going up there." A silver name tag above his shirt pocket said Deputy Chris Bankston.

"Why?"

"Because nobody knows too much."

"He hiked regularly, didn't he?"

"Don't know. Like I said—"

"So he could be anywhere, really."

"Call the sheriff," said Bankston. "The people who know him are worried."

"Who's that?"

"Seriously?"

"Yeah, I know. He's got his share of followers."

"You're in the wrong spot. All the action is in Meeker."

"I'm going to take a quick look around up there. Then I'll be right along. Any news on the fire?"

"Can't imagine anything new. She'll need a month-long rain or an act of God." He paused. "I guess those are the same thing."

THIRTEEN:
THURSDAY EVENING

THEY FOUND NORA BAYLES buzzing around Trapper's Lake Lodge.

"Allison Coil," she said. "Lo and behold. And I mean that in a good way."

"It's been years, how—"

"I'll never forget," she said. "And what happened to you right before and right after you were here the last time."

"Not a fun memory." Allison spent as little time as possible thinking about the death trap and the attempt to end her life through forced hypothermia. Nora had overseen the rekindling of her core body temperature—and her spirits. "I will never forget your kindness."

"And it looks like you need something again," said Nora. "Based on the look on your face, at least. And this young man needs no introduction—Colin McKee if I'm not mistaken."

"We used to fish up here," said Colin by way of explanation.

"Damn good at it too," said Nora. "You and your brothers and your father. What's going on now?"

She turned and led them toward the kitchen tucked back behind the check-in desk. The front hall of the lodge doubled as a rustic dining room and, at least when the cabins were full or when there wasn't a giant fire chewing up the countryside, the kitchen poured out copious quantities of food for hikers, horseback riders, tourists, fishermen, fisherwomen, and hunters too. But Allison knew Nora would be as nervous as anyone else by the possibility that the up-coming season would get crushed by conditions and, now, the fire. Today, they got coffee.

"There's not much left to burn after oh-four and the Big Fish Fire, but I figure it ain't much, and if the fire comes back this way then it was meant to be. If nothing else, I can take a boat out in the middle of the lake and watch. Can't get me there, can it? This whole new fire gave me the heebie jeebies, brought the whole experience right back. Damn spooky, I tell you. Speaking of which, why are you two headed this way when everyone else is fleeing the other?"

Allison laid it all out.

"Right on the edge of the fire," said Colin. "Which seems kind of odd right there."

"And you met up with the ever-elusive Devo?"

"We're not supposed to mention that," said Allison. She was breaking a promise, but she preferred to consider Devo's plea a request. Once the cops got involved and there was a formal investigation, the whole body-discovery part had to be locked down tight. In no way could Allison pretend it had been her find.

If Nora was alarmed by the news of the body, it didn't show. Since Trapper's Lake served as a hub of commerce and comfort on the northern edge of the wilderness, it wasn't out of the question that the dead man had come right past the lodge, or used the lodge as a starting point.

"Any cars parked here that don't have an owner?" said Allison.

"We could look around," said Nora. "Don't think so. Most of the traffic on Marvine Trail starts at the trailhead—but not all, it's true. Possible the guy was a goner before the fire?"

"Hard to say," said Allison.

The call from Nora's landline to the sheriff's office went better than Allison had imagined. Perhaps news of a body meant a welcome distraction for a deputy and the coroner, who were no doubt caught up in the havoc around the fire. They were quick to respond. It was almost as if someone was, in fact, missing.

Arrangements were made with Nora for two more horses and provisions in the morning. A planned 5:00 a.m. departure time would put them back at the body by mid-morning. With the rest of Trapper's deserted, Nora offered to let her and Colin sleep in the main lodge and, at dinner time, served up tangy pot roast and boiled potatoes. Nora refused any offer to pay. Allison checked on the horses while Colin showered, and then Colin set up an outdoor bed on the deck of the lodge while she cleaned up. The makeshift camp on the deck was Nora's suggestion. "No point in being inside," she said. Allison didn't argue.

By the time they were settling down, Allison was stuffed and tired, but unsettled and wary too. Nora had offered a post-dinner "something to sip" and Allison's request for tequila was met with a half-full bottle of Hornitos. Allison vowed on the spot to repay this unassuming angel.

"You're locals," she said.

Stars winked into place. A steady breeze came and subsided. Darkness fell. Wherever it was burning and whatever it was burning, the fire no doubt felt like it had its tank topped off.

"If all goes well, we turn this over to the sheriff and head back tomorrow," said Allison. "We're go-betweens. That's it."

"They're going to want to talk to whoever found him," said Colin.

"I know it," said Allison. "You know it. Devo doesn't get it. Maybe this will be the final excuse to go in and get him."

Fourteen days was the longest anyone could camp in one spot under National Forest regulations, and the next spot had to be at least three miles away from the first. No location could turn into a permanent residence. Allison sympathized with the experiment and the general idea of it all, but she also didn't believe in exceptions, especially when the site was being used for a television show backdrop too. If the cops hired her to find Devo and his people, she figured she would need two or three days, tops.

"They might have to commit to going in and getting him," said Allison.

She turned on her side under a thin, unnecessary blanket. The cover was for modesty since she was down to one piece of clothing. She put her head on Colin's chest.

She smiled and kissed Colin's cheek. *This* was all that mattered. The two of them. Expecting to luck out with both appealing partner and a sane family was asking too much of the universe.

She ran a hand down his chest and found his lips with her own.

"Really?" he said.

"Why?" She rolled up on top of him, brushed her small breasts across his smooth chest. "Afraid of something?"

"What if the camp counselor does a bed check?"

Mild protestations aside, he squirmed his hips around to confirm the fact that his penis had perked up at the possibility.

"So dark there's nothing to see," said Allison. "And I don't plan on making any noise. Do you?"

"Some things I can't control."

She rolled off him to shed the underwear and climbed right back on top. "Ladies' choice," she said.

"Lady?" said Colin. "Think that's a stretch?"

"Maybe." Allison reached down and led him inside her. "But shut up. Try to enjoy this."

"I'll—"

She clamped a hand over his mouth and sat up straight. There was no need to take longer than necessary. This one was a gift. She had plenty of reasons to offer him a little something, but it started with the fact that she liked him best outside the gravitational orbit of the family. She preferred asteroids to planets.

She sat back and watched the stars. She put her hands on his knees, and then leaned forward to bury her head in his neck. She stayed on top and fought his half-hearted attempts to flip her over. They didn't break any records for endurance. He came without all the usual warning signals. It was odd not to hear his usual but brief declarations.

"No camp counselors," she said. "Good job."

"What about you?"

"Go to sleep," she said. "I had a great time."

Like an audible wart, Allison's cell phone fired. She'd given the number to the Rio Blanco Sheriff, but—

"Trudy," said Allison. Two minutes earlier, would she have answered? "How are you?"

"Fine."

With one word, Allison could tell that wasn't true.

"Something's up," said Allison.

"I'm worried," said Trudy. "And alone."

"Where's Duncan?"

Allison sat up, kept her sheet close this time. "I don't know," she said.

"Where are you?"

"At Trapper's Lake Lodge," said Allison. "Heading back tomorrow. I hope."

"Doesn't sound like you've heard," said Trudy.

"Heard what?"

"About Dante Soto."

"Dante?"

Allison had met him. Trudy knew him well.

"He's missing," said Trudy. "They know he was on his hike, one of his regular mid-week hikes."

Dread gripped Allison in the form of a shudder. Colin felt it—or knew her tone. "What?" he whispered.

"Nobody has seen him since yesterday morning—so it's starting to make the news." The shudder morphed into instant, dark sadness and all its accompanying weight. "I got a call from a friend too. People in his circle."

Allison had met Dante Soto at dinner in Sweetwater. She and Colin had been invited to the dinner gathering of the unusual and reclusive Hispanic philosopher-environmentalist with the woman whose line of natural food products and home garden stores were a growing regional success. Later, on a cool March day, she and Trudy drove up to Soto's yurt for a Saturday talk and potluck. "All walks of life," Soto boasted about the attendees—fifty in all. "Potlucks are community," he said. On guard about wading into a throng of self-righteousness, Allison arrived on Trudy's invitation. The idea was facilitated discussion on the future of the West—water, energy, recreation, population, governance, preservation, and how they would and could work together. Given the fact that he rarely stepped out for public interviews or invited people up to the yurt for anything, Soto had no trouble drawing a solid crowd of influential types—bankers, politicians, ranchers, teachers, doctors, miners, water experts, and the energy folks too. Allison had steeled herself for an overdose of self-importance from the crowd, but she need not have worried. Soto's appeal bloomed from the depth of his ideas, his facts, and his genuine ability to pull others into the conversation. If anything, he was self-deprecating, and had found representatives from all the professions who weren't too full of themselves. Soto was happy to be in the fight, but questioned everything.

"He's got a lot of people worried at this point," said Trudy.

Had Allison gone nose-to-skull with what was left of Dante Soto?

"Devo found a body," said Allison. With Trudy, there were no secrets.

"What?"

"And he took us to it. In the fire."

"Was it—?"

"Don't know." Allison sighed. "The body, well, it's beyond anything obvious as far as identification. It's mostly bones, but it's a recently deceased body, I'll tell you that. No way to tell anything else. Awful."

"It's him." Trudy treated her instincts with respect, nurtured the relationship. "Goddamn it," she said. "They got him."

FOURTEEN:
THURSDAY NIGHT

"I'M FERTILE."

A fine *come-hither*.

Cinnamon Nation wasn't prone to wasted words. Until they started procreating, they weren't devolving. He had tangled with her plenty, but always pulled out at the finish. As a community, they had to decide to accept a baby in the same way they agreed to expand the core group of adults. As a community, they had to accept the risk. *Having babies has to become routine,* she would say. *Procreation has to become part of the process. Like hunting. It's all part of toughening up.*

"You've been gone a long time." Cinnamon said it in a caring way. The signals were unmistakable.

How it was determined that Devo would be the father wasn't clear. He feared that the decision said more about Cinnamon than it did about him.

"Did what I said I was going to do," said Devo. Cinnamon had already reclined. And rid herself of her buckskin skirt. "She came right up the trail. Message delivered, dusted my hands. She's all over it."

The hut was dark except for a low-watt lamp on the video camera that cast a dim glow. They needed precious little light to shoot. Ruth and others had shot them screwing a half-dozen times before. How they managed to edit it for television was beyond Devo. In this light, it would be shapes flailing in the dark. It was all beyond his concern, except for the fact these scenes jacked up the ratings and his contract.

"And?"

"And I went up on the side of Marvine Peak to look at the fire. Even from a distance you can see flames. Every once in a while, explosions like a volcano throwing lava."

"I can't believe you wander so far—and aren't afraid of getting spotted, running into people?"

"I have my tricks," said Devo.

Cinnamon raised her knees up, turned to him.

With the evening so warm, Devo was naked in seconds. He kept on the bear-tooth necklace—all 42 teeth from a sow. He put his back to the camera to hide his stiff penis.

"Look at you," said Cinnamon, reaching for it. After a day of running and poking around the ashes with Allison, Devo had taken the time to bathe and was now glad that he did. "Guess you're ready."

"And let me tell you what Allison found," said Devo.

"Do I really want to hear about this Allison right now?" Cinnamon gave his penis a firm squeeze and stroke. It was warm and loving.

Devo took a quick look around to make sure Ruth was rolling. The ratings, if not himself, were about to explode.

She pulled him down on top of her, lifted up her thin hemp shirt so he was skin-to-skin. He slipped inside her, and Cinnamon hugged him close in a way that suggested her heart was coming along for the ride. She kissed his ear, licked it. "So far away," she whispered. "You were so far away but now you're right here, right now. Just us. Look what you've done, Devo. Look what you've started—and look what you're starting tonight."

Inside her. Invited. Welcomed. She thrust her hips in a hungry greeting and reached a hand down to add pressure where she wanted it. She offered a gentle moan.

"Nobody says we can't take top side tricks with us." Cinnamon whispered the words in his ear and then flicked at his tragus with her tongue. Devo felt the shiver in his toes and, if it was possible, felt harder inside her too.

Her hand motored up and down. Her fingertips bounced off his cock. She turned her head to the side, and Devo worked to hang on. He buried his head above her shoulder, tasted the salt on her neck. He arched his body up so there was room for her hand to work. She held her breath and squeezed her eyes. Her hand flew. Devo waited until the waves stopped crashing, then leaned up, looking down at the rhythmic jiggle of her breasts, reflected briefly on the cool gaze of Allison Coil and her trim rear end, and came inside Cinnamon in a way that made him feel like he was tumbling in outer space, lost and gone.

He was nowhere; he was everywhere.

"Sweet," said Cinnamon. "So sweet."

Devo rolled off, stretched out on his back.

"Hope your swimmers are eager and strong," she said.

Camera rolling. He caught Ruth's eye. She smiled and gave a thumb's up. Devo wondered if the crew thought they were producing a documentary on a bunch of farm animals.

"What were you saying?" said Cinnamon. Party over.

"Allison thinks it was arson too." He was still finding his feet back on earth. He told her about the odd campfire ring and the weird potato chip smell. "In the little fire pit," he said.

"You think she'll protect us?" said Cinnamon. "You?"

"She's not like what you're thinking," said Devo.

Cinnamon sat up, pulled her shirt back around her shoulders and hiked up her skirt. Devo inhaled her rich musk, like sweet loam.

"I'm still worried," said Cinnamon.

"I had no choice," said Devo. "And I feel better knowing the hunt for the fucker who started it will begin sooner rather than later."

"You had a choice," said Cinnamon. Was this for the cameras? For staged friction? Maybe not. "We are the tree falling in the forest. Nobody sees us, hears us. Somebody else would have found the guy eventually—right? Now, you could get sucked into this investigation in a big way."

"They can't require testimony out of someone they can't catch," said Devo. "Or find."

"They are going to want you. My prediction."

Devo sighed in the dark, close quarters of their hut. Devo could only imagine the producer's huddle. A reality show about re-wilding gets tangled up in a murder investigation. And an internal dispute flares over whether or not to help modern-day authorities solve the case of the crispy corpse.

"I reacted like any human being," said Devo.

Cinnamon was prepared. "Every single person came here with the idea of heading down a one-way tunnel. Open the trap door and go. We're in a time capsule, launched to a different century. If we get a baby out of tonight, this will be the only world he or she knows. Tougher. More adept. More in touch with the Earth. And he or she will be the first of a new generation. With all the equipment the cops have and the government has, you bet they know where we live. They don't want the hassle of throwing us out, wildfires or not. But if the cops need you, they could waltz right up here and drag you out, then threaten to come after our whole firefly family unless you cooperate. We'll be fucked."

She took a breath. Devo knew she wasn't finished. He preferred sentences. When she got rolling, it was one paragraph after the other.

"It will put a damper on all of our progress," said Cinnamon. "That is, regress. You're our spirit guide, you know, and if you're off and gone on some long trial, all the dynamics around here change. And things are too fragile at this stage of the process."

"A bit of a leap," said Devo. "We'll see what happens. Like I said, they've got to catch me first, and I know one million places to hide."

Devo pictured the trial, himself on the witness stand. To be presentable, he would have to clean up. He sort of remembered what he looked like without the beard and the dreadlocks. Maybe he'd keep the dreadlocks to remind him of the years that had brought him fame and put him in a whole new tax bracket. Some of the disciples were intense zealots who would be fine. Maybe it was time for a new leader anyway. Maybe his departure would be noted, and they would all move on. Backwards. There was part of this that was all so tiring.

Cinnamon turned on her side and put an arm on his chest. Ruth flipped the camera off and stepped away. She would tag-team another one in a minute or two. Every now and then, a moment or two went unrecorded.

Devo felt relaxed but wide awake. He replayed the too-brief interactions with Allison—and how she didn't miss a trick with those keen eyes. He imagined a hotel room and the trial, describing how he first found the body. He pictured real food and the comfort of a hot shower. He was tired of scrounging. He was tired of roasted squirrel. When it came right down to it, he was tired of winters and always wondering if he'd stored enough. He was tired of elk jerky.

And it was true that he thought more and more about the money sitting in his bank account.

Allison had as much wilderness as she wanted, and she didn't suffer.

He didn't need to go all the way back to civilization. He could set up a small yurt in the woods, grow vegetables, and raise goats. He could venture out for the occasional well-paid speech. He could find a woman to join him. He didn't have to abandon his belief in the value of de-evolving. The blackened body in the blackened woods was a gift. A ticket back to the top side, maybe to check things out and see how it was going out there. Beyond.

He might have to force the issue. Perhaps he might not run so fast when they came for him. But it was a ticket. And it might be time to get it punched.

FIFTEEN:
THURSDAY NIGHT

THE SHEER NUMBER OF cars told Bloom all he needed to know—a shudder had rifled through the family.

At least fifty vehicles were scattered in an odd jumble around the wooded lot, which rose to an open ridge where a plump round yurt sat like a spaceship. That is, if blended cotton fabric made for good protection for interstellar travel. On his earlier trip, Soto made a point about shunning the polyester blends.

The cars said plenty about Soto's appeal—an impressive mix of standard-issue country pickup trucks, late-model SUVs, a couple Volvos, a smattering of Camrys and Hondas, and several old-school Grateful Dead buses fresh off a five-decade time warp. Would Soto have approved of all these vehicles making this trip for this purpose?

A small fire in a stone-lined pit pumped puffs of smoke into the air like a priest swinging a censer. A woman's cheeks glistened with tears. There was no need to circle the fire for warmth. The faint breeze felt Saharan, even after dusk.

The Soto clan huddled in loose groups. Low murmurs. A somber tone. Bloom guessed at least 50 folks were gathered in huddles around the ridge. Light from inside the yurt issued a soft glow. In the distance, off beyond Meeker, a ripple of irregular orange surged and danced.

"Who are you?"

He thought the young woman was headed to her vehicle when she stepped in front of him. Bloom would have figured her for one of the Volvos. She had curly black hair bunched around an angular, well-scrubbed face with a strong nose, calm eyes, and a thin mouth that suggested libraries and smarts.

"Duncan Bloom, I'm a reporter from Glenwood Springs."

"This is a private gathering," she said.

"I'm trying to find out if anybody has heard anything."

"You can head back down the road," she said.

"Could I chat with his wife?" said Bloom. Who was this woman? Palace guard? He hadn't anticipated this, despite the well-known anti-media bias in the Soto realm. "She knows me—I've been here before."

"Oh, really?"

Even with the minimal firelight, he could tell she used no makeup. A simple olive-green V-neck T-shirt covered a healthy figure. She wore jean shorts and clunky sandals that looked complicated, like a lesson might be needed to wear them. She hadn't moved an inch. He put her at an indiscriminate age between 28 and 35. All that dark hair made her look older, more East Coast.

"Dante knows my girlfriend, Trudy Heath. And I came here once for a long interview." He wanted to point to the spot in the distance where he had sat with Soto. "This matters to me too."

"Trudy Heath?"

Revealing his connection to one of the region's most progressive leaders in herbs and healthy lifestyles shouldn't be something he needed to make his way as a reporter, but he would try anything to make the drive up here worthwhile.

"The one and only."

"Doesn't matter," she said.

Was a special handshake needed? A code?

"Is there any word from anyone?" He backed up a step. "Is there an update of any sort—has anyone heard anything?"

She paused. *A chink in the armor.* "No," she said. A pinprick stud caught a glint of fire on her left nostril. "Nothing."

"Does anyone know where they saw him last?" He took another slight step back, acceding to her role.

"Look," she said. "We aren't giving out information."

"Would you mind asking his wife?"

Bloom had met her when he'd come over for the one-on-one. It was hard to forget Grette Hansen's lanky height, back-long braids, and stunning Scandinavian cheeks. The Soto-Hansen couple was a hard one for him to get his head around, but it added to the inscrutability of the whole Soto story.

The woman smiled. "I thought I had made myself clear," she said.

"May I ask your name?" he asked without any trace of threat.

She gave it a thorough pro-and-con analysis. "Andrea Ingalls," she said.

"I'm just doing my job," said Bloom.

"I am aware of that," she said. "And what any reporter would say."

"The story will get out," said Bloom. "The police will issue a news release, the whole bit. And some reporters will take that as enough. And maybe his wife will have no comment—that's fine. But I'm interested in the whole story too. You know, the reaction in town. How was this all going over? He must have hit some roadblocks, right? Generated some friction?"

Despite her somewhat stern gaze, Bloom tried to shake off images of buying Andrea Ingalls a stiff drink or a pineapple-kale-blueberry smoothie. Her figure was non-stop. He was plenty happy, of course, but a long interview in a less confrontational setting would be magic. He wanted to know how this woman got here to this place and how much Kool-Aid one had to drink to be in the in crowd.

"My uncle was a reporter," she said. "*Chicago Tribune.*"

"Dante liked the piece I wrote."

"I remember it," said Ingalls. "It missed some fundamentals."

"Even my editor said it was primarily philosophical fluff," said Bloom. "It lacked a sense of how the whole thing worked—what you were doing."

"What we *are* doing," said Ingalls. "This wasn't all about him, even he's—"

The thought put a catch in her throat. She swallowed hard, looked away.

Bloom waited.

She took a deep breath and then strolled past Bloom, down off the ridge and away from the fire. "Follow me," she said.

If there was a choice involved, Bloom didn't see it. He took a glance back at the group around the fire. A phalanx of Soto soldiers had gathered to watch their bouncer's efforts.

Bloom turned tail. At the edge of the light, she grabbed his arm. "Do you have a card?" she said.

"Of course."

"Can you work on deep background—off the record?"

Her uncle, perhaps, had taught her the lingo—though deep background and off the record were two different things.

"Did he piss some people off?" Suddenly they were co-conspirators. Bloom wasn't sure how the tables had turned.

"There was some stuff going on," she said. "All off the record?"

"Yeah," said Bloom. "Of course."

"Then keep walking," she said. "And make like you're walking the plank."

SIXTEEN:
FRIDAY MIDDAY

A TRIO OF MEN worked the bones—one coroner, two sheriff deputies. One deputy took photographs while another searched the charred forest floor. The third hovered over the bones, going ash by ash.

"Someone waiting for him," said Allison. "Knew he was coming this way. Do we know if Dante Soto—"

"If it was Soto," said Colin.

"For a second, let's go with Trudy's hunch," said Allison. "If Soto was a regular on this trail, the killer didn't pick an out-of-the-way spot. You'd think someone ran into the firestarter dude, to use your expression."

"And the other question is did he kill him first—somehow, some way, or restrain him?" said Colin. "Or knock him out?"

Allison blinked. She snapped the trees back from black to health, put the leaves back on the branches, restored the undergrowth of the forest, imagined a confrontation and an attack. Soto's body, if it was him, was far enough off the trail that the killer would have had some cover but any calls and shouts could have been heard by a passerby. The Marvine Trail was a major highway up into the Flat Tops but even during a regular summer that might mean one group of hikers every hour or two.

"Let's go over again how you found him." This was the deputy with the camera and small notebook. He had led all conversations on the journey up. His name was Dennis Dwyer. He had a sandy complexion, crooked nose, gentle eyes…

"Someone else alerted us," said Allison. "Like I said before."

"Who someone?"

She had discussed this with Colin—there was no quarter in keeping Devo's name out of it, and they couldn't pretend they had stumbled on the bones. They lacked a plausible scenario to be traipsing around in the burned-out forest. And they lacked the olfactory power that led Devo to the spot. Plus, Dwyer knew the McKee name well—especially since the arrest of Earl McKee and the severe injury to Deputy Campion. The assault had been a brief topic. It wasn't a good day for a McKee to go crossways with the cops.

"Devo," said Colin. Probably reading her mind.

Dwyer looked at them to see if he was being hoodwinked. "He revealed himself?"

"He found us, led us around to here," said Allison.

"We'll need to talk to him," said Dwyer. "So where did he locate you?"

"We started at the trailhead," said Colin, his head bobbing to the north. "He popped out and flagged us down."

"Like he knew you'd help?"

Allison let the question hang for a moment, remembered the night she had found Devo in a snowdrift and nursed him back to warmth. "We go back," she said.

"So you know how to find him?" said Dwyer.

"No idea," said Colin.

"Perhaps you could help us find him," said Dwyer. "If our suspicions are right, this will be a full-blown murder investigation, and the perpetrator will be charged with starting one of the largest and most destructive wildfires in the history of Western Colorado, at least the past century."

"Dog find anything?"

They had brought a stout German shepherd named Carmen to sniff for accelerants. "Nada." Dwyer had yet to show a flash of levity. It had been a long, slow ride back to this spot.

"We'll have plenty of samples to test too," said Dwyer.

"The fire ring?"

"We didn't pick up on that potato chip thing you were talking about. But if there was anything used to get things going in the pit itself, we should know. But we'll need Devo's statement, and I don't care what trip he thinks he's on or how many YouTube followers he's got. We need to know what he saw, when he saw it."

So go find him, thought Allison.

Dwyer must have read her mind. Or her face. Or her shrug, albeit slight.

"We could do it," said Dwyer. "I'm sure the National Forest guys and the state parks and wildlife guys have a pretty good idea where to start looking. But let's say that our extraction of Devo might not be a delicate operation."

Allison knew he meant scorched Earth. The whole camp would be wiped out in the process.

"With everything else going on," said Dwyer, "we don't want the public relations quagmire that comes with ending their mini *Lord of the Flies* experiment. If Devo could present himself to the authorities as a key witness in a murder investigation, that would be ideal. Might even do him some good in the public eye."

"Is it Soto?" said Colin. "Your gut?"

In the background, the other two uniforms started picking their way back to the trail.

Between them, a black oversized duffel sagged. Each had one end. Allison guessed the bones came out one at a time. It wasn't likely that much would have held together, lacking any connective tissue.

"My gut tells me not to guess," said Dwyer. "But if I did, yes. Size. Location. The fact that Soto is missing. One plus one, two plus two. The math ain't hard."

They got him. Trudy's assertion gnawed at Allison again. It wasn't hard to imagine Trudy reeling at the news. She would be devastated. The idea that Dante Soto was a threat was worrisome, to say the least. He preached relentless neutrality. But he was making progress and no doubt someone's ox was being gored in the process.

"We need Devo," said Dwyer.

She wished she had set a time or date to reconnoiter with Devo. For now, she ignored his request. Let it stew.

The coroner and the other deputy set the bag of body parts down on the trail like it was a load of bricks, even though it couldn't have weighed much.

The other deputy was Steve Twitchell. He was close to forty but had a haircut like a ten-year-old heading off for summer camp. He was shorter than Dwyer and darker. He looked trim and in shape, but this heat could render strength out of the toughest breeds.

The coroner was Alex Rickey. His tone was cool. Facts are facts.

"Was he dead before the fire?" said Colin. "Any indication?"

"We've got more work to do," said Rickey. "There are some issues."

"Such as?" said Allison.

"Such as three nicks on his clavicle."

"Nicks?" said Colin.

"Something sharp," said Rickey. He used his right hand to give a series of soft karate chops to the space between his neck and left shoulder. "One, two, three."

SEVENTEEN:
FRIDAY MIDDAY

STAYING LOW, NOT TOO worried about being spotted so high above the scene, Devo scampered higher up the slope. He had seen what he needed to see. He had put in motion what he needed to put in motion. He had to go about his routines at the homestead. Even though it was hotter and drier than he'd ever seen it, now was when they planned for winter by drying meats, curing meats, and caring for the gardens. Survival was foresight.

He stopped high on the ridge. If any of the five of them bothered to look up, he would have been a sharp silhouette against the hazy-smoky sky. The five remained huddled for a moment, but started to scatter, heading for the horses tucked on the shady and healthy side of the trail. The dog started down the trail like he knew the way, at least the direction of his next meal.

It was odd that none of them sensed being watched. Devo felt as if he could always tell and, in fact, he felt a sudden ripple of concern. He wasn't used to being so exposed, even for a minute.

EIGHTEEN:
FRIDAY MIDDAY

Ash dusted cars parked along the main square. Except for the 100-degree temperatures, it could have been snow. Meeker came across as a hard-working town. Bucolic touches, like the pleasant and well-treed main square, added a splash of Norman Rockwell. But the light, what little of it had penetrated the thick smudge of smoke, looked more post-nuclear than quaint Colorado. Children wore dust masks. They stared, confused. Television and radio warnings were non-stop. Don't exercise outdoors, and stay inside if you can.

Inside the Meeker Café was the smell of smoke. It clung to clothes, penetrated every cranny. A giant slice of apple pie went down a-la-smoke. With black coffee, it was near heaven.

Bloom had filed two fire stories that wrote themselves. When an uncontrolled monster is having its way with your backyard, forcing hundreds of evacuations, the story was a snap to write. Everyone had a comment or a prediction. Between the Lord's Will and government ineptitude, there were plenty of places for any citizen of

Meeker to launch into commentary on global warming or the tactical approach of the firefighters and their battle commanders. The citizens of Meeker had been joined by hordes of looky-loos who got their jollies watching the blaze or recording it for their fire porn. The roads in were all checkpointed now for residents and deliveries, but enough of the crazies had slipped in before the clampdown. The sheer scale of the fire made it sensational, but apparently the cops had their hands full with cases of feisty residents who refused evacuation orders.

The Dante Soto story was harder to pull together.

There was no positive ID. Bloom had heard through a source in Colorado Parks and Wildlife that the body would be back in Meeker tonight, but all Bloom had picked up was the speculation on the street that there was no way Soto could have walked into a wildfire and died.

Foul play, a tame phrase if there ever was one, was assumed. Bloom tried to quiz the sheriff's office, but they weren't sitting around waiting for his call—they had been dispatched to assist with traffic control and the evacuation hassles. Finally Sheriff Christie had answered his cell. The conversation had lasted less than a minute. No official ID yet. The top priority was the safety of the living residents of Meeker. Sheriff Christie wasn't chatty but he wasn't curt either. He invited Bloom to call back as needed.

Bloom filed a story that spelled out the possibility that Dante Soto was dead. He sprinkled it with colorful tidbits from the scene of the yurt—including details about Soto's presumed route and the gathering dread among his supporters, though he'd only viewed the throng from a distance.

Bloom finished scraping up pie goo with his fork, paid a harried waitress with a heavy tip, stepped back out onto the main square and checked his phone—1:30 p.m. The dim, smoky light played tricks with his internal clock. He would have sworn it was much later. Perhaps it was fatigue too. He had snagged a room at the Blue Spruce, but sleep was elusive.

Strolling in the pleasant park around the county courthouse, Bloom hit speed dial.

"Good stuff," said Coogan. "See how tomorrow plays out over there but we need you back here tomorrow night—or we might head you down to Paonia. That fire is proving to be a bitch too."

"Aren't they all?" said Bloom. Could he spend all summer as a reporter breathing wildfire smoke? "The Soto story is the one. He was already a folk hero, so maybe the martyr label is next."

"You'll have to do what you can by telephone," said Coogan.

"How about if I stay here and work the phones?" said Bloom. In their brief time together, Bloom had grown to learn that Coogan could be reasonable. He didn't like to be cornered. "Soto's was the hope, you know. The answer."

Bloom gave Coogan time to think. No pressure. Bloom had grown to love his new newspaper town, Glenwood Springs, and the blank canvas that Western Colorado offered a journalist. In some ways, being downsized from the *Denver Post* was the best thing that had ever happened to him. Of course the relationship with Trudy made it easier to have a positive perspective. He'd never met anyone so moment-by-moment caring, so unconcerned with what others thought and so fucking warm in bed. He'd also never met any woman who felt like a friend first and a lover second. The friend bit enhanced the lover part and that made the friend stuff even stronger. He couldn't describe it.

"Let's take it day by day," said Coogan.

"As always," said Bloom.

"It feels as if we're in the middle of all this shit. But give it another day, see what you can get."

Bloom's next call was obvious. He found an unoccupied park bench and speed-dialed Trudy.

"Allison just called," said Trudy. "She's at Trapper's but said she has to go find Devo—he's the one that found the body. The police want to talk to him."

"Devo?"

The involvement of the most colorful character on the Flat Tops would add a whole new wrinkle to the story. While Devo and his followers were trying to sprint back in time to improve individual well-being and all of mankind, Soto had been trying to strike a balance between modern comforts and the global energy supply without going all caveman. A compare-and-contrast piece could be ginned up on that basis alone.

"How the heck did Devo find the body?"

"You got me," said Trudy.

"Colin was there?" said Bloom.

"I assume so," said Trudy. "Yes, I'm sure of it. Apparently Colin has to head down to the family ranch, and Allison is going back up tomorrow to look for Devo, you know, bring him back."

"Really hard to picture the cops sitting down with Tarzan of the Flat Tops for an extensive conversation," said Bloom. "There's a picture I want to see."

"Poor old Devo," said Trudy. "Always trying so hard."

Once in a while, the four of them had watched an episode of *Latitude/Longitude* together. For every semi-interesting lesson about how to sustain human civilization off the grid, there was an equal amount of squeamish intimacy stuff that had a voyeuristic creepiness to it. Cameras lingered over interpersonal squabbles and resentments. And struggles over leadership. And sex. Bloom always flashed on the movie *Quest for Fire* with Rae Dawn Chong in a cavewoman's garb and the first-ever screw in the missionary position.

In the television series, Devo played the role of misunderstood leader forced to corral a rank and file with a steady flow of new and better ideas. The captain of the journey back in time was losing his grip. Allison always squirmed when they watched it. Colin seemed bored.

The Devo angle would give him something to ask the sheriff about, though he might not want to tip his hand that his sources included the widely known Allison Coil. Now that Bloom had moved up from his Glenwood Springs bachelor pad to all the comforts of Sweetwater, Allison Coil and Colin McKee were neighbors and two of his best friends. Old yearnings for Allison evaporated once he fell into Trudy's embrace and her slow-the-world-down spell, but one of the perks of that world was getting to hang out with the ever-capable and sometimes inscrutable Allison.

"Where did Allison call from?" said Bloom.

"Trapper's," said Trudy. "The lodge."

"That's right," said Bloom. "Sorry—you said that already. Wonder if that's where she'll bring Devo out? Or if the cops will talk to him there?"

"I didn't get the feeling that the plan was, you know, planned," said Trudy.

Bloom had heard, also unconfirmed, that several ranchers up toward Buford had been arrested for refusing to evacuate. Always a perfect Old West/New West tale: Did the government have the right to toss someone off their property in the name of public safety? Maybe he had passed the ranches in question on his ride down from Buford. There had been one ranch with a heavy police presence.

"You coming back tomorrow?" said Trudy. "It's lonely without you and with all these fires. It does make you think about how you'd get out of here if push came to shove."

"Coogan wants me back tomorrow," said Bloom. "And if the fire gets anywhere close to Sweetwater, get down that road fast."

"If you don't come back tomorrow, I might head your way," said Trudy. "Might have to."

"It's chaos up here," said Bloom, "and everybody has to prove residency to get through. Not that I wouldn't welcome the company."

"Reporters?" said Trudy.

"Probably wrangle their way in."

"And delivery trucks?"

"I see where you're going," said Bloom. Trudy's herb and vegetable empire required regular shipments to Meeker, in addition to forty-five other small towns and cities in Western Colorado, all in a fleet of hybrid trucks. "Make it work."

He told her where he was staying. "Isn't Colin's family from right around Buford?"

"Closer to Buford," said Trudy.

"And his family?"

Bloom stood up, some instinct urging him to walk around, maybe head down to the sheriff's office. The smoke seemed thick and chewy.

"What about them?" said Trudy. "Never hear much about them from Colin but there are two other brothers and old-school parents from what I gather."

Bloom could look up the McKee ranch later on his laptop—maybe he could run into Colin and grab a quick local angle from a prominent rancher. Or semi-prominent. Maybe. Soto's demise was the priority. Bloom knew not to spread himself too thin or get caught ten miles out of town when the cops ID'd the body. What would the *New York Times* do? His mantra. Just because he was a reporter for the *Glenwood Springs Post-Independent* didn't limit anything. *Think big. Think bigger. Think bigger still.*

"Yeah, just wondering," said Bloom.

"If that was Dante Soto up there, they are going to be writing about his murder for a long time to come," said Trudy. "It's got to be a murder. I'd put money on it. And I doubt anyone else has the ability to keep his initiative going, especially in a way that didn't seem to be threatening, the way he did it."

NINETEEN:
FRIDAY MIDDAY

DEVO KNEW THIS SECTION of forest well. The critter bounty here was endless—squirrel networks in particular—but this stretch of forest wasn't built for speed. Elk tiptoed through here. So did deer. You could run but you'd be heard. The forest floor was littered with old branches that snapped under foot. The jungle resisted hikers and campers but offered good cover from prying eyes. The forest-topping canopy cut daylight in half. Even in this searing summer, the air here was cooler, more hospitable.

Devo set a course for the homestead. He'd keep an eye out for a fat rabbit or two. It was always good to have critters cinched to your sash when you walked back to camp.

Fuck. That feeling again, that flash.

What the hell?

Devo stopped. Scanned. Waited. Did a slow 360. It was early afternoon and it seemed as if the whole forest was taking a nap. A flicker darted and swooped through the trees on its appointed rounds. A chipmunk stood up on its hind legs, scouting ahead along a fallen tree. *There.* Again.

That weird feeling. Not to be ignored. And coupled with it, an out-of-place scent hung in the air, like tobacco mixed with fresh sweat.

A tree cracked once like an old rocking chair. A breeze rustled the treetops. Far in the distance, a crow barked.

Devo turned his head and put his nostrils up to pin down the scent.

Flash of silver like a flicking mirror signaling an aircraft. Eye-high.

He saw the flash, heard the slow, throbbing whir of a stick cutting air and he ducked.

The whir hung in the air. Devo sprung back up and started to move, chased by a series of glimpses of a thin man, axe blade, axe handle, black jeans, green T-shirt, and dark face. Panic clawed his throat.

Devo darted around trees as he heard the crashing behind him.

What the fuck?

Of course there was nobody faster. Devo practiced by stalking deer and running with them as another member of a startled herd.

He half-expected to hear a gunshot, but none came.

What the fuck? Over?

There was plenty of distance now, and Devo slowed, turned.

What if this fucker wasn't alone?

Twigs snapped.

The man coughed and spat. He was moving as fast he could—faster than walking. Straps on his shoulder suggested a smallish day pack.

His dark face was hidden under the bill of a low-hanging black baseball cap.

Devo ducked behind a beefy, blown-down tree—one of dozens scattered like pickup sticks. His heart thumped hard. He couldn't remember the last time fear jolted his system.

Devo risked a peek. The man had stopped. They were twenty yards apart. He looked fit. He held the blond axe handle in his right hand and the blade popped up above his shoulder. Axe blade on one side, pointed and equally shiny pick on the other. Mean in both directions. The man scanned left. Devo ducked but at the last minute could see the dark, boyish face. The overall physique read youngish. Devo picked up that whiff again—cigars and sweat.

"Mighty quiet around here." He said it like he was talking to himself. "Lots of hiding places. Lots and lots and lots."

What the fuck had Devo done to earn the attention? Had word slipped around that quickly about what he saw, what he smelled, what he found? *Fuck!*

Devo poked his head up.

The man wriggled out of his backpack and unzipped the top. He pulled out a water bottle. He tipped his head back to the sun as he drank, and Devo could see white skin between the camo job and the top of the shirt, a loose gray mesh fabric that looked high-tech with long sleeves and long pants. From his angle, Devo couldn't see shoes.

"Don't think I hear anything moving right now," he muttered casually.

Devo could see how careful Allison and Colin had been keeping their distance. Could this cigar smoker smell him? Probably not.

The axe guy shoved the water bottle back in his pack, pulled out something to eat or chew. He gnawed off a bite and put it back.

This time his hand came out gripping the biggest handgun Devo had ever seen. Sun flashed off the barrel, which looked as big as the man's forearm.

"That's better," he said. He twisted the gun around, studying it. "Much."

Devo wanted to crawl inside his tree, burrow into the earth. His breath quickened and his heart hammered so hard his ribs ached.

There was only one option. There would be no perfect time. He stood a better chance on his feet.

As Devo ran, he heard, "Ha!" and a heavy, metallic click.

When the gun fired, the blast boomed and there was a burst of heat and searing pain.

TWENTY:
FRIDAY LATE AFTERNOON

SUNNY BOY SLURPED WATER. Allison had found a perfect camping spot—one of the 5.8 million such spots, more or less, in the Flat Tops. On the return trip to Trapper's Lake Lodge, Nora had stocked her with enough food for a week-long hunt by four grown men. At least, that's how it seemed. Would Devo be watching this spot already? Would he think he might be needed so soon?

She tended the fire. She kept it small but she had dug a deep pit and a channel for oxygen down to it. Zero chance of escape. It cooked hard. Branches from a snag snapped off easily. A hatchet freed thicker hunks of fuel. Violating the campfire ban? Hell, she was under orders. She was practically deputized.

Colin, at her suggestion, headed back to be with his mother and help out where needed. With Earl in jail, no doubt there was plenty to do. Allison's job wasn't enough for two people. The plan was to reconnect back in Sweetwater in a day or two.

It had been a three-hour ride from the lodge to this spot where Devo told her to send the signal. She had zero doubt she could find

Devo's camp if it came to that, though it would take some work. Nobody could cover ground like Devo, so sightings meant nothing in terms of proximity to his base. Allison knew where she would start to look. With the larger encampment now she was certain she could find the wear and tear. She was sure she could find their trails, hard as they might try to be discreet. Deer made trails, elk made trails, people left all sorts of crap.

She napped by the pond. Her cheeks baked in the sun. She caught a meal-size brookie, gutted it, and steamed it in a tin foil pouch. Trudy had made up a dried herb concoction—heavy on thyme—for such occasions. She sacrificed a wedge of lime from the supplies Nora had donated, careful to keep the lime for its most important use, to squirt in tequila with a dash of triple sec. She used her fingers to pop the fish from the hot skin. Eight nourishing bites and a happy mouth. She mopped the juice from the pouch with a chunk of whole wheat bread and forced herself to sip 32-ounces of water from her Nalgene. A small meadow flanked her pond on one side, and she had built her fire and tied up Sunny Boy at the edge of the woods. When she had downed enough water she followed old instincts around privacy and stepped deep under the canopy of trees to pee.

She scanned the ground for fuel to add to her stash. Then, she stepped back into the clearing. And flinched. Panic flared through her chest.

Your guard was down.

The shape stood still. She stared. Her hands were down, relaxed.

Her nose processed the information, picked that certain essence—extreme earthiness, perhaps.

It was one of Devo's throng.

Allison recognized her from the television show and, in fact, another woman stood nearby, a small video camera held eye-high but away from her head. She was dressed more Colorado outdoors—hiking boots, shorts, and a small daypack.

"No video," said Allison.

The camerawoman was ready. "We can shoot the scene in a way that you're not in it."

"Nope," said Allison. "I mean nothing. No pictures or any part of me, no sound. No blurred face. I'm not in your show."

The name of the Devo follower came to her. Cinnamon. She was compact and sturdy. Her skin was roasted brown like the crust on a pie. She wore crude, minimal sandals and shorts and a vest made of animal hide. She carried a knife in a sheath that hung from a belt and a bow hung from bony shoulders. No doubt the strap that crossed her chest attached to a quiver in back.

"She'll only shoot pictures of me," she said.

"You're Cinnamon, right?" said Allison.

"Yeah." Thrilled to be recognized.

"If she's shooting pictures, she's picking up my voice," said Allison. "No."

The camerawoman brought the camera down to her side. "My name is Ruth," she said. "We can have Cinnamon summarize later."

"But no names," said Allison.

Ruth sighed and nodded.

Was a handshake in order? Allison decided to let Cinnamon and Ruth lead on issues involving backwoods, all-girl etiquette.

With the camera issue resolved, Cinnamon seemed to relax. Ruth yanked a bottle of water from her daypack and started chugging.

"Where's Devo?" said Allison.

"We're not sure," said Cinnamon. "But he told me to come look for you if he didn't come back. We're worried, to be honest."

"Damn," said Ruth. "I'm missing such good stuff."

Allison checked to make sure. The camera sat untended on top of Ruth's backpack, now on the ground. It was pointed the other way.

"The sheriff needs to talk to him," said Allison. "As soon as possible."

"I don't know where he is. But whatever happens in your world doesn't involve us." Cinnamon shrugged her bronze shoulders.

The statement carried an air of finality. And seemed to contradict what she'd seen of Devo when they were together—how interested he was when ensuring action was taken.

"We don't have many rules," said Cinnamon. "But one rule for sure is we don't entangle ourselves with what's happening out there."

"Even if it might help keep your project going?"

"Project" might not have been the most endearing term to choose, but she wasn't sure she cared. The long pause suggested she had landed a blow. Soft, upper-middle class city types didn't need to jump into a time machine and dial up the Westward Movement of the nineteenth century to prove a point. The whole television show aspect made it all so banal and self-righteous, too, and it wasn't drawing the right kind of attention to the Flat Tops. Maybe it was time to kick them out.

"What do you mean?" said Cinnamon.

"I mean the authorities are going to come looking for Devo on their own terms if he doesn't show up. Guaranteed."

"How can you be so sure?" said Cinnamon.

"Really?" The look in Ruth's eyes suggested she was optimistic about the ratings for the episode where the Devo camp gets bulldozed or the day this particular production came to a close so she could get back to having a life.

"Really," said Allison. "They might be waiting for an excuse. This might be it."

The signal fire issued a pop like a gunshot. Ruth jumped.

"Are you working for them?" said Cinnamon.

The question stung, but Allison didn't let it show. "Hell no."

"Then why are you helping?"

Allison figured she could be up on Sunny Boy with all her gear packed and the horse saddled up in fifteen minutes. Maybe they'd like to watch. "Civic duty," she said. "I'm sure your pal Devo—"

"—will not violate our rules," said Cinnamon.

"Damn, this sucks," said Ruth. "What a moment."

"Let's ask Devo," said Allison.

"Follow me back," said Cinnamon. "That's where he'll turn up."

"No," said Allison. "You don't want me to know the location anyway. You bring him here. I'll stay through tomorrow, and we'll see if he turns up."

"And if he doesn't?"

"Then I'll let the sheriff know I tried and see what he wants to do next," said Allison.

"I can't make Devo appear," said Cinnamon.

"Is it unusual to be gone?"

"Longer hunts, sure," said Cinnamon. "And a couple of the others too. Small groups. It happens."

Cinnamon didn't have to say, but the implication was clear—they were hunting elk and deer—bigger mammals that needed several people to pack back to camp. Needless to say, they were flaunting the law.

"But this time he went alone—at least, we know where everyone else is," said Cinnamon. "And when he's by himself, he doesn't usually stay gone overnight."

"I'll give it twenty-four hours," said Allison. "If he turns up, send him here. If not, I'll know he hasn't turned up or doesn't want to talk to the sheriff. Then, they can make their next move."

Ruth folded her hands on her head like a prisoner of war. "I'm killing myself," she said. "Goddamn it."

TWENTY-ONE:
FRIDAY LATE AFTERNOON

Bloom pulled up the news release from the Rio Blanco County Sheriff's Department on his phone. It said nothing new.

Body recovered from a burn area in the Flat Tops. Identification may take days. Full investigation underway. Anyone with information should call *blah blah blah.*

Bloom knew one thing—Soto hadn't turned up. Put two and two together, and you had news. Checking his own story online that morning, the headline read: "Meeker Fears the Worst for Missing Activist; Slide Lake Fire Continues to Roar." The weather forecast called for another week of bone followed by another week of dry. Scanning other headlines, a new fire had popped up near Hotchkiss and was headed into thick forest. It might merge with the one near Paonia.

It was easy to get a feeling in the gut that the world was burning.

Bloom had looked up the address he needed and, using Google maps, set up a walking course from his hotel. He found a modest cottage-like house set back from the street, three blocks from the main square. The front yard boasted a garden so thick with vegetables it would have sent Trudy into paroxysms of delight. A network of misters pulsed spray on the mini oasis. He tried hard not to think about the stack of pancakes and salty bacon he'd devoured for lunch. He could eat breakfast three times a day. It was like cheating on Trudy. He felt as badly as if he had slept with Allison—or anyone else. Trudy wasn't anti-pancake, but that fatty bacon and all the nitrates and delicious salt? Not in Trudy's world. Bloom patted his insta-paunch.

Matching silver cruiser bicycles waited in a decorative rack, unlocked. On top of the cottage, solar panels sucked power from the sky. With the current temperatures, they must be drunk all the time.

He was a full five minutes early for his 1:00 p.m. rendezvous or appointment or tour or whatever this was. Andrea Ingalls had given him the address and time in one of the shortest telephone calls ever.

She pedaled up on a red fat tire bicycle. A powder blue bike helmet kept her curly hair in check. She wore a white T-shirt—another V-neck—and light green shorts. The sandals from the fireside at Dante Soto's yurt had been swapped for orange neon running shoes. Sweat beaded on her upper lip, but she wasn't breathing hard.

"Thirty minutes inside, no more," said Ingalls. "And the couple that lives here—the address—don't exist."

"Got it," said Bloom. "Are they home?"

"Yes," said Ingalls. "But no questions."

"Agreed," said Bloom. "Any word?"

Ingalls knew what he meant. She tightened her lips, looked down. "You know as much as I do," she said.

"You heard about—"

"Everyone knows," said Ingalls. "Everyone knows about what they found up there. And everyone is hoping, you know? Just hoping."

Ingalls took a breath. She daubed at a tear with the back of her hand. It seemed like she needed a thorough cry. What human wouldn't?

The house had been fitted to capture rainwater. Composting was treated like an art. Recycling was a science. The house sold solar power back to the grid "for air conditioning in L.A." Its insulation was upgraded. Structural leaks found and closed. Foam pipe insulation, water heater blankets, door sweeps, and even simple things like clotheslines were installed. The couple, sitting on a back deck under a cool awning, had been shown how to grow enough food on their small lot so half of what they ate was generated in their garden. Trudy would have flipped. Jarring, canning, freezing, storing, labeling—planning. From tomatoes to pickles, they had it all. A new skylight brightened the living room and a new non-polluting wood stove helped with winter heat. They chopped their own fuel in the forest with a permit.

The Soto Experience was part process, part attitude adjustment, and part toxic cleanse for your house and lifestyle. It was also part baptism.

"It's not about greening your kitchen or watching your thermostat," said Ingalls. They were standing in the spotless, cool kitchen. Bloom smelled lemon. And smoke. The tightest house in the world wouldn't keep out smoke. "It's like therapy—it's all about your relationship with the ways you move, work, eat, shop, clean. If you sign up, you are committed for a process that can last weeks or months. You almost feel as if you've got a new member of the family and you'd better be prepared to think through everything you do—and to be more present and purposeful about your relationship with energy."

"Who pays?" said Bloom.

"It's a partnership," said Ingalls. "We want the family to have some skin in the game—it's a needs-based scale. The main thing is changing their habits—much less driving, that kind of thing. It's being more conscious about your needs. And choices."

Several newspaper stories, including his own, referred to the fact that the entire effect was funded by a private foundation—somebody's gamble to see if there was a way to save the planet, one lifestyle and one human being at a time. If he was going to write any more about this, he would need to find out more. *Go to the source,* Bloom told himself.

"How many others like this?" said Bloom.

"Why is that important?" said Ingalls.

"Trying to get an idea of the scale," said Bloom.

"We've passed ninety homes or properties in Meeker," she said.

"And how many of you?"

"A dozen team members."

"And how many houses do you work with at a time?"

"Depends." She had poured two glasses of cold water. The house felt warm—but not uncomfortable. "Depends on how much work needs to be done. It's like therapy."

"And do you know where he had been working lately?" said Bloom. "Not his people, but Soto himself? Think he might have been working somewhere that some people got pissed off?"

"You're jumping to conclusions," said Ingalls.

"I'm doing what you're doing—trying to stay a step ahead," said Bloom. He didn't want to mention the body. He had images rolling in his head, and she must have her own imagination flying.

"The detectives will ask the same questions," said Bloom.

"Police?" said Ingalls.

"They will want to know where Soto had been lately—all his last interactions. They'll re-create his movements the day he—disappeared." He almost said *was killed.* "They will want to know if he felt threatened."

"The farm," said Ingalls. "He had shifted his attention to a farm he bought south of town, other side of the river. He was into the whole D.I.Y. thing—building machines yourself, building your own greenhouses, barns, and even tractors from parts. He thought farmers should be able to work the land and not be running to the bank for a loan for a new piece of machinery. He had quietly bought a farm, and he was starting to get rolling."

"When?" said Bloom. An outsider who wanted to break up the relationship between banker and farmer? An outsider who might make pointed suggestions to the neighbors? Bloom could feel trouble from miles away.

"About three months ago," said Ingalls. "April, I think."

Plenty of time to ruffle feathers—or worse.

"Our time is up," said Ingalls.

Outside, Bloom's phone chimed. He gave Ingalls a sign to wait.

"When are you leaving? When are you filing? Paonia is blowing up—I mean, coming down Main Street."

"Call you back," said Bloom. "Two minutes."

Coogan was saying something when Bloom punched off.

"The old ball and chain," said Bloom. "In this case, my editor."

"How sweet." Ingalls shook her head. "Sounds old school."

"I might go back but Trudy is heading over here. I'm wondering if you might be willing to take her to the places that I was asking about—Soto's experimental farm, for one."

"Not experimental—" said Ingalls.

"Okay, new farm," said Bloom. "And it's possible my friend Allison will be over here too."

124

"Trudy and Allison," said Ingalls. "Who is Allison, a deputy reporter?"

"Two people who care," said Bloom. "Two people who don't like it when shit goes unchecked."

"I suppose," she said. "A bit odd, but they're not official anything, and I'm not officially helping in any capacity, either."

"A friend of the cause," said Bloom.

"If you have to give it a label," she said.

Bloom ignored the dig. It seemed directed at men, not reporters.

"It seems like you're not telling me something," said Bloom. "There has to be a reason you met me here, showed me this."

Soto had injected all his troops with a shot of Anti-Media Bias. Maybe an overdose.

"Were there any problems right before this?" said Bloom. In other words, why was she doing this?

"Problems?" Her question was half scoff.

"Issues," said Bloom. "Situations that might have been festering or new pressure coming from one place or another."

As with Trudy, Ingalls's clear eyes and skin made Bloom ponder the benefits of a diet based on eggplant and couscous. In Trudy's case, it meant a trim body, a clean soul and deep, natural empathy for all creatures large and small. Bloom picked up the same vibe from Ingalls, though the outer shell was turtle tough.

"We've had some moments," said Ingalls.

"Was there a specific situation—recently?" said Bloom.

Bloom took it as a personal challenge to make her smile or laugh, although maybe not today.

"Sure," she said. "We aren't welcomed everywhere. That was one of the things he was trying to overcome, the notion that being green and smart about energy was somehow associated with the left, with liberals. Why wouldn't a smart businesswoman or a thrifty homeowner want to reduce energy use, and what makes them think that learning how to make your own environmentally friendly laundry soap turns you into a socialist?"

He let her question linger.

"We get looks," she said. "We get comments. People know who we are. They point. We go where we're invited, sure, but we mingle in town—shop at the grocery store, check out books at the library."

"Where are you from?" said Bloom. Making conversation.

"Steamboat," said Ingalls. "Born and raised."

"Did you stay down here? Live down here?"

"We all had rooms—motels, hotels, some apartments," said Ingalls. "Soto had quietly bought five small houses. We would share quarters. At first, we spent a couple or three weeks in a motel, getting to know the team, and then we'd find the right fit and move to one of the houses."

"Neighbors were okay?" said Bloom. "Seems like the kind of town where it's supposed to be one family per house, right down the street."

"Nobody has said much," said Ingalls. "At least, to me. Don't forget, the houses and families where we work loved us. We work hard to be as low-key and non-judgmental as possible. Soto always said the norm would shift—that one day it would be more normal than not to have a much more conscientious relationship with the energy being consumed. Then the tide would pull in all the lost boats. In the meantime, we weren't to tangle with anyone."

Bloom gave her space if she wanted to add a more precise answer without being prodded. He pictured the quiet invasion of door-knocking do-gooders and couldn't help imagine the grumbling. Or the pissed-off people. Status quo meant healthy profit for some. Alter the balance? Someone moves into the loss column.

"But you want names," said Ingalls. "That's what the media exploits. He said black, and she said white. Let the readers make up their minds. The media takes no responsibility to own the facts."

"Not all media, not all reporters," said Bloom. "Generalities don't help. If you think the sheriff and the others will pull out all the stops to figure out what happened to Soto, be my guest. Sometimes things move differently. There's more intensity to the effort when there's information out there in public that keeps the process moving forward."

Ingalls's steel casing melted. "It wouldn't take any of us long to come up with a few situations—angry people."

One man had met one of the team at the door with a shotgun raised and ready, screaming nonsense about Soto's effort as a secret government plot to invade people's privacy.

Another team member witnessed a "pretty good fight" between Soto and a key individual from the non-profit organization behind the scenes, based in Chicago. The funder was displeased with the pace of the effort. The team should push harder. The team could entice or incentivize families that had been through the program to bring in new recruits. Soto was having none of it. Participation based on financial rewards, Soto argued, wasn't commitment at all. The exchange got personal, and Soto spent a week in Chicago being contrite. "He came back more low-key, more inscrutable," said Ingalls. "But we kept going."

"Okay, enough." The calmly certain male voice came from behind.

"What?" said Ingalls.

Bloom berated himself for not watching out.

"Charley, I—" Ingalls tucked her lower lip under her upper teeth. "It's not like before."

"Nothing has changed," said Charley. Six-four. He kept his beard trimmed for the city. He wore sandals, a lime green T-shirt, gray cargo shorts, and one of those goofy white-brimmed hard-shell safari caps like he was on safari.

Bloom introduced himself. "I know," said Charley. His hand was damp from sweat. The shake was two-strokes quick.

Perhaps he had been under watch since the yurt.

"How is that?" said Bloom.

"Come on." Charley tapped Ingalls on the shoulder. "Let's go."

"All off the record," said Bloom.

"Until it's not," said Charley. "And then it's all over the papers."

"Someone killed Soto," said Ingalls. She dropped it like a fact, as if she had received a message in a hidden earpiece.

Charley waved a hand like a dad to a child. Ingalls didn't miss the assumed authority. She stood her ground. "He's trying to help."

"And you signed an agreement," said Charley to Ingalls. They were now five paces off.

Whatever reminder was jogged by that statement, it seemed to work. As she headed off, she noticed Charley had turned his back to them, and she gave her first faint smile, revealing a reserve of natural beauty. The smile told Bloom she was sorry. She flashed the thumb of her right hand to her ear and the pinky to her mouth. She shrugged. She danced both thumbs in the air like a speed texter.

Bloom's phone rang again.

It was Coogan. Had it been more than two minutes? Maybe.

TWENTY-TWO:
SATURDAY MORNING

WAITING SUCKED.

The whole plan sucked.

Depending on Devo—and Cinnamon—sucked.

The best thing about the night by herself in the Flat Tops was a night by herself in the Flat Tops, though Allison was also eager to know about the fire or anything new about the body.

She could climb to a ridge and hope for a cell, but the round trip could take hours, and she might miss Devo.

By the sun, it was noon. She plucked another trout from the lake, pan-fried it over her pint-size fire, and she ate the fish with a splash of hot sauce dripped from a bottle she kept in Sunny Boy's saddle-bags. The hot sauce was stored with the tequila, which had sustained a major attack the previous evening. An inch of her precious liquid remained. Didn't matter. One way or another, she'd be back at Trapper's Lodge tonight, with or without Devo in tow. Maybe she could use the lodge again as her base camp crossroads, reconnect with

Colin and head back tomorrow on horseback to Sweetwater, where she belonged.

Allison spotted a blue grouse by the edge of the forest, made a game out of stalking her way up close, and watched the chicken-like bird forage in the tall grass. She groomed Sunny Boy like he was getting prepped for a show, let him have his way with the oats for a spell, and then led him out of the shade to the pond where he washed down his feed with enthusiasm. She stripped to her underwear, took one quick roll-around in the shallow end of her pool to cool off, and laid back on the grassy shore to dry off, her feet and ankles dipped in the water. Even all her years outside didn't mean her skin stood any chance against a Colorado sun at elevation, so she was soon back in the shade, digging out her last pair of clean underwear and a fresh shirt, blue-and-pink plaid. Changing shirts felt refreshing, but she knew it would soon be grimy with horse and smoke and sweat. Maybe getting clean was a minor statement on behalf of evolution, but one thing that would never change was her beyond-broke Lee jeans. A little yin, a little yang.

By the sun, she knew she had given Devo an extra hour to appear, twenty-five in all.

She was up on Sunny Boy when she spotted Devo coming down around the pond, head down.

Allison climbed down and led Sunny Boy by rope out into the hot sun. Devo came around the pond and offered a slight bob of the head to acknowledge her presence. His gait was odd, tentative. A camerawoman trailed thirty yards behind Devo, but Allison waved her off. She stopped where she stood and set her gear on the ground.

"You okay?" Allison asked when Devo was within earshot.

All the birds had been chased to the shadows and the shade. She could hear Devo's labored breathing—a first.

"You've got big-time problems," said Devo.

"Me?"

"All of you," said Devo. He took ten more steps, came up beside her. He looked sweaty but clean. She didn't recoil on first inhale.

"I was watching you and the cops, to make sure the body was getting out of there," said Devo. "And it turned out someone was watching me. On my way back—"

Now Allison realized Devo wore a new or newer shirt, a brown pullover. It was the same kiltish, skirtish thing going on around his waist.

Devo tugged at the opening of the shirt around his neck and revealed a wound, rimmed in dried blood.

"The fucker shot me," said Devo. "Winged me bad. An inch lower, man, who knows?"

Allison tried to comprehend the lightning speed at which the word had made it around that Devo was involved in finding the body.

"He must have been following me," said Devo. "Or got lucky and thought I might come back around."

"He shot you and then what?" said Allison.

"It stung like hell—worse. But it was a lucky shot so I kept running. He tried to keep up, got off two more shots that scared the be-fucking-jesus out of me, but that was the last I saw or heard of him. I've never run so fast."

Devo winced, tightened his lips. He gave Allison the rundown of his feeble attempts to wash the wound and stop the bleeding. Back with his tribe, they had made a poultice of mashed seeds from blue flax, but Devo didn't think it was doing much good.

"Carrying an axe too," said Devo. "Big, long handle, shiny. Had one of those pick heads, like the firefighters use. And, yeah, I got a good look at him. Guarantee he's a cigar smoker. Whoever finds him, he's tugging on a stogie."

"Age?"

"Face in camo, but he looked young. Thin but strong looking, you know? He was wearing this gray mesh thing. Hard to see much other than the axe, but that's what I remember."

"You need a doctor," said Allison. "And now there's two reasons to talk to the cops."

"Cinnamon told me," said Devo. "But I've had worse wounds and cuts than this and I'm not going to town for one lousy interview with the cops."

With one solid punch to the jaw, Allison figured she might be able to knock him out. But it might be difficult to lift him up and drape him over Sunny Boy's rump for the long ride to town.

"They'll come for you, and it won't be pretty. Might mean they come after your whole experiment." She chose the descriptor to get under his skin.

"Let 'em," said Devo. "They should be looking for someone who started a massive wildfire, but instead they come after a small, help-less band of brothers and sisters trying to do the world a favor? Not a wise choice."

"And if you've got someone up here starting fires and smart enough to follow the elusive Devo without him—"

"Hey, I could tell something was going on."

"You wouldn't risk everything you've been doing," said Allison. "Believe me when I say they will come for you."

"Be a hell of a way to finish—steamrolled by the government," said Devo. "The eviction episode."

"And all that money you've got coming in—somewhere. That would be over so fast."

"We'll start over in another place," said Devo. "Take what we've learned and pick a better location. Maybe the Flat Tops wasn't the best choice anyway."

"You don't want to give up so easy. A couple hours in town isn't going to change anything about who you are or how you're put together." She said it, but she knew it wasn't true. She felt as if it took a day of wilderness to wash off each hour in town. "You're in a position now to negotiate. Trade. Get a pledge or a promise to let you be."

"You think I can trust them?"

"Trust?" said Allison. "Hard for me to say. But bring your camera woman with you—record the deal they offer for all your fans and followers to see, and then if they break their end of it, the whole world knows. What I do know is I'm getting up on Sunny Boy and heading back, one way or the other. Someone's been murdered. Whoever killed him also started a blow-up wildfire that might burn for weeks to come. You want to help figure out what happened, come with me. You don't care, then *adios*, and I'll bet the authorities are dragging your tribe and all your asses out pretty darn quick. They might get testy."

Devo couldn't pull too hard with his right arm, so Allison gave him a boost up first and then hopped in front on the saddle. Devo settled in behind her. No doubt Sunny Boy knew he had two passengers, but their total weight was no issue.

Devo wanted to tell the camerawoman the plan, and they walked around the pond, laid out everything to her. She said she'd get on the radio, try to get somebody when they arrived at Trapper's Lake, so they could pick up the story from there. Allison reiterated the standard caveats—she wasn't part of the show.

Allison set Sunny Boy on a course for Trapper's Lake.

After delivering Devo—and there was a chance she'd have to escort him all the way down the valley to Meeker—it seemed reasonable to think she could contemplate getting back to Sweetwater with Colin. Maybe tonight, maybe tomorrow.

She resigned herself to tomorrow. What else could she do?

"Comfortable?" asked Allison. She headed Sunny Boy up an aspen-dotted slope. The leaves shook like rattles.

"Yeah," said Devo. "Very."

TWENTY-THREE:
SATURDAY LATE
AFTERNOON

THE COPS PUT DEVO in one of the shoebox cabins—#5 straight across the road from the Trapper's Lake Lodge. A nurse worked on his wound and gave him a fresh bandage. He declined the offer of a shower, accepted the offer of a pain pill but asked for it to be quartered first. The cops wanted him to stay in the cabin so he wasn't a spectacle. The air inside was hot and lifeless. It smelled like a dozen old dogs had battled for an hour.

Allison hung back, but Devo made it clear to the cops that he wanted her there. He sat on the floor. Allison sat on the side of the bed; the other side was shoved up against the wall. Two chairs ate up the remaining space. Group bathrooms required a one-minute stroll through the compound. No kitchen, no kitchenette, no pink-plastic Easy Bake Oven. Nora dispatched trays of sandwiches and a jug of lemonade. Allison paid for an icy beer that tasted like liquid nirvana.

The ride down was so hot her jeans had likely fused forever to her butt and thighs.

When it came time for the formal interview, the cops placed two chairs outside in the dusty hardpack in the shade of the cabin. A half-dozen cops huddled, but the lead would be taken by a state-level arson detective with the Colorado Bureau of Investigation, Steve Mendoza. Given the late hour, she resigned herself to a day's delay in the trip back home. Either she'd crash at the lodge again or track down Colin to see what was happening at the McKee Ranch.

How long could this take? Careful equaled glacial in copville. The swarm of cops circled-up for a fast hubbub. The History Channel cameraman was told he could shoot wide shots but to stand back, no audio of the interview itself. The cops had their own camera on a tripod to record Devo's statements.

"And another thing," said Devo. The buzz in the huddle halted like a drill sergeant had barked orders. The six uniforms, standing in an untidy arc, stared in unison. "Before I tell you what I know, I need a promise that you'll leave our camp—our homestead—alone."

"This isn't a negotiation," said Mendoza.

Devo's demand seemed off-kilter from his ramblings on their ride down. *Not sure how long I can keep going. Politics in camp. Other agendas. Not the same.* He talked about the network contract and "plot" suggestions from producers for even higher ratings.

"Leave us alone," said Devo. He pulled his feet up so he squatted on the chair like he was planting rice in a paddy. Every move seemed calculated for the cameras.

"There's no plan to do anything of the sort," said Mendoza. "It's not the issue."

"I'll take a promise," said Devo. A touch of petulance had crept into his voice.

Allison admired Devo's spunk but found herself tired of his *schtick*. Putting your own needs above a murder investigation didn't sit right.

"He said that's not the issue," she said, hoping her voice sounded more relaxed than her roiling innards. The Gang of Six turned as one to her interjection and expected her to complete the thought. "You're a witness. That's it, that's all. Another pair of eyes, whether it's Devo or Nick Timms."

She dredged the name like a fleck of gold from the bottom of deep creek. Devo was a failed actor. He craved the limelight. Saving the human race made a clever cover, but still. At the sound of his given name, Devo jerked his head up like she'd poked his soul with a sharp stick.

"And tell them about being shot at up in the woods," said Allison. "And let's not take all day. Places to go, you know."

With a grim stare, Devo launched in, guided by Mendoza's methodical rundown. Mendoza had a series of maps to help. Devo struggled at first to orient himself to the two-dimensional world. He had different names for mountains and didn't spend much time on the trails. He finally found the spot where he had stood when he saw the first smoke. He referred to an individual tree—a reference point—by its name, Abe. "That's its first name," he said. "Won't tell you the whole thing."

The cops weren't moved.

Devo relished the attention. He recounted finding the body and jacked up the drama of being chased and shot.

"Describe him," said Mendoza.

"I remember the axe most," said Devo. "Long blond handle, shiny blade. But on some level, he looked normal. Could have been a day hiker, a man out to fish. Short dark hair, a narrow, long face."

"Age?" asked Mendoza.

"Thirty?" said Devo.

"Height?"

"Medium," said Devo. "Five-ten at the most."

Devo was staring down Mendoza.

"Powerful build, though," said Devo.

Could she call a time-out? Something about Devo didn't seem like he was playing fair.

"Tough. Of course we all sweat hard now. He had no trouble getting around up there. No struggle. I lost him only because I know how to hide, and of course, I know how to run. I got under a downed tree like a salamander. I mean, I had a good head start, even with my shoulder stinging, but he kept coming."

"So the axe and a gun," said Mendoza. "What about the gun?"

"All I can tell you is the thing had a long barrel," said Devo. "Made a racket."

Mendoza retraced his steps over key points—finding the charred body in the first place, whether Devo had touched the corpse. He pressed for any additional details about the shooter, including what he'd been wearing.

"So if you hadn't happened to run into Miss Coil here, what were you going to do?" said Mendoza.

Devo shrugged. "What does it matter?"

"Wondering what your plan was," said Mendoza. His five compatriots stood like a perfect picture of bureaucratic overkill.

"No plan," said Devo. "I would have figured out some way to get the message out. For sure. Got lucky. I wasn't going to let it go, however, if that's your question."

Devo rolled his eyes in her direction, shook his head.

"We'll need you to come to Meeker," said Mendoza. "Go through some photographs. And we'll need you to write a statement—"

"No." Devo stood. "And I don't write. Never could."

"Dictate a statement, then," said Mendoza.

"What about the video recording?" said Devo.

"Mostly to go through the photographs," said Mendoza. "See if anyone looks familiar. The local authorities have some ideas."

Allison felt like she'd missed something—their urgency had kicked up a notch.

"It's Soto?" said Allison.

"As of an hour ago," said Mendoza. "We got confirmation radioed up before you arrived."

Allison felt the weight of it, like she had been handed an anvil. Her stomach roiled. What the *hell*? A minute might have passed—or ten. She stared at the ground. She stared at nothing.

"Suspects?" Allison snapped back to the moment, heard her own voice.

"People we need to talk with," said Mendoza.

"And it's murder for sure," said Mendoza. "The autopsy found cuts in his right clavicle. Three of them. Deep into the bone. Coroner thinks he bled out, died. Fire took most of the body, but not all."

She tried to picture it—the moment. The confrontation. She pictured smart and thoughtful Dante Soto in Trudy's kitchen, clutching a turquoise mug filled with hot blackberry tea. She pictured the assholes who killed Dante Soto and then lit the fire that was torching all that precious hunting ground. If hell didn't offer special rooms where the suffering tripled, it should. She pictured Trudy reeling at the news, and her own heart ached at the imaginary sight.

"The ID?" said Allison.

"Dental," said Mendoza. "And of course everybody affected by that fire would like a piece of the wiseass who set it. Even without the murder, the size of the manhunt would be impressive."

"Jesus," said Devo. "Axe-type cuts?"

"Could be," said Mendoza. "And now you're key, Mr. Devo. You're it. You're the one. You're needed. You don't want this asswipe to set another fire or whack someone else with his axe or shoot someone. What you want to do is come down to Meeker and give us a hand."

Allison tried to imagine Devo being okay with the idea that she would head back home tomorrow and leave him to fend for himself with the cops. He would want her to play escort, handler, and counselor—all in one.

Mendoza and the cops huddled. They checked their phones. Checked their radios. Checked each other. Checked themselves. If anyone saw a flaw, now was the time to say it. Mendoza disappeared for two minutes, came back. He disappeared for an even longer stretch, came back. The sun, an ill yolk behind smoky gauze netting, sank like it was tired of waiting.

Devo pretended to weigh his non-existent options.

"They're not asking that much," said Allison.

"I know," said Devo.

Devo's wishy-washiness felt fake, but Allison couldn't put her finger on it. If it was her, Allison knew she would drop everything for the rest of the summer if it would help track down the axe man firestarter who killed Dante Soto and leveled a giant swath of the forest that would take decades to recover.

"I don't want anyone to know I'm there," said Devo.

Mendoza returned with a plan. They would all go down in the morning. They were gathering files for Devo to flip through. They found a motel room to rent.

"Nobody needs to know," said Mendoza. "Just us."

"One day," said Devo. "Drop me off back here day after tomorrow."

"Do my best," said Mendoza.

TWENTY-FOUR: SATURDAY NIGHT

DUNCAN BLOOM WORMED A hand under her shirt, unsnapped her bra, said hello to her breasts. He attended to them with enthusiasm.

She laughed.

"Thought I was doing a pretty good job," he said. "Appreciative. Attentive. Not rushed."

"It was a hard smile," said Trudy. She played innocent. "That was not a laugh you heard. Not a laugh at all."

"A hard what?" he said.

"Smile. I was so happy that it came out like a laugh. It might have sounded like something else, but I was smiling at your affections. Your talent."

She touched his nose and the corners of his pretty mouth.

"I thought you had to go," said Trudy. "And yet here you are."

"I do," said Bloom. "I'm leaving in approximately three minutes and forty-five seconds."

"What's going to take so long?" said Trudy.

"Talking, obviously," said Bloom.

A full ten minutes later, he was putting his clothes back on. She pulled a sheet up over herself and enjoyed the view. He had needed coaching to take her to the hilltop more than once per session and, it turned out, he had been a master student with a terrific ability to focus. He didn't need to be told twice. At home, in Sweetwater, they had mastered the art of lingering, at least half talk and snuggling. Interruptions were either self-inflicted or indicated poor planning. Time slowed. Duncan had moved to the Flat Tops at Thanksgiving, about three months after they worked together on "the pipeline story," as he called it. They hadn't missed many nights together since. Thus, this reunion came with its own mandatory romp and greeting.

With his jeans on and top off, he planted a dozen soft kisses across her stomach.

"Guess I'll have to finish the job another time," he said.

"You finished, I finished, we're finished," said Trudy.

"There is no end," said Bloom. "As soon as it's over, it starts again with you. Matter of time. Tick, tick, tick."

"You are heading in the wrong direction," said Trudy. "You could stay here in beautiful downtown Rifle and leave at the crack."

"Of dawn," said Bloom.

"Sure," said Trudy.

"You have to say 'of dawn.' You can't just say at the crack and leave it at that. Nobody will know what you mean."

"You did," said Trudy. "You knew exactly."

Bloom wriggled into his shirt and sighed.

"How come you have to go back?" She knew the answer.

"Coogan's way," said Bloom. "His priorities."

Once Soto was reported missing, she had a bad feeling. She knew in her bones he wouldn't turn up alive. He stood for everything he believed, except for all the obvious effort he had put into creating an organization to back his point of view. She was a one-dimensional deal about local herbs and home gardens. Successful? Sure. Visible? Sure. Profitable? Yes. On the other hand, Soto attacked every aspect of this lifestyle and was altering and adjusting people's habits, which had a real chance to make a significant difference, one household at a time. The only thing was he had to push, promote, encourage, and cajole. No matter how gently he worked, those were all verbs that gave her pause. Once he built it, he had an organization to feed and lead. He had backers to please. Goals and targets. She admired his notions, could never have joined in. Nonetheless, she had cried for hours at the thought that someone could feel threatened by Dante Soto. She pictured a thousand scenarios, tried to grasp the sheer violence of the moment. She could see him lying in the woods, peaceful and staring at the treetops one minute, breathless the next. She pictured the fire roaring over his body, the sincere eyes that had graced her own kitchen. She felt the utter sadness of it all. Who would feel threatened? He was a quiet missionary and his only client was the planet.

Bloom straightened his clothes, made a quick round-trip to the bathroom, finger-combing his medium-long hair. He would always look like the out-of-place city boy.

"You want me to talk with this woman, one of his team?" she said.

"Andrea Ingalls," said Bloom. "You won't be a threat, after all. And she likes you and loves your products."

Down to Earth, in fact, had opened a small nursery on the outskirts of Meeker at the same time Soto rolled into town. Her timing could not have been any better as the interest in local herbs and learning how to grow their own vegetables started to climb. The Watt's Ranch Store had carried her brand for years. She was a known quantity. And local—sort of. She tried to minimize the number of trips between Glenwood Springs and Meeker to reduce her overall carbon footprint but managing a regional business required getting around. Her solace was the fuel-efficient hybrid delivery trucks with their spacious front seats, an added perk she did not realize at the time of purchase.

"And she's going to—what?" said Trudy.

"Show you places where he had been working—I guess he had this new experimental farm or something. Andrea said she could think of several situations or people who might be worth talking with."

"I don't have a reason to ask," said Trudy. "You know? No reporter license."

"Ask like you care, which you do. You're asking questions like anyone else and maybe something will turn up. If it does, you tell me about it, and you tell the cops about it and then Coogan sends me racing back up to Meeker, so I'm there when they figure out who killed Soto and set the blaze."

Bloom made it sound easy. Natural. Normal.

"Where's Allison?" said Trudy. "Have you heard from her?"

"Not lately," said Bloom. "Last I heard she was going back up to show the cops where Devo found the body."

Every time Trudy contemplated that scene, she struggled to remain level-headed. It was a challenge. "She must know something," said Bloom. "Especially how the cops are reacting and what else they might have to work with. Have you tried her phone?"

"I gave that up. She never answers. I mean, it never goes through up there. Ever."

"But maybe in this situation," said Bloom. "Even to let her know you'll be in Meeker."

Trudy grabbed her phone from the bedside table.

"Long shot." She offered him a half smile. She would indulge him. "This never works. Never. Ever."

Of course, she hoped the call worked. It was always better to have Allison in the dead center of the mix.

The phone rang. And rang. "Hasn't worked the last ten dozen times I've tried," she said. "I'll leave a message; I guess that won't hurt."

"It's me," said the familiar voice. "Hi there."

"It's her," Trudy told Bloom. "Told you it never worked."

"Who are you with?" said Allison.

"One Mr. Duncan Bloom," said Trudy.

Bloom said, "Ha."

"Where?" said Allison.

"In Rifle now. Both of us. He is heading home, but I'm heading up. What about you?"

"The lodge at Trapper's," said Allison. "We're coming down tomorrow. Devo may have seen the guy who killed Soto."

"Devo?" said Trudy. She couldn't picture it. "Willingly?"

"Kind of," said Allison. "Sort of. He's been squirming. It's possible this won't go as well as they're hoping."

Trudy held the phone down for a split second. "The cops are bringing Devo in to Meeker as a witness. He may have seen something."

"And tell Duncan he's got to get all this through the cops, not me," said Allison.

"You can't use that," she whispered to Bloom. "It was off the record." She liked pretending to speak like a reporter.

"And Devo won't be granting interviews," said Allison. "So don't let your boyfriend get any ideas."

"No interviews," she whispered.

"I've got to try," said Bloom.

"They haven't even told us where they're taking him," said Allison. "Or for how long."

"You with Colin?" said Trudy.

"Plan to find him," said Allison. "He should be around some-where tomorrow, I think."

"How is their home? The ranch?"

"Fine. Untouched. And no army of firefighters, either. The fields look like they always do. I told Devo the whole story—you should have seen the size of his eyes."

"He's right there with you?"

"Staying in another cabin," said Allison. "But yes."

They made plans to meet up at the Blue Spruce the next day.

"Tell her I might have to come back for the party," said Bloom. He had a thing for Allison. All the guys wanted to see if they could crack the shell.

"You okay?" said Trudy.

"Why?" said Allison.

"You sound uncertain," said Trudy.

"Another day in Meeker," said Allison. "Devo wants me to hold his hand. I have no idea what Colin is up to. And a good chunk of the wilderness has been taken down by some asshole who also likely killed a good man. Other than that, all is right as rain, of which we have none."

TWENTY-FIVE:
SUNDAY MORNING

THE "COMPUTER" WAS THINNER than a slice of bread. Mendoza showed him how to scroll, swiping with his fingers right on the goddamn screen. Because he had asked, Devo first looked at pictures of Soto. There were two recent ones. Dante Soto's hair was long and his jaw was strong. He looked serious. There was a shot of him fly fishing, another of him hiking on a stony peak. Devo had heard about these tablet computers from the producers and newbies, but had never seen one. It looked like it could be snapped over a knee. He wanted to pull up an episode of *Latitude/Longitude,* see how they flowed. Mendoza said the tablet was connected to the government's Wi-Fi "hot spot," whatever that was.

"People watch a ton of TV on their iPads now," said Mendoza. "Now they don't even need to sit up on the couch, they can lie there on the couch or in bed, change the channel with one touch of a finger, barely burn a calorie."

Maybe Mendoza was trying to make friends. "Softest damn society in the history of civilization," said Devo.

"Not that I don't disagree with you on that," said Mendoza. "But your methods—"

"Leave my people alone," said Devo. "Leave them out of this."

They would use a motel room near downtown, Mendoza explained, to minimize Devo's contact and keep him out of the limelight. He sat cross-legged in the middle of one thin bed. Mendoza made an office out of the other. The room smelled stale. It had the heavy stink of old and tired. The fuzzy carpet felt wrong on his feet. Ticklish and dirty. He had managed two slices of pizza, but his stomach fought the dense cheese. The spices bit back. Fennel. He wondered how many couples had fucked in this room. The bathroom wafted out harsh waves of mold.

The door remained open in an attempt to generate breeze. Mendoza and the others came and went, mumbling shit and yakking into their radios.

Devo flipped through the pictures. Page after page. These guys were nothing like the guy in the woods. That guy was blond. He had felt bad, lying to the detectives, especially with Allison right there, but he had to protect himself—protect his people—and Mendoza wouldn't deal.

All these guys in the photos were easy to dismiss. Too old, too young, too hairy, too beat-up, too unkempt, wrong entire fucking race. Why would they include a black guy? Devo didn't linger. Glance and flip. He needed one that was semi-sort-of-close.

He felt alone. It was all wrong—the smells, the cops, the expectations, and the pressure. He hated it all.

Allison had taken off. She had promised to check back, but he didn't know when. She had talked to her friend Trudy on the telephone on the way down. They had been escorted down in a big black SUV, a fucking tank for crying out loud. He was alone in his own bench seat, the fourth of four, and he couldn't hear details. She turned around to point out the ranch where Colin had grown up, where his family lived. Except for the crispy backdrop and blackened trees in the distance, it looked idyllic. Devo was jealous. How could you mess up if you had an upbringing like that?

"You're going to watch the room all night?"

Devo imagined the word trickling out. The news could creep out there. *That History Channel weirdo. He's here.*

"Right outside," said Mendoza.

Devo's room was upstairs. The view faced east, but he could see south from the outside walkway, into where the smoke was thick. There were two exterior stairs to the second floor, nothing more than another row of rooms stacked on top of the first.

"This ain't working," said Devo. "He's not here."

"He could be the next one or the next one," said Mendoza. "Keep going."

"These are all suspects from around here?" said Devo. "That many?"

"A mix. Western slope and bad apples from Utah, Wyoming, and the Front Range, a couple anyway. There are networks, you know." Mendoza sat on the edge of the bed, checked something on his phone.

The images blurred from grim faces to tense faces to pissed-off faces.

"You find something close," said Mendoza. "That's okay. Good place to start with the sketch artist."

Devo's head throbbed. And he laughed, to himself. *Hell.* The first months in the wilderness had been weeks of gnarly headaches as he learned to hydrate, to adapt to the new diet, shed weight, and sync with the surroundings. But it had been a long, long time since his head hurt. This was all wrong, and his people needed him.

He made a split-second decision and pointed down at the next picture.

"Yeah?" Mendoza took the computer wafer back.

"Makes my shoulder hurt just looking at him," said Devo. Surely the guy in the photo deserved to be questioned about something. "His hair was shorter and he hadn't shaved lately, but ... Who is he?" He felt guilty about pointing out an innocent man, but this was survival of the fittest. The guy would probably get a good lawyer, have an alibi or something.

By then, Devo would be long gone.

Mendoza tapped the screen and headed to the door. From the outside walkway, he whistled and waved to someone. In a minute, Devo had a new protector, an older cop with short red hair and a sad gut. He gave Devo a courtesy nod but said nothing. He glanced at the gummy pizza, six slices left, and he stood in the doorway with his back to Devo.

Now what?

Now the fuck what?

He felt he was missing something obvious. He was glad to get rid of Mendoza. He sipped water with no ice. It tasted metallic—processed. It smelled bad. Maybe it was the leftover oil from the pizza peppers in his mouth. His stomach was making up its mind about the pizza. The decision might have an ugly outcome. The wall air conditioner throbbed angrily.

A worrisome idea dawned. Identifying the guy wasn't enough. They would need him as a witness.

The weeks ahead snapped into focus. Having spotted the guy in the file—*well*—didn't mean he could saunter back to the homestead *la-dee-dah*. It could be weeks or months. What if they couldn't find the guy in the photo? Devo stood, and grabbed his stomach.

"The pizza," he said when his guard turned around.

He slammed the bathroom door and slammed the toilet lid up so it sounded urgent.

The window was pint-size, not much bigger than a vent, but the frosted pane slid sideways through an open cemetery for dead flies.

It was a straight drop off the back of the motel. Two stories—enough to snap an ankle. The ground fell away behind the motel. That would help with the roll, but it was too far for a leap. His second trip to Meeker was turning out worse than his first, a couple years back, when he found himself at the hospital.

He was never coming back. He would have to wait for his moment, but he wasn't sticking around here. He was going left. The rest of the world could go right, and it could all go fuck itself. Cinnamon was right all along.

TWENTY-SIX:
SUNDAY AFTERNOON

Two messages were enough.

Three looked weak. Needy.

But still, *what the hell, Colin?*

It took ten minutes to walk between the parking lot at the Blue Spruce, where Trudy would materialize, and the motel further east where the cops were keeping Devo. Duncan Bloom was checked in at the Blue Spruce—at least, the room was in his name. Allison covered the loop three times, although she had no idea what she was expecting to see or do. Maybe Mendoza would emerge with news. She altered her route on the fourth loop. She veered north, through downtown. She felt obvious and alone—a cowgirl without her horse, her boyfriend, or a firm plan. The lack of the first two things made her concentrate on the third. Allison bought a cold lemonade from a café on Main Street, noted a television news truck pulling up to park near the courthouse and a trio of over-uniformed cops near the front door. She circled back to the Blue Spruce. This time she decided to stay put outside. She would follow the old rule—if you're the one lost, stay put. Allison found the back of a dirty, blue pickup to lean against and pretend like she belonged. She found herself staring west up the road for the boxy shape of Trudy's delivery truck to pop into view. As far as Allison could tell, she was the only listless human in town.

She stared at her phone. She considered drifting inside to ask if she could use the lobby computer and check for news. She would channel her inner Trudy, pretend to care about the outside world and maybe stumble across an update about Soto. She could do the same on her phone because Duncan Bloom had shown her about apps, but she didn't care for the tiny screen. All the phone did was make her think that if she wanted to stay "connected," she would need occasional access to a wall socket. Carrying a phone had bailed her out enough in the past that owning the device was as basic as packing tequila, but the care and feeding of the thing was almost like a nagging baby.

She couldn't let it die. Colin might call back. Or Trudy. She'd given her number to Mendoza in case something popped up with Devo.

Inside at the Blue Spruce, she explained her electrical needs and was offered access to a lobby side table, an outlet, and a computer. The clerk didn't seem to care. All hands and new faces were assumed to be there helping with the fire and doing something good. If the Blue Spruce was typical, Meeker was a trusting place.

She scanned the news sites.

And there it was on the Denver paper's site—confirmation of what she knew in her bones, of what Trudy knew in her bones.

The would-be game-changing environmentalist had met his fate in the great outdoors. State and others were "saddened" and "shocked." The quotes sounded plastic. Did they really have a clue?

The most heavily used adjective about the fire was "stubborn." Winds had turned it around, so it was aiming southeast, straight to the heart of the Flat Tops. On its current bearing, Sweetwater was in its direct path—days away, but still. "Hell bent and taking everything with it," said one forest official quoted in the *Grand Junction Sentinel*. "Ten percent contained."

Was that supposed to mean she could feel 10 percent better?

The fire's destruction involved too many deaths to count. The forest would rejuvenate and recover. But seeing a big chunk of the Flat Tops chewed up was like watching a friend die every day.

Allison looked up from the computer, checked her phone battery, and spotted a familiar figure standing near the clerk's counter. Jayne. *Garrett's Jayne.*

She stood with that certain disheveled look familiar to motel and hotel front lobbies worldwide. While one of the classier joints in Meeker, any place you could get a room meant you could, well, get a room.

Allison hadn't seen whether Jayne had come down the stairs behind her or from one of the long hallways on the first floor, but she looked like she was waiting for someone and, since she was standing near the door, leaving.

Jayne wore the same-style tapered jeans she was wearing the night she fled half-bombed as the fire roared down to the McKee ranch. This time her wedges were black and her top was a harsh yellow-lime number with a tight fit. An oversized purse dangled from one hand, and she checked her phone with the other. She tortured chewing gum with her tongue for all the world to see.

"Jayne," said Allison. "Hi."

Jayne needed a moment to dial in the name, place the face, calculate the odds, and determine if this coincidence added to her woes or not. Her makeup was rushed. Her spritz was sweet peach. Her look was confused.

"How you doing?" she said. Maybe she was afraid to say the wrong name. "What are you doing here?"

She took a tentative step toward the door, as if she hadn't been waiting for anyone else.

"I know this is a long shot," said Allison. "But by any chance have you run into Garrett's brother Colin?"

"Um, no. Haven't seen Garrett since that night, as a matter of fact. With all the craziness in town. You know." She took one more step to the door and a furtive look around. "I heard his dad got put in jail for something. He hurt someone?"

"A punch, yeah," said Allison. "You don't know where Garrett is, by any chance?"

"You could check his place."

Allison asked for Garrett's phone number, and she made a show of scrolling on her device. It didn't take long. "No. Didn't have it."

Allison noted the past tense. Jayne's feet didn't quite know whether to stand pat or bolt for the door.

"Okay, if by any chance you run into him, can I give you mine?"

"I really don't know how to work these things," said Jayne. A nervous chuckle came with her confession. "There's too much on them, know what I mean?"

Allison found a piece of scrap paper at the clerk's counter, jotted her phone number on it and watched Jayne tuck it into a back pocket so tight that it took some convincing to shove it in.

"I'm trying to head back to Sweetwater but I'm pretty sure Colin is still over here somewhere, okay?"

If Colin surfaced in the next hour, they could grab supplies, fight their way upriver to Trapper's where Sunny Boy, Merlin, and Hercules were waiting and wondering. They could be camping under the stars, alone, tonight. Jayne stared like she was working an algebra problem in her head.

Allison held up her phone. "Suppose I'll try one more time."

Jayne headed to the door, the so-long-farewell pleasantries rendered to the junk heap of civilization.

Allison gave time for the door to the vestibule and the door to the parking lot to close before following Jayne outside. She got Colin's brisk voicemail greeting, "Hey it's Colin—"

She knew the rest and clicked off.

It was a matter of steps from the tiled lobby to the asphalt parking lot. Neither felt right in the boots.

SUVs and pickups jammed the small parking lot, which extended across the full front of the hotel. Jayne headed to an older red F150 pickup. She didn't look around. She had places to go and things to see. Busy, busy bee.

"Hey there." Trudy Heath walked up with a smile that suggested she had found a new way to stretch time. "Right where you said you'd be, though it's got to be cooler inside."

"Where's your truck?" said Allison after the quickest hug ever. No question Trudy Heath was the freshest-looking female trucker on the Western Slope.

"Good to see you too," said Trudy.

"Turn around," said Allison.

"What?"

"We need your truck."

She must have seen the look on Allison's face. Trudy didn't insist on explanations. Trudy Heath was wired with one of those golden switches that allowed her to view the world with optimism and buckets of sunshine until she ran across someone or something that would suck up her entire attention until the dark cloud or menacing asshole was eradicated.

Jayne's pickup was backing up.

"Where is your truck?" With the white side panels, giant "Down to Earth" logo, and its truncated but high-off-the-ground backside, it was usually easy to spot.

"Side lot," said Trudy. "Where the sign told me to park. Who's in the—?"

"I'll explain."

The cab was spiffy and spotless. The windshield's acre of glass gave the feeling of floating near the edge of a bubble. Head-on collisions would involve zero suspense.

"Not your average stealth vehicle," said Allison.

"Where are we going?" Changing plans on a dime was always okay with Trudy.

"Following her." Allison pulled her hat down. The red pickup idled by the front door, blocking their view of the vestibule.

"So far, so good," said Trudy. "How long do you think it will take for her to reach top speed?"

Allison heard a click and a hum when Trudy turned the key, and for a second she thought something was wrong, but when Trudy put the truck in gear and stepped on the brake, it was obvious the motor was running. "It's going, don't worry," said Trudy. "Who's in the pickup?"

"Jayne," said Allison. "And—"

The man who came out of the hotel took the long way around the back. He tossed a bag in the bed of the pickup right behind the shotgun seat and hopped inside.

"And somebody," said Allison. Jayne's rider wasn't Garrett. This guy was shorter than Garrett and wore a dark green bucket hat like a fisherman.

"And Jayne is?"

"Colin's brother's sort-of maybe ex-girlfriend. I'm thinking more ex with every passing minute."

Jayne's pickup pulled out of the parking lot. It rolled a quarter-block east and turned left toward the heart of downtown Meeker. The two-lane street was wide. Trudy waited for a semi to slide past, and then gave hot pursuit at 20 miles per hour.

"What did she do?" said Trudy.

"Probably had some alone time with a new guy," said Allison. "Beyond that, nothing in particular except I didn't like the way she answered my questions. More what she didn't say."

"And where's Colin?"

"Dying to know."

The red pickup was a half block ahead, about to go past the county courthouse. With all the walking around while she had waited, Allison felt like a local.

"When did you see him last?"

"I'd have to think about that," said Allison. It felt like a week.

Jayne treated Meeker's crawling-pace speed limits like the eleventh commandment. She headed north. In a block, the road would climb into the pleasant, church-dotted residential neighborhood stretched across the hill that overlooked the broad valley of the White River.

Mid-block, the pickup's brake lights popped on, and for a second Allison thought they had been spotted—or she had been spotted—in the spaceship-like enclosure that formed the front of Trudy's truck. Trudy slowed, too, but there was nowhere to hide. Through the back window of the pickup's cab, they could see Jayne and her rider both turn and stare at something off to the left.

In front of the courthouse was a confusing scene. A large blue school bus was parked at the curb. It was one of those buses with small, tinted windows. It wasn't for school children. This bus was built for transporting prisoners. At least forty or fifty people jammed around the front door of the bus and beefy bouncer types, all wearing riot gear helmets with shields down, lined the walk to the modest courthouse door.

"Holy—" said Trudy.

"Fuck," said Allison.

Around the front door of the bus, Allison counted at least four television news crews. Across the park, a line of their SUVs and vans, antennas up. This event, whatever it was, had been announced in advance for the media to capture.

"That's Cinnamon." Allison said it matter-of-fact like she might recognize an acquaintance in an unfamiliar location.

Cinnamon shook her shoulders, flailed her hair as best she could with her arms handcuffed behind her back. Trudy lowered the window, and Cinnamon's cries drifted across the park. The afternoon's hot air, laced with smoke, rushed in. Onlookers clapped. Her dreadlocks whipped around. Cinnamon stood no chance struggling against her two large handlers. Cinnamon was halfway to the courthouse when another of Devo's followers stepped off the bus. She was smaller, less feisty, and more resigned to her fate.

"Those motherfuckers promised," said Allison. "They promised Devo."

No wonder they had interviewed him at a motel and not at the sheriff's office, in the basement of the courthouse, so he wouldn't see what they had done to his tribe.

"Guess that's the end of that show," said Trudy.

"Or this chapter," said Allison. "Or season—whatever they call it."

The group arrest would be national news, another Colorado curiosity. Ninety-nine percent of the locals would cheer the eviction. The band of devolutionists on the Flat Tops constituted a flagrant violation of the fundamental rules of the wilderness—you leave it alone. And you don't exploit it for your network television show.

A throaty rumble yanked their attention back to Jayne and her pickup, which shot forward with a sense of excitement.

"I gotta go," said Allison. She popped the door open, slid down to the street. "Follow her and see if she bumps into Colin or anyone. I'll meet you right back here in two hours. If I can't leave you a message on your phone, I'll leave a message at the Blue Spruce."

"Wait," said Trudy. She handed her a slip of folded paper. Inside was one name, Andrea Ingalls, and a telephone number. "Call her. Duncan said she's got information. Ideas. You know, a place to start. One of Dante Soto's people."

Trudy's truck started to move before Allison closed the door.

The sullen parade continued one by one—buckskins and crude moccasins and sadness. It was the perp walk for extreme naturalists snatched from the threshold of their time tunnel. They could have been hippies who rode a wormhole from San Francisco in 1968, but they were tough and built for work. The media soaked up each Robinson Crusoe—and Robin Crusoe—moment. Questions were greeted with uniform silence.

Standing with her camera rolling was the same woman who had been videotaping when she negotiated with Cinnamon.

"Surprise attack," said Ruth. "Dead middle of the night."

"They got everyone?"

"You mean did anyone get away?" Ruth checked herself. "Not for me to say."

"I'm a friend of Devo's. He'll be asking the same question."

"You know where he is?"

"I have a rough idea."

She would need time alone with Devo to tell him about the betrayal. Perhaps they were already telling him. They would want to press charges against Devo like all the others—charge him with trespassing or illegal camping. He was their trophy bull but had to be processed like all the other game.

"No one got away," said Ruth. "Clean sweep. They even had a plan for the goats. They brought in local farmers to help lead them out. Chickens, removed. And they have a work crew they left behind to restore the habitat in that patch. If you know where Devo is, I'm following you."

"Follow me," said Allison.

A fresh round of sweat coated the old round of sweat. Ruth stayed shoulder to shoulder, no obvious sign of strain in the heat. Her tripod rode on one shoulder, camera on a strap over the other. Her ponytails bounced cheerily. How dare they when everything was all fucked up? Since the fire started, she had seen one attempted eviction or forced evacuation up close and played a role in another. Her hunting grounds were getting leveled, and she wasn't up there fighting it. A decent human being had been killed, and she had sent her friend Trudy off to track her boyfriend's brother's sort-of ex-girlfriend and some other guy in a delivery truck.

Five cops stood on the balcony outside the door to Devo's room. In the parking lot, another gaggle of uniforms and one cop car started to scramble, popping on lights and wheeling out of the lot like they were filming a movie.

"There," said Allison to Ruth. "That's where he's being questioned. But you're on your own now, asking to get through for an interview."

Ruth thanked her and set up her tripod for a shot.

Cops made their way back and forth around the south side of the building, pointing and agitated. It didn't take a genius to interpret. Allison slipped around the north side of the pint-size inn. A long white rope dangled from Devo's room. It ended six feet above the dirt. Where Devo would have landed, the slope ended in a dense thicket of brush. The rope wasn't rope—it was strips of sheets knotted together.

Allison pictured Devo scurrying back, clueless that his homestead would be empty when he arrived. But they'd be watching for Devo now, too, since they knew his destination.

Based on Allison's hunch of the location of Devo's camp, Allison gave Devo three days to reach home.

One more thing, all screwed up.

TWENTY-SEVEN: SUNDAY AFTERNOON

THE RED PICKUP JOGGED left, went another block, turned right and then turned right again. Trudy hung back, but knew this was getting ridiculous and risky.

Three deer grazed on a browned-out front yard. Grass in the park, or maybe a baseball field, suffered under the pounding sun. Two men attacked repairs on a trailered fishing boat in their front yard, the guts of the outboard motor in pieces on the driveway around them. They didn't look up or over.

At the top of downtown Meeker, the red pickup followed the ridge back to the east and stopped so suddenly that Trudy had to slide past at the same speed she'd been moving. She risked a fast glance at the crimson mailbox and caught the number, three black-on-gold stickers: 848.

In her rearview, Jayne circled the front of the truck, and her passenger climbed out. She caught a glimpse of his well-brimmed hat before the road pulled her downhill and cut off the view of her prey. Couldn't be helped.

At the next intersection, she noted the streets, 8th and Hill. Now what? There was no easy place to lurk or park or pullover. If she had a sandwich and a book she could fake the look of a tired driver needing a break. She had neither sandwich nor book, and since Jayne and her passenger were out of sight, they could have hopped back in, pulled a U-Turn, and headed the other way. She would never know.

She could be losing them—*right now.*

She could give it another twenty minutes, and then drive back past the house in the opposite direction, make sure the pickup had stayed put. Waiting a block away, without some lunch and props, seemed too obvious.

Three blocks down the hill, the eastern edge of residential Meeker ended at the county fairgrounds. Hill Street dead-ended and turned north onto 2nd Street. Trudy found a spot to pull over and point the truck so she had a view back up the hill. She hid in plain sight with the vague notion that the county fairgrounds backdrop would help her blend into the scenery.

Trudy lowered her windows and snapped off the humming motor. The air-conditioned air vanished in one gulp into the big outdoors. Trudy let the heat swallow her up and took a long glug from a cold water bottle plucked from a small cooler at her feet. She reminded herself not to drink too much. She'd hate to lose a tail because she had to pee, especially if this connected back on even the slightest thread to what happened to Dante Soto.

She hadn't been the one to find his corpse, of course, but she couldn't shake the idea that the skull Allison and Devo had studied in the charred forest had once sat by her fireplace in Sweetwater, sipping Wild Turkey and chatting about the future of the planet.

Over and over Trudy pictured Allison face-to-skull, staring, thinking, looking. With all Allison's issues with death and fate, the moment had a creepy vibe. Trudy had never known anyone like Allison who carried with her the constant warnings of what might be lurking around the next corner, but a high school field trip to Denver had put Trudy in the front row for a harrowing performance of Hamlet with scary, grim actors, and Trudy would never forget the skull plucked from the dirty grave, dripping dirt. Yorrick. The sight had kept her awake for three nights. Trudy had no trouble relating to Allison's fixation, and she felt as if anything she did to help Allison might provide the magic spark of light that would chase the darkness away. After what Allison had done for her, Trudy owed her that.

The red pickup crept down the hill. No rush, no hurry, and no Jayne. Two guys sat in front. A large, round white plastic tub like an oversized picnic lemonade cooler poked above the height of the cab.

When it reached 3rd Street, they didn't look her way. Their rolling stop was a joke. The guy riding shotgun looked younger than the driver, who was the original guy with Jayne, and he had his hand on the dashboard and looked around to check on the cargo. His hair was short and he wore a baseball cap.

The driver turned south. Downhill. The pickup coughed. Its pace was slow torture. She gave the truck a two-block lead and pulled out. The hardest part of this tail might be hanging back and not getting pulled over for driving too slow.

The pickup gave the next stop sign more credence. Houses on three corners, a church on the fourth. He took a left and then a right where it hit a T. The truck hugged the edge of town. Left again, right again, and they were back at the highway. Rifle to the west and Craig to the east. The fact that she hadn't been spotted or that they hadn't grown suspicious about the same white truck staying two blocks behind them told Trudy they were either innocent as spring rain or had so much more on their minds that they weren't paying attention. She guessed the latter.

They headed toward Craig. She let two sedans slip in between her and the pickup, which belched black smoke as the engine strained under the whip. It was a risk, but the battered red pickup wasn't going to be breaking any land speed records. One sedan wasted no time at the town limits to leave the pickup in its dust. The one-car buffer would have to do. The pickup ignored the road to Buford and turned north, climbing past the light industrial buildings on Meeker's fringe. Craig? Steamboat? Further north to Wyoming? As the road climbed, Trudy's rearview mirror provided a panorama of the valley. Behind her, the broad smudge of smoggy haze and smoke turned bluebird skies to a dusty, grim black.

Halfway to where the road would begin cutting its way through rock, the pickup slowed. Going uphill, the driver let the incline work as brakes. The truck plunged off and down a dirt road that roller-coastered its way off across treeless, open country.

Trudy waited at the turn and gave them a one-swell head start. She timed it so she could spot the truck from the top of each scruffy, barren wave of earth before dropping down into the next trough. She checked her phone. No service. She wanted to hear Duncan's voice or at least find out if he had made it back okay. It wouldn't hurt to have someone else suggest a plan here, particularly if this road dead-ended, or if she suddenly came to the top of a rise and spotted them ahead, pickup blocking the road. Trudy felt her breath shorten at the possibilities, picturing rifle shots through the windshield and her truck veering off the road.

Their Sunday picnic pace continued, unerring. Trudy chased the dark daydream away, or at least tried. From the top of the next rise, she spotted the pickup at the bottom of the hill and heading into a long, flat stretch that went gun barrel straight across a bleak plain. In the distance, the road cut into thick woods.

Trudy stopped. She waited until the pickup had covered half the distance across the wide-open gap and then eased her way down. The woods swallowed the pickup, and Trudy stepped on the accelerator. The truck fought the hard-pack washboard with a violent shimmy. The steering wheel throbbed. In her rearview, a Martian cloud of red-brown dust. Did these two never look around?

Inside the woods, the road swept right and then back to the left. Soon she was back under the open skies, and the pickup gave her a profile view as it turned down another road. It was headed toward a squat compound next to a grove of sad cottonwoods. Whatever creek suggested this was a good spot to grow had long-since vanished in the drought.

The entry to the ranch was flanked on each side by two sections of log fencing that amounted to nothing more than decoration or markers. There were no cattle and the low house or maybe trailer, even from a distance, needed a coat of paint and a thorough spruce-up. To the west, a dark red barn faced the house, its big doors flung open wide. A half-dozen trucks and ATVs littered the landscape. The pickup parked halfway between the two structures and two riders emerged. One headed for the barn and the other for the house. Neither one looked back her way.

If anything, the "ranch" raised junk cars and automobile mechanics.

Trudy pulled into the dirt road to turn around. She zeroed the trip meter so she could measure the miles back to the highway. Duncan could figure out more about the owners in an hour on the web than they probably knew about themselves. All he needed was a thread to tug.

There wasn't much more she could do or see. Trudy felt a sudden urge to head back and find Allison, see if there was any way to identify the owners of the rural used car and rust emporium.

Trudy realized one thing—she needed a pee break and the two options seemed to be right here by the truck or back in the woods, about a mile away. Why did she need cover, however, when there was nobody around? She stood outside in the shimmering heat and chose the back of the truck where she could watch the road in both directions. She relieved herself, keeping an eye on the house and both directions on the road. Exposing herself heightened her sense of alarm, though her eyes found no logical cause. The truck idled. She squatted with one hand on the corner of the truck for balance.

As she buttoned up, she cocked her head to a new sound. She was familiar with the truck's hum and pings. This was a new buzz that didn't belong.

She climbed back behind the wheel and reached to put the truck in reverse when she saw the black ring, high in the sky. It bobbled to the right, dropped down and shimmied back over to the left. It was above her windshield. It was a hovering hula hoop at about the same height as any low-flying—

The black ring wasn't high in the sky. It was small, not much bigger than a dinner plate. It sported four conical fan engines, dipped and then hovered midair like a hummingbird. A camera on its belly rotated like a gun turret.

TWENTY-EIGHT:
SUNDAY LATE AFTERNOON

"THAT'S THE PLACE. COUNTY Road 43 dead-ends on this side of the river but you can cross back over before then, near Miller Creek," said Ingalls. "On the other side, of course, County Road 8 goes all the way upriver and clear to Yampa if you want."

Ingalls and Allison were eight miles east of Meeker on a stretch of road that hugged the south side of the White River. The house was clean and sharp, with green shutters and gleaming white clapboards. The grounds were maintained. Everything was in its place. Allison estimated it sat about thirty yards back from the county road.

Allison had called Ingalls from the Blue Spruce, and Ingalls turned up thirty minutes later in her Prius, which looked as out of place here as a horse in Manhattan.

Ingalls was nervous. She explained how she had to slip away, come up with a ruse. She hoped she wasn't being followed.

"It's like you said," said Allison. "Kind of innocent-looking. But it's a big operation."

"Their property goes all the way to the river," said Ingalls. "And it runs about another quarter-mile upriver."

Cattle dotted the broad pasture. Some were in groups and others were wandering and nibbling.

The property was expansive and branded. The trim colors on the outbuildings matched the main house. The field was dissected by sharp-lined fences. Maintenance mattered. A lush garden near the house sported stalks of corn and towering sunflowers. The abundant ground-level defied the heat. Allison guessed tomatoes and lettuce, at least.

"The guy who owns the place, you know, normal. Tall. Fit. One of those fussy moustaches that come down both sides of the mouth. He takes care of himself," said Ingalls. "The kind of guy you meet and think, well, you can stay on top of your game with a little effort."

They were parked in the shade a hundred feet from the road that led to the house.

"I thought Dante Soto concentrated efforts right in Meeker," said Allison. "You know? In town."

"Anywhere around we got a lead," said Ingalls. "And Dante sent me on this one, thought it was what we called a semi-cold call. We had reason to think they would be welcome."

"What do you mean, reason?"

"By the time we knock on a door," said Ingalls, "we have gathered all available public data. We have a profile. Voting records, speeding tickets, civic involvement, anything we can get our hands on—military career, how long they have owned their property, public debts. We check social media, anything and everything."

Allison had seen Twitter over Duncan Bloom's shoulder one day at his office. She thought her head would explode. Her outfitting business had a website—one static page and her phone number over a picture of one of her wall tents and a perfect campfire with Big Marvine Peak rising high above. Not that she would have any business this fall, the way the fire roared. "Was Dante Soto a thing on social media?" she asked.

"We tracked it," said Ingalls. "Mostly positive. Some bottom-feeding haters out there, but most sharing pictures and photos of their utility bills, things like that. Soto paid a guy to monitor social media. We even poked around in the less obvious chat rooms, the sub-groups."

"And this guy?"

"A steady climb in his utility bills," said Ingalls. "Summer and fall and some in the winter but double what they were. So I knocked on the door."

"No calling ahead?"

"Once in a while," said Ingalls. "Not all the time. You know, I could see there was activity around so I did what Dante told us to never do, and that's wander around to the back."

"And when was this?"

Ingalls closed her eyes, ran the calculations. "Three weeks? Late June. Before Fourth of July, I'm sure."

"And?"

"It was middle of the day. I must have tripped some invisible detection thing because as I came back toward the barn—you know, I could hear all of this banging around and the stuff back there. I was greeted by two guys with their rifles up, pointed at my chest."

Ingalls closed her eyes at the memory. She tried pushing a tear back with a finger. It didn't work. Her composure crumbled.

"I thought I was a goner. I mean, the rifles were one thing but the look on their faces and yelling at me to get the fuck off the property…"

Allison gave her space to finish the story at her own pace. Even if nothing else happened, reliving a moment of near death could be as real and as heart-pounding as the first time around. Allison, in fact, had mastered the ability to hang on to one such moment, though it wasn't a skill she cherished or bragged about.

"That was it," said Ingalls. "When they saw it was me, it probably looked like the most dangerous thing I could do was sell them a magazine subscription or Girl Scout cookies. So I left. But behind there—you can see the barn isn't that far behind the house—the strangest thing. There's a school bus in there. At least, there was. The barn didn't look like there was one place in there for animals. There were at least two or three other guys. I could hear a motor running, and you know those sounds like when they use a drill to take the tires off your car?"

"So you left?"

"I can't even remember much of the ride back to town," said Ingalls.

"And told Dante Soto?"

"We have group meetings, twice a week, to review and de-brief. But I didn't want to wait."

"You found him?"

"Right away."

"And?"

"And he asked me if I was alright, which I was. In a way. I'm sure it showed. He asked me a lot of questions. He had me go over it several times, and then we went down to the sheriff's office to put the incident on file. We both went. Dante was underwhelmed, to say the least, by the way they responded. I didn't care—what would they have done? I had gone on their property without permission. By this time, it was the next morning. I wanted to move on. But Dante was riled up. I don't know why. It was the opposite of his thing, not to

172

make a scene. He didn't want to do anything that would draw atten-tion to us. That would detract from our work. He wanted me to drive out there with him and show him the whole scene, he wanted them to pull the same rifles and repeat the threats to his face. Took him a long time to settle down."

Her temperature and intensity had risen. This was either her long-delayed reaction to his murder—or there was something more between them. Allison wanted to use the word "fucking" when she asked the next question, for shock value, but backed off.

"Was Dante Soto more than your boss?"

TWENTY-NINE:
SUNDAY LATE AFTERNOON

AT THE SPEED SHE was forcing her delivery truck to move, Trudy barely held the road. Two ATVs had come flying up from the ranch house or used auto lot or whatever it was down where the dry fields ended and the dry hills began.

Her view had been a quick glimpse in her fat mirror on the shotgun side. Somehow between the bend in her road and their speed, however, the ATVs stayed in the crosshairs of her mirror for longer than she expected, but not long enough to make out much detail. Two guys. Two machines. Tons of speed. Coming after her.

The drone had tapped her windshield three times as she had jerked the truck around, going off road for a minute in the name of haste. She pushed the truck now to pick up the pace with the idea that the drone was buzzing down the road behind her. The steering wheel shuddered. The cab shook. Maybe the drone could shove a bomb up her tailpipe.

The truck skidded on a turn. The crusty washboard surface clutched her wheels and yanked her away from the turn. She cranked the wheel harder, fighting the ridges, which gave out when the road stopped banking. Trudy thanked her stars she didn't have much of a load.

She counted to twelve barreling down a long straight stretch when the two ATVs and their messy clouds of dust came flying into view behind her. She felt an involuntary gasp. Her heart jumped. She put the truck square in the center of the road, a steep slow climb coming up, still straight, and she mashed the pedal to the floor and tried not to think about Allison or Duncan or whatever the fuck the guys on the ATVs would do if they caught up.

Her own dust made it hard to tell if they had closed more of the gap. Her truck tackled the first section of incline like a champ, then strained and groaned. Halfway to the top and it slowed some more, and she remembered these roller coaster dips and climbs ahead and what she could use right about now was another truck or vehicle of any kind as a witness if she was going to get run off into a fence or the ditch.

The truck flew down the backside of the next hill, an unhealthy grade at this speed. She counted to ten before the ATVs crested the top behind her, dark blurs in the brown cloud. Up another wave and down the next.

A substantial ranch house sat to the right. So hard to tell from this distance at this speed, but there was a chance it was occupied. One human would do. But where was the goddamn turn to get down to it? The fence shot on, no gap, no road. Perhaps they choppered in. Perhaps she was losing it.

Another house off to the left but this one was tucked way back against trees, more than a mile. The hills kept coming. So did the ATVs. If she could make it to the highway, then what?

Coming straight at her—another cloud. It crested a wave and plunged down out of sight. The vehicle had a familiar shape, boxy and tall.

At the top of the next hill, Trudy stabbed the brake. The seat belt dug into her shoulder. She skidded. She turned and pulled to a full stop, engine idling. The driver coming her way would have to be alert—and quick—but it was worth a chance.

Her truck covered the middle chunk of road—an ATV could sneak by on either side, but not the truck driving toward her.

Trudy unfastened the seat belt and popped the door as ATVs flew to the top of one roller coaster bump behind her and stopped halfway down the next grade. She ran to the back of her truck waving with both arms as the UPS truck jammed on the brakes. From the top of her hill, she could see both directions.

The delivery driver couldn't be much older than a college graduate. Dust billowed. Airborne grit stung her cheeks. The truck shuddered to a stop, crunching hard on the dirt, and she covered her eyes in the crook of an elbow.

"What the hell?" The driver had his door pulled open, leaned out. Brown shorts, brown shirt, blond hair, and thick blond eyebrows. Tall. "Whatcha doing?"

The ATVs idled and held their ground. One of the drivers shook his head.

"I know," said Trudy. She could see down the hill, the UPS guy could not. "Sorry. I just. I don't know. I think I might have something going on with my engine, and it was the only way I could think to flag you down. Well, flag someone down. I think it's okay, but I'm not sure. It's making a funny sound." That was partly true. It always made a funny sound.

THIRTY:
SUNDAY LATE AFTERNOON

INGALLS, WHO HAD BEEN alternately staring off into the distance and covering her eyes with her hand, turned and looked at Allison dead on. Her lack of a quick denial said it all.

Ingalls's charms were obvious. Whether your leanings ran to Karl Marx or Jesus, a youthful female and an enticing set of boobs could detract from your zeal and throw you off course. Was the gap in ages between Dante Soto and Andrea Ingalls thirty years? At least? She was likely drawn to his star power and charisma, or whatever they called it, in every culture and sub-culture worldwide. Ingalls didn't know whether to lie. The question had caught her off-guard, which was fine with Allison.

"I need the whole picture," said Allison.

"Who are you?" said Ingalls. "And why do you care? And what the heck are you going to do about it, anyway?"

Explaining that "it" was much more than the two rifles that had been pointed at Ingalls's substantial chest might take some work.

"I'm a friend of Trudy Heath's, remember?"

"Don't tell her about me and Dante—"

Even with Soto gone, reputations were in jeopardy. However, Allison wasn't in the business of promising what she would and wouldn't share with her best friend.

Ingalls was entering full melt-down mode. Tears jetted down her cheeks. Allison held Andrea Ingalls's precious secret in her hands. "I don't care what you were doing with Soto," said Allison. "But I think I know better now why Soto might have charged out here and what frame of mind he was in when he got here."

Ingalls stared straight ahead. Her chin quivered, and she wiped tears with her bare forearm.

"I care that whoever cut and burned Soto—"

"Cut?" Ingalls anguish spiked. She hadn't heard. Why would she have heard?

"He was dead before the fire," said Allison. She wouldn't tell her about the axe. "He was attacked first."

"They knew about his weekly hikes," said Ingalls. "His routine."

"And who knew about it?" said Allison.

"Everyone," said Ingalls. "He wanted us to spend time outside the city, up in nature. It was all part of restoring that balance, you know?"

Taking up with twenty-somethings? Not so smart. Advocating that people put down their mobile devices and spend more time under the sun and stars? Sure. Fine. Allison agreed with Soto on a few basics.

"And isn't the sheriff going to find out who did it?" said Ingalls.

"He'll try," said Allison. "And they will start with Dante's whereabouts for the week before he was killed and, if that doesn't get anywhere, the week before that. They will know every movement, and they will end up right here at this ranch, thanks in part to the report you filed about the incident. I'd say tomorrow you're in the first batch of people they're going to want to talk with."

And if the cops up here were any good, and they had a decent reputation, then Andrea's fling with Soto would soon be well absorbed into the story the police would put together. After that, who knew? It could launch itself from the intimacy of this pristine Prius and ricochet around on Twitter and the web from coast to coast.

Enviro Saint Was Fucking the Troops.

Enviro Hottie Saved Energy for Soto.

"I can leave," said Ingalls. There was a flash of hope in her eyes as she focused on a plan. "Denver tonight, out of state by morning."

"That's not going to do much good," said Allison. "They will find you—and it will look suspicious. As in, very."

Ingalls slumped. Dusk approached. It had taken its time arriving, but now the dim light added a new level of serenity to an already quiet scene. Inside the ranch house, a first-floor light popped on, and a quick, dark shape crossed the window.

"Did Soto tell you what happened when he came back out here?"

Ingalls sighed beneath the weight of the mounting woes. Allison wanted her to stop thinking about confessing to the cops too.

"Yes," she said. "Of course. He did the same thing, walked around to the back where he saw them working. I don't know the blow-by-blow but he managed to talk with them, and I guess they sort of apologized for scaring me halfway to hell, but they made sure Dante got nowhere near the barn. Dante saw something he didn't like, I know that. He wasn't real forthcoming with me."

"But he said something," said Allison.

"Not much," said Ingalls. "He told me he was going to make calls until he figured out who was on the property."

This time, it was the light in Ingalls's eyes that popped on. "You think he could have—"

"Provoked them?" said Allison. "Don't know."

But if Soto had made a bunch of calls, it wouldn't take the cops long to go through his records and start talking to the same people and triangulating the questions back to this same ranch house. Another house light snapped on, this one toward the back, and an outdoor light on the back of the house and an outdoor light on the front of the barn.

"Sophisticated," muttered Ingalls. Allison doubted her shattered driver was prone to sarcasm.

"Someone knows electricity," said Allison.

Four men walked from house to barn in no big hurry, where one door opened as if one of the approaching men had punched the button on a remote control.

"Your barn," said Allison.

"That weird school bus," said Ingalls.

If the cops were any good at all, Allison figured they would be out here by tomorrow and no later than the next day. They had their hands full managing Devo's flock and those same hands were overloaded to begin with, given all the scrambling around the fire. While they knew Devo had been attacked, it wasn't as if there was a marauding killer rampaging in downtown Meeker. Soto's killer had waited for him, carried out his work and hung around long enough to know that the body had been found and that there were enough questions to keep the cops lingering long past the point of accidental death. Whoever attacked Devo could have picked up that information on the greasy gossip wires in town and hustled back to the scene to watch the cops sort things out. That meant, of course, that Devo's attacker might already have figured out her name and triangulated her nosiness too.

At some point, however, the cops would know that Soto had kicked up the dust around this ranch. It was the same sheriff's department that had misled Devo into thinking he could horse trade information for his flock's security, but Allison thought the odds were pretty good that at one point or another they would make their way out here east of town.

"You ever get the name of the property owner?" said Allison.

"Dante got it," said Ingalls. "It's a woman, believe it or not. Her name is Bonnie Brandt. But the thing is, the only person with that name anywhere nearby lives in Rifle."

"And you didn't hear anyone use names when you were out here?"

"Dante asked the same thing." She shook her head.

"Okay," said Allison. "Do us a favor. Go back to town, get a cell, and call Duncan Bloom at the newspaper. Did he leave you his number?"

The sigh was minuscule, but there. "I've got it."

"Give him Bonnie Brandt's name, tell him Allison needs to know everything about why she doesn't live here any longer."

"What do you mean everything?"

"He'll know," said Allison.

"What about me?" said Ingalls. "If the cops come around and start asking questions?"

Now three men were back in the open space between house and barn. One lit a cigarette.

"How obvious were you?" said Allison. "And how long had it been going on?"

"Three months." She might be tracking their *monthiversaries*. "We were careful. His farm, well. There are plenty of options. It wasn't like we were slipping away to Denver for weekends at the Brown Palace, if that's what you mean."

"Did he buy you gifts? Text you messages before or after?"

"No," said Ingalls. "And no."

181

"Nobody ever saw you—or might have seen you together? Coffee shop downtown, driving around together too much, anything like that?"

Ingalls shook her head and sobbed.

"Then relax." Allison wasn't going to tell her to lie. "Or try, at least."

Allison opened the door and stepped out.

"What are you doing?" said Ingalls.

"What matters is what you're doing." Allison leaned down to put her head by the open window. It didn't take much leaning. "You're going back to town to make that call."

"And you?"

"Walk around," said Allison. "Wait for the sun to set. Check out the river. Enjoy the night."

"It's—"

Allison didn't hear the rest. Her boots crunched on the dirt road as she started walking, alone at least for now.

THIRTY-ONE:
SUNDAY NIGHT

THIRTY MILES, DEVO GUESSED, to Trapper's.

And another six to the homestead. He'd be lucky to cover it in two days but it could be done, depending on how careful he wanted to be about staying out of sight. He would move at night, and he would follow the river but avoid the river's edge. He had gone downstream first, in the opposite direction they would have guessed. He hid and waited out the day in a grove of cottonwoods by the river. Now he had to circle back. Down here in the farmland south of town, it was all open country.

Moving at night, he had to keep his wits about him. Cattle. Horses. Their mess. Fences. Roads, ditches, streams, camps full of firefighters.

He'd been stupid to think his trip down would be brief, and he kicked himself for the whole diversion—for getting off course and getting involved. Of course he hoped they would find the axe dude, but there wasn't much more he could do. And they wanted him to sit tight so he could make a positive ID when the time came?

No thank you. No fucking thank you. He needed his people. His people needed him.

It was full dark now. Smoke lingered. He'd spent the day in a stand of cottonwoods by a creek at the edge of town. He was thirsty and hungry, but he didn't trust slow-moving creeks that ran through cattle country. He needed water the most. He might have to stay close to the river, which his system should filter with ease. River, yes. Creeks, no.

What he needed was a horse. Even better would be Allison Coil on a horse to give him a ride. Or a car or a truck headed upriver. If he found the right trailer, even, and if it was at a farm looking like it was getting ready or something, he could hop in, perhaps? Take his chances?

Devo slipped through a barbed wire fence, crossed a dirt road. Huddled up against the fence on the opposite side of the road were about two dozen head of cattle, hefty motherfuckers, and Devo gave them a wide berth before finding a place to slip through the next fence and start making his way across the field and its cow patty land mines. A dog barked and kept at it, no relief. This wasn't his game trail or his forest. This wasn't his Flat Tops. And he had a long way to go.

THIRTY-TWO:
SUNDAY NIGHT

ONE MORE HOUR, BLOOM told himself, and he would drive back up to Sweetwater. He knew he'd be alone. It didn't happen much. But the two cats needed feeding and it was his home now. He'd gone from Denver to Glenwood Springs to an isolated hovel on the edge of a wilderness, and he was never more out of his element. Yet, he felt revived. It wasn't how you drew up a career in journalism school.

One day, when big city newspapers figured out how to run their business, he had the vague notion that he'd be welcomed back as the wayfaring semi-familiar face who had developed Western Slope grit and who could bring it all back to Denver in a more elevated role. He hoped they were following his byline. It was fantasyland, but one could hope. Bloom had to weigh the job with all the other benefits, which included Trudy. The session in Rifle's best motel had lingered, of course, all day. A wonderful kind of pain.

One more hour. Coogan was gone. The offices were empty.

He had spent the day doing his actual job. Fires, fires, fires. Updates on the fires. There was no news. Only "more." Another day of battles. Progress was non-existent. Firefighters were in short supply. Aerial tankers were in short supply. Helicopters were in short supply. A section of downtown Hotchkiss took a direct hit. One old-timer died when he tried to stay and fight. Exhaustion, dehydration. There were eight major blazes on the Western Slope alone—but the Flat Tops fire, for its acreage and apparent audacity, reigned supreme.

Bloom cared more about Soto. He wanted to see if he could locate some of the haters.

What he needed was one hater from the underworld to have poked his head above ground, to have made one stupid or semi-threatening comment. Then, Bloom hoped he could follow the idiot back down to his virtual skunk hole to find the whole den of stink, the kind of people who wake up angry and get more pissed off as the day goes on. He wasn't quite sure where he'd start, but "hate Dante Soto" seemed like a reasonable string to enter in his search engine. He was sorting through a couple thousand hits when his phone rang. It was Andrea Ingalls.

It took her a minute to run down the whole story, and it took Bloom a couple of tries to realize that Ingalls had been with Allison, not Trudy. But he soon had the name of a woman in Rifle.

"She asked you to find out everything," said Ingalls.

"And where did Allison go?"

"She walked off," said Ingalls. "I'm worried about her. She doesn't know. It's like that place has eyes. I keep thinking I should go back out there, maybe she'll need a ride back to town."

Allison will figure it out, thought Bloom. "And Trudy?"

"No idea." Ingalls's call left Bloom feeling disjointed and disconnected. He hated both.

Was the Rifle woman old? Young? Dangerous? He drained Ingalls of every morsel of detail. The school bus in the barn seemed whacky, and it wasn't too hard to imagine it had piqued Dante Soto too.

With a half hour of digging around on the web, he knew that Bonnie Brandt still owned the ranch. An obit in the *Rio Blanco Herald Dispatch* reported her husband's death in a farm accident a decade ago. And a story a month before the obit reported the head injury that put him in a coma—one of those heavy metal gates and a gust of wind. His wife had found him. He was sixty-two. The obit said Dale and Bonnie Brandt had one son, Lenny. Every new name represented its own jillion-star universe of data.

Lenny Brandt was arrested at age eighteen for theft of a portable generator and criminal trespass. He was arrested at age nineteen for driving drunk with expired plates and again at twenty for assault outside a bar in Rangely. A neat trifecta—theft, DUI, and assault.

Bloom noted Lenny Brandt's date of birth. He was a late child, assuming Bonnie Brandt was roughly the same age as her dead husband Dale. Whatever he'd accomplished in high school wasn't enough to bubble up beyond the confines of school news, but Bloom found Lenny Brandt on the roster of graduates published in the newspaper ten years earlier.

A chip of granite here, a chip of sandstone there. Bloom felt like he was using a toothpick to bore one of the tunnels in Glenwood Springs Canyon. He checked Facebook—no match. Usually Facebook was the gateway drug for social media. And that was the case for Lenny Brandt too. No Twitter account, no surprise.

With the birthdate in hand, Bloom poked around in his IRB account for all available public records on Lenny Brandt. Bloom may as well have opened Al Capone's vault on national television. There was nothing. He would need Bonnie Brandt. He'd need an excuse to go to Rifle in the morning, and he would need to get lucky to find her too. He pulled her address off the web and then a map program to get a picture of where she lived relative to downtown Rifle, using street view as if he was standing outside her modest house.

It was 9:00 p.m. He'd be home in an hour, as long as he didn't hit a traffic snag in the canyon. With the Western Slope on fire, tourists were scarce and traffic was light. They were working on the road at night where a boulder had punched a hole in the upper deck of the westbound lanes. Repair work meant frequent delays in both directions. Sometimes a 45-minute commute was two hours. Among Bloom's least favorite things about living in Sweetwater was this daily trek. Gorgeous, yes, but he always felt he was playing Russian Roulette with rock slides.

Bloom drove his Camry up across the river and the interstate, windows down. Did he smell smoke or would that smell be with him for weeks after the fires were gone? He made two left turns and faced decision time. Head home or head west? It wasn't that hard of a decision. He reminded himself to call one of Allison's hands, Jesse Morales, and have him check in on Trudy's cats.

THIRTY-THREE:
SUNDAY NIGHT

TRUDY NEEDED A QUICK shower to settle down. Maybe Allison would appear by the time she had dried off and cleaned up.

She was in Duncan's room at the Blue Spruce, reliving the chase and the long and the fake conversation with the UPS driver, who was polite but clueless when her engine started right up and sounded fine. As far as she knew, he had never seen the ATVs, which opted to retreat.

She showered, standing a minute more than the drought conditions warranted. She expected a message from Allison on her phone when she stepped out. Nothing.

By now, Duncan was likely back at Sweetwater. She could try the landline there, maybe catch him before he turned in.

As she listened to the unanswered rings, she felt the peculiar throb of anxiety in her chest. Her throat tightened and the sheer panic of it all came rushing back as if she was right there in the truck on the roller coaster again, losing a race with two bears on her tail.

She started punching numbers on his cell and mulled the implications. Nothing would change between now and morning. If she talked to him now, Duncan would be able to hear her emotions, and he would want to head back over to Meeker to fix things. If he was in Glenwood Springs, he would be an hour away, except for any hassle getting through on the highway, and she didn't want to tempt him to change his plans. She also didn't want him to worry.

The Italian restaurant next door to the Blue Spruce was wrapping up service. Trudy said she would eat anything handy, cold or warm. She downed a cold beer while she waited for the vegetarian lasagna. She sipped a glass of Cabernet while she ate the perfectly seasoned pasta and sauce, thick with mushrooms and carrots. She tipped heavily and walked back, realizing that the best thing to do was to stay put and wait for Allison's return. Maybe she would watch the news and updates on all the fires.

She had parked her truck with the regular cars in front of the Blue Spruce. Nobody seemed to mind. The quick-mix beer and wine gave her a buzz, stirred with fatigue. Her thoughts turned to sleep—one big flop and crash on the bed—but there was something odd about her truck. It sat low.

There was something wrong about the Down to Earth stencil on the side panel. She was used to seeing more of it, even over the top of the giant SUV parked next to her truck.

She walked to the middle of the parking lot, giving her truck a wide berth. Her down-deep nerves fired one collective message— *caution.*

From a distance, it was easy to spot the four rear tires—all flat. She squatted to see if anyone was poking around the truck, but no.

She stood by the front tires and squatted again to inspect the slash at two o'clock on the rubber wheel. The gouge was an inch wide and ragged.

She stood to look around. A throttled-down semi blocked her view for a second followed by another going the opposite way. When they had cleared, a pickup's headlights popped on across the highway, and it pulled a wide, slow U-Turn, blasting her with full high-beams.

The pickup gave a cheery two-toot honk and puttered off into the night.

THIRTY-FOUR:
SUNDAY NIGHT

TWICE ALLISON COIL WALKED from road to river, crossing the fields and ducking under or climbing over fences, keeping an eye out and staying as far from the house and outbuildings as possible. A breeze from the north blew the persistent haze and smoke away, and she guessed the fire, somewhere, enjoyed the nighttime flow of fresh air. It was good to see the stars. The sweep of night sky. Old friends greeted her. Sagittarius, Lyra, and now, the North Star. But it was no longer the North Star in Allison's mind. Per the Ute Indian description it was the Star That Doesn't Walk Around. She liked that better.

The breeze cooled her down. Hunger and thirst each had taken their turns knocking on her door, and each tried to claim they had legitimate reasons to make a fuss. The White River—the White Trickle—was right there, of course. On her second slow sojourn across the field in front of the house, she put her boots in the river and splashed water on her face but didn't drink, given the ranch country and the general lack of agitation in the riffles. On the first pass past the ranch house, she tried to keep a somewhat ordinary pace. It was darker when she returned from the river for the second time. She stopped to watch for movement in the house. The lower floor was lit. She was rewarded with the occasional blur or shadow. On the third trip, she waited even longer and found a comfortable spot to sit for fifteen minutes. She heard some faint country music and men talking quietly outside. She wanted to wriggle across the field like a rattlesnake and crawl beside the house to listen. She wanted to find a way inside the barn, and she even considered a long loop around to the east, perhaps along the riverbank, to approach from upriver. Based on Ingalls's story, they had some sort of security tripwire on the front of the house and maybe the back. The approach from open country might be less guarded. The only issues about a wide loop around were the hour it might take to pick her way upriver. She might be able to get closer without triggering an alarm, but that didn't mean she'd be closer to learning anything.

On her fourth trip past the house, the barn exploded in light. The front doors were opened in too-perfect synchronicity, as if motorized. She counted four men silhouetted against the maw of light.

The bus sat back ten feet from the opening, nose pointed out. If a sporting goods dealer happened along, Allison would have paid the going rate times five for a good pair of binoculars. The men milled around. One of them propped the hood and climbed on the bumper of the bus. He jackknifed his body and his head vanished down in the engine's viscera.

The whole scene looked boiled clean, un barn-like. Her nose said ranch country. Her eyes read industry.

Her phone squealed like a scared pig. A jolt of panic raced through her like she'd grabbed an electric fence.

Shit.

She slipped it out of her pocket and punched it to vibrate before the second squeal finished.

Colin.

Really? Now?

Her heart slammed her ribcage. She stretched out flat, half expecting a searchlight or one of the men to come find the wounded quail that chirped like a goddamn cell phone.

Her phone vibrated.

Green techno letters: *Missed Call & Voice Mail.*

She could text, maybe. She'd need to write a book to describe what she was doing, where she was, and to find out what he was doing and where he was.

11:13 p.m. At least he was still awake and still cared.

No snarling Dobermans on her trail, Allison sat up. The bus headlights snapped on, shooting light pointblank and, had anyone been looking, she would have been nailed. Dead to rights. Snooping cowgirl in the dirt.

She scampered low toward the river. If the bus was coming out, it would turn toward the road, and there would be nowhere to hide.

The motor purred. The brakes snapped and hissed. Two of the men walked backwards in front of the bus like they worked as jumbo jet ushers on the tarmac at Denver International Airport. All they needed were those neon marshalling wands and earplugs. Salt water sloshed at the back of her throat. Imaginary flying ships had the same impact as real ones—they plunked her back to the cold soaking in Long Island Sound when bodies and jet parts were her swimming companions. The illusion made her shudder, and the memory jerked through her body, which was no less immune to flashbacks than her brain.

The sensation flashed and was gone. Perhaps the ugly daydream was induced by her growling stomach. She found a swirl of dirt high enough to provide cover and spread herself down low and prone. If she had a rifle, the rise of soil would have provided a perfect rest for the stock.

The bus crept forward, its two tarmac pilots keeping their distance out front. If the bus was crammed to the ceiling with fresh eggs, its pace would have made sense. One co-pilot, who had been standing in the mini-stairwell, hopped off.

Three on the ground, one in the bus. The bus pulled out to the main road and stopped, its whole body on a steep angle, nose up high.

The bus was painted white or cream, not yellow. She couldn't read the words on the side but there were five words, she knew that much and it sure looked like SUMMER CAMP were the last two.

The bus idled. A pickup pulled around, put its nose up behind the bus and flashed its high beams. The school bus squealed, and the engine whined. The bus pulled out on the road, toward Meeker, and the pickup trailed close behind.

Allison hoped there were three men in the pickup. In the dark, headlights were bearing down on her hiding spot. She had no way to know.

THIRTY-FIVE:
SUNDAY NIGHT

THERE IS A SCARY thing about not having an orthodoxy.

First, you think, *am I right?*

Second, you think, *about what?*

We all know, Allison realized, that all this will end. An asteroid. The rising seas. The ozone. A flash in the sky. Fast or slow, *bye-bye.* That could happen in the next 600 or 1,000 years, a mere blink in time. Or it could happen by the time she stood up in the darkness and brushed the dirt off her jeans.

In the grand scheme of things, a minor course correction in the variety and types of life forms on an insignificant planet in a less-than-average galaxy meant nothing.

Nice try, Earth.

Hope someone else does it better. Hope someone gets it. Hope someone else gives a shit, you know, next time around. Having survived her own random asteroid, she had found a spot in the wilderness where day-to-day life didn't remind her of all the random crap that could go wrong, like drunks speeding through red lights and killing innocents or packed subway trains sliding off their tracks.

The wilderness, ironically, offered order. And maybe that was another problem of having no orthodoxy—she couldn't explain or apologize for how she felt when crap from the city tried to creep onto her stomping grounds.

It pissed her off. And she had learned what to do with the piss. If the school bus was connected to Dante Soto's demise and the giant fire torching the Flat Tops, she had all the reason she needed.

Two ranch house windows glowed. The light from the barn was harsh.

Weariness was eaten alive by curiosity. Three men in the pickup? Two? One?

It would have been nice to know.

Her body's request for nourishment was scolded like a whiny bitch. One more hour and she was headed back, perhaps picking her way along the river to sleep with the water gurgling in her ear and the stars as her blanket.

Allison studied the house for any sign of movement but the place had no pulse.

Three men in the pickup, maybe. And one on the bus. How long did she have?

She stepped into the broad apron of dirt where the barn light pooled and adopted an I-belong-here air. She kept her gait firm. She didn't linger in the high-visibility zone.

One of the doors was so open it felt like an invitation. Wasn't she obligated? Wasn't it customary for weary travelers to avail themselves of whatever shelter they encountered? Allison found her inner Southern Belle, as far across the personality matrix from the particular spot she had claimed, and hoped it would assist in managing any surprises. Innocence, charm, and raging femininity might make an effective cloak should the occasion arise.

The barn was empty, unless tired workers were sleeping somewhere she couldn't spot. Barns had a way of broadcasting the slightest movements, down to rodent level. This one sounded inert.

The insides had been gutted, shrinking Allison even more than most closed-in spaces. The barn was more auto repair shop than home to animals and feed. It took Allison a moment to take in the space—tools and tires and more tools lined both sides of the space where the bus had been parked. Sheet metal, paint, a sprayer on the end of a long rubber hose, a standing propane canister, wrenches. It was a motor head's dream.

Cigarette butts, beer bottles, rags, a pizza box, a giant orange cooler with a Gatorade logo. Where were the calendars with the topless girls? A circle of five metal folding chairs, a matching industrial shade of brown, stood behind where the bus would have been parked. The circle was neat, close enough for its users to hold hands or knock knees. Team meetings? An old leather Bible sat square in the middle of one chair, two black strands of fabric dangling from its pages. Built-in bookmarks. Given that the cover of the King James edition of the Bible was face up, Allison figured the bookmarks marked the tail end of the New Testament. She knew that much. Her parents let Sunday school flag as soon as they felt the basic idea of morals and "do unto others" was ingrained in her soul, but Allison had learned enough to figure out that the Book of Revelations was the New Testament's paranormal acid trip finish. At some point, as a pre-teen, she had learned about Revelation's Lake of Fire references to after-death destruction of the truly wicked, and she remembered being horrified and sleepless for weeks. Beyond death? Beyond "normal" hell was a place with something even worse? As an adult now, she knew better. True evil needed its own chamber beyond where the ordinary sinners paid their eternal dues.

Missing more than anything from this chamber was the universal fragrance that accompanied any well-*animaled* barn—a certain common-denominator pungency that Allison happened to believe was intoxicating. Others might consider the horse-horseshit-hay combo like nature's version of a city subway station. Allison always took the scent to mean only one thing—horses were nearby. There was no such promise here.

Altering the intended use of a good barn should be considered a major zoning infraction in Allison's book, but now it only added to her suspicions along with whatever happened during Dante Soto's last encounter and the weird midnight run of a summer camp school bus.

Allison set her internal clock for three minutes and started a quick circuit, drawn in part by an olive-green tarp draped over a vehicle-shaped form at the opposite end of the barn. The layers of scattered tools and auto repair shop flotsam thinned toward the rear of the barn. She grew more wary with each step that it was a long sprint back to the front. If she was lucky, the rear of the barn might have matching doors in the back or a human-size portal should the need arise to slip away.

The tarp was thick and had seen plenty of use. Even in all this dry heat, it gave off a musty scent like the interior of a stale, old tent. The shape and size indicated truck, but a license plate might come in handy. She half-burrowed under the front edge of the heavy, crusty material to give the front bumper a look, but she couldn't see a thing. The barn was lit by a series of incandescent bulbs jammed against the walls, six to a side, and the resulting illumination was okay for big-picture information but not enough to follow her under the tarp, no matter how hard she tried to keep the front edge aloft. She rolled it all back, needing more effort than she had imagined would be necessary, and burned the numbers from the plate into her brain. 892-XGH. Colorado. The front grill of the truck growled in a teeth-baring grimace, reminding her that as a child in Iowa she used to run from the front yard and hide in the garage at the first sign of a semi or any oversized truck. Their scale and power put a jolt in her system she couldn't explain, only outgrow. Perhaps she had malformed DNA that resisted all things urban, even from the get-go.

She dropped the front edge of the tarp and scurried to the back. The truck sloped in the familiar shape of a water truck or an oil truck and lifting the back corner of the tarp revealed a set of two tires on each side. The rubber was fresh. The treads were deep. She got a whiff of something like smelling salts.

Time to go.

Allison listened for a moment, tried to pick up any telltale rumble or voice. The giant double doors behind her were locked the old-fashioned way, with a pair of two-by-sixes shoved through brackets on each side. She could wrestle them out, no doubt, but she would leave behind a sure sign of her intrusion because she would have no way to close or lock them once she was out.

Steeling herself with the same "I belong here" vibe, Allison started walking, fully aware that hiding places were non-existent, and at any moment a flash of light could race across the front of the barn and the returning bus could corner her like a scared rabbit.

She reached the mini-church and then scampered toward the open door, staying as long as possible outside the view of anyone who might be out there in the dark, staring back. She stopped. She took in three slow breaths, listened again. She took one more scan of the interior, her eyes drawn by a whisper-level whir.

Stuck to the underside of a high rafter, a white round button the size of teacup. A slot in the rounded shell made a mini-track for a white tube that pointed at her like a .44. She tried not to stare but traced the wires that ran along the rafters and down the front of the inside wall.

Fuck.

Allison stepped out into the night.

"Help you?"

The shotgun was the most obvious thing she saw, the butt of it held against a shoulder with the barrel pointed down. The tip of the barrel traced wobbly circles in the air from her belt buckle to her boots.

"I'm sorry," said Allison. "My car blew a tire a couple miles out. I was on the way down from Trapper's Lake. Thought I could walk to Meeker, and then I saw this barn with the lights on and thought I might find somebody."

She pegged the holder of the shotgun at twelve.

He had a boyish shock of blond hair. The arms poking from the dark T-shirt were stick-like, feeble. His jeans hung loosely, and his button fly was wide open. Bare toes gripped the dirt where he stood.

"Sorry if I woke you." She glanced toward the house to see if golden boy had any brothers or sisters or mothers or fathers or aunts or uncles who had also been rousted by her triggering the alarm.

Allison stepped back. Should the pre-teen be unaware of the sensitivity of the trigger that his finger was stroking, she prayed only for a clean hit.

"Why don't you take a seat until my father gets back?" he said.

"No need," said Allison. "I'm on my way. I do need to get to Meeker. It was a long shot to head down this way, didn't pan out. Unless you know someone who could give me a ride."

From all appearances and his crisp speech, golden boy seemed like a polite young man. Educated—or getting there.

"What's your name?"

"Wendy." Allison hoped the telltale pause hadn't been noticeable. Surely he'd cut her some slack for prompt answers, given the shotgun.

"Where are you from?"

"Look, I'm going to go." She backpedaled two steps. The shotgun tracked her belly button. "Didn't mean any harm."

"Wendy what?" he said. Agitation coated the question.

"Didn't mean any harm," she said. "Left everything the way it was."

The barrel wobbled. He wasn't all that strong—yet—but he might be under orders.

She gave him her back. She walked at a non-guilty pace. The night was far too quiet.

No footsteps followed.

Where the hell had she come up with "Wendy"? She feared a deep sonar of her memories would ping off something related to the insipid Peter Pan bullshit, and she decided to look no further. Her heart would no doubt find its regular groove in about a week. She recited the water truck's license plate to herself to see if that scrap had survived the showdown.

She made it to the road, her back and chest free of holes. Six miles back to Meeker. The road would take her there. She glanced up at the black sky and the Star That Doesn't Walk Around.

THIRTY-SIX:
MONDAY MORNING

DEVO COULD LIVE IN a permanent dawn. The crack of light—the *promise*.

Cutting through the burned-out forest on the banks of the White River, the broad plain near Meeker gave way to a narrow canyon. Devo crossed the river where it was shallow. Here at dawn, Devo realized he missed his birds—no robins, swallows, warblers, and chickadees to greet the day. Hiking through a forest scrubbed clean of its undergrowth made for easy travelling, but the lack of birds and critters was eerie.

Now it was dawn, and he would stay low. He knew they were looking. He'd walked all night, and he needed food, water, and a place to hide while the sun was up.

He plunged his head in the water, sucked in cool water until he felt like he would burst. He foraged for berries and spotted a batch of sunflowers huddled up next to a house. He circled downwind of five deer grazing in an open field and risked a half-minute in open country. He yanked one stalk from the earth, a seven-footer. Among the hundred or so available, it would never be missed. He munched on the seeds by the river bank, chewed the blossoms and the leaves, and stuffed a pocket with hunks of the plant for his next meal or a snack, if he didn't find something better.

In this spot in the valley, roads followed both sides of the river but the one on the south bank rose higher to skirt a sprawling farm complex with a half-dozen matching out-buildings prettied up in a green-and-white theme. He had never seen a ranch spread that screamed its brand with so much authority—all the matching paint jobs. The spread might have been airlifted from horse country in Kentucky or Virginia. White wood fences chopped the undernourished riverside fields into chunks of grazing pasture. Dozens of cattle lingered in the morning calm and, further upstream, horses dotted a more open field. The rancher must have had quite the show when the fire roared through. No doubt now any scenic value he could tack on to the property's price had dropped to zilch because the view of a forested hillside had been reduced to thousands of dead-soldier trees and scorched earth.

If someone offered him a horse or a helicopter right about now, Devo thought, he might take it. It had been a mistake to stray from his routines. He'd screwed up, wasted time.

If he was careful, maybe he could cover some ground in the daylight hours too. Maybe.

The sun would come splashing down the valley soon. Devo weighed the notion of stealing a horse, but theft was right up there with murder in terms of putting law enforcement on your tail and, besides, he couldn't imagine figuring out the rigging for the saddle or staying out of sight once he climbed aboard. Instead, Devo found a bushy spot where he could lay low like a dusty rat on the dusty riverbank.

Maybe if he had started to come up with a plan an hour earlier, he might have had something. But now, in fact, three men walked between the main ranch house and the barn.

Voices floated across the dry fields, flashes of sound—no words. One of the three guys talked on his phone. He was taller, had long, unkempt hair and looked kind of lost. He wore a flannel shirt with cut-off sleeves. The middle guy wore a dark T-shirt and darker blue jeans. He carried a rifle propped on his shoulder, and he wore a green fisherman's hat but the brim lacked flies. He looked ready for a trout hot spot, not a ranch. He was a good eight inches shorter than the first. The third guy toted a container for coffee or water, one of those oversized and insulated deals with a handle. He was in-between the height of the other two. He wore a white T-shirt that let the world admire his beefy biceps. He had curly hair and a prominent Fu Man-chu. If Devo had to guess, he would say they were all in the same age range, somewhere in their mid-thirties.

They were agitated about something. Pointing. Pointing back. A word or two jabbed the air with more volume, but Devo couldn't pick it up.

The men turned around like they had been choreographed. Devo followed their gaze. The nose of a large vehicle peeked around the corner where the dirt road met the river road. Shiny metal on the front grill flashed in the first streak of direct sun and the vehicle came into full view.

A school bus.

For a minute, Devo imagined a nightmare scenario—dozens of screaming children being taken for a fucking day at the farm and following instructions to explore and poke around and bring their picnics to the riverbank and all that kind of crap. It wasn't the case. The bus was empty, except for the driver. A person couldn't drive slower if they were in a parade.

At the barn, two of the men pulled the doors open and slipped inside. Vernon Wayne Howell Summer Camp. He hadn't been that far off. The bus performed a slow three-point turn and was swallowed whole by the gaping square mouth of the garage, butt end first. The doors closed by invisible force.

A moment later, the driver emerged from a side door. Ten steps clear of the barn and walking straight toward Devo's perch on the riverbank, the man leaned back, extended his arms like a mime pretending to carry a massive boulder or waiting to catch a falling baby.

And he yelled.

"Fuck!"

He kept coming, straight at Devo, and then stopped. He lit a cigarette. The first two inhales were cheek-suckers. He walked in a mini circle so tight it could have been a ritual dance around a cornstalk. With a cigarette jammed in his teeth, he plucked a rock the size of a golf ball from the field and hurled it toward the river with a Herculean groan.

At the peak of its arc, the missile flashed in the direct sun before darkening again. It grew larger and for a moment Devo tensed as it fell with a noisy squish at the river's edge.

"Motherfuck!" He grabbed his shoulder like he'd done some damage with the hurl. He was pot-bellied and thin-shouldered. His face was gaunt and his head was small.

"Simmer down, asshole."

Devo could hear them now, half again as close. The acoustics were perfect, like a cave that carried voices out of hidden chambers.

"Fuck off." The cigarette smoker knew they were coming.

Devo's guts soured. The bus. The garage. The prize horses. The house. The idyllic bend in the river, a trophy spot. It all made him queasy, and now, fighting men.

The kind of crap he didn't miss.

"Fucking cops." He had the cigarette in his mouth, held both hands up like he was feeling the spirit at a revival.

"Right in Rifle?"

The guy with the fisherman's hat, the shortest, wore a dark T-shirt with an American flag across the front and the words *When You Come For My Guns, Better Bring Yours.*

"Between downtown and—"

The cigarette smoker turned his back, swallowed his words.

"What'd the cops do?" Tall guy.

"Took forever. Paperwork, shit."

"Why did he even fucking pull you over?"

"I don't fucking know, okay?" He took a quick drag on his smoke. "Bored, I guess. I don't know."

"He needed a goddamn reason." This was the fisherman's hat guy. He had to reach up to push one of the smokers' shoulders and the smoker stumbled back. He caught himself before he spilled over. "You're a fuck up."

Beefy guy watched.

On the road, a line of trucks tugged giant yellow bulldozers upriver. Throaty rumbles buried their words.

"I got the ticket, I had to sit there playing it cool. What was I going to do, outrun them in that thing?"

"The hell." Beefy bicep guy decided to engage. "Did you make it all the way?"

"Hell yeah," said the driver. "A little behind schedule, and then I got back to Rifle."

The tall, dumb-looking guy with long hair landed the first punch, straight to the cheek. The cigarette went flying. Devo felt the crack of the fist on bone in his guts.

The driver stumbled and whirled. "The fuck!" The two words came out half-pleading, soaked in desperation.

"First you fuck up with the fire, and Taylor said that wasn't his idea. It was your idea of a bonus something or other? It was fucking stupid. And now you can't drive through a town at night without getting pulled over."

The driver backed away. The blows kept coming, aimed high. Devo winced as each one landed. The driver stumbled down to the river's edge. The bank was a good eight feet above the water, a straight shot down, and Devo wondered if the driver had any sense of where he was or that he needed to watch his step.

He didn't.

One final blow came from Fu Manchu. The half-cry, half-groan at the beginning of the fall ended like flipping a switch at the bottom. The mucky thud came with a short sharp snap, like breaking a stick over the knee.

The driver's legs splayed out in the mud. His head was smashed face down in the gurgling water.

THIRTY-SEVEN:
MONDAY MORNING

HER VOICE SOUNDED STURDY. At seventy-two, you never know.

"Yes, I'm here," said Bonnie Brandt. "Don't have a million places to go, you know. All the heat—stay cooler if you don't move so much. I've got a cribbage game tomorrow if you want to meet the whole crew."

"I'm in Rifle today," said Bloom. He was, in fact, staring at the front of her modest house near the dead-end Coal Mine Road on the north side of the city.

"You think seventy-two is unusual?" She was nobody's special case.

"It's about the research out there about staying active and keeping your mind, you know, working," said Bloom. "By doing something."

The ruse occurred to him during his brief night at the Rodeway, previously the Winchester Motel. He had traded $59 to avoid sleeping on his backseat, which he knew from experience was painful. He'd traded $6.49 for a Wendy's cheeseburger and fries, and he may as well have tried to slurp wet concrete. After so long with Trudy's cooking, the gut bomb punished his innards.

"Use it or lose it. Goes for everything, tee hee." She said "tee" and "hee" in the same low octave as all the others. Bloom liked her already. "What time do you want to come over?"

Now, thought Bloom. Or thirty seconds from now. "Half hour? I know it's short notice. I happened to be in Rifle—"

"That works," said Brandt. "I want to get to the grocery store before too long. Before it's hotter than blazes. Though maybe this is hotter than blazes."

———

"How did you find me, anyway?"

"Story in the paper, the Rifle paper from a couple years back," said Bloom.

"When our cribbage club went to Reno," said Brandt. She might tip the scales at 105. Five feet of feisty with cool blue eyes, a firm handshake, and a spotless house. "Luckiest cards ever. Came home with a trophy barely fit in the overhead. We got some scowls for sure."

The house carried a faint whiff of cigarettes, but no ashtrays. The whites of Bonnie's eyes suggested she was a health nut, but she had the frank demeanor and low rasp that often came with smokers and ex-smokers.

The cribbage conversation didn't last long. How much was there to know? Bloom made a big deal of "not trying to pry" when he asked if she felt like her mind was as sharp, say, as it felt at forty or twenty, and if she had any reason to think that remaining active with a game that required mental activity had something to do with her abilities and faculties today. Bonnie Brandt replied in considerable detail, starting with her "average" career as a high school student and straight into married life and ranch life. She had kept the books on the ranch, she said, and realized when she left that a part of her brain remained "hungry" for things to figure out.

"I tracked every penny every day for thirty-five years and then nothing, so it was like having a muscle but nothing to kick, you know?" She sipped iced coffee, pushed out a smile.

"The ranch was ... ?"

"Outside Meeker," she said. "Upriver about six miles."

"And what happened?"

"Is this part of the story?"

Bloom had uncovered an old, dry well on the back forty, and he dared peer down. Bloom parked his pen next to his glass of iced lemonade and gave her a moment. "Up to you," he said. He had noticed the cluster of photos in the living room of her late husband but had stayed on point until now. The spare, functional kitchen was devoid of sentiment. The window over the sink offered an imposing view of the towering Roan Plateau. How could you live here and not wonder where the boulders would slide and crash when the rains came back?

"Accidents happen," said Bonnie Brandt. "Every day. I'm sure Dale never knew. Knocked out and gone, internal bleeding. You think of the odds or why he didn't hear the gate swinging back or you wonder what was in his mind or on his mind, those last thoughts. But shit happens, pardon my French. We saw enough calves die in the spring, and we saw enough nature in thirty-nine years to know that human beings don't have any special rights when it comes to random."

Bonnie Brandt covered her mouth with her hand and closed her eyes. Her hand tightened into a small fist.

"Of course it's hard to run a ranch all by yourself, but we had hired help for years and I wanted to keep on like that." She had regained her footing. "Not sure why I'm telling you all this."

"Just curious how you got to Rifle," said Bloom.

"How much time do you have?"

Dale and Bonnie Brandt had one son. He was, to say the least, a "hot and cold" sort of kid. What you'd call "mercurial." He had charisma, but could go into long funks when no one could even talk to him. He could be courteous and compassionate, go out of his way for others. But somewhere along the way in high school, Lenny Brandt started falling off with his grades. His anger flashed. He felt excluded, left out, unliked. "He complained about being overlooked." One girlfriend dropped him, then another. He could sail through his classes if he wanted, but didn't try. He smoked pot, and he sold pot, before it was legal. He dabbled in auto mechanics. A self-taught natural. During one of his better times when she thought he might be reconciling on the family front, he repaired a balky tractor that saved them hundreds of dollars in repair. He stripped it down and put it all back together. He learned sheet metal, welding, electronics. He got into hunting—weeks-long trips with two buddies for deer and elk back in the Flat Tops. When he wanted something he would work for five or six months and bear down. He'd stock his freezer each fall with elk, duck, and pronghorn. He acquired a sizable stash of rifles and handguns. He started camping in the deserts of Utah—month-long trips to build up his survival skills and tolerance for heat.

"Funniest thing," said Bonnie. "He started reading. I thought he had turned a corner—Edward Abbey, John Muir, and John Wesley Powell too. Anything to do with Utah and the desert. And then he moved home right after Dale died, and of course I took him in at first. But then these two friends were there all the time. At first they seemed like they wanted to make a go of the ranch, pick the place up. Fine with me. Hired help is one thing but Lenny seemed like he wanted to run the place. Own it. Care about it."

Bloom had grown used to her protracted pauses, knew to let them do their work so she could keep her composure.

"The parties, the beer, the music," said Brandt. "A little at first and then more and more. He had me sign papers and, well, I was being more trusting but pretty soon it didn't matter who owned what. It was obvious I wasn't welcome any longer. The next thing I knew I was looking for a place and wound up here. Housing was a bargain down here when the last boom faded."

They were a long way from cribbage and staying young, but Bloom didn't want to make it too obvious. This was the thread he needed. The names of the son's friends, for instance, and their interests and leanings. Had she ever heard them talk about Dante Soto? And when was the last time she had heard anything from them at all?

"That sounds, I don't know, wrong," said Bloom. "Your own property."

"Never would have happened if Dale hadn't had his accident." Despite the definition of the word itself, she made it sound like "having his accident" had been a choice.

A wave of nerves ruffled his system. Bloom had an urge to come clean, jump to the chase. She might help him more if he dropped the ruse.

Like the old handshake-buzzer prank, his phone zapped the inside of his jeans pocket. He plucked it out after half-standing up.

Trudy.

He hated to not answer, but she would have to wait.

"So you don't see him much?" He decided to keep milking the existing pretense.

"Much?" said Brandt. "At all. I don't exist. Cribbage, eat, sleep, read, take walks when the smoke isn't blowing this direction. I don't sit around waiting for the phone to ring. I go weeks without thinking about him. Try not to obsess. Would I rather be on my own ranch, view down the valley like a million bucks? Hell yes. But I'm fine. Got my cribbage friends and always looking for those elusive 29-point hands."

"Guess I should call my mom this weekend," said Bloom. "And my father."

"You didn't throw yours off the farm, did you?"

"A house in the suburbs," said Bloom. "They're still there. Your son—is he still ranching?"

"I think he leases the land. When it's not so dry, that's premium grazing ground—right along the river."

She blinked twice and stared out with the thousand-mile stare. "Talking about Lenny brings me down, you know?"

"Doesn't seem right," said Bloom. He made a show of putting away his notebook, though he hadn't scratched anything down for half an hour. He snapped his pen closed, too, and tucked it in his pants pocket. He leaned back, sipped lemonade, and hoped he had created enough space for her to fill it up.

She did.

"That boy is best on his own, anyway," said Brandt. "The city riles him up. And by city, I mean Meeker, if you can call that a city. Any place there are rules gets him going, I mean riled up about things like parking tickets. Government's role, all of that, clear up to issues with the United Nations for crying out loud."

"There's a lot of those folks around. Sovereigns. People who believe the government is evil." Bloom stood up, continuing the appearance, projecting only mild interest. Later, when she stopped to think about the conversation, she might realize how much they had talked about Lenny compared to cribbage. "Funny how these people seem to find each other too. They are individualists, but they find strength in numbers."

"He doesn't have numbers, but he has two. You reporters have your sources. Well, I've got my spies up there, and I'm not bad at email for my generation, if you know what I mean." She remained seated. "Lenny and his buddies doing God knows what."

If she was in a memory stupor, she might answer questions as if she was under hypnosis. But with Meeker's size and the ranch location, the name Lenny Brandt would triangulate a whole raft of data, including names of friends and accomplices.

"No girlfriends?"

Bloom kept on with the not-pressing-here approach.

"They come and go. Lenny's most fixated on an older woman. Erica Cross. She's at least forty. Two kids, single mom. Don't know if she is thinking she robbed the cradle or wanted an older son, but she's got ten years on him. Yes, we had Lenny late. Total surprise."

Bloom had plenty. Erica Cross was another point on the compass. No doubt the rats in the middle would all scurry around in the light in between.

Bloom made a show of extending an arm for a handshake, wished her luck on the career in cribbage. He found himself eager to call Trudy and check with Coogan before Coogan was on his butt.

"She seems nice enough," said Brandt. "My sources like her. Got left a bunch of money in her divorce. Can't imagine Lenny could do much better, you know, if he cared about moving up in the world. And I can't imagine she approves of the two pieces of trash that Lenny considers friends."

"Some things you can't figure," said Bloom.

"Wished we had a nice boy like you," said Brandt. "Someone who cared about others—and mothers. Something happened to that boy

I'll never know. It's been six years now of nothing but Lenny, Garrett McKee, and Dug. D-u-g, I kid you not, that's how he spells it."

"McKee?" Bloom said it with more intensity than he intended. It was half-blurt. Unconscious.

Brandt didn't seem to care.

"Garrett McKee," she said. "Of the famous McKee's. I heard Earl is in jail for assaulting a sheriff's deputy. About time someone corralled that asshole."

THIRTY-EIGHT:
MONDAY MIDDAY

"Alone," said Trudy. "No Allison—and no idea where she got to. Haven't seen Colin, though I think he's supposed to be over here somewhere. And no you."

Trudy sat in the breakfast nook at the Blue Spruce where she'd been since 4:00 a.m., waking up after four hours of rocky sleep.

"And I'm headed the wrong way," said Bloom. "Allison disappeared, what?"

"I keep walking outside and looking up the road," said Trudy. "I keep picturing her and I know she's walking. Walking and walking."

"I think we kicked the hornet's nest," said Bloom.

In her mind, all night long, she had rehearsed telling the stories to either Allison or Duncan or Colin, whoever was first. She hadn't seen Allison since she hopped out of the truck to go check on Devo's herd as they were being ushered into the county jail. She kept picturing Allison reappearing as she often did back at Sweetwater, at odd times of the night. Now, as yesterday's strange moments kept their claws deep in Trudy's thoughts, and as much as she had practiced staying calm and collected, the emotion of it all swelled up again and the first words came out pinched and weak.

"Hold on," said Duncan when she started to tell him. "Wait a second. I gotta pull over and take notes." He was giving her time.

"There's an exit right here. Beautiful Silt," he said.

"What are you doing in Silt?"

"I'll get to that," said Duncan. A minute later: "I'm ready."

She went in order—the in-town tail, the drone, the chase, the UPS truck, the slashed tires, the pickup blasting her with light. He had her slow down and asked a million questions.

No, she didn't have a license plate for the pickup. It had been too dark. No, she didn't have an address on the funky ranch with drones. But she knew the spot—east about 10 miles on County Road 15 toward McHatton Reservoir. Yes, she had memorized the in-town address. 848 Hill St.

"What about the tires?"

"The hotel helped me," she said. "A gas station tow truck took it away. They are fixing it now."

"Did you file a report?"

"Done," said Trudy.

"Cops following up?"

"I don't think it's a priority," said Trudy. "And the hotel doesn't have any security cameras on the parking lot. I asked. You saw about Devo?"

"It's unbelievable. Why now?"

"Maybe the fire," said Trudy. "They tolerated it for so long, but maybe they didn't want Devo and all his followers in harm's way. I guess the whole fire has turned back around, heading that way."

"Jesus," said Duncan. "Big story right there. I've got to come back up. I mean, if they know where you're staying—"

It had been a long, unsettling night. "I'm okay," said Trudy. "I'll get the tires replaced, find Allison."

"The Hill Street address will give us a name, of course, and I got some stuff from Rifle."

As Duncan talked, she stepped outside the Blue Spruce into the searing sunshine and again looked up and down the road for a familiar small shape. The main drag, Trudy knew, wouldn't be Allison's first choice for a variety of reasons, including visibility and safety, but the overwhelming sensation that Allison was close wouldn't go away. Duncan cut to the chase on his account of Lenny Brandt, a guy named Dug, and Garrett McKee.

"Garrett McKee?"

The Blue Spruce parking lot wobbled and warped as if she was looking in a fun house mirror.

"Trudy? You there?"

"Yeah," she said it. "So Garrett's girlfriend leads us to two guys who have drones watching their property in the boondocks. Now Garrett's name is associated with the guy who might have tangled with Dante Soto."

"You know anything about the brothers?"

"Not much. Allison doesn't talk about Colin's family but maybe that explains why Colin spends so little time in Buford and as much time as possible on our side of the Flat Tops."

"But you didn't see Garrett McKee yesterday?"

"I don't know," said Trudy. Were any of the guys she had glimpsed Colin*esque*? One of the guys in the pickup? On the ATVs? "What the heck did Soto see?"

"Or say? Or do? Or get in an argument about?" said Duncan.

"Should we find Erica Cross?" said Trudy. As soon as she said it, she knew there was no "we." At this moment, at least, only "I."

"Erica or Garrett or this Dug dude," said Bloom. "But you shouldn't knock on any doors alone."

"I can try to find where she lives, at least. A quick check around, something." She thought she sounded confident. "Can you get up here?"

"One reporter can't slip away unnoticed from a two-reporter town," said Bloom.

"Extended family crisis?"

"Wouldn't fit my editor's definition of family. Though thanks for that."

"None of his business," said Trudy.

"The main thing is it's a small operation," said Bloom. "And almost an hour up to Meeker."

Having her own team of workers and layers of employees she didn't even know, she understood the value of loyalty.

"In fact," said Bloom, "I've got to get back on the highway. I'll poke around more with what we get from Bonnie Brandt. If you can, get the address of that property off Google maps or something."

"It wasn't a super official-looking property."

"You said there was a house."

"Beat-up, small, run down. Back in an area you wouldn't think you could raise or grow anything."

"Then it's a property, and there are taxes. Count on it. Unless you're Devo the Sequel, you're paying taxes."

"Showing a bias?"

"Facts," said Bloom. "If there is a structure, the assessor knows."

Bloom urged her to be cautious and said goodbye.

On the curb, Trudy looked east up the road. She felt the need to be out here, not stewing in her antiseptic room staring at a laptop. The smoky haze heightened the heat, kissed her skin. Ash fluttered. The air could be chewed. Somewhere, the Flat Tops continued to get thrashed by fire. Perhaps Allison had hitched a ride and headed out to Colin's family's place. Was there a chance they had found each other and booked a separate room at the Blue Spruce—or somewhere else? Small town, yes, but easy to get separated. Why hadn't Allison called—or texted? She must know others would be worried.

Looking east, Trudy smiled. A passerby might think "crazy woman" if she was spotted at that moment. After all, she was a woman alone and beaming for no obvious reason. Three blocks away, Allison waved. A boxy cattle truck barreled past but Allison paid no attention. A moment later, the same truck passed Trudy, and she caught the eye a forlorn cow. A plume of farm stench trailed the truck.

All the items on Trudy's "to do" list seemed straightforward— find Erica Cross, retrieve her truck from the gas station, get an address for the drone farm. The toughest one was mere minutes in her future—telling Allison Coil about Garrett McKee.

THIRTY-NINE:
MONDAY MIDDAY

"So Mr. Man of Principles, Peace, and Harmony was sleeping with one of his worker bees?"

"Man is the key word," said Allison. "I've never known any of the other factors to matter."

The shower had been a godsend. An hour's sleep—or two—was the fixation. She had to shake it off.

"A perfectly fine wife." Trudy said it as if she was the one betrayed.

"Appearances," said Allison. "And we don't have his side of the story."

Allison reclined on one of the beds. She had borrowed a clean T-shirt and underwear from Trudy. She would force her clothes back on when the time came, but now the post-shower bliss made it impossible to move, except nibble on blueberry muffins snatched from the hotel breakfast buffet. And sip coffee. Allison's hips ached. She had a stinging blister on a toe, but refused to look.

Trudy was studying MapQuest on her laptop. She was down to the least-hot number of clothes too.

"Wonder if this Andrea girl had someone who found out—a jealous boyfriend," said Trudy.

"Possible. Losing your girlfriend to the guru."

"What did she look like?"

"Not a fireball. More librarian, but attractive. Well put together. Younger side, quiet. One of those aggressively healthy types—and don't take that the wrong way."

Trudy smiled. "Never."

"I'd say youth was her biggest asset. She's a mess now, though. Practically look at her, and she might blurt it all out."

"I wonder if Soto's wife had an inkling?"

"Don't the spouses usually have a hunch?" Allison said it before realizing that Trudy was in a good position to answer the question. Of course, from everything Allison knew, a tender affair with a hunting guide was justified, almost a necessity, given the way her ex-husband George treated her. "Don't take that the wrong—"

"It's okay," said Trudy. "I guess George knew, or assumed I'd try. He was gone for days at a time."

Allison flashed on the moment when she had found Ray Stern's frozen body and his grim, snow-packed face. She shuddered.

"Sure," said Trudy. "The smart ones know. Down deep."

"But do jealous boyfriends get that elaborate? Or jealous wives? Talk about a gentle soul." Allison wanted to switch topics. Adultery was boring. She adored commitment and loyalty from boyfriends—and, by the way, where the fuck was Colin?—but the whole notion of ownership, linked with the biblical scolding and shame thing, made Allison think that a future society would relax about the whole notion of couples and love forever.

"The fire, you mean?" said Trudy.

"And way back up in the woods?" said Allison. "You'd have to wait, right? Wait and think it through. I picture jealous boyfriends blasting away in the city—shoot the dude on sight or shoot your girlfriend for stepping out on you. Right in the house, in a moment of rage."

"You're right. Too much deliberation."

"And if Andrea's boyfriend was from Steamboat or anywhere else, he would have had to spend a lot of time getting in position and would have had to learn Dante Soto's routine, all of that."

"Unless Andrea's boyfriend was one of the others in the same crew," said Trudy.

"All I have to do is ask her, and she'll tell me anything."

"Scratch it."

"Not altogether," said Allison. "Back burner."

"There's one more thing."

Trudy Health didn't do inscrutable. She'd been screwing up the courage about something since the parking lot, one hour ago.

"What's that?" Allison sat up, made a move for her clothes, gave Trudy space.

It took a full minute—a long, empty minute—for the name Garrett McKee to connect and for her head to wrap around the implications other than re-scrambling all the possibilities for the whereabouts of Colin.

"There's not two by any chance?"

"Lenny Brandt's mother even referenced Earl and the assault," said Trudy. "If there's two, we're talking about the same one."

Allison felt a flash of upset at Trudy for waiting so long to tell her, but no doubt Trudy wanted to lay out everything they knew before dropping the bomb. Trudy wasn't the problem—of any kind.

Feeling the need to go somewhere, even if it was out to the McKee Ranch and find Char or Daniel or maybe Colin somewhere ignoring his messages, Allison dressed in a hurry. The jeans balked.

"So how old was this kid?" said Trudy. "The one who saw you?"

"Like I said, maybe twelve. Peach fuzz."

"We need a last name for the Dug dude, and we should be able to figure out who the boy belongs to. Can't be too many Dugs with that spelling who hang out with Lenny Brandt."

And Garrett McKee, thought Allison. Maybe Trudy didn't want to rub it in.

Trudy talked. Allison listened. Trudy came at it from every angle they could dream up.

Allison found herself at the window, staring out at the comings and goings of Meeker, still under an invasion of government vehicles. At late morning, the town looked baked and weary. Cracking the window brought a hot draft that cancelled the effects of the shower and regenerated that special Colorado stickiness—dry but draining. As she was prone to do, Allison blamed the city, in this case town, and the added effects of packing together buildings and cars and trucks in a dense configuration that compounded the heat index. Among all the options Trudy wasn't mentioning was the idea of retrieving Sunny Boy at Trappers and heading across the Flat Tops for the cooler elevations, setting a course for Sweetwater, even if it meant circling far around the fire, and leaving the mess to the town cops and the county sheriff.

Were it placed on the table, however, such an option would be swept from the surface with the impatience of a battle commander growing bored and tired of the lame strategies floated by the underlings. The search for the man or men who whacked Dante Soto with an axe and then lit the Flat Tops on fire wasn't being conducted as a mental exercise or some amateur hour display of clue finding. Her need didn't exist only because she doubted the ability of the authorities to follow through or their capacity to see the big picture and now, with a brother of Colin's in the mix, she needed to know soon. The next minute would do.

"Earl McKee," said Allison.

"What are you thinking?" Trudy had dressed and prepped. She stood ready to go.

"Unless he's been released," said Allison. "At least we know where to find him."

"To ask about Garrett?"

"And pals," said Allison. "Dug, etcetera. Bus mechanics for the religiously inclined and others. Looked to me like they only studied Revelations, did I mention that?" Allison knew she had.

"Twice," said Trudy.

"We should see if Duncan can do anything with the plate number off the truck," said Allison.

"He's waiting on me to figure out the address of the drone farm," said Trudy. "I can see the property on the satellite view, but it's not like it's got a street number or anything."

"But we've got the address where Jayne got out, and he picked up a passenger."

Trudy must have known it wasn't a question. "Duncan can make a lot out of a little," she said.

"What the hell do you need a water truck for? On a farm?"

"On a farm by a river," said Trudy.

"And covered up. And barn-mates with a white school bus taken out for late-night joy rides?"

"So first Andrea shows up, and they chase her off."

"Remember—she said they came out ready for her like they knew she was there. Like they had surveillance."

Allison had given them another highlight reel. *Shit.*

"So she gets out of there but then Soto, when he hears what happened, goes out and gets further inside the barn on his own—and sees even more than you do. The bus is there or something."

"And they've got the whole thing to watch—they know what he's seen," said Allison.

"And he might have let it be in any other situation but because he's screwing Andrea on the side, he feels a touch of manly honor to go out there and find out who frightened his poor little chickadee."

"Men and pride," said Allison. "Topic right there for your life's work."

"And still might not fully comprehend." Trudy smiled. With an ex-husband rotting in jail in Canon City, a man who believed the world and all its creatures belong to whoever saw them first, Trudy once had a ringside seat to maximum hubris. The power and certainty were intoxicating until you started seeing that such powerful egos required constant care and feeding, no worse than the attention showered on a newborn of any species.

It was hard to imagine a man who espoused ultimate neutrality sneaking onto someone's property like a burglar or private eye. The complicating factor, of course, was that the owners of said property had scared the bejesus out of the girl who was making him feel like he was twenty-five all over again. So, neutrality took a break.

"Does Soto even know he was being watched?" said Trudy.

"I didn't," said Allison. "At least, not at first. Maybe drone farm dudes and Lenny Brandt use the same security service—same mentality."

"So Dante goes on his merry way," said Trudy. "Until he meets someone up in the woods."

"Or *someones*," said Allison.

"You couldn't see the name of the summer camp?"

"Maybe Nora at the lodge would remember someone heading up that way the same morning," said Allison, picturing the ambush of Soto. "Too dark, couldn't read the name."

"Rebuilding a school bus isn't illegal," said Trudy. "Think of all the hippies who would have been tossed in jail for that. Maybe these guys are preppers—you know, doomsday dudes. The bus is their bug-out vehicle."

Trudy drifted into the bathroom. She emerged with a toothbrush in her mouth. Trudy was in a new phase of testing homemade toothpaste recipes. Allison was the occasional and reluctant guinea pig.

"They aren't waiting for the big one," said Allison. She tugged on her Ropers. She tried to pretend her feet didn't flinch. It was a thought that required as much fantasy as Allison could muster.

"Maybe the water truck is water supply," said Trudy through a mouthful of suds. "Probably the most precious commodity to come by if you have to strike out for the hinterlands."

"Or wastelands." Allison hated herself for always thinking suspiciously about Bible-thumpers but maintaining a prayer circle next to your acetylene torches in the garage was a sure sign that all perspective had been lost. "The whole Revelations thing is where it jumps the rails."

"If they are preppers, they would buy into the doomsday predictions in Revelations." Trudy was back in the bathroom, rinsing. Allison respected Trudy's fastidious self-care. She predicted the next sight—Trudy flossing. Her friend did not disappoint. "What are you smiling about? Doomsdays?"

"Nothing," said Allison. "Habits, mostly. I'm glad you're here, that's all."

"The world is full of people who think they know when it's all going to blow." Trudy stopped flossing. She looked as cool and fresh as Allison felt sticky and drained. "And sometimes when people get tired of waiting, they find a way to make it happen."

Allison gave her teeth a finger brush with a dab of Trudy's concoction—some weird combination of vegetable glycerin, guar gum, and peppermint drops. If there were three options for societal agendas underway—Trudy's genteel effort to make the world a better place, Devo's search for a wormhole back to the nineteenth century, and maybe some religious zealots' effort to bring everything to an apocalyptic close—Allison knew she would choose Trudy's route, weird taste in her mouth and all.

They were lucky to get Nora on the telephone, but she could not remember any unusual hikers the morning of or the day before the fire. There were one thousand other ways to reach the spot where they found Dante Soto's body besides making it obvious around the crossroads on the north side of the Flat Tops. Allison told Nora not to worry. "But call me if you think of anything," said Allison. "Or see anything." It had been a long shot.

They made a list of all the auto repair supply shops and auto repair businesses in Meeker. The online map showed them the shops on the east side of town where they wanted to start. If you had converted a barn to a NASCAR shop for school buses and water trucks, Allison figured, you'd be likely to patronize the establishment closest to home. When you needed to start somewhere, scraps of logic gave your non-existent fingernails the semblance of a grip.

Before heading out, Trudy called Bloom. Between the sweet nothings, she passed along a list of leads. The water truck license plate, anything more about Dug and so on.

"And that source of yours from Steamboat—she was fucking Soto." Trudy gave the active verb no extra emphasis. "Let that sink in."

Trudy listened for a moment. "Allison got it out of her," she said. "And, yes, she's sure. Allison said she spilled it all."

For the sheer hell of it, Allison tried to get a sheriff's deputy on the line. "It's about your missing guy, Devo," she lied. She wanted to find Deputy Steve Mendoza to see if she could chat some information out of him, though she wasn't sure if she could trust anyone in uniform after seeing Devo's tribe rounded up.

In her spare time, the dispatcher taught ice not to melt. "I can take that information," she said.

"I know Devo is headed back to camp, and I can almost guarantee I know the route he would take," she said. "And I'd like to pass it along to whoever is looking."

"I can take that information," replied the dispatcher, like a recording.

"Do you keep a list of stolen or missing vehicles?"

The water truck bugged her. It seemed so out of place. Even Trudy gave her a look.

"Are you reporting something?" she said. "You're welcome to come down to the station and fill out—"

"In the last couple or three months," said Allison.

"We have missing and stolen vehicles all the time. I see you're staying at the Blue Spruce. We can send a deputy to take your report but—"

"That's okay." Allison hung up.

"I can only imagine how sad Devo is going to be when he returns to his camp," said Trudy. "Nice try. Finding Devo would help."

"And Colin."

Allison tried the McKee Ranch. Char answered.

"Can't say," said Char. "All the confusion, you know? With everyone running around and Earl still in jail, everything is out of whack."

"How is Earl?" said Allison.

"I'm so sorry you had to see that," said Char.

"Is he getting out?"

"They found a judge for the bail hearing," said Chair. "They take their sweet time when it's in their best interest. Have to agree with Earl on that."

"No hearing set?"

"We're supposed to hear any minute," said Char. "Where are you?"

"Downtown," said Allison.

"You planning to stay long over here?"

"No," said Allison. True. Could Char be that flustered at this point? Maybe.

"I'll pass the word if I see Colin," Char said goodbye.

"From what I gathered, Earl is still in jail?" said Trudy.

Allison was already thinking about the questions she would have for Earl McKee and didn't respond until they were halfway down the hall.

"Let's hope."

FORTY:
MONDAY AFTERNOON

DEVO IMAGINED HE WOULD run into a regular old-fashioned tele-phone, a hard-wired type of deal. 911 was still 911, wasn't it? He could leave the details and, hell, he could give an accurate description of where to find the dead man.

Devo had pulled the man over and spun him up on the river's edge. He dragged him to a sitting position. The dead man's head flopped around in a way no head should. Blood and mud seeped from his mouth.

Now, in the garage, time squeezed his chest. He figured the dead man's so-called pals wouldn't take long to return and check on him, no matter what he'd done in Rifle. And he had to figure out some way to alert the cops or do fucking *something*.

A fast circuit of the outside of the bus turned up nothing useful. Devo contemplated flagging down a car or truck and asking to borrow their phone or giving them the information while he waited and listened to make sure they got everything right. Would someone know who he was? Would he scare a driver or two? There was enough traffic on the road that it wouldn't take long to find a willing helper, but the road was likely used by its share of government vehicles . . . and cops . . .

Shit.

A fast circuit of the exterior of the bus—tools and tools, no telephone. No first-aid kit. The bus! Devo hopped on—a sudden image from childhood of the first aid kit on a school bus screwed to a visible spot over the driver's head in a simple metal bracket. Devo had always wondered what was in that box and how it was supposed to help 65 kids without seat belts in the event of a crash. How many Band-Aids could it hold?

This bus had no such box.

This bus . . .

Devo took a second to take it in.

This bus was too simple, too gutted. The driver's seat looked like it was stolen from an old sports car. The cover was ripped and worn. The interior front of the bus was so basic that a vintage U.S. Army Jeep looked like Starfleet Command by comparison. The front console was dark. Two small gauges stared back at the driver—speedometer and fuel.

The light inside the garage-barn was indirect and dim, but the view down the aisle to the back made Devo gasp. Two columns of seats ran down the length of the bus, one on each side and up against the window. The middle seats and the aisle seats on each side didn't exist. In fact, there was no aisle. In its place sat a raised floor about a foot higher than the landing at the top of the stairs where Devo now stood.

Back on the floor of the garage-barn, Devo stared at the name on the side of the bus, this time to memorize it. Vernon Wayne Howell Summer Camp. The name sounded like a place where fun went to die.

FORTY-ONE:
MONDAY AFTERNOON

THE RIO BLANCO COUNTY Detention Center occupied a corner of the upstairs at the courthouse behind a heavy metal door, next to the county clerk's window. The center included a narrow room for visitors to meet with those being held. Allison waited in the plain room for a full fifteen minutes before they brought in Earl McKee.

It wasn't hard to pick up on the "no rush" vibe.

Maybe Earl had to think about it. It wasn't "technically" visiting hours. Allison stated her relationship as "friend" of the detained individual. She was told she had twenty minutes, no more.

The room was windowless and sad. Allison felt trapped. The industrial-tan walls were clean, but the place reeked of fatigue.

So did Earl McKee.

"I can walk all day in the exercise yard," he said. "Have you ever seen an exercise yard on the second floor? Bunch of wire mesh lets the sunlight in above the walls but it feels like a goddamn bird cage out there, and it's hotter than blazes in the afternoon. How are you?"

He wore an orange pajama-like top and matching pants. Allison had only ever seen him in full ranch garb and never without his hat. His hair was thinner and his hairline higher than she might have imagined. Was this the future of Colin's hairline too?

Not that it mattered. Colin no longer existed.

"I'm okay," said Allison. "You alright?"

"Never been so goddamn pissed-off in my whole life." Earl McKee sat on the folding metal chair like he was waiting for a starter gun to go off. "But what can I do?"

"Judge on the way?"

"Believe it when I'm standing in front of him," said McKee. "You hanging over here for a reason? And by the way, before I forget to say anything else, thank you again for that genius bit of work the night of the fire. The ranch is still standing, though Char says she can't look at the view—or lack of it."

"Garrett and Daniel were there too," said Allison.

"And I thanked them too," said McKee. "And those really in charge. Glory and honor and thanks to Him who is seated on the throne."

The line dripped Bible. "Has Colin stopped by?"

Trudy, waiting out in the park outside the courthouse, had encouraged her to be direct. It didn't take much.

"Thought he was tied to your tail," said McKee.

"Not exactly," said Allison. Among Colin's many strengths was knowing not to smother or shadow, two variations of the same sensation. "He's been scarce."

"Called the ranch?"

"Yeah," said Allison. "Today."

"I pictured you two back on the other side," said Earl. "Thought you'd gone."

"I've been thinking we might want to get back," said Allison. "Our defensible space is zero, and if the fire gets close, they won't even give it a second look."

"You've got some people over there though, right?"

"Some people," said Allison. "One." Jesse Morales. The best hand ever. She owed him a call too. "You know a guy named Lenny Brandt?"

Allison dropped the question as casually as she might have asked about the quality of the jailhouse chow.

But she was watching.

"Heard the name."

That hadn't been his first answer.

"Why?" he said.

"You may not have heard, but Devo got involved in the murder—he was the one that found the body."

"Heard that," said McKee.

"Well, since I brought Devo in to talk to the cops I heard Lenny Brandt's place was one of the last places where Soto was doing his—"

"His know-it-all thing."

A slight snarl. Allison pretended she didn't notice. "—and they were looking into what happened out at Lenny Brandt's place."

"Place?" said McKee. "You mean ranch. That's his mother's ranch, just as you go down into the canyon."

For somebody who had only "heard the name" of Lenny Brandt, the information revealed more than Earl McKee should have let on.

Allison shrugged.

"I heard he was living out there," said McKee. "But if Soto had notion to convert Lenny Brandt, he'd have better luck getting the Pope to stop thinking about Jesus. They're looking at Lenny?"

"I guess." It wasn't a lie.

"If the do-gooders would let us get down into the earth and get all the gas and oil and tar sands that's down there and that belongs to us, we wouldn't need pompous assholes like Dante Soto creeping into town, knocking on doors."

"Soto kicked a porcupine or something. He never darkened your door, did he?"

"Uh, no. Probably wouldn't be a wise idea." McKee shook his head. "Your boys?"

They were all grown men, of course, but as sons the "boy" term could last a long time.

"You'd have to ask them. But I doubt it. Don't think either one would have much use for Soto. Or his crew."

If his son Garrett had befriended Lenny Brandt, would Earl McKee know it? It seemed likely, given Meeker's size.

"Only because I heard Garrett was one of Lenny's friends too."

Maybe she was taking some built-up, passive-aggressive venom regarding Colin's absence out on the dad. Maybe she knew in her bones that Earl McKee was guarding information. Everything up to now had been a temporary scratch. This one drew blood. Earl refocused his gaze. Sure, he'd been looking at her. The look turned to study. It was a flash and only for a second, but the recalibration was obvious.

"I don't keep track. They have their own worlds, and I try to let 'em be." He pinched the bridge of his nose with the inside edges of his thumb and index finger and gave a rub, closing his eyes. "Damn smoke. My eyes feel like sandpaper."

The space between them had changed. She could pretend she didn't notice. Or not.

"Any chance Colin is with Garrett?"

"Don't know," said Earl.

"Where does Garrett live now?"

"Mobile home down by Water Street," said Earl. "Last I heard."

"I saw Jayne the other day—downtown," said Allison. She was keeping it vague. Saying "Blue Spruce" might have implied too much.

"Well, if you run into Garrett, best not to mention that," said Earl.

"Why is that?"

She was making conversation, trying hard not to show too much interest.

"What I gather, mostly from Char, the night Jayne was over—the night of the fire—was a strain," said Earl. "It's been a struggle for Garrett, you know, with women. I guess he introduced Jayne to one of his friends, and Jayne decided right there things were over with Garrett. This was a month or so ago, and he's been trying to win her back ever since. He's touchy about the whole thing."

Men and pride, thought Allison. Again.

Should she dance around the issue of the school bus, the water truck, twelve-year-old boys toting shotguns? The book of Revelations?

"Two different boys," said McKee. "Three, of course, altogether. But Daniel and Garrett, *hoo boy*. Once you have children, you'll know, but Daniel makes it look easy, and Garrett just struggles. With everything."

She had a hunch he'd fill the void if she didn't.

"School, work, religion, women," said Earl. "Everything."

No doubt those four things constituted "everything" in Earl McKee's life. Not a healthy picture. "Religion?" she said.

Her least favorite topic to discuss publicly, because her detail on the subject was so thin and because she knew there was no arguing with true believers. When all you had to do was invoke the "mystery" of your faith to escape any logical discussion about the existence of deities, there wasn't a chance for a good debate. She always felt she was punching from quicksand.

"What about it?" said Earl.

"They split up over religion too?" She wanted to see where this would go.

"Over?" said Earl. "They didn't split up over anything. They came out that way, grew up that way, thought that way. Garrett always needed more explanations for things. The world puzzled him. He never felt like he belonged. It was as if Boy Number Two assumed all the burdens of the world, could never get settled in his mind, could never get it to settle down and be at peace."

"And Colin?"

"More like Daniel," said Earl. "Easygoing, just get-along kind of guy. But he took to the wilderness and the hunting like I wanted the other two to do. Some things you can't force. Learned that lesson the hard way."

"Did Garrett ever mention anything about a summer camp?"

She'd been thinking about Garrett's search for answers. The Book of Revelations seemed like a magnet for anyone wanting to find explanations. It could be twisted any which way. The hallucinatory qualities and Magical Mystery Tour prose were so wild they could be ripe for reinterpretation for millennia to come. "There's a school bus out at Lenny Brandt's place. Some summer camp."

"You ask like I've got him on a leash." McKee stood up, stretched. "Garrett comes around every now and then, but he's his own man, and he's been his own man for a long time. I'm the dad, so it's my job to accept him as he is and be a role model, except when I lose my patience with the goddamn cops. He's always been looking for the next thing to get his life to settle down. He might *own* a summer camp, though, and I might not know."

"Know the address on his mobile home?" she said.

"You're determined to find him, aren't you?" said Earl. "Determined to ask him about all of this."

"Looking for Colin," said Allison. "Before I head back."

"I'd try the auto repair shop first," said Earl. "Budgie's Auto, last one on the left heading out of town. Garrett's never home. The auto repair shop is kind of his home base, and tell Carl that Earl McKee sent you."

"Anything I can do for you?" said Allison. No reason not to be civilized. Or pretend.

"Go kidnap a judge," said McKee. "Drag 'em here."

"You've got a lawyer, of course."

"Not that you'd notice," he said.

The lone straight flight of stairs brought her to the simple front door of the courthouse. As civilization went, she had to hand it to Meeker for its straightforward style, efficiency, and modesty. Public buildings didn't need to be ostentatious or complicated. It wasn't hard to imagine that when Soto and his team started knocking on doors in Meeker that some in town recoiled at the notion of being "selected" to test an outsider's agenda. Outside the fancy-ass trophy home communities like Aspen and Telluride, and outside the magnets for alternative thinking like Paonia, Meeker seemed like a lot of cities and towns along the Western Slope. It wanted to keep its collective head down and go about its business. If you believed in change, perhaps the best way was through the old-fashioned, All-American route: retail. The model example of the power of retail's ability to make inroads into lives and homes of the individual was none other than Trudy Heath, and she stood now by a bench near the outer edges of the Plain Jane park that surrounded the courthouse. The guy she was talking with had a familiar and pleasing profile. It was Colin McKee.

FORTY-TWO: MONDAY AFTERNOON

"WHERE ARE YOU NOW?"

Coogan.

"On the way," said Bloom, which was a lie only if "on" meant or implied he was moving. He wasn't. With McClure Pass closed due to the fires, he was supposed to be heading west and then he was supposed to be heading south either over the Grand Mesa or around the Grand Mesa. He was supposed to be "on the way" to Hotchkiss, which was in the process of burning to the ground. He'd given himself a half hour, sitting in the Starbucks by the Wal-Mart in Rifle, to poke around on the Wi-Fi. Sure, the reporter bones squawked at him to get to Hotchkiss. But traffic and checkpoints during the attempt to scramble his way to the action would slow him down, and he couldn't imagine the agony he'd feel if he didn't try to chase down the other leads from Allison and Trudy.

"Going to try the cutoff up and over the mesa," said Bloom. "But if that doesn't look good I have to go clear around. I'm grabbing a quick coffee in Rifle."

That was in case Coogan could discern the lack of road noise. And it happened to be true.

"I don't have to say it, do I?" said Coogan.

"Every minute, yep, got it," said Bloom. Even in the oppressive heat that converted the parking lot asphalt into a pre-heated pizza pie stone fresh from the oven, Bloom liked to sip a scalding hot coffee. He found it cooling. No editor could deny a reporter his java. "On the way."

Bloom didn't bother checking his watch, but gave himself thirty mental minutes—the amount of time it would take before guilt tugged hard and yanked him back to the car.

Bloom logged into his IRB account, the tailor-made database of public records that paid for itself once or twice each year.

The house number in downtown Meeker where Jayne stopped the pickup was owned by Douglas R. Hackl, who had bought it four years prior for the sum of $325,000.

Doug.

Dug?

Bonnie Brandt had referenced her son Lenny, Garrett McKee, and a guy named Dug.

It was possible.

Bloom went to Google street view for an image of the plain, unassuming house that faced north on the hill behind downtown Meeker.

The picture of Douglas R. Hackl, at least the IRB version in data form, was thin. He was twenty-eight. He had five speeding tickets to his name, but none of them were serious violations. He worked with a company called M.E. Construction and according to their website the firm managed industrial-related construction projects across northwestern Colorado. Douglas Hackl had been married briefly, from 2010 to 2012. Ex-wife Daisy Vega was four years older. She was born in 1980. She had a steady job with county public works in accounting. Her lightly populated Facebook page included shots in each of the past six years of the summer office picnic. Hackl started attending in 2009, before they were married. Vega came across as pleasant. She was plump. She had a wide face and a wide smile under a curly bounty of jet black hair. Her smile was unchanged year to year. Douglas Hackl's last appearance at the office picnic had been in 2012, which matched the divorce record. In the last shot, they were both seated behind a table. If the chairs were the same height, Hackl was short. He looked about as happy as a whipped dog. He looked soft. His hair was thinning over a round, puffy face. He stared with a general air of defiance. A hand reached possessively for Daisy's shoulder. One of Daisy's hands gripped a can of Coors Light. The other, on the opposite side from Hackl, was tucked under the table. Based on this shot, Douglas Hackl didn't exist in the mind of Daisy Vega. Daisy's driver's license now carried a new address, also in Meeker.

Hackl had no Facebook page. Bloom took a stab at the high school yearbook and pulled up an online version of Meeker High School. Hackl was there as a junior but not as a senior. His junior year snapshot sported baby cheeks and long hair cut crudely, as if he had done it himself.

Bloom hadn't learned much other than Hackl earned enough money to buy a house and he had connections to McKee's girlfriend or ex-girlfriend or plain old friend, Jayne.

Without a last name or an idea of who to look for, Bloom had no place to start to look for Jayne. A quick search for Garrett McKee on

Facebook found nobody in Meeker to track on social media, which wasn't a big surprise.

Lenny Brandt graduated from Meeker High School three years before Hackl. They could have met there. Still, the small town factor was in play. Everybody knew everybody. It didn't take high school to meet. They were about the same age, big whoop.

Lenny Brandt's girlfriend, Erica Cross, lived her life online. Her Facebook page hummed with news. She posted status updates at least three times a day, sometimes more. Minutia. Observations. Things her two kids said. Dinner menus. Lack of sleep. A new pop tune she adored. The photos were snapshot variety. Two dogs, one cat. "Good day at work." "I'm blessed to have a job." "I hope everyone has a peaceful and wonderful day." Erica Cross looked like she was trying hard to hold onto her teenage girlishness. Pay no attention to these two children, her messages suggested, I'm still a goofy kid at heart. She worked as a dental assistant. Lenny Brandt started popping up in pictures and comments the previous January. He had tight, curly hair and a Fu Manchu that looked like it required daily care. He had a goat-like quality to his long face. He was smile-less, judging from this batch of Erica's Facebook photos, and always seemed to be standing on the edges or in the background like he didn't quite belong. From their photo-posing styles alone, Brandt and Hackl came from separate galaxies. But Erica referred to Lenny in routine fashion. Their age difference, from appearances, wasn't that striking. Lenny's road-weary look made him appear older. Whatever happened to the father of Erica's two kids, one boy and one girl, wasn't apparent. To Bloom, it didn't matter. From what Bloom had gathered from Bonnie Brandt, Lenny's relationship with Erica Cross might have been his first sustained deal. With Lenny's background being such a black hole, it was hard to see or know the attraction. Based on Erica Cross's busy and well-supported life, although no job was obvious, Bloom had a hunch that Lenny Brandt felt like a lucky fuck.

The clock thundered. Hotchkiss burned. Coogan fretted.

One more.

Drone Farm.

He needed a hook into the database. If he could troll all day, no problem, but he didn't have all day. How do you even guess at the number sequence? Zillow helped. About a half-mile from the drone farm and on the opposite side of the road, the real estate website showed a property for sale.

A woman answered at Rio Blanco Realty. No fuss and runaround in Western Colorado—people at work.

"You're the listing agent?" said Bloom, "Correct?"

"That's right."

"And how long has the property been for sale?"

"Six months," she said. Her name was Rachel. "Are you nearby? I'd be glad to take you out there. I can tell you that the sellers are motivated."

"And why is that?" Drones buzzing? Whacky neighbors?

"He has a job offer in Grand Junction," said Rachel.

"I'm in Rifle now." Bloom put on his most serious voice, like he had money. What a joke. "I want something remote, if you know what I mean."

"This is a productive ranch, and, good Lord nobody is going to bother you out there," she said.

"I see a property across the road though, further east," said Bloom. "I'm looking online, of course, but it looks kind of, I don't know, not well put together."

Rachel paused. "I'd be glad to show you the area," she said. "It's really something you have to see in person."

"I like your price, if the acreage is as good as it sounds," he said. "Any idea of the address of the one down the road? I'd like to pull records, if you don't mind, before I drive up there to take a look."

The pause came again.

"It's 4803 County Road 15. But activity around there is way back off the road," she said. "Can I schedule a time for you to come out?"

Bloom declined. The mild ruse was painless. And productive.

Checking the Rio County property tax database, the owner was listed as Guarantee Bank, Town of Meeker. And the previous owner was listed as Daisy Vega.

FORTY-THREE:
MONDAY AFTERNOON

As HUGS WENT, IT was okay. A quick kiss too.

"How is he?" said Colin.

"Agitated," said Allison. "Impatient. Where's Trudy?"

"I told her I'd wait for you while she went down to the grocery store to see if she could pick up anything useful," said Colin. "Local knowledge."

"You're local knowledge."

"Current local knowledge," said Colin. "She wanted to bounce a name or two off of the guys, see if she could figure out if the cops were making any progress."

That made sense. Trudy had a good friend named Brett Merriman who owned the store. Trudy had been a good customer for years.

"Where have you been?" asked Allison.

If it was possible, it seemed even hotter outside than a half hour ago. Smokier too.

"Around," said Colin. "I went back to the ranch at first, and then a friend of Daniel's needed help moving some cattle. His whole field caught a spark, and there was nothing left so we moved about eighty head to grazing land halfway to Craig. Six round trips from twenty miles west of Meeker. I tried calling you the other night but you didn't pick up."

"Busy," said Allison.

"It was midnight," said Colin.

"I wasn't in a spot where I could talk."

"Oh?" said Colin. "Care to share?"

"Everything," said Allison.

Surprised to have run into Colin, she wasn't sure in what order to get to the questions about his brother Garrett. Did it matter? Seeing Colin produced a jolt of reassurance. She hugged him again and wanted to hang on—heat or no heat, sweat or no sweat, sticky smoke or no sticky smoke. Seeing Colin made her yearn for a nap in a cool room. She'd even concede to a hotel, what the hell.

Colin scored two giant iced coffees from Wendll's, and they commandeered a park bench where they could wait for Trudy's return.

"Definitely know Lenny Brandt," said Colin.

Allison had finished a quick recap.

"You and your father both." Allison started with the Lenny Brandt angle of things—the bus and the water truck.

"You were asking him about all this?" said Colin.

"I was looking for you," she said. "And I mentioned some of this, yeah. Of course."

"Did my brother's name come up?"

Again, unprepared. "Which one?" Playing innocent.

"Garrett," said Colin. "Daniel is out of the picture—too stable. I heard Garrett was hanging around with Lenny Brandt, so it wouldn't surprise me if his name, you know, surfaced in the mix."

Colin slurped the coffee, folded his leg on the bench like he had all the time in the world.

"Is he?" said Allison.

"Is he what?" said Colin.

"Buddies with Lenny Brandt?"

"They've known each other since high school," said Colin. "Off and on. When you work auto repair in a small town, you get to know everyone, and Lenny Brandt is one of those guys who is always working on something to do with cars. Garrett seems to make friends for a while. Then things get weird."

"Jayne?"

"Couldn't believe she showed up the other night," said Colin. "I thought that had hit the rocks too. I feel sorry for Garrett sometimes. He tries so hard, it kind of backfires."

"Know where he might be now?" said Allison.

"Why? You want to ask him?"

"I think Soto ran into something or somebody at Lenny Brandt's place."

"Have you told the cops?"

"I've got nothing solid. And I can't say I trust them, after what they did to Devo and Devo's people. The whole thing."

"Garrett might be working," said Colin. "We can go down and find him—his trailer or work or some place in between. Nothing steady in his life, though, so you never know."

"Think he'd tell us?"

"He'd better," said Colin. "But you should at least tell the cops about anything you know."

"Tell them Soto was having an affair too?"

"Really?" He reacted like he'd been slapped, thinking of the implications. "With who?"

The obvious question. "One of his team, a young woman named Andrea Ingalls."

"Any chance she's got a boyfriend, and the boyfriend found out?"

"And staged that whole deal up in the woods?" said Allison.

"Doesn't sound like a jealous boyfriend." Colin gave a good impression of a thinking man. "But if you want to light a spark on the whole investigation, you could talk to the cops or tell Duncan to put it in the paper."

"Duncan knows," said Allison. "And all we have is Andrea Ingalls's claim. It could be a fantasy too. Unless Andrea's boyfriend is a seething, raving hulk who has an axe collection, and until we find out that Andrea's boyfriend found out, well, it's irrelevant too."

"It was an axe?"

"We're putting two and two together," said Allison. She filled him in on Devo's attacker and Devo's escape, which he had heard about.

"So it's back to Lenny Brandt. Seems reasonable. Again, though, the cops. Turn it all over, why don't you?" Colin sighed. He looked tired. "Let's head home."

"You'd be able to leave with your father in jail and things unsettled?"

Colin shrugged. "What's unsettled? He'll bond out, insist on a trial, and that will be weeks or months away. Meantime, he goes back home to the middle of a burned-out moonscape and figures out what to do with the cattle—and everything else."

The semi-permanent taste of smoke on her tongue was all the motivation she needed to think about heading home. But could she walk away now? Every fiber screamed for completion. Deep down, she didn't think the cops could see the big picture—and were probably sniffing around the wrong rat holes. Every time she inhaled, she thought of precious forest going up in smoke and how many decades it would take for the hunting grounds to recover.

Colin sensed her preference. "Then we find Garrett," he said. He glanced at his phone. "Damn things." And answered it.

Allison spotted Trudy making her way into the park. "Char," said Colin.

Allison left Colin to his conversation and headed to meet Trudy, who was already shaking her head.

"Found your guy," said Trudy when she got closer.

"Or he found me," said Allison.

A pink sheen glazed Trudy's cheeks but the walk in the midday heat didn't prompt one complaint.

"How's Brett?"

"The cops are looking for the guy Devo picked out," said Trudy.

"Your grocer knows this?"

"Only by watching the news." Trudy smiled. A flash. "He walks home for lunch—every day. They've got a warrant for the guy's arrest, and he's an outdoor enthusiast."

"You mean freak," said Allison. "Name?"

"Anton Hester," said Trudy. "Thirty-two. Last known address was Meeker. And get this—he hasn't been seen for several days, and Brett remembers that back in high school Anton Hester had an issue with matches."

"A pyro?"

"Spent a year in juvenile."

"So they are going to want Devo back to do the witness thing, and they probably think they've got it all wrapped up."

"If it all fits," said Trudy.

Only if Devo's pick from the photo pile was legit. His descriptions had been a jumble.

"Maybe Anton was in the middle with Lenny Brandt and the others."

"Garrett McKee," said Trudy. "And Dug."

251

"You'd think we would have run across the Anton Hester name before now, but it's possible he's part of the same crew and the cops have found a connection to the same den of bus-driving Bible-thumpers."

At this point of their relationship, looks and gestures didn't require interpretation.

"But what?"

"Not sure Devo is helping the cops as much as they think."

"Seems like Colin might have mentioned the name," said Trudy. "By the way, how is he?" She side-nodded her head in the direction of Colin, who was still on his phone.

"Not surprised at all that Garrett's name has come up," said Allison. "Says we're going to go find him too."

"He thinks we can find him?" She said it like Garrett McKee was the Wizard of Oz.

"Makes sense to me," said Allison. "He should know what's going on in that barn, or if Soto ever got tangled up out there."

Colin walked over, having finished his call. "That was Char," said Colin. "She said Earl called, and they got word that the judge should be here by late afternoon. She's on her way down, and she wants me to stay, show the judge he's got family and all of that."

Moral support for a bail hearing seemed like overkill, but maybe it was another small-town thing. "Daniel coming?" she asked.

"Denver's too far away," said Colin.

"Garrett?"

"She can't reach him," said Colin. "As we know. But that's not unusual."

"You ever hear of Anton Hester?" Trudy asked like she needed to know.

"No," said Colin. "Who's that?"

Trudy filled him in.

"Sounds familiar," said Colin. "They're going off Devo's ID and what else?"

"Don't know," said Allison. "But now we got two reasons to find Garrett—get him to the bail hearing and ask him about Lenny Brandt."

"Stop at Budgie's Auto Repair, and check there first," said Colin.

"What about his place? It's closer, isn't it?" There was no point in extra movement of any kind.

"Char just called and there was no answer," said Colin. "Middle of the day? Not Garrett. He's always off poking around somewhere."

"You'll be here when we get back?"

"Most likely," said Colin.

FORTY-FOUR:
MONDAY LATE
AFTERNOON

"LENNY BRANDT? HE OWES me nine hundred and fifty-six bucks."

Carl Kenyon stopped work on a government-issued Suburban jacked to the ceiling. It filled one half of the two-bay garage, a jungle of dark mechanical mysteries. In the next bay, a second mechanic stood under a behemoth SUV. Allison found herself wondering how often the lifts failed, and how many car mechanics had been found splattered under their work. And why did she see doom in routine? Kenyon continued to poke around the Suburban's sticky nether regions.

"By the way, Earl McKee is the one that sent me here," said Allison.

"What did Lenny Brandt do to you?" said Kenyon.

"Is Lenny around?" she said. Trudy remained in the freshly tired truck. They had decided one-on-one might come across as more normal—*just popped in to see if Lenny Brandt was here.*

"Not except when he's paying down his debt," said Kenyon. "You're talking to me why?"

She put Kenyon at about fifty. Impacted layers of grease and its ever-present companion, grime, coated all visible skin. He had a heavy jaw, spiky ear hair, bushy eyebrows. He came across as busy and wanted everyone to know it.

"Know anything about a school bus?" said Allison. "For a summer camp?"

"Summer camp?" said Kenyon. "Lenny Brandt? Still don't know how I'm involved here," said Kenyon.

"We're friends of Dante Soto's."

The lie felt okay. Trudy belonged to the same community. She knew him, Dante Soto knew her.

"And we know that Dante Soto and some of his people—"

"His network."

"Exactly," said Allison. "That they were out at Lenny Brandt's place before Dante Soto's disappearance. There was some sort of incident."

Kenyon leaned on a wrench as long as her leg and grunted.

"One of Dante Soto's crew said they saw he was restoring a school bus for a summer camp."

The wrench dropped to the cement floor with a deafening clatter. Kenyon gasped like he'd set a personal best for bench press. He mopped his long forehead on his shirt sleeve.

"Try the same questions down at the auto parts places. And tell me again why you're asking. You're not from here, I take it. I recognize your friend's truck, but…"

Kenyon stepped to a high bench crowded with tools on the far wall and, on return, stopped to inspect the progress of a co-worker, a good twenty years younger than Kenyon and more fit, less greasy. He had short hair and wore a baseball cap with a long bill, which seemed out of place under the shadows of the vehicle on the lift. They finished consulting on the SUV's ills. Then, the co-worker made a call from an old-fashioned land line phone that hung on the wall by a Snap-On Tools calendar. Either they had travelled back in time or Kenyon had a particular fondness for the ample brunette featured in April 1993. The calendar was faded. The phone was stuck on the wall between shelf units sub-divided into dozens of slide-out compartments like drawers for the dead in a mini-morgue.

"My friend was pretty scared," said Allison when Kenyon returned to his work on the Suburban. She merged in her mind what happened to Andrea Ingalls and Trudy Heath into one big lump of fear. It was possible they each kicked separate legs of the same angry moose. "And the cops have their hands full."

Kenyon headed to the mini-morgue, slid open an unmarked tray, looked inside, and flipped it shut.

"My wife reads novels about people like you," said Kenyon. Another tray, another misfire. "Didn't know they existed, tell you the truth."

"I've seen the school bus," said Allison. She felt as if this conversation needed a jolt. And she didn't want to watch him poke through all eighty or million trays. "Unless the cost of restoring vehicles has gone way down, I'd say he's got the money to repay you."

"If I owed somebody that much, I couldn't sleep at night," said Kenyon. "When I call Lenny all I get is something about the Bible, though he says he'll repay me. I stopped believing it a couple weeks ago. Now I'm getting ready to meet him in small claims court, where the Bible won't mean quite so much except right at the beginning where you swear to tell the truth."

"He scared my friend like he doesn't even want someone to step foot on the property," said Allison. "Like he had a security system out there."

"Where are you from?" said Kenyon. He located the right washer.

"Sweetwater," said Allison. She could have said "Iowa," but hoped that wasn't what he meant. "Other side—"

"I know it," said Kenyon. "But you're not from there, either. Am I right?"

The question stung like a dagger.

"Iowa," she said. Her voice was softer than she hoped. "But I've lived around the Flat Tops now for—"

"The thing is that up here there are a lot of people on edge, you know?" Kenyon had stepped back to the Suburban's invisible wounds, but now squared her up. "They aren't getting ahead. They don't want to hear anything more about what the government is going to do—or not do."

"You've known Lenny awhile," said Allison.

"He's a good kid. Few issues here and there, but one thing doesn't quite work out for him and, you know, it's easy to get discouraged and start to think the rules you were taught pretty much sucked. And they don't like others poking around in their business—telling them how to live like your pal Soto. Like every breath you take means bad things for the planet. As if those people know—I mean, really know for sure."

"Did Lenny say something?"

Kenyon shook his head. "I've already said too much. I'm filling you in on the mentality."

"And what about Garrett McKee?"

"What about him?"

"Does he work here sometimes?"

"You're looking for him too?"

"His father has a bail hearing coming up, and his brother is trying to find him," said Allison.

257

"Glad to hear Earl is getting out." said Kenyon. "You got your ranch at risk, easy to think you might lose your temper. And I say that even though I know the deputy he smacked. He's got about six weeks until they let him chew food. Eleven hours in surgery."

Allison could hear the crack again and felt the sickening blow as if it had been her own face. Admitting she'd been there, though, didn't seem like a wise thing to reveal.

"Surrounded by all those government workers, government walls, and government laws," said Kenyon. "Ironic."

Kenyon reached up with a wrench into the underbelly of the truck and gave a yank. A solid stream of black oil poured into a bucket propped on a rolling pedestal.

"Help me out," said Allison. "Ironic how?"

"You know, after leading that charge a couple years back to have the county secede from the state. There was a similar effort over on the Eastern Plains—Weld County, I think. All Earl talked about was taxes, taxes—made the Tea Party look like a bunch of pansies."

"Didn't go well?"

"He found some supporters—but only enough to get something on the ballot and then it got creamed by the voters."

In the big scheme of things, Allison told herself, it wouldn't hurt much to know more about her boyfriend's family, to ask an occasional question. Maybe once a month, like paying bills.

"And Garrett?" Allison lobbed it up like a jump ball. Innocuous. Unspecific. Meaningless.

"He was here this morning," said Kenyon. "With all the crews in town for the fire, I've needed the help."

"I mean in terms of his father's attitude."

The oil stream had diminished to a pencil-thin trickle. Then, drops and nothing. Kenyon re-tightened the plug. He wiped his dirty paws on a dirty rag.

"I need the help," said Kenyon. "There's almost nothing he can't do, and if he doesn't know it, he'll figure it out. But he has to work by himself. I mean, running commentary on everything evil, from the White House to the county courthouse. A chip off the old rancher, but no cattle."

Allison's head was busy re-calibrating everything.

She thanked Kenyon and headed back out to the street, eager to bounce all this new information off Trudy, her sounding board.

But Trudy's truck was gone.

Allison spun around, looking up and down the road with the certain feeling that Trudy was moving the truck to the shade or circling the block or maybe she'd made a quick run for gas or supplies or food or...

Nothing.

"What now?" said Kenyon.

"Did you see my friend's truck leave?"

"*You* didn't?"

"How long ago?"

"About ten minutes or so," said Kenyon. "I don't know."

"My friend was driving?"

"Couldn't tell you," said Kenyon.

Back on the too-empty road, Allison stared at downtown Meeker, a mere half-mile away. Add the heat and sweat factor, and she doubled the distance. She had covered this stretch about eight hours ago.

The degree of difficulty was low, but that didn't mean she would enjoy the hike.

FORTY-FIVE:
MONDAY LATE
AFTERNOON

PICK UP, PICK UP, pick up.

Devo sat in the office at Trapper's Lodge. Nora also declined to make the call. He had to punch the numbers. She said something about wilderness regulations, and how she wasn't unhappy about how the feds resolved the matter once and for all. Devo didn't have time to ask questions or get into it.

The phone rang. And rang.

It was the fifth time he had dialed.

Nora stood in the door frame, watching. Her desk was a disheveled affair—notes and doodles on a flat calendar that covered an old wooden desk. Paperbacks overflowed a bookshelf. An electronic device—Devo wasn't sure if it was a radio or something else—played a German opera. The music was odd and out of place. Faded maps of the Flat Tops and one of the whole state papered the wall. The cordless phone would have let Devo wander but Nora insisted that Devo stay put. He was fine with that request.

It was three hours since he left the dead man in the river. He had stayed close to the road, looking and hoping for an opportunity to stowaway on a truck or something heading upriver. At a pullout, he spotted a trailer with six canoes hitched to an old Chevy Tahoe. Dad was out taking pictures of the burn scar across the river. Devo tucked himself inside one of the upside down canoes until the Tahoe pulled out and then rode between the stacks up the long road, his eyes tight and his mouth sealed shut against the exhaust and dust when they hit the dirt sections to Trapper's. He rolled off before they came to a complete stop and wasted an hour lurking around the cabins, hoping for Nora to make an appearance. She was the only one he could trust. Maybe. The cabins were empty. The fire had chased away all the users who wanted to "get back to nature" with their coolers of iced-down beer, packaged hot dogs, and canned beans. The campers and hikers were gone, anyway, but a government presence was heavy. A deputy sheriff paced close to the cabin where Devo had been interviewed by Mendoza. Finally Nora came out to check on something, and Devo stepped out from his hiding spot under a cabin. He gave her a start but he managed to calm her down and explain what he needed. And why. Mentioning Allison always helped. She told Devo about a back door to the lodge and said she'd be there in a half hour, but he would have to find a way to not get spotted—despite the midday sun and acres of bald, barren space between the cabins and the lodge, which sat up on a knoll across from where cars and trailers all pulled in after their long climb from the river.

He had taken a wide circle around, crossed the road to the north where he had plenty of space to wait and watch and then slipped down a deep gulley and worked his way back to the lodge, coming at it from the less-populated side. Nora had kept her promise, and he slipped inside and dialed 911. That call hadn't gone well. The woman wanted his ID. Wanted to know why he was calling from Trapper's when the victim was miles away. Wanted to know why he hadn't called earlier. Devo kept focusing on the location and the urgency. She kept asking for his name. She wanted him to stay on the line. Devo had hung up with a final plea of desperation. He couldn't tell them about the bus—after all, what would he report? The dead guy would lead to the bus—right? Warrants, etcetera.

Pick up, pick up, pick up.

Nothing.

Who else could he call? He would hate to call her boyfriend.

And he didn't know how he would find him, anyway. He would need a last name to even begin to figure that out.

"No answer?" said Nora.

"You don't suppose she's back over in Sweetwater?" said Devo.

"You could try there. Or try to reach Colin McKee. I think I know the ranch you're talking about." She had listened to his 911 call. "Looks brand new, right?"

"A vision," said Devo. "All-American."

"The Brandt's Place," said Nora. "Gotta be the one."

Nora scrounged for a phone number in the clutter on her desk. "Don't know why I'm helping you." Her movements were hurried and quick; agitated. "Don't you think it's all over now—your experiment?"

"Not until they drag me out," said Devo. And if the fire came close to their camp, well, that would be a great episode, if they had to pack and go.

"Here's the number," said Nora, no longer interested in chatting about *Latitude/Longitude.*

"Do you watch?" said Devo.

"Used to. For amusement, anyway." She dialed the number on the cordless and handed him the phone.

The phone rang in Devo's ear and a woman answered. Not Allison. She introduced herself as Charlotte McKee.

"My name is Nick." Using Devo would require too much explanation. Nora gave him a look. "I'm trying to track down Colin or Allison, either one."

"Allison is looking for Colin too," said Charlotte. "It's not routine around here by any stretch."

"Can I leave a message with you to have either one of them call up to Trapper's Lake Lodge and ask for me?"

Nora sighed. Shrugged. Sighed again.

"Only for the next three hours and then there's no point. I have to push off," said Devo. Nora shook her head.

"You might leave a message at the Blue Spruce too," said Charlotte. "Kind of a crossroads place."

"Neither one might recognize my name," said Devo. "Tell them I'm their friend from the woods, and it's urgent."

With Nora's help again, Devo left a message at the Blue Spruce. Then she helped him find the number and call over to Sweetwater. He left a message with a worker at Allison's business named Jesse Morales. No Allison. No Colin.

"Give me a job," said Devo. "I owe you something—some work. I'll clean your kitchen top to bottom. I want to head out at sunset, and I've got a good three hours."

"Head where?"

"Home," said Devo.

Nora started to say something and stopped. "Start over?"

"A few days around the city won't make that much difference."

Nora, for some reason, seemed to struggle with what she wanted to say, how she wanted to approach him. "Your job is to lay low right here to see if anyone calls back."

"I'll leave at sunset if they don't," said Devo. "I'm half-tempted to call back to the cops and see if they are following up on the dead guy in the river. They'll do the right thing, won't they?"

Nora answered with a touch of exasperation. "One would think."

FORTY-SIX: MONDAY LATE AFTERNOON

DUNCAN BLOOM HOPED HE would stumble straight into Trudy. He stood in the parking lot of the Blue Spruce—no sign of her truck.

"Yes, Meeker," he told Coogan on the phone.

"What the fuck?" said Coogan. "Get lost? Take a wrong turn?"

"I called Paonia. I called Hotchkiss. I talked to Delta. I called Ouray and Yampa too," said Bloom. "Fires for all. I talked to state-wide fire command, and I'll talk to the folks here too. The point is there's fire all over, and I'm going to walk into the Blue Spruce, ask them if I might use their Wi-Fi. So I'll send you a story within 45 minutes. An hour, tops."

"Dante Soto?"

"The cops have issued a warrant for the arrest of a guy named Anton Hester," said Bloom. "I need a day on this—a quick story on

Hester and the search for him, and then I've got to follow up a couple other leads. And I'll write the fire wrap-up, including Rat Mountain."

"And that one is threatening nothing more than bear dens and aspen saplings," said Coogan. "All the action is in Hotchkiss—that town might get leveled."

"So might Meeker." It wasn't true. "Anything is possible. I've got some great quotes for the round-up."

Coogan said nothing.

"Trust me," said Bloom. "And when the shit goes down, I'll be right here and all the other reporters will be in Hotchkiss—sniffing each other's butts like they were newborns at a puppy farm."

Bloom found Daisy Vega at home, a modest bungalow on the downtown flats of Meeker's western edge. She lived next to a Baptist church. Her house was tucked back from the street. Based on how fast the door opened, Bloom wondered if she had an invisible tripwire.

Bloom introduced himself, mentioned it had to do with Dante Soto.

"I don't want to be quoted about anything." She cut him off. "But I especially don't want to be quoted about him."

Busy black hair and schoolgirl freckles didn't suggest innocence. That had evaporated long ago. She wore a dark green blouse over longish white shorts, and her feet were bare as if she'd kicked off her shoes after work. She looked like she could be attractive if she put some thought into it. She invited him into a spare, clean living room.

"I don't know what I have to do with any of that anyway." Her eyes were hard, nearly defiant. "I got friends who swear he saved them a bundle and now they run around like the recycling police, but it wasn't for me."

He should know what he needed to know about Douglas Hackl in four minutes flat. Daisy Vega was a talker.

"I don't need to quote you," said Bloom. A postcard-size portrait of an angelic Jesus in a thick frame dominated the wall. "And it's not so much what Dante Soto was pushing or selling. It's about some people he may have run into prior to whatever happened."

"Not about me." She said it like a whip crack.

"Dug Hackl."

"Dug?" She let out a dry chuckle, leaned back on the maroon couch. He had a hardback chair. "He would no more—"

"Not that he used his—their—services, but that Soto's people may have seen something Dug and his friends were up to."

"Well it's gotta be right because Dug was always up to something—not much, in fact, as it turns out, but he always had an idea of what was next. Each week it was some new thing. But that's all I know. We haven't been together for years."

"Is it *D-u-g* Dug by the way?" said Bloom. "That's what someone told me."

"That's the genius I married," said Vega.

"Why D-u-g?"

Vega shook her head. "Fifth-grade spelling bee. Think he was third or fourth and he got pissed off. Said he was going to change the spelling of his name, so there were no silent letters. When he was old enough, he found a judge and switched it. How many times did I have to correct people? I don't know. How did his name came up?"

"Does the name Lenny Brandt mean anything to you?"

"Weirdest friendship ever."

"Goes back, does it?"

"Off and on at first. Then, something clicked, and they were inseparable. These days, if I see either one I know the other is around the corner. Kind of spooky."

"Lenny Brandt?"

She knew what he meant.

"I'm not being quoted."

Bloom showed her empty hands.

"Glenwood Springs, you said?"

"Where my newspaper is based, yes," said Bloom.

"How will I know you don't cross me?" A tear boiled up on her eye, and she stared down at her feet. "Sorry."

"What I write goes online." Once lies started, they came easily. "We already know."

"We?"

"My editors." She looked back up, but didn't hold his eye. "And what happened to Dante Soto is their top priority."

Another one.

"Aren't the police, you know?"

"Sure," said Bloom. "But someone told us about an encounter at Lenny's place."

"Which one of the *places*?"

"His mother's. There's another?"

"Well, he doesn't own it but he spends a lot of time out there— an old junk farm a ways out of town where they rebuild stuff and hang out."

"County Road 15?" said Bloom.

"Back there, yeah," said Vega. "How did you know?"

"Heard about that place too. Who owns it and do you know where it is?"

Bloom knew both answers.

"It's complicated. The bank owns it now. What happened at the mother's place?"

"We don't know," said Bloom. "It seems clear they got run off or chased away. There was a school bus out there. Something to do with a summer camp."

"Summer camp?" She couldn't have been more surprised if he had said hair salon. "That is bull crap right there. I don't think Dug grew up hurting kids. Something changed around Lenny, and it was all darkness. Darkness and doom. Impossible to be around. Besides, what summer camp? Around here?"

"What about this place out on County Road 15?"

"That's no place for a camp," said Vega. "Unless it's a camp for dirt, dust, and sunburns."

"It's not a camp?"

"It's not nothing," said Vega. "It's a hangout. A boy's dream. Place to blow up things and shoot your rifles. You know how boys like to play fort?"

"Sure."

"It's their little world out there—explosives too."

"And you said the bank owns it?"

Vega pushed back a tear. "Now," she said. "Yeah."

"I'm sorry," said Bloom. "I didn't mean to—"

"That was my money, my inheritance, and we were going to fix it up, maybe move out there." Tears streamed down her cheeks. "I was so stupid. Like that loser could do anything."

"But they still use it?"

"The bank is getting ready to evict them all—what I heard. Before they blow the place up. Whatever he's up to now, Dug is doing it with eight fingers. Missing the index and middle off his left hand. Play with fire, you know. All he wanted to do was blow stuff up. They both talked about how things could turn on a dime, and soon it would be every man for himself."

On the three-block drive back to the center of town, Bloom tried Trudy. No answer. Her truck wasn't at the Blue Spruce, and there was no answer from her room. Bloom returned to the searing heat of the park around the courthouse, bought an iced coffee, and sat on a park bench. He wanted to go inside to find out if Earl McKee's bail hearing was underway, maybe find Colin. He didn't want to miss anything outside, either. He'd give the park ten minutes, then he'd head back to the Blue Spruce. He called her office in Glenwood Springs, but they hadn't seen her. A drive out to blow-shit-up ranch held appeal.

To see what? Do what? Confirm the drones? Provoke another chase?

He had forgotten to ask Daisy Vega about Garrett McKee, though there didn't seem to be much dispute about Garrett's connection.

He pledged to Coogan and the gods of journalism that he would make six work-related calls about the fires. If he made a round of calls and stayed around the park or the Blue Spruce, Trudy might turn up on her own. After some routine fire checks, he could get to work on why the cops were after Anton Hester, or maybe figure out if Hester was in the same crew with Lenny Brandt, Garrett McKee, Dug Hackl, and Dug Hackl's eight fingers.

FORTY-SEVEN: MONDAY LATE AFTERNOON

THIS TIME, TRUDY TOOK the roller coaster with care. She hugged the right shoulder at the crest in case of oncoming trucks, and she let her truck shudder fiercely over the rock-hard washboard that rattled the cab like a vibrating bed in a cheap motel. Her passenger hadn't said more than a couple dozen words.

"Drive."

"Stay right at the speed limit."

"Left."

"Right."

"I think you know the way from here."

She'd tried to engage. No dice. She didn't know guns, but the barrel of his weapon flopped in his lap. The last thing she wanted was a jarring bounce to—

She didn't want to think about it.

Now that they were out of town, any quick attempt at escape was useless. If she'd been thinking, she could have jammed on the brakes back where there were people around. She could have created a scene and taken her chances. Of course, the reason she hadn't done anything was the mini-cannon in his lap and the grim look on his weary face.

She would never have figured him for the gun-toting type. He wasn't, in fact, bad looking even with his goofy, wide-brimmed hat. He was on the short side, and he looked soft. He could use a month or two of healthy meals. A sourness wafted from his dark T-shirt that she knew said something defiant about guns, but she didn't want to know. A small black backpack that had yielded the cannon lay at his feet.

Her innards brewed a foul soup that percolated up the back of her throat.

This was all one elongated slow-motion accident, and she was inside the moment, watching it all unfurl frame by frame. The end of the road was where the frames would flicker to an end. She had put herself here. This was her doing.

She feared for Allison back in the auto repair place or, by now, she was at least wondering what the hell had happened to her ride. She feared for Duncan, of course, and hoped he stayed clear of Meeker unless he felt like he wanted to come out to the drone farm and poke around.

Find her body…

Her mind chewed on itself. How to catch him off-guard? How was anything off-guard with that gun?

He didn't respond to questions.

The roller coaster ended. Now they hit the long flat road that curved toward the patch of forest. Soon they would be there. Then what?

All she could think to do was point the truck off the road at full speed and hope to survive the crash or the gunshot. Maybe she'd knock him unconscious—or worse.

There were no answers to her questions. She didn't have much time to plan.

FORTY-EIGHT:
MONDAY LATE
AFTERNOON

Could it be the same school bus? She had him describe the ranch again.

It matched.

"Whatever the hell happened in Rifle," said Devo. "They didn't want to be stopped by the cops."

"You called the cops?" said Allison.

"Yeah, yeah. They should be checking it out now. Or at least him."

The clerk who handed her the note said the message was one hour old. She couldn't shake the image of Devo hanging around Trapper's Lake Lodge or talking on the telephone, like Tarzan riding an elevator.

"How far upriver?" said Allison.

"Where you leave the plain and make that turn into the canyon, where it all tightens down," said Devo. "Five miles out of town? I don't know."

She had him describe the three others again in detail, as much as he could produce. She had him wait while she found a pen and paper, jotted down what she could of the descriptions.

Tall guy with long hair. Camo pants, Fu Manchu.

Shorter guy, floppy hat.

"They meant to kill him?" she said.

"They didn't care that they did," said Devo. "That's all I know."

Fuck.

"And the cops didn't seem alarmed?"

"They asked more questions about me than what I saw," said Devo. "I don't know."

She had him describe the inside of the bus again and couldn't quite wrap her head around the retrofit. Doomsday preppers imagined all sorts of scenarios for storing stuff—water in particular. Why the bother?

"By any chance could you read the name of the summer camp?"

"Vernon Wayne Howell," said Devo. "Sound like fun times to you?"

What the hell? Which way to move? If the cops retrieved a body and found the bus, wouldn't it be over? Wouldn't that be it? That's a big *if.*

Would they put three and three together?

Trudy's vanishing act rattled her core. Trudy had been the one to urge Allison to head into the auto repair place solo to make it less threatening. The clear implication was that Trudy would wait. Where else would she go? Something happened while Allison watched Kenyon work. She had missed it. First Colin disappears and now Trudy. Ironic that Mr. Time Tunnel was moving up the charts for communication dependability.

Ironic, but not enough to laugh.

"You haven't by any chance run into Colin up there?"

"Could have told him all this if I did," said Devo. "Nora helped me call the family ranch, too, and Charlotte said she hadn't heard from him either."

She was expecting nothing more than a dead end, so she wasn't surprised. "How long are you going to be there?"

"Matter of minutes after I hang up," said Devo. "Though I have an oven to finish cleaning."

"Wait." Her heart thumped. "Go back a minute. You said Char hadn't heard from Colin?"

What the hell? Colin had said it loud and clear: *That was Char.* Char said the judge was coming. Char said late afternoon. Char said she was on her way to town. Char said gather the family. She said *all* of that.

"Something wrong?" said Devo.

"She said she hadn't talked to Colin—*in days*?"

"You already asked that," said Devo.

Allison stared up into flakes of fluttering ash. Her stomach wobbled.

"Are you—?" Devo tried in vain.

Colin, right to her face. What the fuck was that? She replayed his sincerity, his casual report. *That was Char. That was Char.* She played it slow, then she played it fast. She tried to think of a dozen ways she might have misheard it. Who else would call the family together? Who had the influence?

Char.

"Where are you going?" she said. She had a sudden urgency to get the fuck off the telephone.

"Back, of course. Forget this ever happened."

"Back where?" said Allison.

Devo paused. "To the homestead." Up-speak. Like a question. Uncertain.

"Nora didn't tell you? Nobody?"

"What?"

The whole valley knew, but she was the one who would have to break the news.

"They cleared your camp," said Allison. "I mean, homestead. They rounded them all up—midnight raid. I saw them being marched into the courthouse—Cinnamon, all your people."

The silence was long. Her thoughts ran to Colin.

"I know," said Allison. "They promised."

"Those fuckers." On the range of whisper to scream, Devo managed both. "Mendoza? That cop?" Snap—*crack.*

"He might have started it," said Allison.

"Out of the billions of acres of government land, we chose to use one tiny patch for a good cause, and they can't stand it." The sadness in his voice gnawed straight into her own. *Home,* after all. "That was our house, and we were way more fucking *wilderness* than the high-tech campers with their sleeping bags and horses and, of course, hunting seasons. Wilderness, hell. More like a twenty-first century weapons conference up here."

He had a point, but Allison didn't know if permanent residence was a legitimate reason to break the wilderness rules because they wanted to ignite a toughening of the collective DNA. "It sucks," she said. Empathy hurt nobody. Devo had been a huge help.

"I've got to go back to have a look around."

She didn't know the difference between sobbing and sniveling, but Devo was stuck somewhere in that zone. His voice crawled high and broke. Years in the woods hadn't wiped out his ability to feel the sting of betrayal and loss. She might be on the same fucking track. "I'm sorry. I have to see it one more time."

Echoes of Earl McKee rattled her head. *Home* has a million connotations.

"Don't you think—?"

A familiar green Camry pulled into the lot at the Blue Spruce.

Duncan Bloom climbed out into the searing afternoon heat. He rolled his shoulders, gave the sky—or lack of it—a glance.

Confused? More than a little. Trudy told her that Bloom was on the road to Hotchkiss, a hundred and fifty miles away. Maybe Bloom had the answer to Trudy's whereabouts.

"Still there?" said Allison.

"What?" said Devo.

"All I'm saying is keep an eye out," said Allison. "They'll want you too. They might be waiting right there."

She understood Devo's yearning. Last requests had their place.

"I know a thousand ways to that spot," said Devo. "And I don't have to walk through it. I need to see it again with my own eyes. Bid farewell."

"Keep an eye out for me heading back in the next day or two. Three at the most. Let me know. Stay in touch."

Devo's frustrations pushed a tear out of her own eye. She flashed on Sweetwater going up in flames.

"Go," said Allison again. "Thank you for all this. Now go."

FORTY-NINE:
MONDAY LATE
AFTERNOON

THEY STARTED WITH THE obvious spots. Bloom ran into the court-house for a quick look around, and they both went into the grocery store to chat with Brett Merriman. No sign of Trudy or her truck.

She called Char, but didn't let on. Char told her what she'd told Devo. No Colin contact, for days.

They prowled in a thorough grid up the hill behind downtown, twelve blocks in each direction. The grid narrowed as it climbed, and each pass was five blocks. Then they took a quick tour of the Sanderson Drive loop at the top of the hill.

They drove past 848 Hill Street, and Bloom explained how Trudy first discovered the house, and how it led to the drone farm. Allison kept the Colin thing to herself, for now.

First, find Trudy. Second, get in Colin's face.

"Eight-fingered Dug," said Bloom. "His ex-wife said he's capable of anything he puts his mind to, but he's drifted from thing to thing. He had plans but no staying power."

They drove past 848 again. Slowly. There were no immediate signs of life. The house was small and unassuming, just a white one-story with black shutters and a green door. A one-car garage was attached. The door was up, but there was no car inside.

"He doesn't have his name on the drone farm, but he does have his name on this one. You have to wonder where he's got the money for this place, you know, even though it's not much," said Bloom. "No obvious signs of support. Like a job. Or a rich family."

"So Jayne led Trudy here and two guys came out later, without Jayne, and Trudy followed them out east?"

"And then got chased down," said Bloom.

"So maybe we knock on the door," said Allison.

"I was afraid you'd say something like that," said Bloom.

"Quoting your basic journalistic philosophy, I believe—why dig through someone's trash when you can knock on the door and ask?"

Allison and Colin didn't hang out and eat dinner with Trudy and Duncan all the time, only when all four were together in Sweetwater. Bloom's tales from the reporter front lines were regular fodder for conversation.

"Start the easy way, right?" said Allison.

"Coming back to haunt me." The fear was fake. "I'd rather drive around and keep an eye out for Trudy. Maybe she went back to the Blue Spruce—"

"Just going to knock," said Allison.

She wasn't sure exactly what she was going to ask, however. The moment would call for improvisation, depending on who opened the door. Bloom might care about finding Trudy, but nobody could outflank Allison on that score.

"We'll both go," said Bloom.

"No," said Allison. "I'll ask for Jayne like I'm looking for Colin or Garrett. And if Jayne answers, fine. She knows me. Just be here when I get back, okay? Keep an eye out for anyone coming up the hill."

The stubby driveway was empty except for a trailer off to the side that held a small river raft, a red four-seater. Both trailer and boat looked new. Allison gave the interior of the garage a quick glance, not wanting to appear too nosy in case she was already being watched. The inside was nearly empty with only a weed-whacker, a case of Coors, trash cans, and a map of Glenwood Canyon on the wall over a workbench near the front of the garage. But it was void of general garage crap.

One doorbell press with no discernable ring.

A firm knock. Then, nothing.

Allison risked a look back around, fearing that Duncan Bloom would have succumbed by now to the same moment-of-rapture syndrome as Trudy. Raptures usually focused on the humans and generally didn't include delivery trucks, but you never know what new tricks religion might have conjured up.

Bloom gave a small shrug as if to say, "Keep trying or don't."

A second knock drew the same nothing. Allison stared at the peephole. She glared for good measure, though only for herself. Maybe she was practicing for Colin. She may as well have been knocking on a rock deep in the woods, where she wished she was.

There was no soft thud of footsteps, no sensation of movement, no weary creaks to suggest an inhabitant.

The door barely opened—just a crack, just a face-width.

It was Jayne.

"You better get the fuck out of here. You and your friend."

"We're looking for Trudy."

"He sees a stranger on our doorstep, he's going ape-shit ballistic."

"Which he?"

Jayne was makeup free in her camo-pattern tank top with a deep scoop showing a mile of cleavage. She was wearing black and orange runner's shorts. In comparison with the kiln outside, the air drafting out from the house would have cooled the North Pole. "Is it Garrett?"

"This ain't Garrett's place. And I ain't with Garrett."

"Someone told me he lives closer to downtown," said Allison.

"If he lives anywhere. How the hell did you end up here anyway?"

Allison couldn't see past Jayne's trim frame, but the cool air may as well have screamed "come hither." Jayne's sheer lack of basic hospitality pissed Allison off, but she didn't need a new reason. Her quiver was full.

"What do you mean?"

"You fucking followed me," said Jayne. "The whole world has gone fucking nuts, just like they say."

"I didn't follow you." Half truth.

"You were looking for Colin then and this Trudy woman now. I don't know who the fuck you are or what horse you rode in on, but I don't think you are telling anyone the truth."

Allison took a slight step back and waited. Tried not to show the sting.

"I am on the way home. But I came here with Trudy, and I want to go back with Trudy." Down to about a quarter-strength in the truth department. "I have lost my friend Trudy. She got crossways with a guy in town after an encounter. Trudy felt threatened. She told me the guy's name, and when she disappeared, I looked it up."

Another slight step back. Allison took a breath.

"Who?" said Jayne.

Look like an idiot? Or look like a smarty-pants?

"Lenny Brandt."

She chose idiot.

Jayne didn't flinch. "You're kidding me, right?"

Allison shrugged. Innocent.

"Lenny Brandt's place is by the river," said Jayne. "Outside of town on the way upriver."

They both heard the car door open. Jayne re-focused her gaze across the street. She opened the door wider in order to step outside.

She shouted: "Stay right there, asshole."

The inside of the house was empty with only green wall-to-wall carpet and not a stick of furniture.

Allison turned around like she didn't care about getting inside or hadn't noticed. She gave Jayne space and gave Bloom the hand signal to stay put.

"He's fine," said Allison. "He's a friend."

Bloom kept coming.

"Nothing is fine," said Jayne. "You don't get it. He comes back, which could be any minute."

"So you're not with Garrett," said Allison. The idiot act was easy. She wanted to keep Jayne's focus off Bloom. "That wasn't that long ago."

"I came out for the party, big deal. A favor to Garrett. Favor, hell, he paid me. I never look a hundred bucks in the mouth, all I had to do was smile and drink."

"Appearances?" Dumb, idiot, clueless—they all seemed to give Jayne more room to expound.

"Hated being seen as a loser—by his father, his older brother, and your guy, too, Colin. Hated."

"It was a show?"

"For him," said Jayne. "I'd already moved on. In fact, Garrett introduced me, and I know he wished he hadn't."

"To Dug? D-u-g Dug? To Dug and Lenny?"

Jayne laughed. "Make it sound like a three-way. Who do you think I am? Lenny's solid with his girlfriend, and I hooked up with Dug. Who told you about Lenny?"

"Colin," said Allison. And everyone else.

Bloom walked up, low-key. "Does she know?" He hung back.

"No," said Allison. She introduced her "friend" to Jayne. "I met her at Colin's family house last week right before the fire."

"And maybe you're no longer with Colin, right?" Jayne offered an eyebrow pop in Bloom's direction. One brow.

"Duncan belongs to Trudy," said Allison. "The person we're looking for."

"Maybe all the McKees are fucked up," said Jayne. "Ever think of that?"

"No." It sounded more defensive than she had hoped. All meant all.

"You ever talk to the dad?" said Jayne. Allison had been thinking through possible scenarios for the empty house, but now came back to Jayne. "I mean really talk to him?"

"What do you mean?"

"To know where he's coming from? You know, what he believes."

"The dad?" said Allison.

"What I said—the dad."

Allison shook her head. "I didn't think you were around that long."

"Twenty minutes with Earl," said Jayne. "One on one, if he trusts you. I mean, that's all you need."

"He's fucked-up how?" said Allison. *What had she missed?*

"Going somewhere?" said Bloom, noticing the empty house.

"None of your business," said Jayne.

"Is Dug around?" said Allison.

"Could be around here any second, matter of fact," said Jayne. "Would not be pretty. Or good."

"Daisy says he's got another place out east, some sort of—"

"You talked to the ex?" said Jayne. "You're looking for your friend and you, what, bumped into the ex on your search?"

Jayne lowered her sights on Bloom. Maybe she was more comfortable arguing with a man.

"What's your two's deal anyway?" said Jayne.

"Why is the house empty?" said Allison.

"Look," said Jayne. "I got no idea about your friend."

"What is this other place Daisy talked about?"

Bloom's cell phone clanged.

"Go ahead," said Jayne. "Take it. Maybe it's her."

"Actually," said Bloom. "It's not. But I've got to take it."

Bloom turned on his sneakered heels and put the phone to his ear. He drifted away.

Jayne shrugged and stared. "Your turn."

"I'm missing something." Allison said it with as much sincerity as she could muster.

"I'll say."

Allison flashed on the night of the fire at the McKee's—Jayne working hard to get plastered, then taking off when the shit hit the fan. Where was Colin that whole time? Since the fire, the skin that held her world together had been peeled off with a pair of pliers, one patch at a time. People think you get lost in the woods? Try the city. "Fill me in," she said.

"You're not from around here," said Jayne.

Did the Meekerites have a secret handshake she needed to learn? Was it that obvious?

"Iowa."

"You don't know your boyfriend's family?"

"We live on the other side."

"Ask him questions, poke around, hang out?"

She and Colin made appearances at the McKee's when summoned for occasions, special or not. The words "family" and "obligations" were not a happy couple.

"No," said Allison. "Not really."

"Well, you might want to focus on the *really*."

"Fill me in."

"Why should I?" Jayne added a dismissive semi-snarl to go with it.

"Because I need a shortcut." Allison heard a snap to her voice. Patience scampered off. "Because time is precious. Always has been and always will be. Because my friend is missing. Because your pal Dug and Lenny and Garrett McKee are up to something with this school bus, and because Dante Soto saw something at Lenny Brandt's ranch and got himself killed. And if that's not enough, because whoever killed Dante Soto lit a fire so big it will take a good chunk of the Flat Tops about a century to recover, and the wackos killed one of their own and left him to die in the river."

Allison took a sharp step forward. Jayne flinched. And blinked.

"Who?" The news left her rattled. "Really?"

Allison felt Bloom's presence behind her, but she didn't turn around.

"Not like I have names," said Allison. "But if you know anything that will help us find Trudy, I need to know. I need to know right about now. And if you know anything about Garrett McKee or Earl McKee or what the hell is up with Lenny and Dug, I don't need it right now—I need it about ten minutes ago when I first knocked."

Jayne shook. Her gaze flitted back and forth to Bloom. She stared at the ground, backed up another step to the house, then did a slow 360.

"Did Earl McKee make bail?" said Jayne.

"Yes," said Bloom. "That was part of the last call."

"Then all is well," said Jayne. "I only know pieces myself, but tomorrow is Colorado Day—right?"

"Day after," said Bloom. "August 1."

"Even so," said Jayne. "You're too late."

FIFTY:
MONDAY EVENING

THE DRONES SAT SIDE by side on the beat-up couch like a pair of circular dung beetles.

They stared at her. Trudy was on the floor of a mobile home that looked like it hadn't been mobile for a long time. The floor was slick with grease. The space smelled as if a squirrel had crawled into a wall and died.

Her insides churned. She had struggled as they dragged her inside, protested when they tied up her hands and protested harder when they tied up her ankles. Then she was ignored as she asked questions and tried to make conversation.

Her passenger—her kidnapper—squatted at her side. He said nothing. He pulled out three stick matches from his pocket and a cigarette. He retrieved a rubber band and a small sheet of paper. The paper was green and square. He rigged the cigarette and matches with the rubber band. The matches overlapped the filter, so the heads touched where the tobacco would burn.

He pantomimed lighting the cigarette, striking the imagined match with the three-fingered hand. It was clear the match heads would catch fire as soon as the cigarette burned down, then the paper, and then ...

He placed the device on the arm of the couch next to the drones, headed off with one evil bug in each hand.

He came back a minute later with a bag of potato chips. Picnic-size. He held the inside up close as if she was the one-woman audience for his magic act. A chemical version of barbecue flavor wafted her way. Trudy's heart thumped. Her wrists burned. She could see her hands turning white, anxious for blood.

He placed the open bag on the armrest of the couch and made sure enough chips were piled near the front of the bag and then positioned the cigarette-match-paper device near the pile. Next he pulled a shabby brown curtain away from the frosted window and let it hang over the bag of chips. The curtain's pleated valance touched the ceiling, made of faux paneling for that cabin-in-the-woods effect.

They didn't use names, but the other one was Garrett McKee, who had come into the mobile home twice and never looked her way. He had that same McKee look but was taller than Colin. His gangly frame made for awkward movements. His hair was longer than Colin's, but he had the same eyes and nose.

They were busy. They didn't answer her questions. They didn't make conversation.

She wasn't tied to anything. She could move within the confines of the greasy-floor mobile home. They came and went enough that she didn't have time to wriggle on her butt or fish-flop her way to the door and try, somehow, to open it. With her teeth?

How long did a cigarette take to burn when it wasn't being smoked?

288

Besides her burning wrists and ankles, there were other problems too.

First, they had parked her truck in the barn. The barn was a long way from the road. And who knew what other defenses they used, though maybe the evil bugs were now back in service. The barn would be hard to approach from any direction.

Second, the water truck. It had to be Allison's water truck. They seemed to be working on it. All Trudy had was a fast glance. A ladder climbed up the side, and the top was popped open. They didn't seem to care what she saw.

Trudy figured her driver must have come to town for supplies, for something, and spotted her truck, spotted her. Maybe they knew Allison was inside Budgie's Auto Repair. Maybe not. The driver must have left his vehicle in town. Maybe it was the pickup she'd spotted the first time. He had been carrying the backpack with the gun—what else was in there? Why had he gone to town?

Third, the bags of fertilizer. Not enough farm, no crops in sight down this tired stretch of sad land.

"Ready?" Her kidnapper with the cannon had a high, thin voice. She might forever be afraid of men who wore fishermen's hats. "One more ride."

FIFTY-ONE:
MONDAY LATE
AFTERNOON

"Too late for what?" Allison heard the snap in her own voice, felt the urge to lose it. Jayne flinched. Maybe she saw a minute into the future, saw the worst. Didn't like her odds.

"I don't know much," she said.

There was no need—yet.

"But you know enough," said Bloom.

"Where's Trudy?" asked Allison.

"Never met her," said Jayne. "Haven't heard of her."

"Then what the hell is going on?"

"They got plans," said Jayne. "They are leaving—like really leaving. Gone. They've been practicing. For years. I couldn't tell you where or how they are going to do it, but they've got it all set up with supplies out in the desert. They've got a bunch of them out there, and they've been loading them up and getting them ready for a long time."

"Running from what?" said Allison.

Jayne tried a smile, but it came out with tears. The tough-girl thing collapsed. "That's the part I don't know. They don't tell me nothing. Dug likes me around, you know, the obvious. He's okay. Lenny ain't as bright as he wants you to think—a couple of screws loose, I do believe. But they don't tell me nothing. Except I hear Colorado Day, and I know it's all coming down. I hear enough, you know."

"All coming down?" said Allison. "What the hell?"

"Something to do with the canyon over by Glenwood."

"Glenwood?" said Bloom.

"Sometimes I can see the problems they see," said Jayne.

"Other times?" said Allison.

"I can't hate my country as much as they do," said Jayne. "I've tried. Some of the things they say, you know. You can't keep track of all the hate. And I'm not saying the little guy doesn't get screwed, but they live in that dark place, you know. They want to be heroes to people I don't want to know."

"The map."

Allison said it out loud, found herself back inside the garage long before Jayne and Bloom followed.

The relief map covered the southern edge of the Flat Tops. Someone had handwritten the key spots along the highway as the road climbed from Glenwood Springs east—No Name Tunnel, Grizzly Creek Rest Area, Shoshone Dam, Hanging Lake Tunnel, French Creek Viaduct, Bair Ranch Rest Area. Up and down the canyon, dots of pencil and faint lines from the same pencil, maybe, and a pen.

"You two have about one minute of luck left," said Jayne. "I do not want to be here if he comes back, you know. Out of the blue."

"Where is Dug?" said Allison. The ongoing threat of his furious, imminent return was losing steam. "Where is he—right now?"

"And what's up with the empty house?" said Bloom.

Jayne's lips tightened. One teardrop erupted from her eye and raced down her cheek. Her chin shook. She glanced from Allison to Bloom and back. Allison found the tear calming. It gave her strength.

"What the—?" said Bloom but Allison put a hand up to stop.

Jayne needed no further prodding. All they had to do was wait. Another tear chased the first. Same eye. And now the other one. Allison made a point of not moving. Not a scratch or blink. Allison's racing heart found a better groove. Who had Devo found in the creek? She pictured the school bus in Rifle, the cops stopping it late at night. The driver was the guy Devo found in the creek. Lenny Brandt? Garrett McKee? Dug Hackl? Another?

Jayne struggled. She'd flipped. Allison could see it in her eyes. But she struggled.

"Something is bothering you," said Allison.

"They promised," said Jayne. Those two words needed a great deal of effort, but loosened the dam. "They promised I could go with them."

"Where?"

"They said I'm not ready," said Jayne. "I am ready."

"Where to?" said Bloom.

"They've got it all planned out—way deep into the wilds, the desert," said Jayne. "Gone. They have supplies—guns, food. You know, stored out there. They have the water all figured out. They have everything all figured out."

"Dug," said Allison. Calm reigned, but she made sure Jayne knew her patience was thin. "Where is he—right now?"

"All I know is it's all started now," said Jayne. "I know it started because they fucking left me here, and what I am supposed to do now?"

"If you were to go look," said Allison, keeping logic and reason well within reach, "where would you start right this minute?"

"I know two of them have to go straight across the Flat Tops," said Jayne. "That's the beginning. Phase One. Phase Two is everything that happens after."

"After?"

"The big event. That's what they call it."

"Horseback?" said Allison.

"Fastest way," said Jayne. "Garrett has access to horses, but I know horses ain't Dug's thing."

"Which way are they going?" Allison was already plotting the speed at which Bloom's Camry could shuttle her to Trapper's. Or wherever. She needed Sunny Boy. He would understand.

"The wilderness scares me."

"Where?" Allison practically barked it. "Which way?"

"The straightest, fastest. They did lots of trying to figure that out," said Jayne. "That's why they kept Garrett around—because he knows the Flat Tops so damned well. Like his brother."

Like his non-existent brother, thought Allison. Like his *poof adios so long farewell* brother. "Colin?"

"Well, Daniel knows his way around up there, too," said Jayne. She'd recovered some composure.

"But he lives in Denver," said Allison. "Somewhere down there." It was all one big blurry blob of city.

"Yep," said Jayne. "But that's why they needed to keep Garrett around, because he's experienced up there. He's not your guy. Who is? But Garrett is under a lot of pressure to prove himself, even though his buddy stole his girlfriend."

"You," said Bloom.

"Me," said Jayne. A moment of pride. "But then they cut me loose, left me here. Split. I'm a sucker. A fool."

"It's Dug and Lenny," said Bloom. "This is their deal?"

"You could say that," said Jayne. "Dug's the leader, that's for damn sure."

"Here's the deal," said Allison. "We are going to leave here. We aren't coming back for a long time. Could be days, could be weeks, could be longer than that. If we find out later that you knew what these guys are planning, and you didn't tell us, I will come back here and make your life miserable. I don't know how, I don't know when, but it will happen."

Jayne shook her head. "I don't know. They run around, I don't know."

"The other place? Out east?" said Bloom.

"Where they fool around," said Jayne. "But Phase One? They are long gone. All I really know is Lenny is the driver. I don't know what he's driving, but I heard that here and there. And they might need another driver too. There might be a fourth."

"Anton Hester?" said Bloom.

"That guy is a loser," said Jayne. "No way. Two horses, two vehicles. Over and over. All I heard. Two by two. Come marching in, you know, two by two. Like the ark. They had to draw straws for who was doing what, but two by two. That never changed."

FIFTY-TWO:
MONDAY NIGHT

"WE HAVE TO CLEAR the drone farm first." Bloom drove down the hill at a good clip, rolling stops at the intersections where the signs demanded more. "What if they're out there?"

"We need to get me on a horse as soon as possible," said Allison, "right after we call all this in."

"Or stop and see the cops first?" said Bloom.

"We can try." Allison's head swirled with possibilities. "If you see a Colin-shaped figure out there anywhere, would you let me know?"

"Dante Soto ran into a shit storm," said Bloom.

"And more." Allison brought out her phone. Low battery—but enough. She punched Colin's number. Voicemail. Trudy's. The same. Char?

"Still no Colin," said Char.

"Has Garrett been through?"

"Earlier," said Char.

"Doing what?"

Bloom pulled in at the sheriff's office, an entrance off the back of the courthouse. It was after hours. They might have to ring the bell or try to reach Dwyer on his cell.

"He took a couple of horses, said he was going riding later," said Char. "I guess that later would be now. Crazy to go up there with the fire still doing who knows what."

"Riding with who?" said Allison.

"You okay?" said Char. "You sound tense."

"I plead guilty," said Allison. "Was Garrett with a guy named Dug Hackl?"

"Didn't tell me," said Char. "Dug wasn't here. Not this time. Of course Garrett is welcome to borrow horses whenever he wants. Just good to see him, you know, motivated about something, getting excited."

"Did Earl make it out okay?"

"He's home," said Char. "Thanks for asking. Want me to put him on?"

"I need Colin," said Allison. "And if you know which way Garrett might decide to head?"

"This trail, that trail," said Char. "I don't pay much attention, I'm afraid."

Bloom was at the sheriff's door. He pulled it open. Allison popped the Camry door and hustled to catch up with him.

"Thanks, Char," said Allison. "Gotta run."

They found Dwyer in the cramped basement office. He looked tired. Bloom introduced himself. Allison didn't have to.

"Nothing for you." Dwyer to Bloom.

"What if we trade?" said Bloom.

Dwyer's head bobbed. As if to say, "see what you got." It took a minute to run down what they had and what they had was disjointed.

"We got that call from Devo," said Dwyer. "And by the time our deputy goes up to the place, there's no dead body, no dead body in the river and no school bus or anything strange at all. Nothing. *Nadaville*. Maybe he's getting us back. You know, from what we could tell, we don't think old Mr. Devo knows he's got a surprise waiting for him when he returns home."

"Nobody?" said Allison. "No *body*?"

"Must have been a miracle healing," said Dwyer. "Oh yeah, your pal Trudy is missing. How long? Not even twenty-four hours?"

A rhetorical cop, just what she needed.

"Anton Hester?" said Bloom.

"What about him?" said Dwyer.

"Got your man?" said Bloom.

"Yes, but the investigation is continuing," said Dwyer.

"And what next?" said Bloom.

"We continue the investigation," said Dwyer. "I don't know how it works in Glenwood Springs and down there in Garfield County, but we don't usually lay out our investigative strategy for reporters."

Back in the Camry, Allison could feel her own uncertainty and Bloom's too.

"You want to check the drone farm," said Allison.

"I want to find Trudy," said Bloom. "You know they must have spotted her—someone who chased her down. Something like that."

"But if Jayne is right, and events are already rolling—and if Char is right, and Garrett and one of his buddies already have the horses…" She let it dangle.

"I'm going to the drone farm," said Bloom. "Like, now."

Bloom wheeled the Camry past the Blue Spruce on the off chance. No truck. They didn't even bother checking inside.

The drone farm made perfect sense, even after dark. But every minute counted finding Garrett McKee and, well, there was this lingering matter of finding little brother Colin.

"I hate to even suggest it," said Allison.

"Split up?" said Bloom.

Trudy, Allison told herself, was resourceful. Fairly brave. Smart on her feet. It killed her not to look for Trudy first. Bloom was no less determined.

"Hate to say," said Allison.

"Where is Sunny Boy?" said Bloom.

"At Trapper's," said Allison. "I have a hunch the guys headed straight up Marvine Peak Trail. It's easy, even at night, puts them right in the middle of the Flat Tops, and then who knows where the hell they're going."

From Trapper's, she'd be coming in from further east, hoping to get lucky. With the fire, there wouldn't be riders up there risking themselves. Allison tried to imagine a straight line from the head of Marvine Peak Trail south to Hanging Lake, slightly southeast. The route would cut across the big Grizzly Creek drainage to Dead Horse Creek. A thirty-mile ride. What about the fire?

"One problem," said Bloom. "Getting you to Trapper's."

"Drop me there?" said Allison. "I don't think Meeker has got a Hertz."

It didn't take much figuring. It was the only way back to Trapper's, unless Allison stuck out a thumb and whatever ride came by might not get her all the way up to the lake to Sunny Boy.

Bloom stopped to top off the gas, snagged two bottles of water and a bag of beef jerky. "Loaded with chemicals," said Bloom. "Don't tell Trudy."

He headed out on the highway, turned right at County Road 8. "Doze if you can," he said. He drove hard. Allison's mind ran ahead to the ride—all the things she didn't have. She'd have to find more water around Trapper's and nibbles of something for nourishment. Sunny Boy would need feed. He couldn't go two days straight. Or all night. Wake Nora? How else? She'd be damn lucky to be anywhere close to Marvine Peak Trail by dawn. She had to take it one step at a time, gauge the fire. In the distance, in her mind, she imagined the fire licking treetops. Those orange lollipops. *That sound.*

She closed her eyes. She told every stupid "what if" question that surfaced to go back to its damn hole and stay there. Some wouldn't stay put. She slipped below the surface for a minute here, a minute there. She felt the curves of the canyon. Bloom found an AM Radio station out of Denver, and she half-listened to the national talk show, *Coast to Coast.* The subject tonight was increasing your sensitivity and awareness to the energy fields around you. The host took it all very seriously. Trudy would have taken it very seriously. Allison tried. She slipped in and out of consciousness. The smoky night air and the radio chatter whirled together with her thoughts—Jayne, Glenwood Canyon, Colin, Trudy, the map, the empty house, the desert caches for Dug and Lenny and maybe Garrett. There was Devo and the guy who was in the water but was gone when the cops got there. The whacky bus and Devo's description of the retrofit. She flashed on Revelations. Perfect fodder for a Doomsday freak. Phase One. Phase Fucking Two. Was Jayne telling the truth? Maybe they should have gone up the other side of the river to see if there was any action at Lenny Brandt's place, just to make sure.

The threads of information spun and tangled. As soon as she went to grab one, it jerked up higher and out of reach. She needed the threads to braid together, show her how they fit.

Bloom punched the Camry to its limits. Allison pretended to put her head back but kept her eyes open a crack, sure that a buck would leap out and the next thing she'd see would be the windshield blowing apart and the deer smashing in bloody bits. The fire had chased the critters down. You didn't need to tap some unseen energy to know the wilderness was in shock mode. All creatures great and small scrambled for new homes, new turf, new ways, new neighbors and, most importantly, new prey.

"Can't," she said. Sitting up.

"You tried," said Bloom. "I'm afraid you've got a long night ahead of you."

"You too."

"I was looking at the map earlier," said Bloom. "I'm going to cut across the field on foot."

"Some of those preppers," said Allison. "Booby traps and trip wires."

"Do I have a choice?"

Ahead, the McKee Ranch—much sooner than she expected. They were much further upriver than she realized. Maybe she had dozed.

"Slow down," said Allison.

She pictured Earl back home and wasn't sure she was ready to see him again. Should she call Char again to see if she'd pick up? Would anything have changed? She said she would have Colin call if he turned up.

Bloom pulled to a full stop at the top of the long road that led down to the house, one dim light on the porch, another in an upstairs window. Allison didn't have to ask the time. It was pushing 11:00 p.m. She could smell dank smoke and the bitter blackened forest, like an old campfire times one billion. Her gaze followed the road out to the barn, where the lights were brighter than the house.

"Down there." She pointed.

Bloom didn't hesitate. The Camry bounced the quarter-mile across. Shadows of cattle, black against black. Eau de earthiness and real bullshit brewed with smoke. She caught a glint off the magic livestock tank, the one that brought her a flash of temporary fame among the McKee clan. She wondered if they all wouldn't be a lot better off had they let the whole thing burn to rubble. No punch-out of the sheriff's deputy. But a burned-down McKee house wouldn't have changed Devo's discovery. It wouldn't have caused the cancellation of Phase One or Phase Two. What the hell?

Bloom pulled the Camry in a circle, so she had to look through Bloom's open window to see down the gullet of the well-lit barn. A long way down, one man stood from a crouch. He lifted a rifle that looked as big as a rocket launcher. It was Colin.

FIFTY-THREE:
MONDAY NIGHT

WRISTS TIED, IN PAIN. Ankles tied, burning. And duct tape over the mouth.

Kind of cliché, Trudy wanted to say. *Don't you think?*

She suppressed panic. Tried to keep her wits.

She had to keep her wits.

It was a requirement.

They had her lie down on her side. Then the wrists were lashed to the legs of one seat on the bus and her ankles lashed on the other side. Her hands were tucked back behind her, up high. She couldn't straighten her legs. The urge to pee rose—and faded. She assumed the hunger pang was more about nerves than real need. She rode on a metal surface—right leg, right hip, right chest, right shoulder all slammed down. Her hips ached, her ankles throbbed.

They were waiting a long time. An hour? Two? She guessed it had been at least two. She had been alone for two hours, lashed up in the bus. Two hours to think of options. Two hours to think of things to say.

They let her lie there, alone.

"Let me ask one question," she said when the driver showed up. With the duct tape, of course, it didn't come out well.

It didn't come out at all.

"What was that?"

There was a light on in the bus, enough to see it was a new guy. He had a sharply cut Fu Manchu but hadn't shaved in days.

"Let me ask one question," she said again behind the duct tape. Could he sense her calm disposition?

She had a hunch the new guy was alone. It had been a couple hours, at least, and nobody had been coming and going. She heard the water truck pull out, seen the blast from its headlights illuminate her cage, this strange school bus with one row of seats on each side running down.

He pulled the duct tape up. Her lips burned.

He didn't take it all the way off. She could feel the piece flopping against her cheek and she tried a small smile.

"What was that?" he said again.

"I want to ask one question," she said.

"Make it good."

"I wonder," said Trudy. "If you know that this isn't going to work? That my friends right now are telling the sheriff everything, and they are on the way out here right now. Your best bet is to stop now and deal with things the way they are. You haven't really done anything yet…"

The tape went back on. He pressed hard and shook his head.

"Jesus," he said. He went back to the driver's seat.

She heard the bus rumble to life and start to move.

He looked up in the overhead mirror and stared at her, shaking his head.

FIFTY-FOUR: MONDAY NIGHT

"WHAT THE HELL?"

She muttered it to herself, opened her door out of instinct and walked around the front, holding up her hands in the "stop" motion, elbows locked.

What were her hands going to do?

Colin...

Was she that bad a judge? With a gun that size, they'd be blown to smithereens.

"What the hell?" Colin shouted. "Scared the crap out of me." He lowered the rocket-launcher or whatever it was.

"I might ask you the same fucking question."

She sensed Bloom behind her. She felt the tingle of adrenaline firing her nerves as she walked. The scene went flippy-floppy. Blurred. Maybe she was tapping invisible energy.

Colin grinned. "God, it's you."

She couldn't force a grin if she tried.

"Can you put that gun, or whatever it is, all the way down so we don't blow a hole in the roof?" said Allison.

The interior of the barn was dark, stalls up and down both sides and Allison sensed the presence of the horses. One muffled snort. A heavy blow from another. She kept her gaze locked on Colin, who stood behind an open storage closet, the door about chest high.

"Check this out," he said, as he pointed inside. He put the gun down. "Duncan—how are you?" he said.

She'd never seen him this nervous.

"I know what you're going to say," said Colin.

"No you don't," said Allison.

"Like where have I been," said Colin.

"For starters," said Allison. She stood right up next to him. "You said it was Char that called."

"What?" said Colin. Did he expect her to be clueless? "When?"

"At the courthouse. Earlier. You stepped away, said Char called because Earl was going to have his bail hearing. But it wasn't Char. She hasn't seen or heard from you in days. In *days*," said Allison. "You're right here at your own house and don't stop to say hello?"

"Maybe—" Colin started to say.

"Who was on the fucking phone?" said Allison. "And what the hell are you doing?"

She glanced into the storage, a neat row of rifles standing on their butts—twenty? Thirty? A military vibe to most of them—assault weapons with the fat magazines, flash hiders, metal where there should be wood stocks.

"Goddamn armory," said Bloom, taking a closer look.

Allison wanted Colin to answer.

"Loaded for bear." Bloom was in awe. He pulled out another weapon to inspect it. "Somebody sunk a fortune."

"It wasn't Char," said Colin.

"No shit," said Allison.

"It wasn't anyone."

"What the hell?"

"I know Garrett is in some stuff."

"No shit," said Bloom.

"I needed time," said Colin. "I've been trying to find him—he's getting sucked into something bad, and I want to keep you from the mess, the whole thing, all the fucked-up stuff he's dealing with."

"You answered your phone," said Allison.

"So?" said Colin. "I was trying to buy time. There was no ring."

The little faker. She could add actor to his talents, if she cared about the list any longer.

"What mess?" said Allison. "Where did Garrett go? And who is he with?"

"Wait," said Colin. "You think I'm doing something to *help* him?"

"If you didn't tell me about this mess, as you call it, you may as well be." Her voice rose. She found herself a step closer, and she'd practically been hat to hat already. "You think that I expect your brothers to be McKee brother clones of you? You think I couldn't handle it?"

"He's part chameleon," said Colin. "He can change colors on a dime. It's whoever wants him in his club."

"Lenny Brandt," said Allison.

"Dug Hackl," said Bloom.

"Them," said Colin. "At least this week. Garrett can get awfully riled up, you know."

"Where is he?"

"He wouldn't tell me," said Colin. "But he seemed so damn happy that I know something is off. Something's wrong."

"Where did you see him?"

"I ran into him when we split up," said Colin. "I came down, and he was out here in the barn. I came out to muck the stalls and check the horses. He wouldn't say much except he was high. Even though I know he doesn't touch drugs or anything like that—his own system produces enough. He knows he's wired funny, and that stuff whacks him out even harder. He wouldn't say a thing. He just kept boasting. Said an opportunity had come along and, yeah, he mentioned Lenny Brandt."

"He was poking around back here in this storage?" said Bloom.

"That's the thing. He didn't say squat about anything. He was putting some of this hay in his pickup, the weed-free stuff. And he was heading up to the woods, but he wouldn't say when or what for."

"Woods?" said Bloom.

"Flat Tops," said Colin. "Same thing to Garrett."

"That was Friday," said Allison. "I headed back up to get Devo on Friday." How she pulled the day of the week out of her ass, she might never know.

"Yep," said Colin.

"And all weekend?" said Allison.

"Like I said, I was helping a friend move cattle when I ran into Garrett again at the hardware store. We needed a part for a hinge on a gate."

"When was that?" Snap to her tone.

"Sunday, mid-afternoon."

"Alone?" said Bloom.

"Nope," said Colin. "Some guy I'd never seen before."

"And?"

"White guy. He looked real young, I don't know. Early twenties. Powerful looking guy. White guy, yeah, but his face looked greasy like he'd been up hunting, which, of course it's not the season. He looked drained, sweaty. Well. It's so early. He was tall, six-two maybe. Six-four?"

"Gray mesh shirt?" said Allison

Colin did a double take.

"What did Garrett say?" said Allison.

"Not much," said Colin. "Same shit-eating grin, still flying high."

"His pal?" said Bloom.

"Didn't get an introduction," said Colin. "How did you know about the shirt?"

"The guy the cops have in jail, Anton Hester?" said Bloom. "The guy Devo ID'd? Based on the mug shot I saw, that's a long way from blond hair."

"I heard about the Anton Hester arrest," said Colin. "He another run-about loser. Couple years ahead of me. A high school dropout bottom-feeder."

"Careful," said Allison. "You sound like your dad."

"Sorry." Colin offered an ever-so-faint smile. Looking for an inch. She gave him a resting bitch face.

"But Devo picked him out," said Bloom.

Allison pictured Devo in the room, flipping through photos while the cops milled around waiting for him to say "ta-da." It wasn't hard to imagine Devo figuring an easy way to get them to leave him alone, to put down their guard while he slipped away.

Was there a test she could run to check Colin's *bonafides*? Would good faith show up in his DNA? Allison was willing to take a blood sample the hard way if that would work. Maybe she'd be able to taste it if she chomped on his neck.

"Garrett asked about you," said Colin.

"What?"

"He'd heard you were the one to go back and bring Devo in," said Colin. "You know, bring him down. He asked if there was a chance you might join the crew up there, give up the city life. He thought it was real funny. Laughed at it, for real. His friend didn't think it was so amusing."

"His friend say anything?"

"Yeah. His friend said 'let's go.' That was it. Never broke a scowl."

Garrett's riding partner came into view. Soto's killer. Devo's attacker.

Two by two.

"The shirt matches how Devo described him," said Allison. "Size. Height. Except when Devo saw him he was carrying an axe."

"Soto," said Colin. "His shoulder. By the way, how is Trudy?"

Maybe that was his *bonafides*. He cared enough to ask.

Allison felt the clock. *Tick-tick. Tick-tick-tick.* Time eating itself. Relentless.

"We can't find her," said Bloom.

Colin's horse took in a sharp breath and his face contorted to genuine worry. "The hell?" he said. "Where was she last?"

Allison went through the whole thing. Kenyon. Budgie's Auto Repair. The truck. And then the vast void where the truck was once parked.

"I'm going out to Dug Hackl's place," said Bloom. It took him a minute to describe the location, why they thought it was a problem. Why they thought it needed to be checked. "First thing is to get Allison back on Sunny Boy at Trapper's."

"Go," said Colin to Bloom. "Get out there. Now. I'll take her to Trapper's. That is, if she trusts me enough to let me drive."

FIFTY-FIVE:
MONDAY NIGHT

TRUDY FELT EACH WAVE of the roller coaster.

The bus inched along. No big rush, no big hurry, no chance of sliding off. *Crept* was more like it.

He'd enjoy it more if she struggled. The ropes were solid, and the knots were tight. There would be no point in struggling, only agony.

She took an inventory of *now*.

Allison had taught her this. She had described a long, wet hike after Sunny Boy had been cut loose when she was following the trapline bunch. Yes, it sucked. Yes, it wasn't ideal. Yes, it was uncomfortable. Yes, various things hurt, including her ankles, wrists, and hips. Yes, there was pain, but she was alive. She had her head. She had her eyes. She had her wits if she chose to use them.

She wouldn't think about Duncan. Or Allison. Or Colin. Or Sweetwater. Or her business. Or her team. Or Dante Soto. She wouldn't think about anything but now. If she kept her wits, she could look for an opening—any opportunity.

The roller coasters ended.

If it was possible, the bus slowed even more, came to a stop.

The dashboard lights put a slice of his cold eyes in the overhead mirror, and she watched as he looked right, looked left, and then right again.

He waited for a minute. Then the bus roared, and he pulled out like he owned the world.

FIFTY-SIX:
TUESDAY EARLY MORNING

THEY ROUSTED NORA. SHE woke like it was dawn and time to make coffee.

Nora gave Colin a horse named Ella. "Fearless," said Nora. "Strong like a bull."

It was 2:00 a.m.

"You called the cops?" said Nora. It was smoky dark. The night was still. Nora operated like it was midday.

Ella was a chocolate mare with a flax mane and tail. Allison stroked her cheek, patted her muzzle.

Colin kept his head down, helped Nora. Lodge light caught the edge of their launch pad.

"There's a million ways to get across." Nora had likely ridden every one. "You'll need one other thing."

She returned a minute later, and Allison started to protest but thought better of it.

"It's a Kimber," said Nora. The rifle came with a scope and, of course, Nora had a scabbard to go with it. "You know, strictly for the bears. You never know." A box of cartridges for her and a Smith & Wesson revolver for Colin.

"I'm good," said Colin. He waved it off. "But thank you."

"I'll take it," said Allison. The sight of the stash in the McKee barn was still fresh in her mind.

They were ready.

Allison knew the route around to Marvine Peak Trail. It was her best guess. Garrett hadn't told Colin a thing. On the long, torturous ride up, she had pressed him for any detail. Any overlooked scrap of Garrett insight or wisdom. Allison played the hard ass. She was the wronged, the hurt. It wasn't a hard role to muster.

Everything Colin said lined up, but she couldn't cave.

Nora scampered for headlamps, water, sandwiches, homemade elk jerky. A whole sleeve of Fig Newton's. "Your favorite," she said. "It's a long way across. Pace yourselves. Ella knows the trails."

Allison didn't want to make it all the way across—she wanted to catch up with Garrett and Mr. Axe long before their destination.

They circled Trapper's Lake in silence. Ella took the lead. Sunny Boy trusted Ella, sensed her knowledge. He kept up through the sections of the trail still recovering from the Big Fish Fire where the forest was open and even when it started to close down. They climbed up and around to skirt Big Marvine Peak. The first hour slipped by. It felt good to be back on a horse—back on Sunny Boy. She imagined him equally thrilled, sunshine or no. Allison tried to breathe. It wasn't the smoke—it was her pissed self she was trying to exorcise.

Allison studied the space that was Colin's back, up ahead in the blackness. She would have to relent at some point. Or would she? His gesture was noble. In a way, it was protective. She tried to imagine what she would have done, and she couldn't be sure. Her family was stable, boring even. A source of normalcy, back there in Iowa. She had no idea what it would be like to have family members who had flown off the rails. Who were unpredictable or desperate. She imagined that Jayne, to Garrett, had been a step up. A chance. She represented hope, and she had slid across the dance floor to Dug Hackl. That's the way of the world. Allison tried to think about what would keep Garrett in the loop, having been jilted and left there by the likes of Jayne? Something had kept him in the Brandt-Hackl orbit, and it had to be substantial. Meaty. Maybe he was used to seeing girls slip away, out of his grasp. Maybe it was a familiar feeling. Maybe, in Meeker, there weren't many other places to go.

"We got a plan?"

A voice from ahead.

A voice trying to find a bridge, a way back. There was a toll on the bridge. But even Allison didn't know the fare. The price fluctuated wildly.

The complicating factor was fatigue.

"Maybe we wait until dawn," said Colin, reading her mind. Did the unctuous cowboy think he knew her? "See if we can pick up any signs in the morning. I'd hate to run straight over a sign."

"At the junction with Marvine Peak," said Allison.

She sounded authoritative. Decisive. Leader-like.

"You as whipped as me?"

"Been a long day," said Allison. "For sure."

"Then we take it easy," said Colin. "Let daylight be our friend. We don't want to get trapped down in a spot with the fire. And we don't want to come stumbling across Garrett and his buddy."

The simple dream of laying down brought a jolt of pleasure. It didn't jibe with the ever-accelerating clock in her head, the one that made each tick shorter than the last, but she couldn't argue with Colin's logic.

Colin flipped on his headlamp, found a clearing.

Sleeping bags rolled out.

Saddles off the horses, a tree post for each. Room to graze.

This summer, night rains weren't an issue. They glugged some water, shared the same bottle. Allison drifted off for a pee. No announcement needed. This was their routine, like an old married couple getting ready for bed, he headed out in the direction of his sleeping bag. She headed off to hers.

She walked further this time, just because.

She breathed as hard as she could, sucking up her ire and trying to let it go.

Trying, but not succeeding.

Picking her way back, she saw Colin sitting cross-legged on his sleeping bag. His headlamp pointed down to a spot about a foot in front of him. In the center of the spot sat two plastic coffee cups. He drizzled a teaspoon of liquid on top of what was already in the cup. When he was done, he rolled lime in his palms to excite the juices and then sliced off a wedge. He squeezed it over the cup and repeated the process for the second cup.

She matched his cross-legged pose on her sleeping bag. Smoke choked the night air. Four stars struggled to assert themselves but weren't having much luck.

We're still up here. The universe is a big fucking place.

You're fire ain't jack compared to ours.

Love is hard to find.

"I deserved it," said Colin. He held up a cup for her and she sniffed it—honey, citrus, woodiness. "I know."

They thudded plastic cups and sipped.

He put a hand on her thigh, and she didn't push it away.

"You've got a gun?" she said. Colin took a sip of his drink. "I borrowed a little something from my brother's stash."

FIFTY-SEVEN:
TUESDAY EARLY MORNING

THE PLACE LOOKED DEAD, but how would he know?

It was zero dark thirty. It was nobody's time. They could all be in there, sleeping. Bloom imagined the bozos all passed out, caricatures of themselves. Drugs and drinking. A stench of self-assurance. Maybe some pot, though the whole Lenny Brandt religion thing probably wouldn't go for that.

Bloom had waited in the dark, scanning the place with binoculars borrowed from the night clerk at the Blue Spruce, who had to be dinged to the counter using the call service bell. "Rocky Mountain Raptors," she said by way of explanation that her pair of binoculars was so handy. "Those birds built this country."

He'd left a crisp twenty for her troubles, promised to get the binoculars back.

He could see a faint, steady glow at the end of the long driveway. The plan was to circle around on foot, through the god-knows-what kind of field. Blackness. At least it was all dry.

Circle around, why?

He peered into the darkness. The faint glow filled a small portion of his field of vision. Details were impossible beyond a sort-of house on the right and a barn, or something, on the left. From his angle, the house looked more like two or maybe three low mobile homes side-by-side, maybe connected somehow in a way he couldn't quite make out. Too many maybes, not enough detail. Not one straight line. The whole thing sagged. Weeds and bramble had no enemies.

The place looked—

Wait.

A figure crossed the opening between the buildings.

Walking…

Headlights popped on from the barn, and they wasted no time, picking up steam and charging hard up the road. The headlights were up high, wide, definitely from a truck.

Bloom had his window down—the cool night air was necessary, despite the smoke—and he could hear the gears.

Shifting. Quickly. Hard. Growling.

It roared up the road, and Bloom realized his vulnerable spot.

He couldn't snap on his headlights now, in order to hide behind their glare. It would be too obvious. He couldn't, out of the blackness, start driving. And he didn't have time to turn around without using his headlights—he would risk running into the ditch.

Better would be a stalled old piece-of-shit Camry. An empty stalled old piece-of-shit Camry.

Bloom popped the door before the truck made the corner. He rolled out and flattened himself on the road. He pulled the door shut above him. He tucked himself underneath the carriage, and he could see the truck coming his way, picking up steam.

And braking. The brakes squealed and hissed.

A wave of dust washed over the Camry, flew into his eyes, shoved grit down his throat, and a door opened.

Holy hell.

Would his pounding heart resonate off the dirt? The truck's engine pinged and hummed—nice cover.

Boots on the ground—*right there*—and Bloom saw the flashlight beam flicker and dance on the dirt. He wondered what signs, if any, he had left inside. He felt the binoculars clutched in his hand and thanked his lucky fucking stars.

What else? Sunflower seeds, burger wrappers, a notebook—he couldn't be sure.

The boots turned and ambled back. He half-expected to see the boots turn around again and some asshole squat, to peer under the car. It didn't happen. Door shuts. Engine revs. Truck in motion.

Bloom gave it an extra moment, rolled out and sat up. Touched his racing heart.

He stared off down the road at the fading shape of the rear lights, the two top ones closer together than the bottom two. All four were red.

The water truck.

Bloom waited to stand, to make sure there was no strange movement or shadow in the guy's rearview.

He shook the dust off, spat in the field to get the sand out of his mouth. At least, the first layer. He glugged water and rinsed his mouth, wiped his eyes.

He looked back at the drone farm and raised the binoculars again, steadying his hands.

The view reverted to its dead self, though Bloom had lost confidence in his ability to gauge what was happening at the end of the road. Whatever lick of tiredness he had felt between the McKee

Ranch and downtown Meeker and driving out here had vanished in a surge of adrenaline.

Screw it.

Trudy...

He snapped the Camry to life, gunned the car to the top of the road heading down to the drone farm.

As he turned the corner, he didn't need binoculars to see a bloom of orange flame flickering in the window of the house, or whatever it was.

FIFTY-EIGHT:
TUESDAY EARLY MORNING

FLAMES LAPPED AT THE ceiling and flared at the fresh rush of oxygen. The curtains billowed in swells of fire. The cheap sofa burned across the top like a picture-perfect campfire log, the seat cushions yet to get in on the action.

The air carried a whiff of potato chips; grease. The fire cooked hardest on the right armrest of the sofa, where it must have started. A blackened pile of—what?—burned merrily. The front room was empty, and Bloom skipped past the flames to two back bedrooms—cheap old mattresses on the floor, piles of crap and clothes, magazines scattered around, no time for an inventory—and a pint-size bathroom. The next two trailers were all open affairs, scummy and clutter-filled. Lots of crap. No people.

It was all old, sad, and filthy.

Outside, Bloom moved the Camry closer to the barn, left the engine running and blasted his headlights into the barn.

Trudy's truck stared back at him, parked about forty feet back from the front of the barn.

Trudy ...

Behind him, fat angry flames filled the mobile home. A window shattered and fire chewed the walls.

The cab of Trudy's truck sat empty.

Figuring out the latches and sliding locks on the back took a furious minute, but the doors finally popped open. Empty.

"Trudy!" he shouted. Then he ran. He yelled her name twice more, a sound coming out of his chest he'd never heard before, as much volume as he could muster fueled by gut-level panic. He squelched the urge to vomit.

The barn, more like an auto mechanic's paradise than a place for animals or ranch work, was dead. He checked the truck again—no keys. Rolling it outside might save it.

The mobile home spat orange jets.

A bucket and water? Or a hose? A fire extinguisher? It was hopeless. There was one good thing. Down here in the scruffy and treeless butt-end of scrubland, the chances of starting another forest fire seemed remote.

A thudding explosion buckled Bloom at the knees. Flames shot up, stretched up, twice the height of the mobile home. The home's cheap, dry wood popped and crunched under the assault. An invisible giant snapped two-by-fours over his thigh. The sky filled with swarms of crackling fireflies and a surging fountain of sparks pumped straight up into the breezeless dark.

His cell phone coughed up a weak signal.

"Yes, I'll wait here—or as close as I can." The signal was spotty. The roaring fire didn't help.

The fire, at least, was illuminating more of the area around the barn and the home, and he peered off into the moonscape scrub.

Another explosion thumped Bloom's chest. His ears squealed at a mean frequency. The shower of sparks surged and thickened. The walls of the first trailer caved in on each other. Shuddering sheets of raw heat threatened to knock him down. He could forge steel. The second trailer was starting to go.

He popped back inside the Camry, door handle like a stove top.

He drove to the county road, where he could wait and flash the approaching fire trucks. Or truck. An all-volunteer department, if Bloom remembered correctly. Bloom guessed it would be thirty minutes, maybe more.

In the distance, the roof of the barn burned. From Bloom's angle it was like a neat orange parallelogram floating in the black sky.

FIFTY-NINE: TUESDAY MORNING

No cell. No surprise. Allison knew the routine up here, but she had to check. It wouldn't hurt to find a National Forest—somebody on the line to see if they could get a read on the fire, some indication. She would hate to be walking into a fire trap. She knew that routine. She wouldn't mind a call to or from Bloom to see how things went.

Trudy.

It was dawn. They had awakened at the same time. Allison, at least, had slept like she was shot with anesthetic. She had travelled to a dark hole and burrowed down inside, and then, blink, she was awake.

They had camped along the Oyster Lake Trail in a section of pothole lakes and stunted willows. The Oyster Lake Trail, the longest on the Flat Tops, started near Buford and cut a meandering path through the northern heart of the wilderness. They had camped by Twin Lakes—so named because one was three times the size as the other and the big one was ovalish, and the smaller one was shaped like an arrowhead. Must have been somebody's idea of humor. Behind them, to the east, Trappers Peak soared to 12,000 feet and, closer, Big Marvine Peak stood about as high. Dull apricot haze coated the dawn. Allison fixed up her kerchief as a filter over her mouth. How much ash had she ingested in the past four days?

The way she figured it, Garrett and Mr. Axe had three options. Marvine Peak, Ute Creek, or Oyster Lake Trails. All three options would bring them to the intersection at Doe Creek Trail, no more than a quarter mile west of their campsite.

From there, they had access to all points south. Of course Garrett and Mr. Axe could take one of many trails south once they'd climbed up on the plateau. But Allison guessed they wanted to stay as far east as possible, due to the fire. That would mean Marvine Peak straight into Doe Creek and a straight run to the south. There were dozens of options, but the fire, in this case, might be their friend. It might limit the options of their prey.

If Garrett and Mr. Axe had ridden all night, they would have slipped south already. If they had kept a more reasonable pace, she and Colin might have beaten them to the crossroads.

Colin led the horses to a pocket lake and gave them the option to drink. This was routine—water them up when possible.

Conversation took a backseat to gestures and punctuated questions.

"Fig Newton?"

"Apple?"

"Your phone getting a signal?"

Colin took two of the cookies and half the apple after she sliced one open. His phone was as useless as a skipping stone, like her own.

"Garrett have any preferences?" said Allison. "Favorite routes?"

Questions like those two might lead to a full-blown verbal exchange.

"And all you've got is that map on the wall of the garage?"

"And Jayne's confidence that something involved Glenwood Canyon. Lots of dots and marks around Hanging Lake," said Allison. "Around there."

"He knows the fastest ways across," said Colin. "Sort of a matter of which way the fire blows, I suppose."

"I'm thinking Doe Creek," said Allison.

"To wait?" said Colin. "Or chase?"

"First, let's see if we spot a sign. Anything," said Allison. "There can't be too many others up here."

"None foolish enough," said Colin.

The Marvin Peak Trail turnoff came first. It was another hundred yards to where the Doe Creek Trail headed south so, briefly, travelers heading north or south spent a minute or two on Oyster Lake Trail. The two trails looked like they lined up on some maps, but no.

"Fifteen minutes," said Allison.

Against her better judgment, she let Colin go. He would scout back up Marvine Peak Trail no farther than where it started heading down toward Marvine Lake at the headwaters of the creek. The first stretch was all open plateau.

She would go the same distance down Doe Creek. And then they would meet up again back at the Doe Creek intersection with Oyster Lake.

In theory.

Allison preferred to walk. Colin, with eyes like a Pentagon satellite, could spot stuff from the saddle.

She tied Sunny Boy to a tree. Their tight group of four mammals was split in three. Leaving Sunny Boy was also not taken for granted—she had once returned to such a spot to find his rope cut and no trace of her horse. She would never forget the rest of that afternoon, slogging through a pounding rainstorm until Colin had popped up on the horizon like an apparition. Sunny Boy, heading back to his barn on his own radar, had been found and secured by a pair of hikers.

The best thing, she knew, was to not focus on Colin. How much would she punish him for trying to protect her from a crazy sibling and his loosely defined crew?

A shot of rain overnight or the previous day would have been perfect, to soften the trail, to allow the earth to give under the weight of a couple horses. Rain? This summer? It might never rain again, the way it felt. A smoky reminder with each inhale. Sitting on a rock, cross-legged, she pointed her binoculars up the trail, which climbed up to a wide saddle at the edge of an unnamed butte. She was a thousand feet below the summit of Big Marvine Peak, over her right shoulder, but the top of this plateau was likely 10,000 feet in elevation. Right at home. The haze chopped the vistas in half, but she felt wonderfully small. She focused first on the farthest spot on the horizon. She caught a blurry flash of horse flesh and the shape of a rider. In her binocular-extended view, they were the equivalent of out of the corner of her eye, not dead-center. The motion took a second to process, to hold its hand up and say "over here." And then it was gone. It was half image, half feeling. But it was there. She tried closing her eyes to replay the loop, slow it down. It was a bay. The rider wore a cowboy hat with a rolled-up brim. The horse was moving with purpose. The loop lasted a second or less. She followed the trail back through the binoculars, keen for any bobbing horse or similar flash, her system now perked up on a surge of adrenaline as sweet as strong black coffee.

On her knees, Allison did a piss-poor downward dog. She stretched her back and cocked her head to see if the morning light would catch fresh tracks. She side-headed her view at dirt level. Strong sunlight, a dependable commodity most summer mornings, would have been welcome. Instead, she got weak sunlight filtered through ash and haze. Walking on sunshine, in fact, might just be possible with this chunky air.

There were plenty of crusty tracks, both horse and human, but most were faint and ancient—but not all.

She picked up a fresh set, one right and one left with sharper definition, the edges less windblown where the hard soil had succumbed to recent weight. She stood to see the pattern and picked the set, the right hind leg stepping beyond the impression from the right front leg, and she worked her way down until she found eight sets of prints she liked—even and recent wear in the chalky, dry dirt. There were two distinct horse tracks. The trail turned to single-track width, which meant nose-to-tail riding. But eight hooves didn't take up that much room as long as the fresh ones could be sorted from all the others.

"We're chasers," said Colin. It had been fifteen minutes on the nose. He arrived grim-faced, matter-of-fact. He knew she'd seen the same news bulletin in the dirt.

"Agreed," said Allison.

"They must have camped somewhere too," said Colin. "Afternoon start yesterday, crack of dawn today."

"I caught a flash of one horse through the binoculars," said Allison.

"Color?" said Colin.

"Chestnut, black tail."

"Could be Taz."

"One of yours?"

"Garrett doesn't have many favorite things," said Colin. "But Taz is one of them. That horse is quirky like him."

"Rolled-up brim on his hat," said Allison.

Colin nodded. "Garrett's thing."

Back on their horses, they crossed Doe Creek and climbed the low saddle. Wildflowers did their best, given the conditions, to perk up the scenery.

As the trail topped the saddle, they tied their horses to willows and snuck up on foot to the top and glassed the trail ahead. The plateau fell away. The trail cut west and hugged the woods. The binoculars turned up nothing human or horse.

The first two miles stretched out over the top of the broad plateau. They peered into the woods. The trail pulled them down. The creek cut its own canyon where it would join the South Fork of the White River. Their trail brought them to the head of the next canyon east. From the top, they repeated the binocular time maneuver, sneaking up on foot to avoid putting two silhouettes against the sky.

About halfway down, two horses moved at a hearty walk. The bay was in back, following a gray, slightly larger horse.

"I can't see detail." Colin whispered his first words in an hour.

"Ditto," said Allison.

This time, they had three whole minutes to pick up what they could, but even in the zoomed-in view, the four mammals were only specks.

They watched until the horses rounded a corner. They were there one second and gone the next.

In fact, Allison had no idea what she was going to do and how she was going to do it or where she would pick her moment. At this pace, if they kept moving all day, they'd be deep in the southern flanks of the wilderness, maybe close the canyon by dusk. It would depend how much they stopped whether the horses would get breaks.

A long afternoon nap would be perfect. Or if they could sleep somewhere tonight.

With this much light, even with the diffused version of sunshine, they couldn't just ride up behind the two riders, tap them on the shoulder and say "Excuse me." Without any discussion, they climbed back on their horses and started picking their way down the canyon.

There was no rush. Surprise belonged to them.

SIXTY:
TUESDAY MORNING

BLOOM PLED WITH THE sheriff's office for a jailhouse interview with Anton Hester. They wouldn't consider it. He wasted an hour trying. Maybe, they said, after Hester was arraigned. But they couldn't guarantee it. *Come back another day.* They claimed he didn't have a lawyer, either, or a public defender assigned.

Bloom argued that it was Hester's decision. The cops didn't budge. And, besides, the fire in the woods. Always the fire. They were stretched thin, yada this and yada that. What did whatever was happening up in the woods have to do with opening a door and letting two people have a conversation?

Anton Hester's version of events would have been interesting to hear, to see what he knew about where Dante Soto had been killed, how the fire had been lit. And why. Did Anton Hester know Lenny Brandt or Dug Hackl? Did he know what they were up to? Bloom was sure he could write a story saying the cops had the wrong guy in jail.

For his part, Bloom could do nothing but drive around. He kept his eyes out for Trudy's truck—yet there was no truck to find. By the time the fire truck had arrived at the drone farm, he had watched it burn for a half hour, and he had seen the explosions when the fire found the fuel tanks on Trudy's truck and the other vehicles too. Neighbors had gathered on the county road. It was a spectacle. The interviews with sheriff deputies had lasted for a couple of hours. He was reacquainted with Deputy Chris Bankston, whom he had met on the road to Dante Soto's yurt, it seemed, about a month ago.

Deputy Bankston absorbed it all. School bus descriptions. Water truck descriptions. They issued a bulletin about the missing Trudy Heath. Bankston expressed interest in talking with Garrett McKee, Dug Hackl, and Lenny Brandt and said they would most likely be opening a formal investigation. "But we have a guy who confessed," said Bankston.

Bloom drove. It was late morning. He called Coogan on speed dial, taking the time to lay it all out.

"Jesus," said Coogan. "Do whatever you need to do. Nothing else matters."

"There's some weird shit going on. I don't mind saying that I have never been quite as worried about someone as I am right now." Bloom's voice sounded unsteady, dry. In fact, He could go blocks without seeing anything. He had driven the main drag several times, one end to the other on the highway, and found his mind straying to terror.

"She must have been in the truck at some point," said Coogan.

"And might have been in the water truck that went right past me," said Bloom. "The cops know what vehicles to look for and some of the signs point at Glenwood Canyon. We spotted this one map in the house of Dug Hackl's girlfriend, and it was all about the canyon."

"Jesus," said Coogan.

"The cops here said they would alert the cops down your way," said Bloom. "Just damn hard to tell what they think of my info. *Fuck*. It's right there, but we can't get our hands around it. And the weapons, the drones—these people have money but nobody freaking works."

———

There was only one dentist in Meeker, which made it easier. The "office," a converted house, was three blocks east of the medical center.

Erica Cross, the receptionist, asked him to wait for her outside. She had a lunch break in twenty minutes.

"I've never talked to a reporter." Erica didn't seem unhappy about the prospect. There was something upbeat about her presence. She was easy to spot from her Facebook profile pictures, shorter than Bloom had pictured but just as youthful. Bloom had to remind himself she was the mother of two kids. Curly brunette hair tumbled to her shoulders. Her eyes were green.

"I'm not doing a story right this second," said Bloom. "I'm looking for a friend and I think Lenny might know something."

"Friend of yours?"

He mentioned Trudy's name but it didn't have any impact.

"I'm sorry," she said. She slumped in sympathy, as if searching for a suggestion where he might look. She wore white slacks like a nurse and a pink smock with a medical vibe. She looked air-brushed, immune to the infestation of smoke.

"Do you know where Lenny is? I think he might be able to help."

"I'm afraid that I don't," she said. "Lenny and I broke up a couple of weeks ago."

"I'm sorry to hear that."

Jayne had been abandoned. Now Erica? Bloom's chainsaw stomach still churned, but at least he was doing something. Finding Cross seemed like a natural loop to close.

"May I ask, without prying, what happened?"

"Do you think it's related?"

They were standing on the sidewalk. The weary sky continued to digest an endless supply of smoke. Where was it all going?

"It might be," said Bloom.

"It was between him and me," said Cross.

"Like I said, I'm not doing a story." He was sure his desperation showed. "I'm looking for my friend."

"He never came around," said Cross. "Lord knows I tried. I considered it a sort-of crusade, you might call it, to get that guy to smile. To see the world in a different way, do you know what I mean? He's so sweet underneath—and bright too. He can be so good with my kids, with our pets. Might not look like a cat lover, but he is one for sure. Go figure."

"Did you spend time out at his ranch?"

"Oh no." A puzzled look on her face. "That was his world. Basically, in the end, I told him he had to choose between his dark friends or me. For so long there it was all the politics—big plans, you know."

"Politics?" said Bloom. Didn't seem likely.

"Secession." She whispered it like someone might have been snooping. "That group that got all torqued off about the legislature down in Denver. Something to do with electricity. Somebody down there wanted to tell the cooperative up here what percentage of renewable energy they were required to offer. My father is on the board, and he wasn't too crazy about it either. But it wasn't like the sky was falling. Front Range politicians, all Lenny Brandt could talk about besides the Book of Revelations, much as I tried to tell him there were other good parts of the New Testament. It's not like he didn't believe, but I could never get him to relax, you know, to enjoy life. Is your friend a friend or a girlfriend?"

"Girlfriend," said Bloom. "Lenny Brandt was involved in the secession movement?"

"I've got to go meet a friend for lunch," said Cross, "but, in a word, yes."

"With Dug Hackl?"

"Dug got him in, I guess," said Cross.

"Anton Hester?"

"I never heard that name until I heard it on the news. Let me ask you this, does your girlfriend add to your day—or take away? Say, like the Lord. Does the Lord add to your day or take it away? It's a dumb question, right? He always adds to your day."

Facts are facts.

"Not even a close call," said Bloom.

"You wouldn't stick around, right, if it was the other way around? It would get to a point, right?"

Bloom nodded. "Sure."

"That was my situation with Lenny."

"Was he still in a group talking about secession?" Coogan had dispatched Bloom to talk with the early ringleaders. The effort attracted a mix of local politicians from several counties trying to figure out a way to band together and place a measure on the county ballots. They wanted to start the 51st state. "That was before the last election, a year ago."

"They kept meeting," said Cross. "But they kind of went underground, and he wouldn't tell me anything about what was going on."

"Garrett McKee?"

"He was in there too," said Cross. "On the fringes. They let him hang around."

"Let?"

"I heard all this from Lenny, of course. And I really have to go."

"I know," said Bloom.

"Nobody really knows what happened. But at some point, Earl McKee got laughed out of there. Earl McKee is hard core." Cross backpedaled. She shook her head. "Makes the secessionists look like a bunch of softies."

"And Lenny?" Bloom stood his ground, didn't want her to think he was going to stalk her to her car.

"Don't much care," said Cross. "But from what I heard, he has his own plans to disappear. I don't expect to see him for a long time, if at all."

SIXTY-ONE:
TUESDAY MORNING

THEY BROUGHT HER WATER. They led her out to a crude bathroom. They were parked in a large garage. The school bus was dwarfed by a warehouse-like industrial interior. By her calculation, they had driven for an hour before they had stopped, deep in the middle of the night. She wasn't sure if she had slept. She wasn't sure about much. Worry fought with hunger and fatigue for her attention. She slapped each complaint down, in turn, and they kept coming back, kept whining.

After her bathroom and water break, they came through and checked the windows and sealed them up. She heard tape being ripped—over and over for an hour.

Or longer.

She had no idea whether it was midnight or dawn.

Or later.

They said nothing

She could hear them working their way around the bus, banging on the outside. And still the hard tear of ripping tape. The heavy-duty kind.

And then the smell of paint and the soft hiss of spraying. Off and on.

Pssssst.

Psst.

Pssssssssssssssst.

SIXTY-TWO:
TUESDAY AFTERNOON

GARRETT MCKEE AND MR. Axe didn't look around.

They let Doe Creek Trail dump them into South Fork Trail, and they kept riding, down through the Meadows, a lush stretch sheltered by high limestone cliffs. Aspen groves shaded the trail up on the bench of the South Fork River itself.

They picked up Coffee Pot Road, a stretch that usually brought up the four-wheelers and the ATVs all the way from Dotsero. With the fire and the road no doubt blocked off, the road was clear. It headed south and climbed up the west shoulder of Triangle Mountain to the broad saddle at Indian Camp Pass. In the long southbound straightaway, Allison and Colin hung far back—checking with binoculars to make sure Garrett McKee and Mr. Axe kept moving.

Trails intersected at the top of Indian Camp—Allison knew this spot like the back of Colin's hand.

Dry Sweetwater Trail came in from the east, around the north side of Triangle Mountain. She could be home in three hours, tops, if that was on the agenda.

Trapper's Lake Trail came in from the north, but these boys weren't bouncing back that way.

Coffee Pot Road, one of the many Jeep trails that fingered and crisscrossed their way up into the southern flank of the Flat Tops, would pull them south.

They still had a long way to go—ten miles to the head of the creeks that cut southwest from the towering Flat Tops and plunged into dark canyons on their way to the Colorado River.

Grizzly Creek. West Dead Horse Creek. East Dead Horse Creek. French Creek. Tic Gulch.

West to east.

Take your pick, boys.

They wouldn't make Glenwood Canyon by dark unless they pushed—hard.

Sunny Boy labored. He was a willing soldier, but she could sense his forbearance. Ella sweated to a lather, but at least the air wasn't humid.

At the top of Indian Camp Pass, they let Garrett McKee and Mr. Axe go.

They left Coffee Pot Road and dropped down to the west, where they found a spot along Buck Creek for a break and shade for the horses. Adding more gap couldn't hurt. Both horses were strong, but a rest would do them good.

Or maybe she was thinking about herself.

She decided on twenty agonizing minutes. *Go slow to go fast.* She hated that saying in the business world. It made zero sense. Out here, it just might mean something. The horses drank first, then dozed standing in the relatively cool shade. She nibbled jerky, drank water. Colin did the same.

SIXTY-THREE:
TUESDAY AFTERNOON

HE WAS THE SAME kid who held Allison at gunpoint. He stared out through the screen door, a couple paces back.

Bloom studied the boy—blond hair, scrawny. Age matched what Allison had said, about twelve. No shotgun.

"Ain't here," he said.

"Is anyone else?"

"I'm not even supposed to answer the door."

Bloom drove back around to the county road, headed upriver to the McKee's.

Charlotte McKee answered the door, flustered and tired though Bloom had no point of comparison. She looked as if the last thing she needed was another disruption.

"No idea," she said when asked about the location of Earl McKee. "Took off yesterday morning and didn't come back. He said he had business in Glenwood Springs and then might have to head over to Parachute for something. Said he might not be back."

She had let him inside for a glass of lemonade. They stood in the kitchen with the view of the bombed-out forest. Bloom couldn't help notice the suitcase, packed and ready to go by the bottom of the stairs. Fresh name tags—hers.

"Las Vegas," she said. "Another reason I'm not worried about Earl. It was his idea, to get the hell out of dodge. Now if it's 100 degrees in Meeker, it's got to be 118 in Las Vegas, but do you know what I'm going to do?"

She smiled and shook her head, giddy. "I'm going to get myself a big old bucket of tokens and an icy cold gin and tonic, and I'm going to sit in the air-conditioned madness with all those bells going and after about two drinks I'm going to go up to my air-conditioned room and close the drapes. I'm going to ask for black-out drapes. I'm going to put the television on some white-noise food channel or something, and I'm going to sleep until dawn or however damn late I want to. Just think—that air conditioning is out there, right now, just waiting for me. It would be a crime to not go use it, don't you think?"

"Sounds good," said Bloom. It actually sounded hideous.

"Nothing growing here this summer, anyway," said Charlotte. "We have help to watch after all the animals. So there's not much to do up here anyway but inhale smoke and watch the depressing view."

"May I ask something?" He said it with patience, to not alarm her. He said it like he had all day to wait for the answer. He didn't.

"Sure," said Charlotte, who had already asked to be called Char. Ironic name, thought Bloom. Maybe *sh-ar* was different, when you spoke it, than *ch-ar*.

"What happened with Earl and the secessionists?"

Char snapped to attention. "What do you mean what happened?" she said.

"He was involved, right?"

"Until he wasn't."

"It didn't go to the ballot, right?" Bloom knew the answer.

Char seemed to shrink. "There's no point in going back over all this old ground," she said.

"Something happened," said Bloom.

"What does any of that have to do with any of this? With today?"

"You've done well for yourselves, haven't you?" Bloom tried to avoid coming off as offensive or prying.

"Again, what?" said Char. "We have no complaints. Two fine sons and one who struggles, about average."

"Money wise," said Bloom.

"Earl McKee picked a good spot by the river, and the river has been very good to us," said Char. "The cattle and horses, everything. But I don't see the connection."

"It was a tough time for Earl," said Bloom. "Last fall. Before the election."

"One of the toughest. He was so disappointed when they packed it in. Earl had all sorts of ideas. Not a fan, as you might have gathered, with what goes on in Denver. Or much of government anywhere. He wanted to keep pushing. All I know is he came home from the last meeting, and it was the first time in a long time, right after that, that Garrett started to come around more regularly. I am sorry about your friend. I'm sure she'll turn up."

"Thanks," said Bloom. "Do you mind if I take a quick look in the barn?"

The storage compartment with the rifles was empty. No surprise—Trudy wasn't out here either.

Bloom drove to Meeker in a fast daze, hugging the turns and flooring it in the straightaways, putting the nose of the Camry in the middle, so it flew straight down the two-lane. He cut the corners, startled oncoming drivers and drew angry, long honks that tailed off behind him as he cruised.

"Trudy!" he shouted to the inside of the Camry.

He couldn't imagine leaving Meeker without her.

By the time he reached the sheriff's office, it had been four long, unproductive hours since he'd chatted with Erica Cross.

"No reports," said Deputy Bankston. "We've got everyone on alert. We've sent her picture to the news media and—"

"The school bus? The water truck?"

"Every cop in Colorado has the information. State troopers and Cub Scouts," said Bankston.

"Security cameras along I-70?" said Bloom.

"They exist," said Bankston. "It's going to take some time to go through the material, see what we can line up. And you're not positive that's the way they headed, are you?"

"I can't be certain, but there was some sort of night practice run, and it ran straight through Rifle, I know that much."

How could a water truck and a school bus disappear?

Bankston didn't mention the fire as the Big Distraction, which was a relief.

"Trudy is with them," said Bloom. "I know it." He cleared out of his room at the Blue Spruce, including Trudy's clothes and things. "Wherever you are," he said out loud, "be smart and stay cool."

It was dusk when Bloom hit the high spot in the road halfway between Meeker and Rifle. He pushed the Camry past the comfort zone, happiest when he was a good twenty miles over the speed limit. The steering wheel shuddered. The night closed down. There were no checkpoints. The Rat Mountain Fire, according to the long rundown of Colorado fires on the radio, had moved east.

SIXTY-FOUR:
TUESDAY NIGHT

THEY CAUGHT GARRETT McKEE and Mr. Axe climbing off trail. They had left the Grizzly Creek chute and headed to the top of a treeless ridge. Colin spotted them with binoculars at the last gasp of light. Allison would have sworn she saw a puff of smoke rising from the head of the rider on the gray horse in front.

"Dead Horse Spring on the other side." Colin was more familiar with this terrain, well outside the wilderness boundary. He kept his voice at a whisper. "From there, the creek drops straight and then picks up East Dead Horse Creek at Hanging Lake."

From where they sat, passing binoculars back and forth, the two horses reached the top of the ridge as darkness swallowed them up.

"How far down from there?" said Allison.

"Four miles," said Colin. "Maybe more all the way to the highway."

Still no cell. The bottom of the canyon was 1,500 feet below, down one of several steep-sided slashes in the limestone cliffs.

"They've got to stop." Colin said it in a matter-of-fact way. Garrett and Mr. Axe had pushed it hard.

"I would," said Allison. "We're going to have a hard time following them down the canyon at night." The walls of the canyon would broadcast any noise, the faintest step or rattle of a bit. Their pair of prey could stop, wait thirty minutes, and pounce.

Back on their horses, they cut higher across the broad swale at the top of Grizzly Creek and snuck in the dark to the top of the ridge, further north up the ridge than their prey had climbed. Near the top, Allison climbed down and Colin followed suit. Below the ridge line, they led their horses on foot at first and then tied them off. She brought the rifle out with care. They stayed low as they crept further, stars and a faint moon useless behind a night sky thick with smoke and haze.

At the top, the ridge flattened out, and they veered south, Allison's mind's eye was a rough gauge to estimate where they would intersect the route the two had taken.

Allison caught a whiff of cigar, almost sweet against the standing background scent of smoke. It was the equivalent of a tincture on the breeze. She ducked like she was avoiding bullet fire. Colin dropped too. She found his shoulder in the dark, pulled him close and put a finger to his mouth, just in case his nose hadn't worked as well.

Allison's senses fired. She stared, half-hoping for a handy flash of lightning to illuminate the scene or for instant powers to see in the dark. She held her head near the ground to see if she could pick up the guttural rumble of men. She flared her nose to confirm the cigar, and there it was again, human as could be. Cliché, she thought. *You're a walking cliché.*

A red ember to go with it. The pair were stopped, at least for a moment. The lit end of the cigar throbbed in the night, pulsing as it got sucked. Allison figured two hundred yards down the slope. The

cigar's red knob bobbed in the same general circle, and Allison realized they were looking through scattered trees.

How did Colin feel about chasing down his brother? How did
she feel about chasing down Colin's brother—with Colin? She had
stewed on the possibility all day, and here they came again. They
were reasonable questions with no time to think through and all her
"work" on the questions had gone nowhere all day so why would
now be any different? She knew at this moment she was glad she
wasn't alone. What the hell was their plan?

Two against two. Either they took advantage of their upper hand,
the surprise factor, or they didn't. They could wait to screw up—or
take action soon. But what else were their prey packing besides
whatever blade of choice Mr. Axe preferred? They had been close
enough one time that Allison believed she could see rifle scabbards.
She had used the scope on Nora's Kimber, which was a dandy. But
still, they couldn't be sure. Given the well-stocked compartment in
the McKee barn, it was hard to believe these two weren't armed to
the gills.

A fire flipped on, like hitting a switch. Perfect, knee-high flames.
Whoosh. And then the flare subsided and the fire cooked a neat stack
of chopped wood like a Hollywood set, too perfect.

The fire was small but lit up the scene. With her naked eye Allison could make out a trail just fifteen or twenty yards off to the
right. She wanted to use the scope but couldn't pull up the rifle for
fear of producing a dead-giveaway reflection. Garrett McKee, with
his rolled-up brim cowboy hat, stood to one side of the fire. He
munched on a sandwich. The light flickered off aluminum foil in his
hands. Mr. Axe Man wore a baseball cap with a long bill. He poked
the fire, walked into the darkness on the far side of the ring of light,
and emerged again with two more sticks of pre-cut wood like the
bundled crap you could buy in front of the grocery stores. The wood

was dropped on the fire and two words came rumbling up the slope, clear as if Colin had said them. "That's enough."

Allison's heart thumped against the ground. She put an arm around Colin. She couldn't imagine for a minute doing anything that would put him in harm's way.

They had to be smart, but they also couldn't delay.

Trudy...

Dante Soto...

And this, said Jayne, was Phase One.

With more fuel, the fire had bloomed. The two firestarters were forced to step back and Allison wondered why they had bothered starting one at all—they weren't cooking anything, and they didn't need the heat. More cliché, perhaps. Just something you did.

But the wood stash—the fuel had been waiting.

Dead Horse Spring had been their destination all along.

Colin tapped her on her arm and grabbed it. He used her own arm to point to the edge of the light under the trees. The firelight was dim under the canopy, like staring into a basement with a dim bulb.

When the light flared, she saw what he had seen—horse tails and horse butts.

They were standing with plenty of distance between them, maybe on a rope hitching rail between trees. From this angle, she couldn't be sure. The problem, however, was obvious.

There weren't just two horse butts. There were four.

SIXTY-FIVE:
TUESDAY EVENING

BLOOM COULDN'T GO ALL the way home. Sweetwater would be too far from Glenwood Springs and Glenwood Springs was already too far from Meeker. He didn't know whether he was in the right spot at all.

Coogan brought a six-pack of cold beer to Two Rivers Park, a strip of used-to-be greenway and a baseball diamond across from where the Roaring Fork joined up with the Colorado, which drifted out of the mouth of the canyon. A softball game had wrapped up and people were out milling around, trying to catch a cool breeze by the river. It was 10:00 p.m.

The beer tasted fine, but Bloom had no interest.

"I called Rio Blanco County myself," said Coogan. He had switched out wire-rims for contacts a month earlier and complained about them every day. He was in his mid-fifties and had three decades of newspaper experience under his belt. He seemed rattled and worried. "I talked to Deputy Bankston, and he gave me the rundown. I have to say they are taking this seriously, at least if tone is any indication. He asked about you."

"Me?" said Bloom.

"Just to assure them that we know you're credible. A casual question. They were tracking down this Jayne and Lenny Brandt, all the others you mentioned."

"But they're all gone," said Bloom.

"They're looking through the rubble from the fire too," said Coogan.

"The place was deserted," said Bloom. "Guaranteed."

"The point is they're working on it," said Coogan.

"How do you make a school bus and a water truck disappear?" said Bloom.

"There's more than one road out of Meeker," said Coogan. "And the back roads of Rio Blanco County are not Times Square when it comes to security cameras."

The *Post-Independent* had all the information up on the web, at Bloom's urgent insistence. The version in the morning paper might be too late. People who saw the bus or the truck were urged to call a Meeker number. All leads were welcome. Anything was welcome.

"I can't sit here," said Bloom. He refused to picture Trudy in any particular situation or condition. At least, he tried not to concentrate on *what ifs*. He'd already fought off tears. He had to pull off the highway near New Castle on the way back and let them flow. He cried like a baby. "And at the same time, I don't know where to go."

"Okay," said Coogan. "Doctor's orders here. Drink half that beer, and I'm going to ask you a question."

"What?" said Bloom.

"You'll see." Coogan didn't play games. "You can chug if you want to, just drink half."

To Bloom's taste in editors, Coogan ran too much toward crime and cops. Bloom preferred politicians, the environment, health care, and economic development. But now? He wanted the best cops in

349

the state. He wanted to know they were trained and hungry and that they knew every investigative trick of the FBI and Scotland Yard combined.

Bloom chugged. The canned IPA tasted dry and fruity. "Okay," he said.

"Start at the beginning," said Coogan. "Start from when we talked —you are on the road coming in from Yampa when the fire was blowing up. Everything you can remember. Nice and slow."

"Now?" said Bloom.

"From the top. Nice and easy."

Coogan sipped. Bloom talked—and sipped. Bloom was on his third can of beer when he recounted the decision to split up with Allison and head to the drone farm.

"Over and over," said Bloom. "It's just like any damn fucking economic development story—follow the fucking money. Drones, buses, water trucks, and that arsenal, I'm telling you. Where the hell is all the money coming from? Lenny, Garrett, and his buddies—I mean, you are not talking about investment bankers here. Shit."

"Hang on," said Coogan. He had his phone out. "What was the name of that summer camp?"

"Vernon Wayne Fucking Howell," said Bloom. "I told the cops. They know what to look for."

And he realized that Coogan was doing what he should have done a long time ago.

"The hell," said Coogan.

It was dark, but Bloom didn't like the look on Coogan's face.

"I knew the name rang a bell," said Coogan. "That's David Koresh—the name he was born with."

SIXTY-SIX:
WEDNESDAY EARLY
MORNING

Mr. Axe sharpened his blade by the fire. It looked like a Pulaski, as Devo had said, only a bigger custom job. They each had a flask— no sharing. Allison guessed bourbon. More clichés. Garrett had checked the horses. Mr. Axe lit another cigar, put his head down against a bedroll and laid down by the fire, but kept smoking. Both were prone. Allison used the rifle scope to watch. Mr. Axe looked familiar but she couldn't place him. She knew she had seen him, but where? When? He looked younger than she'd been imagining. And, she assumed, butt ugly.

Dante Soto...

Trudy....

Bloom must have found her by now, right?

They heard words exchanged, couldn't make out any sentences or meanings.

"Allison."

It was Colin's first word in hours.

It was the first word in hours—period.

Colin said it at sub-whisper level. It was three syllables of almost nothing. Lips by her hair, his mouth pointed down the chute between their bodies.

She gave a look she hoped said "what?" In the darkness, it didn't do much good.

Colin nodded where they had been looking, only maybe Allison had drifted off for a minute. Or ten.

Mr. Axe wasn't there.

"How long?" she wanted to say. But didn't.

Garrett McKee slept. The fire had dimmed. He had his head on a bedroll and now she saw what Colin spotted—that he had taken the second bedroll and crawled underneath.

Candy ass…

The air was still warm, by any measure, but Garrett McKee needed a blanket. She hoped he had passed out.

"How long?" This time she said it, but at the same sub-whisper level too.

"Thirty," said Colin.

She had slept.

"What the hell?"

And what if Mr. Axe had heard something, spotted something, sensed something? And was now circling around in the dark?

Up here? Coming for them?

Allison sat up, shook grogginess from her head.

"Let's go," said Colin.

There were still four horses.

"He had a daypack," said Colin. "And the axe."

"Did Garrett wake up? When he left?"

"No."

"Our horses?"

"I checked them," said Colin. "They're fine."

He had found their horses in the dark and picked his way back to the same spot, all without waking her. Colin was a helluva scout.

She had really slept.

"When?" she said. Garrett still hadn't moved.

"Just now."

If Mr. Axe was coming back, then the sooner they got to Garrett McKee the better.

She carried the Kimber in both hands. Their pace down the slope was steady. The scrub was low and the ground, of course, dry. Maybe Colin knew something about how his brother slept. Colin led the way, his pace pushing the envelope.

And then it hit her. She wanted to grab Colin's arm, retreat, re-consider, and *recalibrate*.

Her thoughts tangled in an ugly knot. Somewhere deep, her head had been busy matching images. Maybe it was a game brains played.

In this corner, Mr. Axe.

In this corner, the guy working on the SUV at Budgie's Auto Repair. Carl Kenyon's co-worker.

Same dude.

Allison lost a step. Of course there was a huge "but…"

It was stuck in there somewhere but Colin was almost to Garrett, gun in his hand. Forearm tensed. Allison scanned the edge of the light, spun around. Was this a trap?

Nothing, at least, to *see*. He could be in the woods.

Nobody.

Garrett stirred. Colin covered the last five long steps across the flat to the dimming fire, and Allison told herself a gap between the two of them might be good.

It would require two good shots from the darkness.

Take me first.

Allison found herself trying to recall the conversation with Carl Kenyon so she would unlock the tangle before the sniper started firing.

There was no time.

"Where is he?" Colin stood over his brother and pointed the gun in his face. He gave Garrett a dead stare.

"Well, well," said Garrett. He looked around. "Oh, I figured she couldn't be too far. Change of tune?"

"Where is he?" said Colin.

"Going to shoot your own brother?" said Garrett.

"Where is he?" said Allison. She flipped back Garrett's blanket. His hand was wrapped around a semiautomatic. She jabbed a boot on his wrist. He flinched, but didn't call out. Colin picked up the handgun, stuck it in the back of his jeans in one smooth move. "And where is Trudy Heath?"

Garrett McKee shook his head. He stared at Colin, ignored Allison.

"I don't know anyone named Trudy," said Garrett. "I'm pretty sure."

"Then where the fuck is your buddy?" said Colin.

"*My* buddy?" Garrett sat up, crossed his legs in the dirt. The campfire light was dim, but it was enough to show Garrett McKee was scared of nothing. "Oh, sure, Colin. Calm as could be a day or two ago and look at you now. *Agitated.*"

"Where?" said Colin.

"I told you to keep to your business," said Garrett. "And we'd keep to ours."

"Where the fuck is he?" said Colin.

"What time is it?" said Garrett.

"What the hell does that matter?" said Allison.

"If you want to know where he is," said Garrett. "Then it matters."

"Say, three thirty," said Colin.

"Then you're too late," said Garrett.

"Stop with the little fucking games," said Allison. "Did he go straight down Dead Horse Creek?"

"What do you mean by straight?" said Garrett, seriously, but a wisp of a smirk to go with it.

"Listen, asshole brother of mine—"

"—go ahead and shoot me. You still lose. You still lost. Already. If it's three thirty. I wouldn't know. I've been sleeping. If it's three thirty, you lost."

There were still four horses. "On foot?" said Allison.

"What's it to you?"

"Everything," said Allison. She stepped in front of Colin, shoved the butt of the Kimber into Garrett's shoulder. She shoved. He rolled back, straightened his legs. She could see him give. It was in his eyes. Like a worried dog. "What did Dante Soto know?"

She had no time for questions. Fetching Sunny Boy would take twenty minutes. She'd need to bring Ella, too, because it made sense to not have Colin leave Garrett, for any reason, once she was gone.

She was ahead of herself, already itching to go.

Garrett looked at Colin, at her. Back to Colin. "Nosy motherfucker, that one," he said. "And his people."

"Did he know the plan?" said Colin.

"What plan?" said Garrett, back to being stupid. Looking at her. She was standing over him. Her view was all rifle and Garrett's face. Straight down the barrel. "You want to see the plan? Go to the bottom of the canyon now. I still think you'll be too late. You'll be able to see the plan. Hear it too."

"Fuck you," said Colin.

Earl McKee, for crying out loud, sent her to the auto repair shop, where Trudy was last seen.

She couldn't get her head around it. Not now.

"Fuck you," said Garrett. Brother-to-brother verbal depth. He looked at her. "Why you?"

Of course, it was the question of the decade. At least, the question had lasted that long.

She hadn't been able to answer it on her own, so she wasn't going to try now.

"Because Dante Soto is dead," said Allison. "Because the cops don't quite have the big picture. *Yet.* Because when your asshole buddy killed Dante Soto, he started a fire that's still torching wilderness. Because my best friend on the planet is missing. And because I'm alive and I don't know why. In that way, I'm just like you. And that thought scares the fucking crap out of me."

SIXTY-SEVEN:
WEDNESDAY EARLY
MORNING

BLOOM FINISHED HIS UPDATE, posted it on the website himself. The story included a recap of Vernon Wayne Howell and the shootout and disaster in Waco, Texas, and the fifty-one-day siege of the Branch Davidian compound by federal and state law enforcement agents. In the end, seventy-six men, women, and children were killed. So was David Koresh, the Revelations-thumping leader of the sect, organized around the sect's firm belief that the Apocalypse was nigh.

Timothy McVeigh, who observed the siege in 1993 from outside the armed checkpoint established by federal authorities, was photographed by a local college reporter from Southern Methodist University. McVeigh was sitting on the hood of his car. He was selling bumper stickers. Among them:

> *A Man with a Gun is a Citizen.*
> *A Man without a Gun is a Subject.*

McVeigh, who later would be executed for his role in the Oklahoma City bombing that killed 168 people and wounded 680 more just two years later, told the reporter: "The government is growing bigger and more powerful, and the people need to prepare to defend themselves against government control."

Bloom's story mentioned McVeigh's religious beliefs. McVeigh wasn't as tied to Revelations as David Koresh, but McVeigh often said his favorite book was *The Turner Diaries* by William Pierce. He had copies of pages from it when he was arrested. The book was associated with what was known as the Christian Identity movement. Essentially, "regular" Christianity was too pro-government. "Regular" Christianity overlooked the harsh living conditions in rural America. Christian Identity offered scapegoats to blame, in other words, the government. It gave them a revolutionary purpose. The movement, however, insisted on whites only.

Lenny Brandt, Dug Hackl, Garrett McKee, and some asshole with an axe, it seemed, had formed their own branch cult to pursue their warped view and, perhaps, blow something up.

It was 5:00 a.m.

August 1. Colorado Day.

Coogan had hung in there all night, calling the Rio Blanco and Garfield County Sheriff and the Glenwood Springs police—even though they had no firm evidence or indication that the action would go down in Glenwood Canyon. A map on a wall in Meeker with curious dots did not constitute a plan. Coogan had assurances from the Garfield County Sheriff that they were working with state transportation to review highway camera footage east of Rifle. There were cameras in Silt and Canyon Creek, just west of Glenwood Springs. There were cameras in the canyon at No Name and Hanging Lake Tunnel. And there were one million places to hide two vehicles between Meeker and Glenwood Springs, even using the predictable route through Rifle.

The sheriff, Coogan said, had positioned deputies along the highway coming into the canyon from both directions.

And still no Trudy.

Bloom had one of Allison's hands, Jesse Morales, check their house and feed the cats. He called back with the predictable news—no Trudy. And no sign of any struggle or problem either.

"Somebody had money," said Bloom. Coogan pulled up a chair by his desk. Coffee steamed in two giant cups between them, the best convenience store coffee in town. "And another thing is the auto repair connections. The drone farm was a used car emporium, almost a junkyard, and the barn out there was no regular barn for horses and hay. Ditto for Lenny Brandt's place. And then Trudy vanishes outside an actual auto repair business in Meeker. What do these people do?"

"Three loners," said Coogan. "At least, the three we know. Not mainstream guys with mainstream jobs."

"No jobs," said Bloom. "All three in the cracks—though I guess Garrett McKee did some work at Budgie's Auto, but part-time auto repair among all three of these guys?"

"Dante Soto saw something," said Coogan.

"Saw enough," said Bloom.

"And maybe they've got a network down in Rifle or New Castle, you never know, where they pulled over for the night."

"Warehouses and barns," said Bloom. "Any place big enough for two good-size vehicles."

That might reduce the one million hiding places to ten thousand between Meeker and Glenwood Springs, which was a significant reduction in the number of places to check, but still.

"But let's assume they haven't hit the highway yet—that the transportation department footage hasn't spotted anything yet," said Coogan.

"That would mean Rifle," said Bloom. A downtown Rifle café called Shooters hit the national news when its waitresses started carrying weapons on their hips as proud supporters of the state's "open carry" laws, which allow each city to set its own restrictions.

"An appropriate launching pad," said Coogan.

Thousands were down to, say, hundreds. The main I-70 interchange at Rifle was home to a cluster of industrial-looking buildings, and there would be other options in the city, which was primarily residential but had its share of medium and small businesses too. They might not need one building for both vehicles. Two might work just as well.

Bloom punched in a search on his browser. "Eighty-seven auto repair listings in Rifle—truck and car," he said.

"But knock out the chains from the list," said Coogan. "And skip the places that just do auto glass and oil changes, and take out the auto parts stores. They come out to change your windshield wipers but they don't have a big garage out back."

Bloom printed out the list. It felt good to do something.

Down to twenty-five.

"Take out the gas stations," said Coogan. "Too small, too much traffic."

Down to sixteen.

"And the towing companies." Eleven.

They scanned the list together, knocked out one with an address in Vail, another address in Silt and one in New Castle. Vail was a search fluke; Silt and New Castle would have required time on I-70. Eight.

Bloom pulled up the Secretary of State's website. Was it possible some name would jump out among the registered agents, the articles of incorporation? The state database could be friendly, but it was easy to conceal true owners.

Bloom started going down the list. AQM Custom Repair. Bill's Auto Repair. Dawkins Complete Auto.

Bloom picked up the phone. Coogan gave him a look.

"Lenny Brandt's mom," said Bloom.

"It's early," said Coogan.

"Actually, it's late."

She sounded chirpy as noon. "Age and sleep," she said. Bloom had her on speaker so Coogan could hear. "I thought you might be one of my walking friends. Is that article getting published?"

Coogan shook his head. Bloom cut to the chase.

"Friends of Lenny's in Rifle? I was thinking later—you asked a lot about Lenny and my husband."

"I'm still writing the cribbage story," said Bloom. "But I was also looking into something else. And now my girlfriend is missing and, well, we think Lenny is involved with some weird stuff, and that's why I'm wondering if he's got any friends in Rifle—maybe an auto repair business or a buddy down there. A religious friend. Or anti-government friend. Anything."

Bloom sounded desperate—and he knew it.

"Hardly had my first cup of coffee," she said.

"I know."

She was quiet. He heard a spoon stir a cup, pictured her clean kitchen.

"It's funny after all that time and now you're asking this morning," she said.

"Why is that?"

"He was here last night," she said. "Knocked on the door. Thought I was dreaming. He looked real different, gaunt and tired."

Bloom wanted to ask a million questions, but tried one. "Was he with anyone?"

"No," said Brandt. "But he was real quiet and later, when I was thinking about what he was trying to say, I realized he was trying to say goodbye, that I wouldn't see him for a long, long time. He was beating around the bush, but that's what he was trying to get across in his own way."

"Did he mention where he was staying? Was he staying in Rifle?"

"Wait a minute," said Brandt. "Yes, he said something. I asked him if he wanted to spend the night here, which would have been plenty strange, but I had to offer. I mean he looked like he'd need a week of eating and scrubbing just get him back to civilized. But that's when he said he was staying over at a place in West Rifle, and he said he had a friend there that owned a business. Auto repair, as a matter of fact."

"Name of the business?"

"You don't even need a cribbage brain to remember," she said. "West Rifle Auto. The only reason I asked is I've been looking for—"

SIXTY-EIGHT: WEDNESDAY MORNING

THE FIRST TWO MILES were hell. And dark. Allison didn't know the trail. Sunny Boy didn't know the trail. She could feel his reluctance, so she pushed through her own.

Bad news ahead. Allison knew it. Based on the distance she had covered, a troubling hunch further soured her worried state.

With a first gentle crack of light, she started catching glimpses of the cut in the canyon ahead. From the dark shadows and the fact that she could make out the rugged jutting outcroppings on the other side of the river, she knew that the trail would plunge like a waterfall. Steep trails down canyon walls often meant loose rock and tight switchbacks. Neither was a good scenario for stealth or horse safety. She might have to leave Sunny Boy—again—and hoped she could make it back or send word.

To someone.

To who?

Earl McKee. There was the real brain hurter.

Duncan Bloom's question about the money? *There's your answer.*

Earl McKee had sent her to Budgie's Auto Repair because that's where Mr. Axe worked.

Simple. Easy. She fell for it. May as well have held a flag up that read, "I'm poking around in your shit."

Maybe Earl called down to Budgie's before he was put back behind bars, but Allison also remembered a call came in while she was there and how casual and relaxed Carl Kenyon had been, taking their sweet time and drawing out the conversation.

And Trudy paid the price.

The hell…

Earl McKee? That line he quoted about glory and honor and thanks. She would bet anything it was from Revelations.

Did Colin know that too? The gun-in-your-face act with his brother seemed plenty real. But what the fuck did she know? What about Char? Daniel?

The hell…

It hadn't come together until she was a mile down the trail, wracking her brain to sort out the story.

She'd left Colin with Garrett. Maybe that was another ruse. Colin had Ella and all four of the other horses were there and the idea was that Colin would keep an eye on Garrett and figure out something with the horses, so in the worst case none of the guys coming up the canyon would have the mobility they were expecting.

That is, if her effort failed.

Now, Mr. Axe.

Ahead and on foot. She didn't want to crawl up his back, give him a chance to turn the tables. And she couldn't let him get too far ahead.

They came to the edge of the void, the first step a fucking doozy and no indication where it turned or flattened out. Sunny Boy stopped. Pure animal instinct, like her own.

SIXTY-NINE: WEDNESDAY MORNING

Two cop cars flew by like two fighter jets, side-by-side coming up in Bloom's rearview mirror Then the one in his lane slowed and pulled in behind the other when they passed him—*pffffft, pffffft.*

No sirens. No lights. And they didn't look over.

Out in front, they went back to the shoulder-to-shoulder model, and Bloom gave the Camry more juice.

Or tried. It was already pushing ninety. The steering wheel throbbed. The body of the car shook like an alignment was about ten years past due, which was the case.

New Castle.

Silt.

Traffic was light and the sun was coming up. Smoke fuzzed the sunrise to mush. Garfield County might never see the sun again.

Bloom glanced at the eastbound lanes—pictured a school bus and water truck lumbering their way toward the canyon.

Eighteen-wheelers, RVs, cars. No school bus. Maybe they were in time. At the risk of having the Camry fly apart, Bloom whipped the engine harder. It was too early for speed traps and, if the pair of flying cop cars was any indication, the sheriff and Rifle police should have their hands full.

Bloom called Coogan, who had called the sheriff's office while Bloom raced to his car.

"They are probably already there by now," said Bloom. "I'm between Silt and Rifle."

"You see cops?"

"Two just shot past me," said Bloom.

"West Rifle Auto Repair," said Coogan. "The owner's name is Leonard Crosley but no real story that's obvious through any database, at least based on a quick-and-dirty search."

"Part of the network. Sympathizers. Friends."

Bloom hung up. He eased the Camry down from full throttle for the last two minutes to the West Rifle interchange.

All the development at the interchange was south of the highway along the river. Bloom flew down the ramp, cut back underneath the highway, ignored the stop sign, turned onto the frontage road. West Rifle Auto Repair wasn't hard to find. A white steeple topped a church that sat next to a sprawling, fenced-in yard full of semi-trailers, a couple of giant tow trucks, a line of RVs, and several dozen used vehicles with orange and green neon "For Sale" signs covering their windshields. An unadorned industrial building sat in the center of the lot with its massive garage doors rolled up.

Bloom guessed two dozen cop cars in a haphazard array. Lights swirled on about half. He parked on the frontage road and hopped out, running.

Four uniforms surrounded a man backed up against a tow truck that was the size of a small house. He was leathery, tall, and skinny.

He had a knob nose and a small, shrunken face. He wore overalls and a baseball cap. He shrugged, took a drag off a cigarette, pushed his hat back to scratch his forehead.

Where was Trudy? Was there a chance it was all over?

Bloom circled around for a look inside the garage, felt a hand on his bicep.

"Easy, big fellow," said Deputy Randall DiMarco, a good source. "I heard you were in the middle of this."

"What's the story?"

DiMarco shook his head. "Check it out for yourself."

The school bus sat deep inside the building in one corner, nose facing out. The water truck sat in another, face-forward too.

"Where's Trudy?" said Bloom.

"No sign of her," said DiMarco. He was tight-lipped, unexcitable. "Or the drivers for that matter. But we've got the vehicles—recently painted. But something happened—they changed their minds or something."

"Changed their minds?" said Bloom.

He could smell the paint. The water truck sported fresh maroon. On the school bus, a light blue barely covered "Vernon Wayne Howell Summer Camp." Given the rush, they were impressive paint jobs. Professionals.

"They knew someone knew too much," said DiMarco. "We're certain the paint work was done somewhere else, but we'll find it. And plenty of indication they were making a bomb—the compartments in each vehicle were retrofitted, and there's a mess of high-nitrogen fertilizer. I mean, it's all over the place."

"Changed their minds?" said Bloom. "Maybe they just changed their trucks."

SEVENTY:
WEDNESDAY MORNING

DOWN.

Her boots worked like mini surfboards on the loose rock, which was unavoidable in spots. She held the Kimber low in one hand, then both, then the other. She fought to stay out of the main gulley of the trail where the rocks proliferated, but there wasn't much room on the sides to quiet her footfalls or reduce her chance from slipping. At times, she surfed—and hung on.

The trail switch-backed down at a precipitous rate. She stopped every four turns, listened ahead.

Or gave him an easy, standing target.

She scanned the woods, she watched the trail. Where a pint-size spring burst from the cliff and puddled on the trail, she spotted three clean prints, two lefts and a right from serious boots. A horizontal tread pattern in front, four diamonds on the heel. The heel bore weight. Two inches separated front from the back sections of the print, and the prints were fresh. The trickling water had started eroding their mark.

Now that she knew the pattern, she knew what to look for. But spotting the occasional print fragment didn't matter. He had two options. Up. Or down.

She half-jogged, half-surfed.

Her thighs burned. Her toes, jammed down in the front of her Ropers, started to bitch. Sweat slicked her back and down where she carried the Ruger, tucked into her belt. The light, flat canyon light might stay like this until the sun popped overhead for a couple of hours in the middle of the day. The light was okay, but the sight lines sucked. He could be several staircases straight below her—depending on how the trail zigged and zagged—and she might never know it. She could round a corner and, *boom*.

The top of the canyon floated higher. The walls pinched in like they wanted to grab her. The trail shot north for a long stretch, putting her back to the canyon's mouth, and it turned on a hairpin. The grade relaxed and put her on a long straight-away toward light. In the distance, she could see the high cliffs on the opposite side of the river, a half mile away.

And she heard him.

A rattle like a snake—but louder. It sounded like a mini rockslide, no more than two seconds long, like a heavy load getting dumped from the back of a truck. The sound started clean, ended clean. It was soft and distant. He was moving, and a healthy gap remained between them.

SEVENTY-ONE: WEDNESDAY MORNING

THERE HAD BEEN A few moments where Trudy thought it might be a matter of outlasting them. Of being cooperative, not struggling, not complaining—too much. The longer it took them to paint the water truck and the school bus, the better. They still didn't say much but they brought her a peanut butter sandwich when they realized she hadn't eaten all day and they seemed less focused on her—and more panicked about their plans.

Something had gone wrong.

Trudy heard the shouting. The tension was electric. It was close to entertainment, but maybe more of a distraction from her own miseries—burning hands and ankles from the rope and, when she wasn't eating, her taped-up mouth.

They had kept her in an inside office for a long time, on an old black beat-up couch that was fake leather, the kind that grows sticky and squeaky in the slightest heat, that carries layers of spills and gunk. The windowless inner office baked. She sweated. She knew she was ripe. One tiny oscillating fan rattled from its high perch on the far wall. Its attempts at cooling were lame.

Hours had slipped by. Outlasting them was key.

Then she saw the two matching panel trucks. They were the same brown as UPS, but no markings. They sat side-by-side between the school bus and the water truck.

She was given a well out-of-sight spot to sit on the cool metal floor. The dashboard was up high. The window on the sliding door on her side was up high. The driver, her eight-fingered friend, sat on a pedestal seat. Up high.

She had a good view of the brake and gas pedal. She was lashed to a hook and couldn't stand. A big deal was made about watches and timing. Her truck would get a twenty-minute head start. Somebody had run the calculations.

They had heard, from what she gathered, something about roadblocks. What if there was a roadblock?

There had been a third guy around who seemed to know the most. He had overalls and a baseball cap like a train engineer with gray and white stripes. She was hopeful at the talk of roadblocks. Maybe she could make a scene and try something. Try anything.

Clearly, they had to ditch the school bus and the water truck because the word was out. They needed a back-up plan—and they had to scramble to make it happen.

Roadblocks were good. Would they check every truck? Panel trucks, not so good. Her place on the floor of the truck—horrible.

Her eight-fingered pal had cleaned up as if he'd been to a spa. He had a brown uniform, shorts, and top. He'd nicked his chin shaving. Coconut shampoo. He looked fucking *presentable*. She heard them rehearsing their lines—they were delivering the trucks to Denver, not delivering packages.

Once they were on the road, all she could see was hazy sky through the big window.

"You really don't know?"

For a second, she thought he was talking on a phone but he was talking to her. He looked down and repeated the question.

She said nothing. But she didn't really have an option.

"You think Dante Soto saw something?"

She nodded. She uttered the word "maybe." She wasn't sure how it came out.

"Soto saw something." His hair flew in the breeze from the open window. The road was noisy. He almost shouted. "Nosy asshole. Yep. Him and his people. But it's way more than that—way the fuck more than that."

He shut down.

She caught flashes of the high canyon walls. She predicted the arrival of No Name Tunnel, the first one going east, almost to the second. She knew every outcropping by heart.

The next tunnel would be Hanging Lake—much longer.

But from the shards of conversation, Trudy knew they wouldn't stop in the eastbound bore. They would drive to the Bair Ranch rest stop, turn around, and head back. If their timing was right, they would arrive at the same time as the trailing panel truck broke down—mysteriously—near the mouth of the eastbound bore.

Outlasting them hadn't worked. She had missed her one chance, back at the auto repair place in Meeker. If she could figure an angle, she'd have to put up a fight.

SEVENTY-TWO:
WEDNESDAY MORNING

AT THE JUNCTION WITH the Hanging Lake Trail, Allison moved as fast as the rocks and chute allowed.

The trail was usually thick with hikers, but the fire had closed all routes heading toward the wilderness, including the short but steep jaunt to Hanging Lake, which was a curious body of water on the edge of a cliff. One in a thousand hikers took the fork that headed up the unforgiving pitch of Dead Horse Creek.

Where was he?

Allison kept up her pace. The woods were thick in the bottom of the canyon. The gap across was no more than thirty yards in spots. The light was indirect and dim. The creek was quiet. This summer, there was no flow.

The plunge from the top had left her soaked in sweat. She craved a drink. Her thighs screamed in protest from playing brake.

She strained for a sound. She waited for a flash of him. Big sky teased. A footbridge took her over the creek bed, too noisy for her pleasure. She ached for a glimpse of the highway. She knew she was nearly all the way down, but the trees were thick and unforgiving. There were no true breaks.

The school bus .... The water truck .... One for each bore. Her head went dizzy.

She stopped at the top of a rock knoll, the last tree-lined drop to the river. The whirring sound came from behind. Maybe because of what she thought might happen to the tunnel, she was ready.

She ducked, juiced by panic. She rolled on hard rock and into the scrappy scrub oak.

A flash of silver, a quick view of the blond handle, and she heard the blade slice air and then sink with a mean *thunk*.

She rolled, popped up again on her feet. He pulled the axe out as she raised the Kimber. He kicked her hand, and the rifle skidded off. Her left hand stung and throbbed.

There was no time to size him up in detail, but two things were obvious—his powerful size and his cold look, like he wasn't working at all.

She faced uphill. She couldn't risk a glance at her footing. She backpedaled, stumbled and reached for the gun in the sweaty small of her back. Before she could put a firm hand around its grip, he kicked again and she spun, careening. She needed both hands to break her fall, and she heard a guttural bleat of desperation.

Her own.

She landed face-first. She skidded on loose rock, and her wrist caught and she rolled over on her side, desperate to get a grip on the gun and yank it out. Her palms screamed. The silver blade flashed.

He stood over her. She wriggled away and yanked at the gun. She found a useful grip but sensed that her timing was off.

A second here, a second there.

He swung the blade up, and it looked like the kind of arc you'd need if you were chopping tree trunks, not little old *her*. His forehead sprouted an instant ugly 3-D welt.

Dead center between the eyebrows. The welt was wet and shiny and big.

Blood splattered and rained down on her face and sweating, heaving chest. The booming shot faded.

SEVENTY-THREE:
WEDNESDAY MORNING

BLOOM RAN. THE ROAD swept right across the river toward the eastbound bore. Cars were jammed up and parked, drivers out. Cop cars and trucks were stuck like flies in amber with nowhere to go. There were two lines of cars with their motors off. People running out of the tunnel, too, and he could see the panic on their faces. Kids in the arms of mothers. An elderly couple, both caning it. A wheelchair. People helping people. Cries.

The road coming out of the westbound bore was empty, of course, and there was always the chance ...

The highway lanes were separate, girders on both sides and a good ten feet between. And a long drop to the river.

"The other way," said a guy ready for fishing, his hat full of flies.

"Why?" said Bloom. He knew.

"Accident in the tunnel, one of those UPS trucks. Somebody smelled the fertilizer." He tugged on Bloom's arm to get him to turn around. "At least, that's what I heard."

Bloom shook him off.

A sheriff's deputy with red hair and a green approach tried to deliver the same message.

"The tunnel is being evacuated." His thin voice was ineffective.

The cop wasn't prepared to handle desperation. Bloom shook him off. "I'm looking for someone." He said it much too late for the cop to hear while he ran.

SEVENTY-FOUR:
WEDNESDAY MORNING

TRUDY COUNTED HER BLESSINGS. The count started with people. Allison and Duncan. She thanked previous lovers for taking her in. For dealing with her issues back when she was more fragile. For showing her something new. For letting her try new things. She thanked Sweetwater. She thanked all her employees—hard workers. She thanked her customers. She thanked the plants and the flowers and the trees and the herbs.

And, she realized, she better thank Glenwood Springs and even this canyon, which had always scared her with its soaring roadways and steep-sided canyon walls. In all her trips through, however, she had never seen one falling rock. And now this.

She wasn't sure there was any circulation in her wrists. Her ankles throbbed. She was so tired of breathing only through her nose.

The driver was gone. Cars stopped honking their horns about five minutes ago.

She had heard shouts and yelling at her eight-fingered driver. It must have looked like a pretty stupid piece of driving, how he had swerved and jammed on the brakes.

He had slowed, but barely, before veering sideways and shutting down both lanes of traffic.

Cars crunched into each other behind them. The tight space amplified the tire squeals, the violence. He didn't say a thing. He slid open his door and left her.

He didn't give her a second look.

It was quiet.

She picked up a low-grade buzz, something electrical. Orange lights dotted the roof of the tunnel, far overhead.

She started her list of thanks all over again.

SEVENTY-FIVE:
WEDNESDAY MORNING

COLIN'S HANDS AND SHOULDERS shivered. She'd been there.

It wasn't about choices or doing the right thing or desperation or anything else. It was about the fact that he'd taken the life of a human being, albeit a monster.

Mr. Axe had ended up face down, sprawled down the slope. She had used her phone to call the police, once she got her heart rate back. Down here, the signal was fine. It had taken her several run-throughs with the dispatcher to get all the details across. They scrambled down the final rocky pitch to the paved walkway.

Civilization? Maybe.

Straight ahead, a short section of the elevated highway deck and the east end of both bores—westbound and eastbound. On her left, the highway cut around the corner of a towering butte. Cars and trucks jammed the short section of highway, meaning that the back-up was now miles long. If the west end of the tunnels looked anything like this one, cops would need choppers or parachutes to get close.

"What about Garrett?" she said.

"I left him." Colin carried the dead man's axe. "He might need untying in the next few hours. I left him a bucket of water so he can lap it like a dog."

"Sunny Boy?"

"With Ella," said Colin.

They were going back up and would need to leave soon. It would be like climbing an elevator shaft with no rope and bad footing. Four miles to Dead Horse Spring might take half the day. They would go together.

"And your dad?" she said. She had wanted to tell the cops about all of that, too, but one step at a time. They had their hands full, to say the fucking least.

"I was trying to keep you from all that stuff. He went crazy when the secession thing fell apart and practically blew back in his face. They laughed at him, and he went off the deep end. When I saw him and Garrett so close, working together after all those years, I knew Garrett had pulled him into his shit."

"Keep me from *knowing*?" The fury started in her toes. "Keep me? From knowing?"

"I was trying to get them to shut it all down," said Colin. "Stop before it was too late, but I had no idea they were planning something like this. No idea."

If she had known to be wary when she was chatting with Earl in the jailhouse, she might have gone to Budgie's, but she would have gone with her eyes open and with Trudy at her side.

Trudy ...

Allison knew where to find her.

East end or west? Take your pick.

The only way to reach the highway deck was to the right—down the paved trail, through the long parking lot for Hanging Lake hikers, and up the ramps leading to the west entries of the tunnels. To reach the elevated highway deck on this end of the tunnel, they'd need a fifty-foot ladder. She was fresh out.

The traffic on the highway wasn't going anywhere. Mr. Axe wasn't going anywhere.

Should they each take one tunnel? Allison guessed it was fifteen minutes to the mouth of the east entrance to the tunnels, if they jogged. It didn't matter.

Two matching men appeared in brown uniforms, shorts, and shirts, wearing heavy black boots and carrying large backpacks in tan desert camo.

Allison tugged on Colin's shirt and pulled him back out of sight. The men waved up the hill, signaling as if "come on" or "let's go," but the thick trees at the mouth of the canyon made hand signals useless.

Allison swung the Kimber around and lined them up in the scope. They had wide-brimmed hats. All sorts of crap dangled from their belts.

They walked, but stopped now and then to peer up the slope, trying to figure out what the fuck was going on—and what the hell had gone wrong.

SEVENTY-SIX:
WEDNESDAY MORNING

SHE LINED UP ONE chest, then the other. Each carried a rifle at the ready. Each rifle sported a forward-curving magazine. The weapons were stubby and black. They looked like AKs.

The men trudged. The heat and the backpacks took their toll. They kept looking over their shoulders or backpedaling a few steps, perhaps not wanting to miss the moment when the tunnels blew.

She passed the Kimber to Colin. "Is that them?"

Colin needed no time. "Hackl is the smaller of the two, on the left. And, yep, Lenny Brandt. I can give them something to think about."

"One guy gets away," said Allison.

"Or lives long enough to get out his phone," said Colin.

It would be an easy shot. The two men stopped and turned around. Brandt dug something from a pocket. A phone rang—fucking loud. *The Ride of the Valkyries* in full orchestra mode.

She dug the ringing phone from her jeans, one of the two they had taken off Mr. Axe. Her hands fumbled to kill the damn noise. She pressed the only green button and listened.

"What the fuck, where are you? Come on!"

Brandt held a phone to his ear. He looked up the flat trail, straight at their position in the shade and dark, several trees deep in the woods.

"Make it happen, make it rain, come on!"

She punched it off.

"Hackl this time." Colin had the Kimber. "Now he's dialing."

Hackl punched with a finger. Even with her naked eye, she could tell what Hackl was doing. She yanked the Kimber from Colin. Maybe he thought she only wanted to see.

She jammed the butt plate to her shoulder, aimed, and squeezed.

The Kimber boomed and kicked. With its feather weight and no muzzle break, she expected nothing less.

Brandt buckled. Her right ear needed a moment. She had sailed the shot off to the side.

There was no need to rejoin the killing ranks. *Yet.*

She sprinted, Kimber pointing the way, and her heart thudded hard. She sensed Colin—his footfalls, his easy breathing on her flank.

They were both going for their rifles, but too late and too slow. *AK-47s not ready for action. Eh, boys?*

Hackl was first to get his rifle up.

She screamed: "Don't move!" He played deaf.

She skidded a reckless round at his feet. Hackl spun around, stumbled.

Brandt was trying something. Reality refused to focus. It back-pedaled in blurry bobbles of fuzz. The scene went hazy.

Should she just kill a man who wanted to kill many more?

Brandt fiddled with his weapon. He looked up in time to see Colin giving him the less lethal end of the axe, the whack like a hammer on bone. Colin switched his grip, so when Brandt rolled and came up on his back, he had a good idea that Colin would use the sharp end on second flail.

Brandt moaned. The axe told Brandt and Hackl all they needed to know about one of their team.

Colin grabbed Brandt's rifle and shoved it away. Brandt's dead face tried to show he felt nothing from Colin's whack, but she saw him fight the pain. He sucked air, clenched his jaw.

Allison lined the Kimber on Dug Hackl's chest.

"Rifle," she said. "Toss it."

"What the fuck?"

"Now."

He had black hair that fell to his shoulders, likely well past UPS regulations. He had baby cheeks, fair skin, and a permanent sadness in his eyes. He put the rifle down on the walkway. Allison grabbed the AK-47 by the tip of the barrel and yanked it away.

Colin flung the axe aside, switched to his Ruger to cover Brandt.

"Backpack," said Allison. "Off."

Hackl didn't move.

"By the time I count to one." She chambered another round. The backpack fell with a heavy thud.

"Too bad about your friend," said Hackl. "She told me all about you. You know, before."

"Before what?" The scope of Kimber found Hackl's sweaty nose.

"Sheriff of the Flat Tops. Just as she described. Just a little thing. Thinks she's tough. Thought I saw you inside there at Dale's place, chatting away."

Brandt moaned again, from the depths of pain. Colin hadn't held back.

"Where is she?" said Allison.

"Tied up," said Hackl.

Colin dumped Brandt's backpack out like a yard sale. He found a coil of rope and sliced off a hunk with his buck knife. He yanked Brandt's arms behind his back. The knife sliced Brandt's shirt, and

Colin ripped it over his head. Colin lashed the ankles together, then strung a length between the ankles and wrists.

Hog-tied. In about one minute flat.

Colin gave Hackl's backpack the same treatment. The guts of their loads included clothes, knives, dehydrated food, ferrocerium rods, blankets, compasses, LED flashlights, hacksaws, can openers, first aid kits, collapsible fishing gear, and water. They were stocked, but Allison wondered if they would have ever made it up the steep incline of Dead Horse Creek carrying so much weight. She figured one heart attack and one case of severe dehydration.

Brandt clenched his jaw in pain. "Where is she?" said Allison.

"Occupied," said Hackl. He took a step back.

"Where is she?"

"Fuck you," said Hackl.

"Is that what they teach in Bible School?" Hell seemed like a real place. Hell seemed too easy.

"He's the Bible nut." Hackl bobbed his head at Brandt.

"Where is she?" said Allison.

Hackl shook his head, took another half-step back.

He opened the palm of the hand with a full set of fingers, the right. He showed them the world's smallest cell phone—a silver keypad and not much more to it.

"Now you let us go," said Hackl. "Or I start dialing. We'll have a good view. And your friend? Well, she's in your hands."

"No," said Allison. "You put that down, or I put a round in your chest."

Hackl cradled the gizmo, punched a number with his thumb.

"Cold blood is tough," said Hackl. He glanced down at his hand to check the numbers. "You might think it's easy, but—"

She was too close for the scope to be of any use, but she lined up the barrel of the Kimber and tracked down Hackl's arm—bicep, elbow, forearm, wrist—in a flash. Her aim settled on the palmed phone.

And then it was gone, replaced by a burst of red spray.

She was used to the sound by now—and the recoil.

Hackl stood there.

Blood dripped. One finger—the index—was gone. The middle dangled by a string of flesh.

"Son of a bitch," said Colin. Couldn't he have said *nice shot*?

Allison's whole body rattled, scalp to boots. She took a breath, tried not to let it show.

Hackl buckled to his knees, pulled his wounded hand into his body and reeled from the pain.

"Son of a bitch," said Colin again. This variation carried a happier tone. He was digging for the first-aid kit.

"Not easy," said Allison. "And it's not so hard, either."

Colin checked Hackl and patted him down before he went to work. He found a sheath toting a mean-looking Bowie knife with a black handle and prominent crossguard.

"And Soto?"

Hackl looked up. Blood dripped onto his chalky legs. The look in his eye said he was still playing games. "Who?"

She wanted to wipe the smirk off his mug with a shot that would graze his cheek.

"Soto," said Allison. "Tell me."

"Who is asking?" said Hackl. Colin unwrapped a roll of gauze; Hackl could apply his own first aid. "You're not even from around here, are you? What rights have you got? And if you think you're an unofficial agent of the government or whatever, then fuck you. The government—"

"What did Dante Soto do to you?"

"Meddling fuck," said Hackl.

"Did he find your plans?" said Allison. "He know about this—the tunnels?"

"He saw what he saw," said Hackl. "Does it matter? He was a government fucking agent getting his nose in our business. Another one. Comes in sandals, but they may as well be jack boots."

Government?

Hackl must have seen the question on her face.

"Yeah, government," said Hackl. He rocked to the pain. "Or another one of your quasi deals. Foundations or some bullshit but all controlled by government types doing government business and the goddamn government agenda, and the government's getting bigger and fucking bigger. Pretty soon they'll know when you wipe your dainty ass." He must have practiced snarling. "Go look it up, you little self-serving bitch. You thought he was a fucking angel from heaven, dropped out of the sky to save the fucking planet? Give me a break. You didn't smell a rat? That's the problem, the government comes around and everyone goes to fucking sleep on morphine. Walks in lockstep. Fucking *succumbs*."

Hackl pointed at Colin. "Hell," he said. "Even his dad knew Dante Soto was a fucking government agent."

"And that's where you got the money," said Allison.

Hackl gave her a demented smiled. "You need resources, you know? When it comes to fighting the government, you're slingshotting grains of sand off a grizzly bear's hairy ass. All I'll say is that Earl McKee is a mighty generous man."

Hackl bent over at the waist in nearly childlike pure agony. He screamed: "My fucking hand."

"Yeah," said Colin. "Now you have a matching pair."

SEVENTY-SEVEN:
WEDNESDAY MIDDAY

"HOW DID YOU—?"

Trudy squelched the urge to cry.

She'd been waiting so long for that moment that would be the end, wondering and half-crazy imagining what she would see, what she would know, wondering how the logical part of her brain would process what was happening before it ceased to have the capability to function.

Stupid thoughts, crazy thoughts, manic thoughts, desperate thoughts—black, black, black. She struggled and wriggled because she had to, not because it made any sense.

A flurry of steps, something banged on the door, and Duncan Bloom's face hovered upside down above her.

With the tape off her mouth, he started to work on the rope.

Sweat coated his face, dripped off his nose. A pocket knife made quick work of the rope.

He helped her run, arm around her shoulders.

The tunnel ahead was empty.

The road curved and dropped.

Her legs balked, but felt the relief too. Something to do.

"We're going to make it," said Bloom.

She didn't look back.

SEVENTY-EIGHT:
THURSDAY MORNING

THE ROAD FROM RIFLE to Meeker was thick with pea soup fog.

Except the fog smelled like campfire and there wasn't enough moisture on the whole Western Slope to soak a kitchen sponge, let alone produce fog along a thirty-mile stretch of highway. Colin drove their rented pint-size sedan in Glenwood Springs.

After the long afternoon of interviews with a variety of uniforms and agencies—both counties, state level officials, and others—they stayed at the Best Western Antlers. They had taken two rooms—one for Trudy and Duncan—and one for her and Colin.

Allison had, so far, kept her issues with Colin from infecting the reunion of the foursome. Pizzas arrived. So did a case of cold beer. They ate and sipped beer and talked until midnight. How could her heart freeze out a guy who had saved her life? Logic, she supposed, didn't apply. Would she have been in that situation if he had been more upfront in the first place? Her head swirled. She let him sleep in the same bed, but that was all.

Garfield County Search & Rescue was dispatched to pick up Garrett McKee from Dead Horse Spring. The sheriff's office found an outfitter to retrieve the four horses. Allison told Jesse Morales where to find Sunny Boy and Ella. Then he would ride the next day to return Ella to Nora at Trapper's Lake Lodge.

The Denver news stations had gone into round-the-clock coverage, with the occasional break for an update on the fires. How many times had they shown the video of the two UPS-like trucks being towed at a snail's pace from each bore of the tunnel? How many times had they shown the bomb squad guys giving the all-clear signal? How many times had she seen aerial footage of the miles-long traffic jams—cars empty, drivers and passengers huddling outside on the highway—on each side of Hanging Lake Tunnel?

Also in heavy rotation—Brandt and Hackl, both handcuffed and being marched down the hillside with Hackl in his boxers. That clip preceded the shot of the dead guy in a body bag. He was being identified as Taylor Corbett. Twenty-nine. His rap sheet started when he was nineteen. He was from Arizona and had moved to the area—Rifle, Craig, and Meeker—just six months ago. From their conversations with the cops, they learned that Brandt and Hackl were being pressed to identify the location where they'd dumped the dead guy Devo had found in the river.

Bloom had spent some time at the newspaper. Trudy had spent two hours at the hot springs, soaking. When sleep came, after a final round of beers, it was delicious.

In the morning, following breakfast and another round of showers, pampering and laundry, Trudy headed back to Sweetwater and Bloom headed to work. There were plans to put Bloom on national television—satellite interviews with the networks.

Allison insisted on the return trip to Meeker and she wanted Colin with her.

The ride north was quiet, punctuated by the occasional comment about the fires or some overlooked detail from the day before. Dog houses are lonely places but Allison wondered if Colin knew that she had felt equally exiled and just as distrusted.

They found Charlotte and Daniel McKee outside the courthouse. Gabriella had stayed behind in Denver. Charlotte sobbed and sobbed.

One son in Garfield County jail, one husband in Rio Blanco County jail, and the details of their conspiracy still trickling out.

"We'd like to see him," asked Allison.

"As long as he wants to see you," said Daniel. His crisp button-down white Oxford shirt looked fresh from the dry cleaners. His jeans were for show, not work. If he had come straight from Denver, he must have used a back road; I-70 reopened when they were eating breakfast. "It's his call. He's in a chatty mood, all things considered. We left him fifteen minutes ago when the cops came."

Daniel drove Charlotte back to the ranch.

"Did Daniel know?" said Allison. They waited outside the jail, upstairs, on a bench in the hallway.

"I don't know," said Colin. "I really don't know. I know you think I know, but I don't. All I know is Daniel lives way down in the city, and I don't think he and Garrett had much to do with each other after that situation in the woods, whatever happened up there when dad dumped them out and told them they were on their own."

"But how did he get here so fast?"

"Drove all night," said Colin. She had stayed on the outer loop of conversation and had taken a call from Trudy, too, so hadn't heard all the chatter. "Kremmling to Yampa and the county road to Buford, stayed at the ranch last night and was there when the cops came to get Earl."

"Trust him?" said Allison.

"More than you trust me," said Colin. "At least, right at this moment. I can't change what I did or why I did it."

They waited. Her mind swirled with the idea of granting a pardon. She wasn't sure how that would feel. Artificial? Perhaps. An hour slipped by, and they were escorted back.

"So it's not just my boy," said Earl. "It's the girlfriend too. I guess you found Garrett."

Fuck you crossed her mind.

"Eventually," she said.

"And you found a whole lot more, from what I gather."

Colin cut to the chase.

"What are you telling the cops?"

"All I did was help my son," said Earl. "Gave him some money— I've been telling the cops, just trying to help my boy. Some kids find their way in the world, others need help."

"And you know that's bullshit," said Colin. If Colin was trying to soften her up, he was doing a decent job. "Garrett and I were alone. Night before last. We were alone for a long time. He said you knew what they were going to do with the money—everything."

"Did he now?" said Earl. "The word of a wild and crazy dropout up against mine," he said. "Well, okay."

"And mine," said Colin. "Based on what Garrett told me. You knew what was happening—right down to the plan for Dante Soto. I know you knew. Garrett knows you knew—and Lenny Brandt and Dug Hackl. Same thing. That's a lot of witnesses."

Earl McKee studied the ceiling for an escape hatch, and the floor, perhaps, for a trap door.

"It's all fucked up," said Earl. "I mean, don't you see? I did what I was supposed to do—I worked my ass off. I did everything the way you're supposed to do. And what did I get for it? Nothing. Paid my taxes and all they want is more and more and nobody pays attention. The people who put this country together, out here working our butts off. And now, gun control? Letting all these damn immigrants come pouring over the border, so we can pay for the health care, give them good schools? So we can, what? Deal with their crimes and let them rob us right and left? The government is the aggressor—every fucking day. They are chipping away and chipping away. And here I am, an old rancher with nothing left, and I've given the government half—for what? Show me, for what? I'm two dogs down. I raised them from puppies until they were old and gray. I buried them both. Almost twenty years each and things ain't going to change for the third—they are going to get worse. Mark my fucking words. I am sick and tired. It's bullshit. Somebody had to send a message. You know?"

Silence remained the theme on the ninety-minute drive to Trapper's Lake.

"Whatever money he gave to Garrett and his buddies must be the last of whatever he had," said Colin. "Mostly, I feel for Mom."

"She might have to sell the ranch," said Allison.

"Which was a whole lot more valuable before the fire."

They drove past Brandt's place, barely visible across the river. They drove past the McKee's and didn't stop. Colin didn't even suggest it.

Allison insisted on thanking Nora—and more. Nora got a full rundown and profuse thanks for the horse, rifle, gun, and provisions. Allison explained that Jesse would be bringing Ella back the next day, and she would send a check over for the weapons, now in police custody.

"Can you imagine my business if those tunnels blew?" said Nora. "You can send a check if you want, but I'll rip it to shreds the second it arrives."

Colin took a call from Daniel and then another from the Garfield County Sheriff. Allison asked for another round of favors to Nora. "Do I look busy to you?" she said.

Allison ate a turkey sandwich on the patio with Colin. When it was time to go, a Strawberry Roan named Hilde was packed and ready with food and camping supplies. Allison wouldn't need much. She didn't care if the trip home took two days or ten.

She hugged Colin, and he held her, hard. "I didn't know it all," said Colin. "I knew a bit. But I didn't know it all."

She kissed him. She hadn't decided for sure, but she kissed him.

She watched him walk away, down the dusty road. Someone had to drive the rental back, right?

"Hilde is short for Brunnhilde," said Nora. "You know about her, don't you?"

"Not really," said Allison. She was thinking *not at all*.

"In Wagner's opera *The Ring*," said Nora. "It's one of the operas in the cycle. The Valkyrie. Brunnhilde is a Valkyrie."

The Ride of the Valkyries—Lenny Brandt's goddamn ring tone. The tune had haunted her sleep.

It would take too much to explain, Allison thought. She'd keep the coincidence to herself. "Didn't know that," she said.

"You know about the Valkyries, don't you?" said Nora.

"Not really," said Allison, still thinking *not at all*.

"Yeah," said Nora. "In Norse mythology. The Valkyries are all women. They are out there on the battlefield, but they don't fight. They decide who lives. And who dies. They are the choosers of the slain."

ABOUT THE AUTHOR

Mark Stevens lives in Denver. He worked as a reporter for *The Christian Science Monitor, The Rocky Mountain News, The MacNeil/Lehrer NewsHour* and *The Denver Post*. He has also worked in school public relations. He is a member of the Mystery Writers of America, Sisters in Crime, Rocky Mountain Fiction Writers, Southwest Writers, Western Writers of America, and the Colorado Authors League.